GENESIS:

Forlorn Raider Book 1

TRAVIS LAUGHLIN

This is a work of fiction. Names, characters, places, and incidents either are the product of the author's imagination or are used fictitiously. Any resemblance to actual persons, living or dead, events, or locales is entirely coincidental.

Copyright © 2021 by Travis L. Laughlin

All rights reserved. No part of this book may be reproduced or used in any manner without the written permission of the copyright owner except for the use of quotations in a book review.

First paperback edition October 2021
Second paperback edition October 2023
Third paperback edition June 2024

Book design and internal illustrations by David Oakes
Chapter Icons and Map by Katherine Murphy

ISBN 979-8-48-046247-0 (Paperback)
ASIN: B09GNV56N5 (eBook)

Table of Contents

Prologue: Driftless Dreams 4
Chapter 1: Throne Room Parade 8
Chapter 2: Continuing Countenance 18
Chapter 3: Directionless Direction 30
Chapter 4: The After-Party 40
Chapter 5: Dauntless Farewells 52
Chapter 6: Elfless Lorelei 64
Chapter 7: Dark Reveries 72
Chapter 8: Marauder's Glory 82
Chapter 9: Esoteric Naif 92
Chapter 10: Forina's Contract 102
Chapter 11: Golden Goliad Gladiators 120
Chapter 12: Frigid Night Blues 130
Chapter 13: Illicit Nightmares 144
Chapter 14: Awkward Riposte 154
Chapter 15: Midgard's Inundation 166
Chapter 16: Prosaic Management 176
Chapter 17: Jumbled Confidence 192
Chapter 18: Lightfall Part I 202
Chapter 19: Lightfall Part II 218
Chapter 20: Lightfall Part III 230
Chapter 21: The Dark Marble 244
Epilogue: Reascend Red 260

GENISIS:
THE KNOWN WORLD
Unknown
Teritory
Elvanian
Republic
Elvania
Tuscany
Empire
Tuscany
Alvernia
Sovereignty
Alvernia
Alvernia
Superior
Alvernia
Minor

Prologue: Driftless Dreams

This round of silence was dwarfed by the sound of violence. The dead were overtaken by the dying and their reluctant, temporary replacements on the battlefield. An elven archer burned to death beside me while the last remaining human vanguard buckled under the pressure of the enemy's vast numbers. There were as many of them as there were leaves in a forest. When one fell, thousands more took its place. This bastion of civilization was all that remained between us and the endless darkness brought by the enemy's tide.

Marleen was screaming my name repeatedly, her calls cutting through the chaos. Each call was more desperate than the last. As she took it upon herself to seal one of the enemy's portals opening next to us, it cost her an arm. Blood splattered endlessly across my face and the ground. Yet, her attention remained concentrated, focused, and diligent. Why was she fighting so hard to win? We stood no chance. Not a glimmer of hope remained in the soldiers. Not a smidgen of uncertainty remained in anyone's mind that death awaited us all.

Her lips pressed against mine. These were our last moments together. "Raider, my love. We did everything we could do. There isn't much we can ask past that. I need you to focus on me. Focus on the sound of my voice and bring your eyes to mine. That's it... now look at me. Laura is gone. The last defendable tower fell on top of her while she was trying to protect our flank."

The trance I was in brought me to look across the field full of demons. Behind the waves and waves of black miasma-filled creatures was the tower Marleen spoke about. Laura was buried under it along with our children. It was coming back to me now. She took our son and our daughter to hold the only remaining defensible position left in the entire world. While she did that, Marleen and the last remaining mages were attempting to cast a spell. What was that spell again?

Marleen slapped me to regain my attention. "Raider. The spell... it was successful. Isn't that great? We will meet again. This time, we will hold the answers in our palms. There is no way for us to be blindsided again. Not this time. We will win. It's you... just remember... we can't let Alvernia fall! It's the chain that breaks the link."

I replied, "Marleen... I don't... I don't remember what's going on right now. What spell? Why is Laura dead? How... did we get here? Weren't we... just... in the Throne Room?"

My eyes were drifting lazily down to the ground. There I was, watching a fuzzy pool of blood forming under Marleen. At first, I didn't know what it was. But after a few seconds, the dripping reminded me of an event I saw not too long ago. What was his name again? Another memory I can't piece together, but it was so important.

She pulled my chin back up again. "It must be a side effect of the spell. Shion! Shion, he is fading! We are going to lose him before the spell takes effect. Can you do something for his mind? Stabilize him somehow?"

Another mage in black robes approached. She was a different... kind of... something I can't recall. She looked so familiar. Her hair, her ears, and her earrings. Even her scent has an odd flavor that tingles the senses.

My body slumped over onto Marleen, who struggled to hold me up. "Marleen? What is happening to me?"

She cried out, "Hang in there. We need you to hang in there. We have no hope if you give up on us now! You're the only one that can fix this!"

My eyes were cracked open only slightly. It took every bit of my energy just to do this much. Marleen commanded the black-robed mage. "I'll spend the remainder of my mana to erect a dark barrier. While I do that, you need to encase yourself with him in as many earthen barriers as you can muster. We must buy time! We only need but a moment!"

The mage replied, "Leave it to me. Our time together was... far too short. I'll miss you, Grand Mage."

Marleen smiled as she vanished behind the earthen walls that sprouted out of the ground all around us. My hearing was fading as fast as my vision. The walls blocked out the last bit of the sun I would probably ever see. That didn't stop... the cries of pain and agony coming from what few survivors were still alive outside.

A large talon crashed through the four or five layers of earth walls this mage had made. It pierced right through her chest, spraying blood all over the walls and my body.

When she fell on top of me, she smiled the same way Marleen did before she vanished. A single stream of blood rolled down the right side of her mouth. "Raider, you will make this right. Don't let it come to this again. Don't let... them..."

I figured it out. She was an elf, too, just like...

Chapter 1: Throne Room Parade

A strong punch hit my ribs, followed swiftly by an angry whisper. "Stop daydreaming, asshole. The King is asking you a question."

It was Laura, somehow reaching my ribs while kneeling in front of me... a feat easy to accomplish when you're as ruthless and dominant as that woman. It took me a second to get my bearings. I couldn't quite remember just what was happening. My memory was a little fuzzy... it seemed extremely important, like something I shouldn't forget.

She hit me again, followed by the King obnoxiously clearing his throat. Yeah, I get it. Whatever you just said, I clearly missed. Now, please move on so I'm not further embarrassed in front of all these nobles and other people I could care less about. This cold ass floor hurt my knees, even for someone as young as me. I would rather follow the cracks in this less-than-adequate foundation than listen to more useless prattling from those who are supposed to be more important than me.

His Majesty, the great 'King Forsythe the Pacified,' rests on his luxurious chair, high above us lowly 'plebs.' I suppose we are all noble here. I'm also a lowly noble now, barely holding the rank of knight, not that the rank means a lot for my station. Lately, we seem to be called in front of him as a form of publicity stunt for the kingdom. All the real conversations dealing with any important matters always take place after we dismiss from the Throne Room and reconvene inside the War Room immediately afterward. I understand placating the public and the nobility occasionally, but this has been happening every day and is starting to become a burden for everyone.

What makes this worse is that this will probably continue to happen in the foreseeable future because nobody is coming up with any solutions to our problems. It's almost as if the King truly believes he can showcase his generals off enough to whisk our economic and military woes away. I'm not sure what he is even saying while kneeling here because I've heard it so many times before. The only line that matters for anyone except for Laura comes when he announces that we are dismissed. That phrase is something along the lines of,

'Supreme Commander Laura, gather the war council and convene inside the War Room.'

Giggling could be heard from behind me. It was Marleen playing around like she usually does, never taking anything seriously. When I wandered my eyes from the floor cracks back to her face, she winked at me. "You might want to pay attention, hot shot. He's going to get angry if he calls you again."

I hadn't heard a word the King had said, so it's possible. My mind isn't all there right now. Half because I was looking for those golden words he would say to Laura and half because my mind was in a complete fog right now. Could it be the pain in my knee from kneeling for so long? I'd rather be complaining to my fiancée about this garbage while taking a nice long stretch around the castle. Laura, however, might stop us from galivanting and taking it easy. She is constantly riding me on all kinds of trivial matters. Not that it is entirely her fault, as I know that hounding really comes from above her.

Just as I was getting wrapped up in my thoughts about what I was going to do after this, King Forsythe, clearly agitated at my lack of attentiveness, blatantly singled me out. "Raider, if you will be so kind as to humor me and pay attention instead of having your imagination get the best of you. We must discuss the increase in demon incursions! Laura informed me that the number of attacks from the Unknown Territory continues to increase steadily. I want to hear it from you because you will be held accountable if even one Alvernian is killed due to your complacency."

He throttled his voice down a notch. "Now, are we still on track for our supplies for the winter, and do we have enough soldiers? If our supply chain and soldier counts remain adequate to last through the cold, then can we count on the mana levels inside of each fort's ManaBank to remain steady as well? They are just as critical as ever for protecting our soldiers from the Unknown Territory's miasma as well as keeping our magical items operating. I know I don't need to mention this to you, but we must remain vigilant."

Comments like these make me die a little inside. How many times have we had a ManaBank run out of mana? How many times have our barriers failed on the front lines? Better yet, just how many times have I allowed our soldiers to run out of food, weapons, or clothing? I know we are facing a potential shortage in the next six months to a year, but the answer is still never to all those questions. I wonder if he asks me this because he thinks my captains can't manage their forts or if it really concerns a total lack of confidence in my abilities. Sometimes, calming down and constantly telling myself this is all for a grand show is the best play here.

I replied to his redundant line of questioning, "Your Highness, the latest reports sent to me over the last several weeks indicated we barely have enough supplies and soldiers to see us through the winter. However, with correct rationing, we can still maintain all our obligations unless something unforeseeable happens. As you know, the potential shortage is due to several of our supply lines being intercepted by the mindless raids from the Unknown Territory and increased robberies along our main roads. The bandit's activities are swelling everywhere within our borders. Their constant attacks against our caravans are a rather new development and will require more patrols behind our front line to solve the problem."

I continued, "As I have for the last year in my position, my devotion to monitoring and addressing both situations won't falter. Should any of these party's attacks not be resolved, it will cause us to have to cut down on our presence in all areas, and that cannot be allowed to happen. One last thing of note would be the increased tours of duty for our soldiers on the front line. Simply put, our soldier's length of stay in combat-ridden areas is well over double their original contracts. This is slowly causing desertion, eroding morale, and, most importantly, affecting our overall fighting readiness. None of these are going to cause immediate problems, but if we neglect these issues in favor of focusing on other ones, this will prove to be disastrous."

There are several issues with what I just told him occurring behind the scenes. These problems tend to run in the arena of 'open secrets,' and everyone knows it. The first problem involves the general in charge of the Royal Guard, Claire, being appointed as an appeasement offering to the nobles. She's shy, timid, avoids almost all conflict, and doesn't have the backbone to support the rest of the generals. She comes from a proud merchant family that may as well oversee most of our merchant guilds. To sum up, making them happy is almost like making the rest of the greedy nobles who benefit from them happy as well. She has long blonde hair, a killer body, and all the right connections. Her one fault was her glaringly poor academic scores when she was in the Military Academy with me. None of our peers consider her a 'General' but more of a trophy wife-to-be in general's clothing.

    Don't get me wrong, she has always been nice to me and everyone else. However, she would be far better off being on the sidelines than being in her current role. Secretly, all of us hope she gets reassigned or decides to retire early. The best-case scenario would be her getting married off to another noble house and dropping out of the military altogether to raise children or something. Nobody says anything because we want to keep our jobs and not have her family run us out of town. I suppose this means we also lack a backbone to some extent. That lack of a backbone keeps her in her current position as the General of the Royal Guard, which severely undermines all efforts related to our 'elite.'

    Our second major problem revolves around our 'allies' from the Tuscany Empire, who were supposed to send us aid through food, magical items, and soldiers. Those bastards sent the first shipment of arms and a few thousand soldiers about six months ago and then fell dead silent. Alvernia hasn't received anything since then, which has caused immense pressure on our economy and military. This all goes back to what they promised, and what they sent us was as different as promising a lake but getting a pond. This has soured relations with them as our predicament, and it only worsens. And so far, whenever we reach out, we are given the runaround by their diplomats.

    Our kingdom is located closest to the Unknown Territory in the southeast. The Tuscany Empire is relatively safe to the west and has been protected by our country from demonic attackers for as long as anyone can remember. With the recent increase in threat emanating from the Unknown Territory, we had a council between our country, Alvernia, the Tuscany Empire, and the Elven Kingdom to the north, Elvania. When the council was concluded, the Tuscany Empire sided with us when we pleaded our dire case to them. They began aiding our nation with any resources they could spare in order to keep the status quo. To me, the original deal they made was a joke. It seemed more like they were buying time than assisting the whole of the world from certain death.

Even with their agreement with our nation, the Empire ignored anything involving the Elvanian Republic. The Empire has a history of having smugglers illegally cross into Elvania and kidnap elves. The elves being abducted and sent all over the Empire has been done for decades because elves are thought of as less than humans, only fit for slavery. Once they are enslaved, all kinds of horrible things can happen to them. Sometimes, they are forced into military service for their magical capabilities; other times, they are forced into prostitution. The business is extremely lucrative to the smugglers and merchants involved, so the number of incidences continues to go up despite Elvania's border security 'increasing' exponentially.

Elvania continues to try to resolve this issue without going to war for their own reasons… possibly to strike and kill when they get the chance. Not that it matters, as Tuscany continues to ignore them. This causes them to have no formal diplomatic ties with each other, and it doesn't look like this will change anytime soon. There is also the fact that the Empire's government, including 'The Emperor' himself, is run by human supremacists who share the same view as their public that all other races are inferior. None of this, though, was the main reason for them aiding only us, at least according to them.

What caused our current situation was King Forsythe's decision to act last year on the Empire's word and place additional forces and resources on the front line. We turned over the entire way we fought because of their promises. Training timelines and expertise exposure, more rations to increase morale, higher pay for those on the front lines and in forts, and so on and so forth. When the Empire failed to continue to deliver its goods, it placed us into the predicament we now face. Overages in deployment times, a rapidly draining treasury, and equipment we can't easily replace.

The easiest thing to do now would be to send an envoy to the Tuscany Empire and have them give us what they promised. But that will never happen because we have no real leverage to force them. That means this situation turns an easy solution into an impossible one. Moreover, they could reply by telling us this is the way it has always been, and these problems aren't theirs to begin with. That being the case, they aren't necessarily wrong. Even if our country does falter, the Empire could just come in and pick up the pieces to expand its territory. There's no real way the Empire loses.

What they are missing is that if the attacks continue to intensify and we must withdraw from the front line or our country falls, it might be too late for the Empire to repel any of the demon attacks by itself. From what our intelligence networks have gathered, it's obvious the Empire has enormous numbers of spies, but do they know just how much effort we put into keeping everyone safe?

Also, from our monarch's point of view, King Forsythe might not realize that the Empire did all of this to put us exactly where they wanted us. It's not difficult to realize that the Empire set a trap and lured us in with a few sweet promises and outdated equipment. I know it; the King should know it, and the other competent generals for sure know it. I would go so far as to say even my fresh-out-of-the-academy knights know it, but nobody will say anything negative about the Tuscany Empire because we don't have the strength left to back up those statements in public.

"RAIDER!" A booming voice interrupted. "What is with you today? Why are you ignoring me so openly in my court?"

I started speaking out loud from my internal monologue. "If we weren't fighting an invisible war of attrition with the demons from the Unknown Territory, then it's easy to see our forces crushing the Empire, no problems. Along that same line of thought, we also continue to weaken our lines of defense against the Empire and the Elvania Republic to supplement our forces on the front lines. Doesn't this seem too circumstantial for even the blindest of individuals? At this rate, it would not be surprising if the elected noble council just decided to reduce all our combat strength and then expect all of us to do less with less. It's already hard enough to do my job as the General of the Eastern Front without being handicapped further by bureaucrats and politicians."

Voices sundered around the room. I just fucked up, and I knew it. They echoed phrases like, 'THE ARROGANCE!' and 'HOW DARE HE!' for several minutes. The King's face went pale as he put his hand over his face to decide how to handle the truth so openly. While he thought about handling what I just said, part of me thought it was good to be rebellious. None of those assholes were really all that shocked. However, their acting was next level. Haughty pieces of crap, all of them.

The King took a deep breath and said something I never would have thought would come from that old man. "Raider, I'll get right to the point. We are short on time, and there are more pressing matters than your outburst. Should we attempt the Hero Summoning Ritual? We are short on trainees coming out of the academy, our treasury is all but exhausted, and our supply lines are being cut. Just about the only resource we can still pull from, aside from our agricultural surplus, is the mana in the Alvernian Royal ManaBank. There aren't many spells we can use to solve our problem with it, and increasing the number of magical items attuned to it won't help in the short term. We need something drastic, permanent, and immediate."

Dead silence fell across the room as everyone understood exactly what this meant. I'm not one to put my faith in magic, which is saying a lot because I am engaged to a magician, but this would be gambling on the random summoning of someone from who knows where. I would need to verify with Marleen on the specifics, but the research behind that nationally guarded spell is lacking tremendously. This 'Hero' could come from another world, dimension, or parallel world without guaranteeing anything. They could be twelve or eighty. They could also arrive to instantly hate all of us because we took them away from anything and everything they have ever known or loved. What happens if this person turns against us or resents us? People naturally follow a hero because of their immense power, so even uttering anything about a hero summoning might cause a civil war.

And if that were to happen, even if we happen to quell a civil war, the devastation would be unimaginable to the point of not being recoverable. And there's one more thing while I am entertaining this idea. Summoning a hero means we would practically deplete our National ManaBank and would not be able to cast large-scale magic for offense or defense if we get into a bind. In essence, our king is willing to bet the entire nation on this garbage, and he wants my approval for it. Why not just ask Laura? She ranks higher than me, and she would agree with anything he says. The King knows how much I disapprove of relying on magic, so he antagonizes me publicly. It's no wonder everyone in this room fell silent. Nothing was written about the First Summoning, so there isn't much to support this decision. From what I've heard, it was successful, but nothing else has been made public.

I know I am being baited into this response, but I'll go for it anyway. "Your Highness, forgive my ignorance of magic, for my knowledge is limited. If it were up to me, I would rather use all that mana from the National ManaBank to create high-grade magical items for our front-line troops to reinforce their strength. In my opinion, it makes more sense to take our time with something that we know works and play the long game. If we are pressured and must fall back while we prepare, then we can even withdraw from our forts bordering the Unknown Territory. This would give us time to rebound when our soldiers are properly equipped."

He replied with heightened eyebrows. "Are you suggesting we abandon our garrisons instead of using our resources to fortify them?"

I clarified, "Not at all. What I am suggesting is… only if necessary… we reconsolidate and bet our money on a winning hand. By doing this, we can then use supplemental troops from the Northern or Western fronts to create a task force intent on suppressing thieves and bandits. This would allow us to create one outward movement and keep all our enemies in front of us instead of trying to rely on a half-baked scheme. Summoning a hero is far too risky for me and should be for anyone else. We would have better luck in one of the gambling dens than placing our faith in a random foreign power to solve our own messes. Remember, no matter who is summoned, none of our problems are theirs. This person could show up and cause just as much damage to our forces as they do to the enemy."

The King then looked at my fiancée, and I knew we were in deep shit right away. "Although uncouth and a little brash, General Raider may have a point. General Marleen, your betrothed seems to lack the same resolve you have when it comes to placing the kingdom's hope in magic. There is no way an Elvanian of such an ancient White-Elven bloodline would agree that this is a reckless course of action. In addition to being one of the most highly skilled magicians and researchers, you are one of only two in Alvernia to reach the rank of Grand Mage. Given your expertise and background, what do you have to say on this matter?"

That sneaky bastard is pandering to my one weakness. You didn't call Laura, Ian, or even the useless Claire to support your crazy ambition. You call on the one person who can affect my nightly activities and will obviously side with your ridiculousness. He isn't a bad king. In fact, I'd even be willing to name my firstborn after him. However, as a ruler, he knows how to get what he wants and make it look good in front of everyone else.

Marleen, being an expert magician in both persistent and non-persistent magic, would always side with an outcome that favored depending on magic as a solution. That's because, at its heart, magic can be considered a true roll of the dice, and magicians have the largest addiction to it. No two outcomes are ever the same when using any magical spell or when creating a magical item. So, the King and Marleen would probably think, 'Why not take the gambling to the max and summon a hero?' as if it's the logical choice. To some degree, they are right because the summoning spell could be considered as dependable as casting anything else.

Where we differ is that I focus on the potential outcome of casting a spell, not the methodology used to cast the spell. Because mages focus on the methodology, they get a form of gambler's high when casting. This means the larger and riskier the spell, the more of a rush a mage can get from successfully completing it. Spells can fizzle, succeed, kill many people, or even kill nobody. What's important is that the King wants a specific outcome, and my crazy-ass elf bride-to-be will take part in it if it gives her the rush that she's looking for.

Truthfully, participating in powerful spells isn't the only thing to get Marleen off. She has had periods where she obsessed about clandestine adventures, theoretics, metaphysics, and even the composition of my body... as odd as those sound. That's why she is so eager to participate in this next-level proposition. I swear, marrying a mage is like marrying a junkie that has no real help of ever recovering. I am going to be hitched to one of the most successful mages, so the road ahead of us is going to be a long one.

I can't see her face while she kneels behind me on the floor, but I can practically hear the drool hitting the marble one drop at a time. Ok, I suppose I can stop acting like this is all bad. The side of her that is willing to take risks is what made me originally fall in love with her. Her crazy ideas and magical intuition have given me many unique experiences over the years. However, this time, we will be talking about an impact that affects every single citizen of Alvernia.

Marleen looked up to meet the King's eyes and replied, "Your Highness, please forgive Raider, as he tends to hate the very idea of magic. He thinks deep down that every problem can be ushered away with battle tactics and a sword. I don't believe he intends to have any ill will, but rather, he is trying to provide alternatives before we decide. In his defense, tactics, and steel, with minimal magical support, are usually enough."

    Marleen took a sizeable pause before she continued. This meant she was up to no good.

Chapter 2: Continuing Countenance

Marleen chuckled after leaving us on edge. "Despite the usefulness of the blade and my future husband's renowned battle prowess, I agree that a hero summoning would be the best for our Kingdom. It grants the highest probability of success with the smallest overall expenditure of resources. Our National ManaBank would replenish its supply far faster than our coffers, recruits, supplies, or diplomatic ties. Should you give the word, I will personally oversee the summoning and make sure it is a success. I guarantee results on my very life."

King Forsythe stood up, obviously happy at her predictable response. "Very well, General Marleen! I am glad to see that most of us are on the same page! We will reconvene to discuss this further in the War Room in the next half hour. Laura, Ian, and Clare. I expect you to help Marleen in convincing her husband to join the rest of you in support of this endeavor."

Now that I think about it, I believe the King was a well-rounded mage in his prime. I've only been to the Royal Magical Academy a few dozen times, and I'm sure I've seen his portrait there somewhere. Is it possible his urges as a mage resurface, which is also a primary influence on his decision-making? Probably better to leave some of those words unspoken. I'm already on his naughty list today… in addition to all the other times I've found myself on it.

After making his point, the King abruptly departed the Throne Room. His absence gave us a much-needed, although brief, break before heading back to meet him. Everyone stopped being all formal and began to congregate in clusters in the middle of the room to discuss what had just transpired. The nobles were still appalled at my 'outburst.' They distinctly made it a point to avoid including me in any of their circles while they mumbled loudly enough for me to overhear their condescending tones.

They didn't faze me. I pondered aloud, "What the hell was I doing before this meeting?"

Taking advantage of the chaotic conglomeration of nobility, Marleen rushed over to me to express how excited she was that her plan had worked all too perfectly. With her expressions, it was hard to tell who was leading whom in that charade just now. How many times does a twenty-four-year-old mage from a foreign country get to perform one of the hardest spells? To her, it was probably a badge of honor to be able to use almost all of a nation's stored mana. She will put that one on the list of accomplishments she has lying about the house someplace. I can see it on her permanent bragging portfolio, 'Hero Summoning Badass,' or at least that is what she is probably thinking.

    To break me from my internal monologues, she looked left and right to make sure nobody else was looking and licked me from the bottom of my jaw all the way to my hairline. This was normally her way of reconciling or breaking me out of deep thought. She knows I hate it, but it always makes me focus on her annoying quirks and forget about our disagreements. In a way, she is far more manipulative than the King.

    Pushing her away, I wiped my face off while chiding her. "I get it; relax already! I'm not angry with you. Besides, how often do I need to tell you that we are older now? Have some respect while in public, at least. We are in some of the highest-ranking positions in the Sovereignty. Don't you think you can finally show a little class? Where did you even get that stupid habit of yours anyway? It's not like it's an elf thing, an Elvanian thing, or even an academy thing. I've told you countless times to cut it out. What would happen if someone else saw you acting like a child?"

    She absconded from my comments, "Stop being so obstinate and just roll with the flow for once! You're taking the joy out of the little time we get together! Every time something exciting happens, you try to tell me all the boring minor details that could go wrong or get someone killed. And deep down, I know you love my affection! When we first started dating five years ago, you didn't mind entertaining me. Admit it! Back then, you didn't mind anything we did while alone! But now... you're a sour soldier. Rugged to the bone!"

    Marleen was clearly too giddy to contain herself. She was practically squealing in delight. That aside, she was right about our relationship. One day, out of the blue, she just licked me, and that is what triggered me to ask her out. Who's ever heard of an attractive White Elf with long blonde hair, perfect curves, and bubbly personality talking to a human casually? It can be odd sometimes because I am tall for a human, while she is much shorter. I'd estimate she's short for any race. But in my opinion, for an elf, she is the perfect height. Who can turn that down? A rare species of elf wanting to engage in a relationship with a human is generally not something that happens. White Elves and Green Elves are almost exclusively found in Elvania, and White Elves specifically are a small fraction of their population.

Anyway, the whole thing was too good to be true. I would have been a fool to turn her down back then. If you asked me, aside from her long ears, hair, and incredible figure, what attracted me the most... it would have to be her unassailable intelligence. She tends to conceal her intellect behind her eccentric personality when in public, but she might be the most intelligent person in the kingdom. I still don't know what she sees in me, but we are clearly a very compatible couple, especially with how well we get along. Maybe it's my short brown hair, slightly muscular build, or my height. Sincerely, she could do much better, all joking aside.

But who am I kidding? The only thing she probably cares about is my cautious personality. I tend to be the voice of reason, while she is a go-getter that never looks back. Not to brag, but if I had not stepped into her life, I bet she would have exploded a thousand times over by now because of some experiment or miss-casted spell. They would call her the 'Crispy Crunchy Grey Elf' because her skin would have transformed from pale to charcoal by now.

"Helloooooo? Raider?" She was knocking on my head with those small, bony fingers of hers. "Stop zoning out all the time. What's with you today? It's as if you aren't... yourself. Are you wrapped up inside your head again?"

Her face pressed against mine as her eyes moved up and down, giving me a once-over. "Wait a moment... what happened to you?"

I caught Laura forcefully ending an inelegant conversation with some noble vying for her attention with sweet words. When she was close enough, she sharply snapped, "Alright, you two, cut that shit out in public. Feel free to do whatever you want when you return to wherever, but right now, we need to discuss our plans moving forward. And by plans, I don't mean getting 'Hero Summoning Badass' on your record, Marleen." She glared at Marleen because she knew exactly why she was going along with the King's request. But Laura isn't much better. She would support that man to her very grave if he asked it of her.

This glare triggered a contest of wills between the two women... a contest they got into so often that I was better off ignoring it. Laura would call Marleen 'childish' or 'lackadaisical,' which would cause Marleen to try to rub Laura's ears while saying she was 'too serious.' This would provoke another reaction, and then another, and then another. They were used to me backing up to my own devices as they went at it.

Unfortunately for Laura, everything in her life has always come down to loyalty and duty, which is what caused her to butt heads with both Marleen and me. That is probably how she got to her rank of 'Supreme Commander' so quickly, that die-hard attitude of hers. If you took away the loyalty aspect of why she was supporting the King, we are more alike than she cares to admit. She would entirely refute this whole thing as a propaganda stunt to bolster the public's opinion of the Royal Court.

But, then again, that conversation would never come out into the open because she would consider it borderline treason. In a way, she depends on me to be her silent voice without coming forward and telling me that is my role. I'm calling it now; her damn sense of duty will cause some serious consequences one day when I'm not around. My main hope is that when it happens, those consequences aren't irreversible.

While I am thinking about Laura, she is generally considered one of the most 'untouched' beauties in all of Alvernia. Her blood-red hair extends halfway down her back, and she usually keeps it in a ponytail unless she goes into combat. She's a little taller than most of the others at about five foot eight, but I swear she can stare me down like she's taller than a two-story house. She always wears her traditional silver Alvernian plate armor with gold trim and a red cape while she is in public. And, she never goes anywhere, not even the bar, without both of her artifact blades on each hip.

The reason for her attire and weapon loadout being over the top has to do with her feeling the need to represent the country in the best light. She takes her station very seriously, which also gets on my last nerves. At the same time, she expects us to always wear similar attire while on official duty. Whoever came up with the dress code must not have thought about comfort, that's for sure. Nobody wants to be covered in plate armor from head to toe when it's scorching hot and humid out. That woman, though, doesn't give a damn what others think.

Laura has a million nicknames as well, but among them, some of my favorites are the 'Red-Headed Berserker,' 'Blood-Blade Babe,' 'Blood-Red Dead,' and her most notorious one, 'The Blood Dancer.' Her red hair is a little rare for an Alvernian, which is the reason for such a focus on it. Another unique feature is her naturally slightly darker skin, which is what really sets her apart from most of the other women, especially nobles, who try to remain as light-skinned as possible.

The only tribes of women I know of with skin that color come from the southern Tuscany Empire or the far eastern side of Alvernia in the Desolate Plains, where the desert seems endless. There are a few in Lorelei as well, but not many. Even given this, she has always said she is an Alvernian native, born and bred. But with her hair and skin color two-hit combo, she has become somewhat of the ideal poster girl that nobody dares to cross due to her combat prowess. Although she is still young, pushing thirty-two or so, she has seen more combat with humans and demons than entire forts. That's how she eventually became known as the 'Blood Dancer.' She is named amicably after how beautifully she cuts a path through any enemy that opposes her.

Laura has never once thought of the consequences when she gets into a fight, verbal or physical. That thoughtless recklessness is what landed her a job as an instructor at the Military Academy when she was very young, far before her current position. She often hurt students bad enough they couldn't even walk off the training field because she was 'caught in the moment.' That's how the whole 'berserker' and 'blood' nicknames started. This makes her ruthlessly careless in combat, but aside from that, she can be one of the most caring people on the planet for those she considers friends.

That leads me to another darker memory of mine. Once upon a time, when I was fifteen, and she was my outrageously out-of-reach twenty-six-year-old aggressive instructor, we even dated in secret. But she broke it off when she accepted her new position, so all of that is ancient history. Now, she treats me the same as all her other subordinates when we are in the public's eye with that untampered attitude of hers.

Confidently, I addressed her, "Laura…"

She stopped her feud with Marleen to cut me off, "That's Supreme Commander in public, you dipshit. Wake up before I demote you or personally give you the worst detail I can think of. Or better yet, let's go to the training yard when we are done here. I have some new techniques I learned from some random wandering swordsman, and I want to try them out on you."

In an attempt to be as monotone as possible, I stagnantly replied, "The Honorable Supreme Commander… your Highness Laura…"

Laura crossed her arms and replied while smirking and rubbing her chin. "Better… but work on it. Anyway, continue…" If there was one thing I could count on, it was how awkward she made me feel when she wanted to put me in my place.

I tried again, "I don't care if it gets me in the doghouse and forces me into the arms of the women in the brothels for a whole month! We cannot let him go through with this outlandish idea! The concept of using that spell is unheard of in today's age, and I'm tired of everyone pretending it isn't. It will burn our country to the ground! Damn it, Laura, you need to support me on this."

Laura has a good sense of reason; she understands why I am so against it, and I know deep down that if given enough time, she will side with me. Not that this will have any ultimate bearing on what the King decides. I think he's looking for all five of his generals to agree with him to feel confident about his actions. Even he knows that Ian and I are the only two who would publicly oppose him.

Marleen, joking, stepped in, "If you go to brothels for a whole month, just make sure they aren't elves. That way, when I finally forgive you, you will be crawling back, begging me for that little something only I can give. Remember that shocking surprise last time? I think I keep it interesting!"

She was, of course, joking. I don't think she would ever forgive me for being unfaithful to her for a single second, not that the subject has never really been an issue between us. If anything, she was a little too frisky at times, and I could use a damn break. I wonder if all her race was like this. That is another one of those questions I shouldn't ask.

Speaking nonchalantly, I tried to get under Laura's skin. "Marleen, are you talking about what you do with your mana to surprise me when we..."

I was interrupted suddenly by Laura, who is not the bashful type. If I remember correctly, Laura was even wilder than Marleen regarding the bedroom. "Cut that shit out too. Who do you think you two are kidding? We all know you two aren't the closest thing to frisky. Pretending otherwise would do a disservice to your kind, Marleen. If you want a good story, then listen to my share of estranged and disorderly engagements. By the time my story concludes, you wouldn't want to try my resolve or my vigor."

Marleen knew this wasn't an idle threat... and sadly, neither did I, but for other reasons. Once Marleen settled down, Laura smiled and backed off. "But again, we are in public, so knock it off. We need to all get our minds right for the upcoming meeting. Head to the usual spot to entertain our illustrious and all-knowing ruler. We need to hear out any additional details he may have omitted from his speech. I know you two are desperate for more information about why he wants to move forward with the Hero Summoning Ritual. Especially you, Acton."

After that, Marleen and I decided to head off to the kitchen to grab something quickly before heading back into another long meeting. It's not unusual to see us in the castle together since we have had offices here for the last year. We know all the staff, their families, and what they do inside the castle. Speaking of that, we rounded a corner into a deserted hallway except for one snappy-looking butler standing outside one of the doors. He was holding a towel and slightly bowing at his waist.

As we approached him, both Marleen and I said in unison, 'Good Morning, Seventeen,' and continued walking. Seventeen is the Keeper of Shadows assigned to me that oversees my intelligence, counterintelligence, and odd jobs. We have known each other since long before I assumed my current post due to his family connections at the Military Academy. He would occasionally drop in and be a guest speaker and brief us on the importance of intelligence gathering in the field.

Things like bringing in Keepers, or their families known to pass down their trade from generation to generation, were done to encourage interest in utilizing assets off the battlefield. Too many blockheads after the 'upper echelon' seats only wanted to wield a sword and tell people to go die instead of using resources, like Seventeen, at their disposal.

His identity was never disclosed at the time, but when I was appointed as the General of the Eastern Front, I knew who he was right away. One could say we have known each other just as long as Marleen and I have known each other. To me, that makes him basically my family since my real one was never there for me. He is easily the most dependable and trustworthy person that reports to me. I would entrust my life to him without a second thought.

It's become quite the game for Marleen and me to recognize him in one of his disguises whenever we cross his path in public. Nonchalantly, we greet him and keep going like nothing is out of the ordinary. Not that there are dozens of people who dress up in random costumes, but he tries his best to blend in with his surroundings. If we correctly guess it's him, we win, and he owes me a minor favor. If he wins, he gets one minor favor from me during his next report. If you asked me how this little game got started, I don't quite remember. It might have been during my first and only year with the Royal Guards, about two years ago, when he pulled one over on me. To him, fooling people with disguises is a hobby he can get a few laughs at.

We ended up wagering that the next time we met, I would see through his 'dirty schemes.' Since then, it has become a silly contest back and forth. Most of our little competitions are good fun, so Marleen wanted to get her pointy ears involved, too. So far, he has only won twice, and both times, he requested a different pair of undergarments from one of my captains, Leah Douglas. His unnatural obsession with vampire women is startling... but I don't dive into his personal fantasies.

That gets awkward because I have known Leah since I was in the academy. She thinks I am into weird shit when Marleen isn't around. Luckily, since she is a vampire, I exchange blood for her silence whenever I pay her a visit. So far, she hasn't spread the rumor mill to Marleen, so everything is working out fine. I also don't visit her at her fort that often, just whenever fort checkups are needed a few times a year. That makes things a bit easier, and fewer questions are asked.

Seventeen started chuckling after he lost this round. "General Raider, the same mead as always, I assume? That honey is becoming quite rare, you fiend." He started his over-accentuated nobles bow to me. His fake butler routine has started to shine, I'm impressed.

I replied, "Yeah, I'll take that along with that dragon's egg you are trying to hatch. Don't think I don't know about it. How did a slimy guy like you get ahold of something so valuable? Swindling the vagabonds out of their money?"

It's never a dull moment with Seventeen around. I know more about this man than I should or even care to admit. The thing with the dragon's egg is mostly a joke, too. We don't know what that egg is, but he has had it forever under a heated lamp. That man raising a dragon should scare the entire world. Imagining him riding that damn thing into battle with the Empire would put me in an early grave from laughter.

Seventeen continued with his butler impersonation. "Very good sir, General sir. As for the services you requested this morning, you will find them with your bottle of mead in the kitchen. I hope everything is to your liking. I expect to have additional services available for you within the next week."

Excellent, this means the information I requested on the Empire has arrived! And a whole week early at that! It is outside of my jurisdiction to request anything other than information pertaining to my post. Specifically, it is about demons or bandits and their activity. However, with those Imperial assholes going back on their word, it puts my job and my people at risk. I'm not about to let that happen without a fight.

Truth be told, there is only so much I can do outside of my domain of responsibilities. Once something is within my domain, I have the full authority second only to the King and the High Mage. Not even Laura can intercede in my efforts without a damn good reason. Seventeen knew this investigation was a risky assignment for his subordinates, but he stayed the course and got it done. I respect that man and hope to never make an enemy of him or any of his underlings. The world of shadows can be a very mysterious and treacherous place that is hard to survive. However, Seventeen was born for it, effortlessly flourishing with his assigned tasks

Seventeen also has me thinking about what the other Keeper of Shadows is like for the other generals. Every general and even most of the captains each have a keeper assigned. All of them work independently of each other. This was done to avoid favoritism or corruption from one party to another. Are Seventeen's skills and personality amazing, or are they all trained that way?

I asked Marleen once if she had one assigned to her, and she insisted she didn't. I don't doubt her sincerity, but I sometimes wonder if she can't tell me because she was originally from the Elvanian Republic. Put differently, maybe the King doesn't fully trust her because of her national origin. That can't be the case because Marleen was put as the 'General of the Northern Border' with Elvania. This was done to help encourage peaceful coexistence with them. Or maybe she doesn't have a keeper assigned her because we trust Elvania too much?

By the time Marleen and I had arrived in the kitchen, all the staff had left for their breaks. Royalty, nobility, guards, and even the castle's servants ate some time ago. It wasn't quite time to prepare lunch, which put us in a predicament. We were both hungry because we were up late last night and slept through breakfast. We decided to instead wait for lunch and look around for what Seventeen had left for me. He can be a sore loser, so he likes to prepare my rewards in awkward places most of the time as a sort of revenge.

One time, the reward was in an oven, and another time, it was next to the toilet with a sign that said something along the lines of 'For Toilet Raiders Only.' What a clever man he is, always thinking of outdated puns involving my name. When we found what he left, we realized he didn't even try to hide my bottle this time. It was right next to a chicken head. Or wait, that is a male chicken head.

Marleen started laughing before I even figured it out. Sometimes I hate my life. She, of course, had to snicker, "He got you good this time, you cocky general you. I feel like you got off light today; last week's toilet humor was sourly delightful!"

I replied while rolling my eyes and grabbing the bottle. "You know, only you and Seventeen think any of this is nonsense is funny. Just give me the booze and call it good. There is no way that other keepers are this ridiculous. Nothing he does is even really 'cloak and dagger'! It's all just for show, but I suppose it's alright if he is having fun. Who am I to get in the way of the old man's enjoyment?"

"You mean give me the bottle, and I might share some with you if you get down on all fours and bark like a dog?" Marleen phrased that as a question as she snatched the bottle from my hands.

"Hold on, wait a second. Let me see that bottle." I returned the bottle from Marleen and noticed his signature red thumbprint on the bottom of the label. So, it appears his report is on the inside part of the mead label, which is not bad if I do say so myself. Taking the label, I rolled it up, placed it into my satchel, and then handed the bottle back over to Marleen. Even though she will be my wife, I can't share any of my reports with her or anyone else by the King's proclamation. Sometimes, he can be a little paranoid, but that's fine. He doesn't get the title, 'The Pacified', for no reason. It may as well be 'The Ultra-Cautious,' given how much he tries to avoid regicide.

"So about getting on all fours for this mead..." Marleen said jokingly.

I decided to play along, "Save it until later tonight, Miss Horny Ears. Or you can at least wait until after the war council is over. Damn glutton."

Chapter 3: Directionless Direction

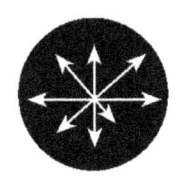

      If the Throne Room and the War Room were competing for the biggest waste of time, they would come up in a dead tie. Both are large cold rooms full of condescending, manipulative assholes. And every single one of those bastards likes to make decisions without knowing what they are making decisions about. The mood in both rooms has always been serious because everyone seems to have a chip on their shoulder, perks of their bullshit statuses that they like to shove down other's throats. So, no matter what I say, my opinion is overruled one way or another. Every conversation I contribute to usually begins with everyone listening to what I have to say and swiftly ends with abrupt interruptions that contradict any and all presented evidence.

      It's always as if I am the only ultra-conservative voice of reason that errors on the side of caution while everyone else wants to charge headfirst into everything. Why would you want any ground to stand or pass verdicts about when you can see your own reality? At most, I get patted on the head as a way of those in charge stating, 'That's cute, thank you for your opinions, now go sit in the corner.' A great example was when I presented last week about the demon attacks that killed over fifty farmers far behind our front line. It was 'reworked' into the public report as fifty mercenaries adventuring into the Unknown Territory.

      Are things like this done because they don't respect me for earning my way into nobility and my background is of a humble, commoner origin? Is it because they all have something to prove to the King? It doesn't matter because it happens every time, and the King allows it. That is probably why most of these conversations make me want to tell them to shove it. To round it out nicely, I would have to interrupt their pointless ramblings without a clear way to solve any of our problems.

      The only official with any real authority that has ever taken me seriously was Laura… not publicly, but in private where others couldn't hear her. The problem with Laura is that she is always playing politics while balancing her sense of duty. I believe she does this to protect herself and every general underneath her, so I ultimately draw the short end of the stick even when I express myself in her presence. She is my reassurance that nothing is reassured.

I don't fault her for the way she reacts. Being a political entrepreneur is exactly what the Supreme Commander position is supposed to be in a nutshell. She is basically an overhead for her direct reports. Sheathing her swords and taking up the silver-tongued word to protect us from all non-military personnel. Clad in shining silver armor, she funnels only the important information in the form of missions or objectives. It's a tireless job that I thank her for doing every chance I get... when she isn't chewing me out for something. All this builds up to make the Throne Room a parade for the nobility and the War Room to be extremely taxing on my nerves due to a lack of consideration for my solutions.

If there were any upside at all, it would be that nobility are infrequently invited to the War Room, so half of my headaches end before we even arrive here. But that still doesn't stop me from thinking, 'Here we go again... same old shit again', as I struggle in vain to do the right thing and help the kingdom and my soldiers out. That ringing question of, 'Is this all worth it?' probably won't go away anytime soon, but if I don't look out for my people, nobody else will either.

I don't know how the other generals behave outside of our high-level therapy sessions, but I can say for certain that none of them put themselves out there for their subordinates the way I do... and that includes Marleen. I would be willing to bet the other generals might say the same about me as well, for a different reason. Even though I am very vocal, the impact of your policies and actions often can't be seen for two to ten years down the road. Maybe I am being a little arrogant, but I don't care what they think of how I lead. Does this make me a hypocrite for judging them and not caring if I am judged? Yeah, probably. But on a long enough timeline, they will see that most of my decisions are the right ones.

"Alright! Quickly take your seats so we can begin." King Forsythe is opening the meeting like he usually does. His relaxed composure couldn't reflect his overall attitude any better.

As soon as I took my seat, he pointed me out. "I know what you're thinking. And yes, I have things I care about in the world, regardless of my relaxed posture. You know damn well those nobles and their bickering wear me out something awful. Day after day, their shenanigans cause me more headaches as they distort the truth. Part of me wishes I would keel over and let one of my absent sons take over. At least then, I'll have some peace! If it weren't for my loving wife, I would have no heaven at all!"

That last line was a lie, and he ceaselessly argued with Queen Olivia. I only know this because the Queen has been close to me for a long time and tends to dote on me, unlike my significant other. She does this purposefully in front of her husband, again painting a target on my back unnecessarily. This only makes matters worse because his daughter and I have also gotten along a lot better than he would like.

Between the two of them causing hell for me when the King is around, he pays me back double whenever they are absent. This makes his War Room 'sanctuary' an arena of fun when it comes to antagonizing me. Yet another reason why my ideas will never get through to anyone when it counts... like today. Kind of makes me laugh. Just the thought of both his wife and daughter cracking the whip behind closed doors is enough to make me want to come here and deal with his provocations.

King Forsythe cleared his throat as he scratched his head. "While I am on the topic of you, Raider... your little outburst may have done better than I initially realized. It lessened the impact of the grave news. Leave it to them to be more concerned about reputation than survival. So, thank you for going along with the usual show. As always, you make a great, willing sacrifice so Marleen and I can compete against you. I thoroughly enjoy watching your torment in pure delight. But on a more serious note, this kingdom benefits substantially from your efforts. Just know that regardless of what we decide going forward, everyone appreciates your leadership and guidance for being so young. All those old men downgrading you because of your birth is all to make themselves feel better, so don't pay them any mind. I would easily trade one or two dozen of them for you any day of the week and twice over when deciding our best course of action."

He's exhibiting unusual behavior this morning as he never panders to me at all during these 'meetings.' Moreover, the usual back and forth in the Throne Room was very short and to the point. I am starting to get nervous that his mind was made up a while ago and is about to tell us more unsettling news. It would be his style to act first and then ask for support later if he knew an unfavorable result was guaranteed, the cautious old bastard.

Not that he needs to gain my support... but keeping me around has made his life significantly easier than when Claire held my position two years ago. Plus, he might also be thinking that if he irritates me too much, he will then make Marleen upset and might lose her favor. Keep going down that rabbit hole, and in his mind, it might be displeasing two generals for the price of one. However, dividing and conquering us by playing to our desires one at a time is just smart. Like I said before, this is a cunning old man.

King Forsythe's speech patterns seemed hurried as he spoke. "The High Mage, Laura, and I have decided to move forward with notifying each of the other bordering countries about the increase in demonic activity from the Unknown Territories. We still have not received any word from the Elvanian Republic regarding activity along their border, so we will operate under the assumption that our allies can support themselves. Up until now, we have used dispatch riders to communicate our intentions to both the Tuscany Empire and the Elvanian Republic."

He had an unnatural pause in the middle of his speech. "But... due to the severity of the situation with our supply and soldier shortages, we need to stress the seriousness of the situation we find ourselves in more so than ever. Therefore, all of you will be sent with small contingents to the countries that border your area of responsibility. Each of you is to inform the other kingdoms of our situation, gather information, and clearly express our need to summon a hero to survive unless we get immediate aid."

He slammed his fist onto the table and raised his voice in anger. "We simply cannot afford to send our usual messengers! They aren't taking us seriously enough based on their lack of responses! We must, and we will, express that our situation isn't anything less than harrowingly grave! While they sit in their forests and their castles and lap up the life of peace and solitude, we die by the dozens every day. OUR PEOPLE! They are dying for the sake of everyone, and they couldn't care less!"

Quickly, his demeanor changed as he recomposed himself. "Laura and Claire will remain here and continue with their regular duties. Nothing will take priority over commanding the Royal Guards and the security in and around the capital. Ian will head to the Empire to see if they still intend to give us the shipments they are behind on. Ian, I need you to be successful... we need you to be successful. I cannot stress this enough. Marleen, you will go to Elvania. Do what you must, including relying on your family connections. The rest of us are forbidden from crossing the border since we are human. We can thank the Empire for that, but no use in dwelling on it. Raider, you will go on one of your normal rounds and check out each one of our border forts to verify the reports you receive are accurate. I expect Ian and Marleen to be gone about a week, and Raider, two weeks at most."

    For the first time since I was appointed to this post, I'm genuinely worried. Things have got to be far more dire than the King has been letting on up to this point. The 'usual rounds' he mentioned didn't exist until I started them last year. None of my predecessors even left the capital to check on the front line. Instead, they would only communicate by letters three or four times a year and play Armchair General while the captains took care of all the real responsibilities. It wouldn't even be an understatement to say every general at every post was more of a figurehead than an actual leader.

    When I took command, the first thing we needed was a real account of the situation along our most dangerous boundary. Since then, it has become expected for me to make one of these rounds to check on things every six months. Mostly, these visits aren't formal inspections. They include receiving reports, shaking hands, and going on a few patrols to confirm the integrity of the information that has been passed up the chain. This was the only solution I could come up with to establish an effective feedback chain. Now, he wants me to go on another one of these rounds several months early.

    I am in no position to ask for more details, but for all his top generals to be dispatched at the exact same time makes no sense strategically. If one of the other two countries has been masquerading as an ally but secretly has nefarious intentions, this would be the perfect time to strike. Quick and decisive actions would be able to kill the general assigned to the border with that country, cause chaos in our ranks, and put the entire burden of leadership on those stationed locally. As a commander looking to invade another country, it would be impossible to ask for a better circumstance unless you could maybe assassinate the remaining leadership figures. In other words, he is out of his mind.

    For that smart old man to give this directive… means he is either planning something he doesn't wish to disclose or is privy to additional information he doesn't wish to divulge. I have absolute faith in Seventeen. However, if the King knows something that even he doesn't know, then he is damn good at hiding it.

    Personally, out of the three of us being sent to other countries, I would be most concerned about sending Ian to the Empire. Ian is loyal, determined, and, overall, a damn good general. However, as a safety measure, I would have sent him first and had one of us back up his post while he was gone. As it currently stands, Ian is being sent to the Empire, and nobody is looking after his line of defense in his absence. There isn't any way to stress how much of a stupid decision he is making.

    Piecing together what went into the decision to send Ian won't ever resonate with me. The only move that made sense was sending Marleen to the Elvanian Republic. The King understands how important it is to cooperate with the elves. Elvania's patience with human-run countries is on very thin ice. They aren't exactly angry at Alvernia, but there are several factions that control their country that loop all humans together as being responsible for the Empire's enslavement of elves. Therefore, Marleen is the only person in a significant leadership role that we can send. In addition to her background and whatever family ties she has, Elvania's reluctance to listen to our story might outweigh their willingness to listen if we send her as a representative.

    Their prejudice is completely understandable once you learn just how awful the kidnapped and enslaved elves are treated in the Empire. Put simply, elves traditionally have had a passive culture and have avoided having contact with most humans for the past several decades until those idiots started abducting them. This is also why almost all elves, aside from the nomadic Grey Elves, which are their own society and culture, are very rare in Alvernia.

    Against my better judgment, I decided to speak out of turn. "Your Highness, why would you make such important decisions without the entirety of the council being present? Only Laura and the High mage were present for such an important decision? And if I may, why would you bring up the hero summoning publicly but then dismiss the War Council on errands immediately afterward? Doesn't it seem like you are trying to conceal your true intentions from us? We were all appointed to your inner circle for precise moments like this when you should lean on our input for guidance. Today's events aren't like you."

His right eye flinched as I spoke, a tell-tell sign I caught onto him. Now I'm sure of it. He wanted to gain internal support to cast the Hero Summoning Ritual while we were out gathering consent abroad. He has used a similar version of this 'bait-and-switch' tactic in the past by having us all focus on something he makes a spectacle while doing something else. Maybe a pride thing as a ruler?

Our kingdom is a series of independent regions that all support Alvernia. None of the other regions are suppressed by force but instead willingly cooperate out of the necessity for safety. Making sure they are all on board and feel their support isn't going to be wasted is essential to ensure future peaceful cooperation. I'm sure he thinks if he drops the idea of us summoning a hero to the other regions, then they would be less likely to think our king was making decisions without them. By sending his generals out to also declare our intentions to the other nations, he can avert a possible misunderstanding, which might lead to a war... or the other countries casting their own summoning magic in retaliation.

Laura didn't even give the King a chance to respond. "Acton, I think you are forgetting your position. Your job is to execute what is told to you by those above you. Just because you have a history with His Highness doesn't mean that stepping out of line won't have severe consequences! This decision was made, and you will abide by it! Do I need to put you on display in the arena? Thirty lashes for disrespecting our King? I'll be damned if my student and my subordinate is going to disrespect our sovereign ruler!"

And in steps hostile Laura. Man, have I missed you... but not really. She is a crude and blunt hammer when what is needed is a knife. If she is this hardcore about the King's decisions, I'll have to drop all my lines of inquiry to become the epitome of a loyal servant. This doesn't make me feel any less like I'm walking into a dark alley with no illumination source. This eerie feeling of a monster jumping out from the shadows to bite me is getting stronger, and I don't mean Leah.

The King placed his forehead back into his palm. "That's enough, Laura. I admire the inherent idealistic nature of youth so much sometimes. That nature always tends to radiate from the brightest and most promising of people. Raider shouldn't have his life considered for trying to do the right thing. I'm not a damn tyrant. I know you two have a long past together, dating and what have you, back to when he was a young teenager. That doesn't mean you shouldn't cut him some slack. I can't tell if you are lashing out at him like a mother or a lover most of the time. Either way, stop suffocating the poor guy. Don't get me wrong; I thoroughly enjoy watching a good lover's quarrel now and then."

Laura's eyes lowered in displeasure. After a half-hearted chuckle, he continued, "Now, as for you, Raider... like Laura said, this was done for a reason. We are not trying to cut you or any of the other generals out. What we are after is the protection of our people. With that, make sure you depart as soon as possible. Marleen, make sure to take special care of Raider. It might be a while until you can see him again, so you never want to part on bad terms. Ian, spend some time with your wife as well. Laura, get a boyfriend or something to vent your pent-up anger on. You're getting older and need to settle down! You're thirty-two already, and you don't have many years left to bear children, after all."

King Forsythe went back to laughing as he was finishing that last comment. Nobody knows why Laura hasn't ever tried to settle down. Lately, the King has decided to use that as his primary point of harassment at her own expense. She could have almost anyone she wanted with her looks, so there's something else blocking her from moving forward with her life, and I have a sneaking suspicion I know what.

After standing up from his chair, King Forsythe leisurely headed for the door. He stopped right before it and turned around to question me again. "Raider, have you ever thought about what you want to do with your life if we ever defeat the demons? And by that, I don't mean having kids, getting married, and doing your duties as a soldier. What do you absolutely want to accomplish with your life?" A cold chill ran down my spine like this might be a farewell question from him. Almost as if I should put all my effort into answering him sincerely.

I replied, "Your Highness, I haven't given any real thought to my personal needs for a long time. Any answer I give you will more than likely fall short of your expectations."

He didn't face me when he spoke. "Then try to be the best. For you and those around you. When the whole world turns against you, your allies abandon you, and you find yourself estranged with no possible outs... that's when it matters."

He removed his crown and gazed at the jewels in it for over a minute. "For a long time now... too long... that is... well... never mind. You won't always have people above you or next to you as you get older. People die, they move on, they find love, they turn their backs on you. If you ever need motivation, look to yourself and find your courage."

I asked, "Your Highness, I don't understand what you are asking of me."

His hands fiddling around with the crown eventually stopped. He was getting sentimental and choking up. "Time will tell for you more than others. Never give up, no matter how bad things might get in your life. Put another way, when you die, make sure you've become a legend worthy of being remembered."

He then glanced at me one last time before leaving the room. This was the shortest, most precise meeting he had ever held. We went in and sat down. He told us to disappear from the kingdom for a while, and he singled me out several times. What a day.

Chapter 4: The After-Party

After the King had left the room, the rest of us collected ourselves and began to talk again. Ian jumped up from his position across the table from me and ran over to violently pat me on the back like I was his son-in-law. "Damn, boy! When did your balls get so huge? I thought we knew each other, but after that stunt, I'm looking at a different man! For sure, I thought you were done in when you slipped up in the Audience Chamber. Taking on the King and then having him defend you against Laura is a new one. Teach me your secret magical techniques for wooing royalty and women, young one."

What a snide guy, but I love him and wouldn't trade him for anything. He's always been like the cooler older uncle I never had. Knowing him, he might even be liquored up and wanting to throw a party before we all take off into the wide world. Somewhere, somehow, he always has something on him to get sauced up. He hides it well, except for his breath. He also becomes very clingy as the day goes on with those to which he has taken a liking. Every time we go down this path, he eventually makes Marleen jealous to the point of trying to outdo each other. Laura then tries to break all three of us up while Claire continues to sit in her chair, maintaining her completely oblivious nature, as always.

Speaking of Claire, it comes across as no surprise that she didn't know what to say. Instead, she did what she always did and smiled back while playing with her hair. When our eyes finally met, she nonchalantly stood up and exited the room like she had accomplished something by being noticed. It must be nice to live in your own headspace every day.

I hope that woman never changes because she will really make the perfect obedient wife for some random noble or another. Just like Laura, there aren't many nobles in this country that would turn her down. If for nothing else, then most people would marry her for her political connections and her looks. Personally, I hope she applies herself and at least begins to look around for a suiter. Last I heard, she told her family she wouldn't agree to any arrangement meetings until after she had finished her first tour in her current position. But there's always that glimmer of hope she will start looking earlier than expected. The longer she takes, the more it hurts our overall readiness for combat. Maybe I can start setting up double dates to lure her into an early marriage?

    Just Laura, Marleen, the High Mage, and I were left in the room. I never learned the High Mage's name, but he was keen on whispering something into Marleen's ear before he departed. He was an elderly man with a long-flowing grey beard and countless wrinkles, always hunched over and supporting his weight on his staff and very quiet. The man never raised his voice, even when displeased. The little I knew about him was his unusual magical affinity for the fire element. Where most mages that wield fire can do small things like throwing fireballs, illuminating dark areas, and making a temporary wall or barrier... he could bend and twist the element around his body in a grandiose display. In other words, he ascended to his spot amongst the thousands of other mages because of his elven-like control over his element.

    Whatever that guy said made her light up so bright it was blinding. Her smile made me feel she was a mix of anxious, happy, and energetic, all rolled into one energetic elf. But, based on how Marleen has overacted in the past, I thought it would be best to ask her later when we got home. Even Laura was paying an unusual amount of attention to Marleen right after the High Mage spoke to her.

    Laura's downturned facial expressions showed she wasn't surprised at Marleen's giddiness. It was almost like this was a secret party everyone had already arrived at, and I wasn't invited. Laura's hand was on her face, her elbow on the table, and she projected a slight frown. Her disposition was only amplified by her impatient tapping with her other hand. Laura, Marleen, and I have been in an unusual trio for almost ten years. Secrecy was a divider that had never existed in the past.

    However, if I am reading the room right, Laura is beyond a little peeved at whatever Marleen has just learned. This just reaffirmed my earlier decision not to bring it up until later when we are at home. Laura's voice saying, 'Learn to read the atmosphere, asshole,' is already echoing in my head if I don't keep my mouth shut.

    Now that the three of us are alone, we will typically have a really good time together. The outward façade was no longer needed, so we could be ourselves. Often, this can turn into an unexpected, memorable after-party. Frequently, we end up in pubs, arenas, on patrol, or even in the barracks. But no matter what happens, for the last year since Marleen and I got appointed to general-level positions, we have always found a way to make it a unique experience. On a personal level, Laura and I are extremely alike, even though she is eleven years older. Our major personality differences can be derived from her ferociousness in battle and her attempt to take the mature adult approach in public. Appearance is everything to that woman.

 I tend to approach almost everything the same way except for the difference in persona projection. I don't like hiding or disguising my intent behind a fake personality. To her, however, that is an essential part of who she is on many levels. Even then, neither of us is like the eccentric and outgoing Marleen. That is why Marleen will take the lead in suggesting what to do or where to go whenever we make plans on our days or evenings off. Laura is a party animal and will go with the flow if she can fly incognito. The problem with that line of thinking is that everyone already knows who she is because of how she dresses. Who wouldn't notice the highest-ranked person in one of the local bars or restaurants wearing a red cape and heavy metal armor?

 Aside from her attire, we have been at this so long that now the people in the places we go to naturally know how to separate what she does on and off the clock. So, if those around us continue to act discreetly, then Laura has no problems letting her hair down and having a good time. There are times that I'm sure she feels like the odd person out, but she doesn't let on that she minds. Luckily, nothing awkward happened between Laura and Marleen due to our past relationship. Marleen knows that Laura and I are close at one point, but she doesn't know all the intricate details. Coming back to reality, I had almost let it slide that Laura had just casually threatened my life a few moments ago. It might be that she's trying to put distance between our group.

 She decided to stop her nervous tapping and speak up. "Hey, you two. I want you to know this is nothing personal, but everything is about to change. I want both of you to be prepared to do what it takes to be successful and don't get yourselves killed no matter what. I am not at liberty to disclose more than I already have, but by the time you get back from your assignments, everything will be made clear. Take care of yourselves and spend these next two nights doing things only young people can do. Just don't... don't get yourselves killed. We have a very long road ahead of us."

She then locked eyes with Marleen. "And... if you die before Raider, and I die of old age, then there won't be any point."

Laura didn't even give us a chance to respond before she unexpectedly stabbed her dagger into the table. Her unceremonious departure quickly followed. This ominous display was in line with what I was observing, but stabbing her dagger with her personal crest on it into the table was unexpected. It made me wonder if she was hurting or if she was trying to make a point. Being alone is a hard burden to bear, and even harder if you never ask for help.

Being in my early twenties might be another root cause for overthinking everything that has transpired today. I took the dagger from the table and put it into my belt loop until I could see Laura again. The King wants me to make a name for myself, and Laura was so focused on Marleen that I seemed like an estranged outsider. I'm too inexperienced in all this political drama bullshit, throwing my head in circles.

Life in the military was supposed to be much easier and more straightforward than all this nonsense. The King and Laura claimed I moved up way too fast because of my natural talents, although that seems unlikely given my mostly 'armchair' status around the capital. Laura could also be acting odd because of our history together, but jealousy isn't her style. Perhaps today was just another way for Laura to show her unusual affection? Could she be devolving into a hostile sentimentality? She was never like that in the past.

I'm having flashbacks of our first time together when she countered one of my attacks and hit me much harder than was necessary, knocking me out. I was hurt bad enough that there wasn't much I could do but lay there helplessly when I finally came to a few seconds later. And while I was lying on the ground and unable to resist, she stripped me down and took her time enjoying herself for hours while we were in the middle of the training yard. It was as if she was unleashing years of pent-up rage, anger, and hostility on me all at the same time with no other care on her mind. There are still physical scars where she clawed me. Most of them riddle my rib cage and the low parts of my back. Calling this an emotionally scarring moment wouldn't be doing justice to the state of mind I was in for weeks afterward.

This made for a very awkward first experience with the opposite sex, but I eventually came to terms with it when we started dating. She didn't care that those relationships were forbidden between the instructors and students. It's not like I am complaining, but Laura never knew how to give people 'choices' when her mind is made up. This very well could be her way of turning over a new leaf while trying to be a better person.

I was so caught up in my thoughts that I didn't even realize Marleen had her head propped up by her arms while gazing into my eyes. "Still daydreaming, are you? Something happened between this morning and now to distract you, didn't it? You really aren't acting like yourself at all."

She still had that blinding smile while patiently waiting for me to respond. Honestly, she is too good to me. Marleen knows when to and when not to interrupt me when I'm rolling in the deep. She finally dispelled the daze I had going on and said, "So, are you going to ask me? Huh? Huh? Go on! Ask your soon-to-be amazing wife what she knows! Ask her about the wonderful news that has fallen upon her and cloaks her in everlasting power! I bet you can't wait to learn what good news has come her way! Grouchy pants Laura doesn't seem to like it, but I know you will! This is so great! There is so much planning to do and so little time! Maybe there will be a party as well, with lots of food and all our friends. I'll for sure invite everyone from the Royal Research Academy!"

I replied, "Okay, Marleen, settle down. What are you even talking about? Take it nice and slow so I can understand everything piece by piece. You tend to get overly excited and jumble your thoughts into a massive word soup."

It's cute when she tries to rush herself and stumbles over her words. However, those around her can never get a direct answer unless she is told to take it one sentence at a time. She has a bad habit of going around in circles without directly responding to the questions that are asked of her. A good example was when I asked her to explain 'magic' to me. Four hours later, I learned nothing and was drunk on information… and alcohol.

She put on a pouty face while acting irritated. "Are you so blind you didn't even notice the High Mage talking to me just after the meeting ended? Dense General Raider is your new title! Slayer of demons, protector of virtue, dense as rocks! This is going to cost you major points with me, mister."

My subdued eyes and half-lowered eyelids didn't budge. In response, she instantly grabbed my hands. "Everything just happened! Everything I have ever wanted is going to finally come true! We need to tell everyone! All those long hours researching magic and pushing for further understanding of our universe will bear fruit. There is so much to do. First, the texts I'll get access to... then there's researching intermittent elements and people. But wait... the priorities. That must come first... the pylons. Yes, those."

It's times like this that I must interrupt Marleen, or she will keep talking until I die of boredom. "Moving on... I was going to ask you about that when we got home. Laura was getting impatiently upset the longer she saw the High Mage speaking to you. So, what's going on? I bet it has something to do with elves having more magical affinities than humans or something else mildly unimportant."

This time, she looked peeved, so I quickly continued, "Anyway... since you are the only White Elf in this kingdom that any of us have met, I bet that man just wants to exploit your natural abilities. That, or maybe he wanted your help due to your magical prowess like usual? It must be nice having attained the only Grand Master's red robe. He can just push his weight around however he sees fit now. He has been depending on you more and more lately, and it's starting to get under my skin. Tell that man to figure out how to properly research magic on his own or get someone else from the research institute to help him who isn't engaged to me. There are plenty of 'expert' black-robed mages lingering around the Royal Research Academy, where he can siphon the life out of one sip at a time. May as well be a vampire, damn old man."

I said it because it's been building up inside me for a while. The more she gets pulled away from random shit that guy asks her for, the less time she can spend with me. Call it selfish, but sometimes it feels like we could go days without getting quality time together because of some stupid random project or another. It just occurred to me that this might've been what was putting Laura on edge as well.

Could it be less about what was said to her and more about Marleen's future time allocation?

Marleen often gets displeased at my general lack of knowledge about magic, mage advancement, and magical research. I've become somewhat notorious among her peers because of how little I depend on it tactically and practically. This causes me to focus on areas I have more control over... like supply management and process improvement. It's not that I don't utilize magic on the battlefield, I use as little of it as is necessary to complete each mission or assignment. As far as everything Marleen is specifically involved in, such as researching new spells, item enchantments, combining magic, the mystery of the universe, and so on... it falls flat on my 'I give a damn' meter.

What? Because all the little theoretical details that haven't been proven couldn't possibly affect things like hand-to-hand combat, sieges, or casualty care. I'm not downplaying what she loves doing, but for someone like me who must focus on the applicability of the 'here and now,' the mage world will always place second. Because of what she calls my lackluster attitude, Marleen is always sure to correct me, even if she knows my intentions are noble.

She patted me on the head while getting a smug look on her face. "Please try and keep up, dear. Remembering a little about mage progression before making your overarching generalizations might do you some good. A mage's ranks are displayed according to their robe color. Novices who aspire to be mages but haven't entered the Royal Magic Academy of Alvernia wear white robes. Once accepted to the academy, they become trainee mages with blue robes. Surely you remember my dark blue robe that was oversized?"

I replied, "Oh, right. An elf wearing robes designed for humans always gave me a good laugh. Not that we spoke a lot back then, but you really stood out amongst all the others walking around. If I remember, you used to trip over that baggy thing before you got it tailored to fit you a few months later."

She hit my arm. "That wasn't funny. I was brand new and struggling to make friends! Nobody would approach me, and then I would fall on my face. How embarrassing!"

"You were really cute back then. Then I got to know you..." She interrupted me by hitting me again.

"Anyway, let's forget that… you know, forever." Marleen forcefully got back on topic. "After those blue robes, mages are granted purple robes upon graduation from the academy to signify they have a basic understanding of magic. Those robes are given with the title 'Mage.' Every set is custom-made, with each mage's elemental affinities embroidered along the edges near the hand openings and middle seams. In my case, my robe has always had water and wind alternating along the edges because those are the two I can use. Well, I can use earth magic to a lesser degree, but I don't claim it on my robes because it's not my forte."

I stopped her before she kept going on. "Does this story have a point? I'm sure you have told me this a dozen times over the years. What does it have to do with what the High Mage tells you? I may be ignorant of mage ongoings, but that doesn't mean I am entirely ignorant."

Marleen continued, "I'm getting there, Mr. Impatient."

She cleared her throat and pulled her professor's glasses from her robe, carefully placing them at the end of her nose. "After taking some tests and promoting to the brown robe, only those most distinguished get the highly coveted, rarely attained, black robe!

"Uh huh…" My eyes drifted down her red robe attire and back up. "You got them before graduating, so next, I suppose you will tell me that you're even more of a prodigy than you tell me every night."

Sighing, she grabbed her wand from her robe and thumped me on the head. "Let me finish! Those with black robes are the only ones qualified to lead mages in the military or on important research projects. The title we earn, 'Master Mage,' is hard to get for a reason. They have proven their expertise in magic proficiency to such a degree that they aren't required to report to anyone. That is, of course, unless they decided to opt for military service, like yours truly."

I chuckled, "You report to me."

Marleen replied, "Interrupt me again, and I'll give you a good licking in front of Laura! Yes, I attained the Master Mage title before graduation several years ago. Since then, I've been the go-to for the High Mage. Half because of my abilities and half because of my knowledge. Since he and I are the only two in Alvernia to get the rank above Master Mage, Grand Mage, he also believes he is saving face by leaning on me more than others. But in truth, he has acted as far more of a father figure for me. I rely on his wisdom as much as he relies on my abilities."

When I get nervous or don't understand something, my foot begins tapping on its own until she puts her hand on my thigh to stop the noise. My tapping continued for half a minute until she did just that, prompting me to speak. "I got it. He wants you around because he can't find the answers on his own, and you want him around because he has experience that can help develop you. I would say this is more of a master-student relationship than a father-daughter relationship. He has his pride, and you have your ambition, but not much is different between you two than between Laura and me."

I asked, "What is he again? An earth magician or something of the sort? What would he want with a wind and water mage? Oh, I got it! He couldn't make mud pies all alone, so he wanted you to soak his dirt in water. What an efficient way to provide service to your customers! You two have such a fantastic business strategy already planned out!"

I sarcastically kept on while her face was clearly drowning in disappointment. "Just promise me I can be the most renowned house husband who cares for his wife's mud pie delivery bakery. I can see it now; I'll clean the house in a maid uniform and play dress-up after your long days to cheer you up. Not a bad retirement strategy."

Marleen started to tear up. It seems I took my jabs went a little too far, ruining her good mood. She mumbled, "First of all... he is a fire mage. And second, you aren't being very nice right now. I was trying to tell you about some good news, and you just kept going on about his dependency issues. Nothing he said has anything to do with asking me for help... by the way. You jumped to those conclusions all on your own."

"Come on now! You can make fun of me for being a 'cocky general,' but I can't try your magic mud pies?" This was my dodgy attempt at keeping humor around so it wouldn't get too serious. She can go from happy... to excited... to pouting in the blink of an eye.

Marleen somberly replied, "Blame Seventeen for that, not me."

She suddenly snapped back into being chipper. "Anyway, the High Mage said that after I get back from my trip to Elvania, I am all but guaranteed to be the next High Mage! He was set to retire a while ago but wanted to maintain the position until another mage earned their red robes. He had all but given up until I earned mine last year!"

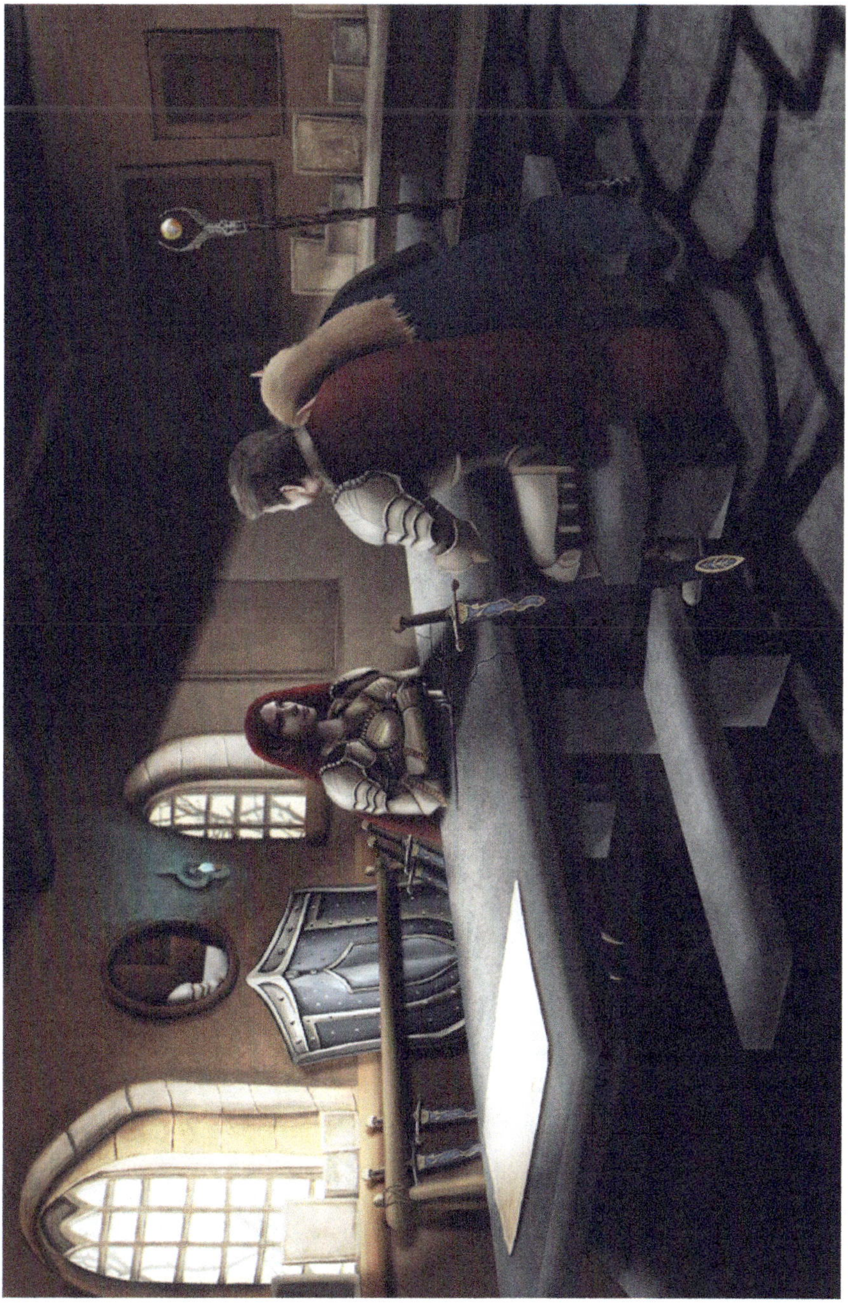

Chapter 5: Dauntless Farewells

Marleen's news was horrible for me. I didn't even know where to start. "Hold up. What the hell do you mean, 'you will be the next High Mage'? What about you being from Elvania? Can't anyone else do it instead of you?"

She looked dejected and jaded. "The King and High Mage Oliver didn't mention anything about where I came from since I am an official citizen of Alvernia. Besides, this isn't anything new. Since I earned my robes, they have just been waiting for the right moment to make the transition. The delay may have also been because both wanted to ensure that appointing such a young mage wouldn't be a problem. In other words, they were evaluating me. According to them, I'm the youngest one to ever be appointed to the position since the recording of Alvernia's history!"

Hiding how upset this made me was getting harder with every word she spoke. "Great… now you can be married to the royal family just as much as you will be married to me. You know the High Mage is a political position entirely controlled by the royal family, right? I'm sure Princes Karl and Wilhelm will love to have you under their thumb when they inherit the throne. More than that, their kids and their kid's kids will be taking advantage of you. Don't get me wrong, I'm happy they recognized you… but this…"

She interrupted, "At first, I was also sad because I thought I would have to give up my position as a general and diplomat along the northern front with Elvania. But when I voiced my concerns, they said I could keep that role as well for diplomatic reasons. This means I'll be the youngest person to hold the High Mage position and the only one to ever hold it while being heralded as a general! I couldn't ask for a better opportunity so early on in life. Think about how great this is for us. When we get married, we are set for life. What is there not to be happy about?"

I sharply shot back, "You are being controlled by the state, for one. But I'll support you no matter what you choose to do."

It's hard for me to be excited hearing that because it means she will keep distancing herself from me for her own life goals. It's not necessarily a bad thing because it makes her happy and gives her a sense of fulfillment for her passion. My only hope is that she doesn't get so caught up in her aspirations that she leaves me behind. For as long as I can remember, I've always thought her abilities would exceed mine. Repeatedly, I would ask myself why she sticks around, given how many others are interested in her.

Instead of further souring the mood, it was better for me to keep joking with her to hide my true feelings. "More things to add to your accomplishments, huh? Well, when you become the next High Mage, does that mean I can occupy the role of househusband? I can learn to cook and take care of farm animals."

Marleen didn't like that one bit. She fired back, "Get real for a moment! This is a magnificent chance for both of us! Just... don't let anyone else know just yet. We need to iron out some final details after returning from our diplomatic missions. How about we... well, since... we have been engaged since our graduation three years ago..."

"You want to call off our engagement?" I jokingly interrupted in a mournful manner.

She threw her arms around me. "No! How about we set a wedding date for when we get back from our trips? Will this help set your mind at ease? I can tell you're worried!"

I replied, "No use in concealing it. You always see right through me in the end. You know I'd marry you tomorrow if you would let me. Genesis and our duties be damned! If you are ready to make it official, we can tell everyone when we return. I still wish that I had that optimistic outlook on life that you have. My approach is way more pragmatic as I take life as it is thrown at me. For example, you plan to have the wedding when we get back. You take joy in the inevitability of it heading our way. For me, happiness will come only after we finally get wed and settle down from this crazy life."

She rubbed her face on mine while squealing, "What's the rush? We have all the time we could ask for! Enjoy the little things in life. Between last time and this time, I won't make the same mistakes again."

She said something weird just now. "In case you forget, I'm human... I don't have time to enjoy 'all the little things.' And what do you mean last time and..."

"Why don't we head home and have some alone time?" She insisted as if to overwrite her slip of the tongue completely.

Reluctant to let go of what she said, I agreed after a small pause. "Let's do that. I'm not looking forward to departing from you again so quickly. Perks of the job, I guess. I also need to look at what Seventeen gave me and sift through the stack of endless reports sitting on my desk."

Marleen changed to jealousy. "Always going on about your stacks of reports. You never see any stacks of reports on my desk! And you never see me spending long hours mulling over useless information for days on end! You need to learn to delegate that work to people you can trust. You're so worried about how much time we get together, but you put me behind some paper? If I were you, I would try whittling down that work before worrying about my position change. How can you possibly hope to spend alone time with me at this rate? When we have kids, it won't get any better, you know."

She's always good at flipping any conversation to make it look like I'm the bad guy. Cautiously replying to her, our eyes met. "Marleen, dearest…" There was no way to refute her. She does have a way of getting out of our conversations smelling like a rose.

Marleen interjected, "Oh, here we go, some old married couple we are! Let's hear it!"

I ignored her attempt at misdirection, "You don't have stacks of reports because the number of reports necessary to maintain the one northern garrison properly is almost nonexistent. Furthermore, about our love life…"

At this point, Marleen acted like she was in her own little world. "Uh huh, you do more than me… so on and so forth…" I suppose this means I should just ignore her quips about how much time we have to get intimate.

Redirecting the conversation, I put on a faint laugh while changing the topic. "…furthermore…trust isn't something easily earned by one's direct reports. I know that I can do the job assigned to me, but I haven't had enough time to vet out potential candidates to pick up a lot of these other tasks and relay information I would consider critical. The only two close enough to me are Sergeant Alex Doraleski and Seventeen, but neither one of them is an officer. And even if they were, trust isn't the only important thing I'm looking for when I delegate tasks. Competency must also be proven over time. I've been in this seat for a year; give me a little bit, and I'll vet out the correct people. Maybe if you helped me solve all my problems, I could progress my househusband plan."

Marleen's posture shifted from hugging me to laying back in her chair, indicating I was making excuses in her eyes. So, as expected, she ignored almost everything I said. I don't mind our little skirmishes occasionally, as it keeps me sane while warding off the boredom of the same old routines. There are days I wish this would continue forever, and to hell with the rest of Genesis. But I realize that is selfish and would be shirking my responsibilities with the impending turmoil on the horizon.

Maybe if the other countries contribute their fair share, we could eventually pull off a stable life together. I might even get to do some traveling outside the country once in a while. Elvania might even be a fun destination for our honeymoon. However, I doubt they would treat me any differently, even if married to one of their own. It's far more likely the opposite would happen, and they would look at me with scorn. There aren't many White Elves to begin with, which might prompt them to try and kill me instead.

Elvish culture and their people are bizarrely amazing. There are attractive men and women everywhere… by most human standards. But like a sword, that beauty comes as a double-sided blade. As beautiful and elegant as their people are, they are just as haughty and pompous. It could be that elves think they are superior to all other races because they are one of the few races that can have multiple magic affinities. I suppose if I could wield three or four times the elements of other races, then I would be an insufferable asshole too.

However, these affinities only apply to some of Elvania's population, like the White and Green Elves. The Grey Elves, which comprise the bulk of their commoners, have no magical affinities because they cannot resonate with any elements. That makes their particular race even less attuned to the magical elements than most humans, which can have an affinity for one element at the most. I'm making assumptions here as this is all secondhand information I overheard from Marleen when she was drunk one night. Imagine being the only species of elf in an entire country that can't use magic at all. Top that off with being made as the primary front-line soldier… fate can sometimes be a cruel and unyielding force.

For the next two days, we got all our affairs in order. Preparing for our separate trips took much longer than either of us had anticipated due to constant changes in mission constraints from Laura. For that entire time, it was endless paperwork, organizing our personal guards, and verifying appropriate chains of succession. Here, we were supposed to be taking some time off and enjoying ourselves, but the only fun either of us got to have been during the evening after we were exhausted. Well, at least we made the most out of that, so it wasn't all bad. During our last night alone together, Marleen decided to have a serious conversation before we fell asleep. She snuck a heavy-hitting topic in and caught me completely off guard. This woman always tried to keep everything happy and lighthearted, which made it even more emotional.

"You do know that if I become the High Mage, I will have authority unmatched by anyone except for the King. Yet, you're steadfastly resistant to it for the fear of losing me." Marleen opened with that statement while lying on my arm in our bed.

I tend to cherish these times more these days because they are becoming increasingly rarer. She gets so wrapped up in her work that she often sleeps at the research academy when it gets too late. At this moment, I feel like the luckiest guy in all of Alvernia. If we could just stay like this and not go anywhere or do anything. The problem comes with human ambition. If the demons weren't a problem, then the Empire would be. If they weren't a problem, the elves, the mermaids, or some other group would take their place. Another hill, another fight, another war.

"And what would you do with all that authority? The more power you have, the more responsibility you gain. Everything leads to spending more time in service to other people, or something like that." I said while slowly brushing her blonde hair behind her ears.

She replied, "Ever since we first met, you have known what I always wanted."

I quipped, "To sit on the magic throne over all the other inferior mages?"

Marleen whispered, "Keep that up and see what happens. It's the thrill of exploration... the anticipation of the result, the rebound of the spell. Sitting at the top is but a minor stepping stone to much grander things. Guiding this and the next generation of mages with infinite resources at my disposal... that's what it's all about. Think of all the secrets we could learn to improve people's lives! You can't possibly expect me to pass that up. I need to find out everything I can about this world. The amount of information we have attained hasn't even scratched the surface."

Marleen closed her eyes and snuggled up next to me. She's playing off my sentimentality again, like a musician playing the lute. I asked cautiously, "And what happens when you find all the knowledge there is to find?"

She whispered, "That wouldn't be possible in a thousand of my lifetimes. When the first spells were discovered, then mana was discovered. Afterward, civilizations found the ManaBanks and formed cities around them. Then we understood how ManaBanks absorbed mana and stored it to be used for later. Not long after, their runes were decoded, and their mysteries were unlocked. Now... we have found something else. Something... astonishing and marvelous."

"What could you possibly want to know or discover about this world that would improve things so much? You'll live for hundreds of years, so why not take it in stride? Selfishly, I would prefer you to spend less time on your hobbies and more with me before I die. Save all your time-consuming passions for your fourteenth husband. That way, he loses time with you instead of me." The truth about our age differences was a sorrowful reminder of how temporary our love would be for her. If she were back in Elvania, she could find a partner to spend hundreds of years with instead of fifty to eighty. Probably more fifty than eighty because I'll be old as shit by then.

To try and salvage the mood and my dignity, I quickly added, "Or better yet, skip the fourteenth husband and go find yourself an elf or a vampire after I am gone. They can match your lifespan, keeping your husband's turnover rate low. Wait, I have it! I'll become a vampire, just for you. Now I just need to convince Leah..."

She punched me in my side and said, "I don't like that woman. She always tries to get her fangs into you whenever I turn my back. And besides, what if I found the secret to extending your life through magic? Then you wouldn't need to become one of those bloodsuckers, and I wouldn't need a fourteenth husband. I've… already almost lost you once."

I pondered aloud, "There you go, saying weird things again. You never lost me, and you know it. As far as extending my life… what if my lifespan is enough for me? What would a human even do with all those extra years? Eventually, I would run out of things to do, and everyone else around me would be dead."

Marleen continued, "Come back to reality. When we are together, we can make anything work. Are you saying being with me for a thousand years would get boring?"

"Did I say such a thing?" I asked.

She raised her head to look at me briefly before nuzzling back to my side. "Anyway, nobody has ever tried to answer any of the hard questions. All anyone ever cares about is war and the 'Unknown Territory.' These are temporary problems… we need to look at the bigger picture. Why not focus on the less in-your-face things that this world seems to be detracting from?"

I smiled. "This is one of those theoretical conversations, isn't it? Come on, Marleen… it's our last night together for a while."

Marleen ignored me. "Like, what do we truly understand about this world? Do we even really know what magic is or why ManaBanks can store mana the way they do? Do we even understand why things like a 'Hero Summoning' exist to begin with? What is a 'Hero,' and why do they have so much power just by coming to our world from some other random place? Doesn't it seem like the world we live in, Genesis, almost pushes us away from asking these things by supplying us with constant 'life or death' situations to focus on?"

"Are you saying…" I stopped for a moment. "That you think Genesis is alive…"

By this point, she was starting to ramble while nodding off. Sometimes, when she is drunk, she does this, but this is the first time she is just pouring her heart out while sober. The news about becoming the next High Mage has been hitting her hard, it seems.

She continued, "Maybe the world is alive? What if it thinks for itself, and answering these questions would be detrimental to its continued survival? Are there other worlds like this one… ones that the summoned come from? Regarding the inhabitants, it's as if everyone is just content to have things continue to exist the way they always have."

Marleen paused for a good minute. "Is living day to day, falling in love, or raising a family enough to justify our existence here? What even are the 'Unknown Territories,' and why are they guarded so fiercely by so many demons?

She was half asleep but kept right on inquiring aloud. "If there are that many demons... why don't they all just invade at once and wipe us out? Instead, they continue... to hold their ground... with few incidents. Why did... why did I do that to you? To leave me... to... please... stay... wi...t.h.... me..."

I replied quietly into her long, pointy ears, hoping to get one last jab in before she fell completely asleep, "As long as you want me around, I'll be here. I may not understand your fascination with some of these things, but I love you. If I wasn't here, who would look after you when you get lost in your work? Who would... corral our kids?"

When I heard her loudly breathing, I finished with, "Who would live off your hard-earned money?"

She punched me one last time before we both fell asleep.

The next morning, we had our separate caravans outside waiting to pick us up. Marleen was going as an official representative of Alvernia, so her escort consisted entirely of Royal Guards. Those flashy bastards are the most stuck-up of those who went to the same classes as me, so I recognized all of them. I was somewhat concerned for her safety, but she could easily take all of them on at once with the flick of her wrist, the twitch of her wand, or the pointing of her staff. Their ridiculously detailed gold flashy armor and signature winged helmets wouldn't do anything to protect them from that kind of magic ripping them apart.

I, on the other hand, traveled lightly because I had to go a long distance. Gaudy armor is impractical for everyday use and does little more than weigh you down unless you're on the very front line of a battlefield. Not to mention that I don't like unnecessarily extravagant armor that signals to anyone within a five-day horse ride that you're somewhat important and should be targeted.

My detail only included about a dozen soldiers in light, black, or brown leather armor. Each rider was also equipped with two explosive short spears, a sword as a backup weapon, and enough provisions to last about a week. The only exception to our loadouts was the giant shield I always carried on my back because it was an indispensable artifact given to me by the King. These were men and women; for the most part, I kept close to me whenever I went outside the capital. I personally purchased their equipment as a reward for their loyalty and support, so I know it was top-notch.

This can be contrasted with Marleen's escort, which had twelve carriages containing gifts, attendants, and fifty highly trained wingtip knights. The gifts are understandable, but my guess would be it was the King who wanted some of our elite soldiers guarding her for the awe factor. Marleen usually likes to keep it low-key when traveling, but it isn't surprising that she would be overridden for a visit like this one. What's comical about this arrangement is that the elves will probably make all of them wait at the border except Marleen. Imagine some of our most distinguished knights all hanging out for days on end, doing nothing, and guarding all those goodies with some random border guards. Watching that would be priceless. I bet they don't say more than three words to each other... and not because Marleen is the only one who knows the language.

We embraced one final time before setting out on our respective paths. After doing the same routine for over a year, we have become accustomed to having to be separated for short periods of time. I'll miss her, of course, but with her wanting to get married upon my return, it gives me something to anxiously mull over during my long ride. Thinking about her only makes the distance and the time hurt that much more. Her earrings, hair, and necklace I purchased for her on our first anniversary. All of it blends together in a mess of painful mental deterioration.

Hopefully, she can keep the bragging to a minimum when she returns from Elvania. I'll have boring stories about my tedious time in some run-down forts run by corrupt nobles, vampires, and mercenaries. Meanwhile, she will have tales of how grand the cities of Elvania are, how elegant their Queen is, and how tasty the cuisine was when she ate it. Her face will turn bright red, her cheeks will be flush, and her eccentric personality will draft a cascading shadow over my reserved one.

    I need more friends after listening to myself think. I'm realizing my future wife gets to do all the fun things while I only have my ex-girlfriend to get drunk with occasionally. And all she does is demand to whip my ass as compensation for my sob stories. And every time that happens, I must consult all the traumatized bystanders to apologize for everything that woman does. Maybe I'll offer those poor saps my life savings next time to round out my self-sympathy.

GENESIS: Lightfall

Chapter 6: Elfless Lorelei

The first planned stop is Fort Goliad. It's about a two-day ride away if we only stop to let the horses recover. The weather is looking to be in our favor, albeit slightly cold, since that is the season we are entering. Of all our front-line forts, Goliad is the best-supplied all around and the most secured by far. Their reports indicate there are few incidents, the soldiers have high morale, and there has been no loss of civilian life in over a year anywhere around or behind the fort. So, why come here at all? I know they are lying about everything.

If there was one fault to be found at Goliad, it's the fact that it gets most of the fresh recruits right out of the academy, and only the most well-off nobles get leadership positions. This causes an oversaturation problem with young men and women out to make a name for themselves in the lower and upper echelons. What do I mean? The newly minted officers, specifically the nobles, who want to improve their prestige, take their fresh 'out-of-the-academy' soldiers on reckless excursions instead of just adhering to their regular patrols. As one can imagine, these engagements get soldiers injured or killed unnecessarily. The officers then turn a false report that says their squad was 'mercilessly ambushed' by demons, and only a 'few' were injured or died. The rest of the report highlights the 'heroic leadership' that got the rest of them through the horrible ordeal.

This, in turn, gets them promoted by other officers who are in on it... usually by being paid off or getting favors exchanged. After a few times being labeled as indispensable officers, they are replaced by another new officer who does the same thing. If I've seen it once, I've seen it a dozen times. By the time I get around to visiting the fort, all I hear are the newly promoted officers singing their praises while our recruits are the ones barely holding it together. All this amounts to Goliad being my least favorite stop when doing my checkups.

When I visit, and they know well in advance, there is a typical cadence their leadership follows. For this reason, I tend to be very incognito and spend a lot of time with the soldiers before introducing myself to their superiors. This allows me to bypass the gloating of their superiors and get a true sense of things around Goliad. This is to see if the fake reports they submit to me have any adherence to reality.

I can do this in many ways, but the easiest way is to hang out in the barracks or the local pubs strategically positioned around each garrison. Newer soldiers never recognize me, which is exactly the way I like it. I can introduce myself as a transfer or a soldier stopping over for a few days while heading to my next duty station. Doing this gives me some of the best 'war' stories I have ever heard. Soldiers just being typical soldiers is always a good time when they don't have a boot on their necks. Almost always, their stories begin with, 'No shit, there I was,' and end with one man wrestling fifteen demons or telling some officer or another to shove it when they get shitty orders. It would be hard not to call this some form of a sick hobby as much as I enjoy listening and egging them on.

Well, perhaps there is more to listening in on the stories than just hedonistic pleasure. I am trying to incorporate a feedback loop outside the chain of command. But as anyone can imagine, that is extremely difficult given how our forces are siloed in remote locations. They are poised to be partial to their direct chain of command while loathing those above them. Part of that is because of potential reprisal reasons, and part of it is because they might fear what those above their chain would do with the information. What was the old saying? Things can always get worse.

We set out half a day ago and have been riding since then. I made a bad judgment call to push through while there was a bit of a tailwind. This superseded ambition wore the horses down to a crawl just about when we arrived near the closest town to the capital, Lorelei. Stopping here is a bit of a luxury that I tend to make time for because of the local taverns, odd people, and their famous red wines. Suppose taking a break at the lake just within eyeshot of the town will have to do today. Damn time crunches.

While reviewing the route before our stop, I realized I still hadn't read Seventeen's letter. More than a realization, it was deliberately delayed because of the contents. The encrypted piece of paper specifically asked me to 'Open when outside of the city.' I think we are far enough out that I can read what he wrote without worrying about anyone else. When he writes that phrase on the outside of his letters, he means that the information is critical enough not to disclose to anyone, even those closest to me.

As I was thumbing the outside of the envelope, my horse stopped when it noticed two broken-down coaches blocking the road. Our horses are trained to be cautious from birth at the slightest sign of something being out of place. 'War Horses,' as they are called, are the best anyone can find in any country. Elves generally don't use horses, and the Imperials may as well be riding overweight cows or hogs into battle with how their steeds fair in combat.

I'm putting a lot of stock into the horse's warning, but it isn't as if I'm oblivious to how bandits operate. There is a chance that some helpless merchants or traders are looking for some support. However, given the reports I received about this road regarding recent banditry activity, it being traders seems highly unlikely. The coaches are too perfectly placed, and there are hills just high enough on each side to conceal additional thieves. The tall grass around the hills is also a dead giveaway. If I were a bandit, all that would be left would be to send someone out to get us to peacefully surrender our shit. When we let our guard down by complying, they would capture us, string us up, and then gut us. To get more victims, they would leave our bodies in the nearby woods.

Oh, here it comes. Some moron walking out in front of the carriages with a smug look on his face, hands on his hips, and concealed weapon along the back of his belt loop. The unknown man addressed me because I was the point man. "My name is Barlo, and I'll cut right to the chase. Dismount, surrender your arms, and kneel if you want to surviv…"

He didn't finish before I signaled for a combat maneuver. I threw my short spear through the middle of his chest while yelling for a right flank movement. This tactical gamble assumed the small hill to our right, and the long grass behind it didn't conceal too many hostiles. Acting quickly is the only way to minimize the risk of being counter-attacked or enveloped. Hesitation delays tempo, audacity, and ferocity… all necessary components to being successful in combat. Break the opponent's movement, never let them recover, and destroy them in their entirety.

Textbook, straight from our doctrine taught in the academy. When outnumbered and under-geared… hit hard, hit fast, sweep from the side, and follow up with a fire mage to ignite any spears left in and around enemy positions. The ensuing ignition would cause the spear to explode, sending shrapnel to cut through the bastards. It is a wonderfully sick sight one would love to behold. I appreciate every second of it.

After the first spear was thrown, the unit executed the maneuver with excellence. We shifted our weights to the right, pushing our tired horses to their limits as they galloped up and over the small knoll. The animal's heavy breathing, the screams of the dying bandit, and the silence of pure discipline from my men reassured me there was nothing to be concerned about. When we crested the top, we split into two smaller groups of five men each. My sergeant, Alex, ignited the spear before we got too far away. The moment his fireball hit the hilt, the weapon exploded, ripping through the carriages and setting them ablaze. Ten to fifteen men rolled out of the sides to spend their last minutes alive in pure agony.

I raved, "Nice shot Alex. One in a hundred chance a mage lands that spell so perfectly."

Alex rarely shows facial expressions. "Why do they always hide in plain sight like that? I'll never understand humans that masquerade as others."

"What, did his armor give him away? Or was it the obviously concealed blade?" I asked.

"It was his posture. His blood would have tasted bad." Alex signaled to the five riders on his side of the hill. "Raider, I'll take these five for the right wheel. Take Lacia for your mage. She's raw, but she won't let you down."

For mounted cavalry tactics, we prefer to split into two 'wheels.' One moves to the right and one to the left. The purpose is to surround the enemy while pelting them with spells, arrows, and spears. Kill as many as possible, then hastily retreat if we run out of projectiles and mana. If we can manage an even fight, we draw swords and charge from both flanks. When executed correctly, the fight is intoxicating. It will get you drunk right down to your core.

Luck was in our favor. There weren't any hostiles on the other side of the hill on our side. They placed their ambush by lining up only on the left side of the road over that small hill because it was closer. When the carriage ambush was foiled, they stood up to charge us to find themselves on the other side of a bonfire and nowhere near melee range. That left about twenty or twenty-five total, including the injured survivors with protruding shrapnel too concerned with survival to be of any use in combat.

My team went north, while Alex took his to the south. He left before me, which meant he was locked in combat before we were. To combat us, the bandits also split into two groups. The ones that went south charged with small axes, swords, and shields… but no projectiles. They were dead before they even understood what was happening. A firewall, two explosions, and many arrows later… there wasn't a single life left breathing.

Our side faired just as well. No casualties on our side as we rained arrows and spears down on them. Lacia, the mage assigned to me, used water magic to take their legs out from under them. The force behind her waterball spell took their legs out from under them as they ran. Non-moving targets take the fun out of things. A few who refused to fight made a break for it in the opposite direction. We gave chase only to be stopped dead in our tracks when we crested the hill on the opposite side of the road.

A giant brown and white wolf, probably four people tall and five to eight people long, grabbed one of the fleeing bandits in its mouth and bit him in half. The torso of the man slid down the wolf's throat, followed by a huge gulp. Blood trickled down all sides of its face. Its eyes rotated to meet mine as it stood still.

I whistled to Alex's group just about the time they rallied to the south of us on this side of the road. "Yeah, no thanks. We don't need to become dog food today, boys. Regroup quickly at my rear. We can't outrun it, but we can make its food so hard to kill that it becomes not worth it."

Alex shot up a red flare to notify any garrison in Lorelei that we were in trouble. I've never seen a wolf anywhere near this size. Some of our oldest legends talk about them even existing… Red-Lycans. They are said to have been wiped out long ago in a series of decisive battles. The Alvernian flag has a white and brown giant wolf as its primary emblem after one of those legends. How the hell is one of these alive in the middle of our country after not a single report of one for a thousand years?

When the other group hastily met up with us, we started our retrograde. The mythical creature sat still, only moving its eyes to follow my movements. The unmoving death bringer… exuding killing intent, able to wipe out everyone with ease, and yet... still motionless. That is, it was until the last bandit that was sitting still turned to run away from it. A giant paw swiftly followed, crushing him into a bloody mush pile.

The wolf looked back at us one final time before darting off into the woods in the opposite direction. What the hell even just happened? A Red-Lycan appears in the middle of a field, kills those who are trying to kill us, and then disappears.

Alex directed the soldiers as soon as he saw the threat was cleared. "Begin scouring the battlefield for survivors. Bind them and get ready for interrogation. Lacia, come with me."

One of the men replied, "Sergeant, almost all the bandits are already dead. Only a few were unlucky enough to survive our onslaught, and that wolf is still breathing. And of those, most aren't in their right mind. They are endlessly screaming from being burned alive or shredded by metal shards. Of those still making noise, we culled five without hope of living long enough to be tortured for information."

Receiving a blade to the heart or neck was a rare privilege they shouldn't have been afforded. It allowed them to avoid what would come to those still alive. While looking around, we found two people with minor injuries. One had pissed themselves, probably because of the wolf, and the other one was as stern and steadfast as they come. If he wasn't bound, I'm sure he would bite my head off with his temperament alone.

Really sucks for these two that every unit-sized formation always has a water mage. When water mages are trained, they receive special lessons on the most excruciating ways of torture. Technically, every mage has a way of torturing, but water mages are unique in that they can keep the subject alive for long periods of time while not inflicting any permanent damage. This is done by constantly drowning their intended target but stopping just shy of death. Give the victim a few moments to recoup, spill what they know, and prepare for another round of suffocation. Very efficient and not terribly time-consuming. The record for holdouts when we were introduced to this in the academy was about two minutes.

The first of the two was held down to the ground while Lacia started working her magic. I hope she takes her sweet time while I start thumbing through Seventeen's letter. Too much all at once is distracting. Makes it hard to read when you hear muffled gargling or the criminal breaking to beg for their life.

She just started, and I already hear him pleading in and out of his choking. "STOP! Please! No, I don't…"

I distanced myself from them and sat down under a nearby tree. When my eyes reached the piece of paper, I scrolled across the word 'severity' in the first sentence. Please don't be about giant wolves popping up all over the place; my heart can't take it.

"Raider, I hope when you read this, you are sitting. The severity of the intel I have come across won't be easy to digest, much like that chicken head I left you. The Empire's main army has been mustering around their capital in close-to-invasion strength over the last year. Their training regime has changed from battle tactics against demons to fighting techniques suitable for humanoid targets. Most of their recruits are commoners from their countryside, so it will take at least half a year, if not a full year, to get them into shape. This could only mean they plan to expand their borders with either Elvania or Alvernia. It's no secret they have no love for the elves, but invading our country would be far easier given our depleted military strength. The Empire also seems to have made elves hate all humans so they could invade Alvernia and Elvania wouldn't interfere. After all, in the elves' minds, humans fighting humans is a win for them. The more of us that die in a conflict with each other, the more likely they are to be able to get back their captured citizens and live a peaceful life.

There is more troubling news. I'm sorry and loath to be the one to tell you. Marleen is a double agent for Elvania. There's no way this intel is wrong, as I lost several good men validating its accuracy. This is not to say she is inherently hostile, but she has, without a doubt, lied about her past and her position within the Elvanian Republic. I fear you could be embroiled in conflict from all sides, with nobody backing you up except the Supreme Commander. If there is one thing I can guarantee, she always wants to be on your side no matter how she projects herself when others are around. Please prepare yourself for when you return as you may have to compete with the Eastern Front, Tuscany, Elvania, and maybe even Marleen.

I'll be in your corner until the end,
17"

Damn it! It hasn't even been a full day since I left, and suddenly, the woman of my dreams is some spy? How can that even be possible?

A cry echoed out behind me, "Stop! Please, no more! I don't know anything! Grglgrglegrgle..."

"Someone shut him the hell up, I'm trying to think!" Yelling won't make me feel any better. The beating of my heart, the hatred welling up as I decide who to believe... all of it just gets to me. I don't even get to enjoy watching Lacia do her thing. I'm so angry right now.

Not only can I not confide in Marleen, but the only one I can seek guidance from is Laura? There is no way Seventeen doesn't know she is wrapped around the King's little finger. Moreover, Laura has known Marleen for as long as I have, and they are very close. Trust my ex-girlfriend over my fiancée... what in the hell could have led him to that conclusion?

"Please! Please! No more... I'll talk... grglegrgle..." If that man doesn't shut up, I'll kill him myself.

"Just let the man talk. I think he's had enough." I paused before continuing. "I need a few more minutes before I come over."

I might be going about this the wrong way. Marleen and I are about to get married; I think I would know her better than anyone else, wouldn't I? To what benefit would she have to marry a human, even if she was a double agent? I'm sure just eloping with a human once would be enough to get her severely ostracized. Her status would decrease, or she might even be exiled for marrying someone from our species. Would she be willing to destroy her social standing for her long life just to accomplish a spying mission? That doesn't suit her at all.

The screaming, drowning, gargling, and overall unpleasant noises continued in the background. "I thought I said to stop drowning him! Seriously, cut it out."

The headache I got from the torture mixed in with Seventeen's news overwhelmed me. I pinched my nose and leaned back. The steady wind bounced off my face and hair to create a mildly pleasant experience. I could still feel the heavy eyes besetting me in the background.

It had to be the mage waiting for my signal for them to speak... so I gave it to them. "Please, come over here. Stop being so bashful."

Chapter 7: Dark Reveries

"General Raider..." Lacia timidly said. She was a newly minted, purple-robed mage. That meant she hadn't been out of the academy for too long and was getting her feet wet. This could very well be her first unit and assignment. She seems shy and way too formal for my taste, but it doesn't bother me if she is good at her job. As long as she doesn't leave like the last two water mages. Every one of them is so obsessed with getting their black robes that they are never long for the army.

"How many times is this now? Call me Raider when we aren't in front of the nobles or another unit. I hate formalities when we are out in the field. Also, stop killing that guy while speaking to me. I told you twice to relax."

She looked startled. The pool of water floating around the man's head dispersed to fall onto the ground. "I'm sorry, General Raid... I mean, Raider."

Her nervousness was worsening my headache. "There's no way we can attempt a civilized conversation while he's screaming for his life. Mistakes are fine, especially when you're new. Next time, listen to my voice before you continue with your interrogation. And stand at ease. Being so uptight all the time will shorten your life."

She aimed to please me by proving she wouldn't slack on the job, even when addressing her commanding officer. Her attitude, posture, and mannerisms signal she has at least a little ambition to progress in the ranks. If she can learn how things are done around here, she might end up being a great addition who isn't just using us for her next promotion.

One more thing that sticks out... water mages are mostly used in our kingdom for agriculture or are placed into the military for defensive magic. If we can mold her mind to have a soldier's mentality, and away from how most mages think, we will have a real winner for years to come.

She squeaked, "Please forgive me, I did not mean to be rude. My name is Lacia Orleans! Thank you for talking to me!"

I sighed, "It's quite all right. Now, what did you need, Lacia?"

She looked at the man who had passed out from torture and then back at me. "This man here..."

I interrupted her, "This criminal. Don't confuse common thugs with the hard-working men and women of Alvernia."

She continued, "Right! I'm sorry! I mean this criminal. Well, he said there are three safe houses near here that some of his collaborators have been using to store raided goods."

"Those must have the supplies from the two caravans I heard about last week. Perhaps some of the merchants wear them as well. Come to think of it, that report also said the merchants were abducted as well. Did he mention anything about selling people into slavery?" My line of questioning is half to get her to think about further questions to ask and half to get the information I care about.

She looked hesitant to answer. Alex stepped in on her behalf. "We will get that from him, Raider. Stop harassing the poor girl."

I chuckled, "Alex is coming to the rescue! I'm just having a bit of fun. Lacia, if he can give us the rough locations of each safe house, along with how many should be inside, we can act on the locals' behalf. However, dealing with them at our current strength is another matter that could take several days."

Alex responded, "Raider, not that it's my place to say, but we should notify the local garrison and continue our mission."

"Noted!" My reply was more chipper than I intended it to be. "With that being said, we have an obligation to act for the people's sake. It's a slight detour; what's with that sour look?"

Alex sighed, "Try not to let your enthusiasm affect your better judgment. Think about what General Claire would say if she found out."

He's not wrong. The Royal Knights fall under Claire and, along with them, the supervision and training of town garrisons. Rumor has it that they were separated originally until some general a long time ago wanted more power. Now, we find them rolling up under the most useless person to ever occupy the position. If I were to approach them, it could easily be seen as overstepping my authority. And if Claire O'Connor found out, it would be more of a hassle than just solving the problem without their help. The juice just isn't worth the squeeze.

There is one loophole that we could utilize. If we can convince the garrison to support our cause without me invoking my rank... that would mean they decided to aid us of their own accord. The garrison has the authority to act in the best interest of the people they protect, including linking up with other units outside their chain of command. This is way more common with independent cavalry or mage units, but the principle is the same. There would be nothing that ditzy blonde would be able to do even if she did find out. That paperwork would go right from one pile she doesn't read into another pile she never read. Another unwitting report written by one of her captains or lieutenants that never crossed her eyes.

"Lacia, immediately leave with two riders and my crest. Take this note to Lorelei and inform them we need fifty men to put down some pests. They don't need a lot of equipment; they just muster with a light loadout similar to what we have. We will provide them with explosive spears as primary weapons; anything else they bring is also fine. The main things they need are a horse, a satchel, and enough rations for two days just in case things drag out. If they press you as to why, then tell them it's because we saw a big fucking wolf and don't want to die alone."

Lacia was aggressively nodding. Alex spoke on her behalf. "You're just going to tell them to join you instead of trying to get them to assist on their own?"

My eyes shifted from top left to top right, carefully avoiding his. "Well, that would be the normal play, but I bet most of them don't even know who they report to up the chain."

My eyes snapped back to Lacia. "The key here is… acting. Act like you're in charge, and you are in charge. Got it? What they don't know won't hurt them… and we're doing this for their own good anyway. As for the rest of you, don't say anything to them when they arrive. If one peep or loose comment tips them off, I'll throw you in that damn lake over there. Seeing as Lorelei is within eyesight, I expect them to be back by nightfall with my reinforcements."

"Alex, is that guy still alive? Wake his ass up and let me have a look at him. Playtime is over; now we must begin our preparations for our raid tonight." I headed over to the incapacitated bandit who had been tied to a log. "What's your name, thief?"

Alex lit a fire under his chin, instantly snapping him out of his slumber into a panic. He was clearly out of it from the torture he had just undergone. As he replied, he nervously stuttered, "Sir, please let me go! I've told you everything I know. Make it stop! I was trying to save my family…"

I replied, "I won't ask again; what is your name?"

"I'm… I mean my name… name is…" My sword slipped through his neck before he could finish.

This was a bit of mercy I learned from my time serving under Laura in the Royal Guard. This bandit was going to be put to death regardless of what happened. Why go through the bullshit of taking him back, formally charging him, delaying our trip further, and so on. We can't afford the time to do all that shit. The longer he remained alive, the longer he would have dwelled on his impending doom and drained our supplies. As savage as I can be when someone's time is up, it's best to let them move on as quickly as possible.

"Alex, burn his body with the rest of the criminals and their carriages blocking the road. If there is any useful cargo, load it up on horseback. When the reinforcements arrive tonight…" I noticed Alex tapping his foot.

"If… the reinforcements arrive tonight, we will systematically begin the purging operation. If they decline our offer, we will move on our own as covertly as possible. After the operation is over, we will get a few hours of sleep and set out for Goliad by dawn. I don't want this minor inconvenience to impact our timeline." The troops saluted and began to make camp while we waited for our riders to return.

The camp had barely been set up when dusk arrived. My small unit tends to get antsy if they sit too long. The phrase 'busy hands keep a soldier honest' couldn't be more accurate for this bunch. Restlessness gets people into trouble as they find roundabout ways to pass the time. A few were already wrestling with onlookers when our lookouts spotted a large cluster of torches off in the distance. The two or three hundred they saw were a far cry from the fifty men I requested to back us up.

The chances of this group being hostile weren't exactly zero. Six light cavalrymen pitted against two hundred of anything may as well spell our doom. The only way we would be able to face off against all of them would be if our furry protector showed up again.

I mumbled, "Alex, you don't happen to have any large chunks of meat on you, do you?"

Like everyone else in our unit, except our water mage, who sticks out like a sore purple thumb, he wears the same leather armor that I usually wear but with an oversized hood. This makes it hard to see his face and pale skin clearly. His most noticeable features are his vampiric glowing red eyes, visible for a long distance during the nighttime. He's a Green Elf, but since he never removes his hood, I can't ever see his long, thin ears or green hair. I tried joking around with him in the past by asking him if he tied his ears behind his head, but the jokes always fell flat when he ignored my provocations. What fun is having a Green Elf vampire in your unit if you can't ever see their hair or ears?

"Talking to yourself again, Raider?" Alex's monotone responses never get old. He probably knew what I was thinking.

He added, "Instead of hoping for the wolf, would you prefer I scouted the situation? It would be a better-grounded option."

Yeah, he knew what I was thinking. Always weird running into a vampire. His last name, Doraleski, is a signature name for vampires. It's like all the ones I've met over the last five years have one of five last names that have been recycled because they couldn't think of anything else on the spot. I don't know much about them, but Leah is as aggressive as they come, and Alex is the most passive person I've met. Overall, they tend to keep a low profile whenever possible.

Speaking of vampires, they aren't all that rare in Alvernia. Being a subspecies of Elves and humans is an amazing feat. 'Crime rate' wise, they contribute nothing to the overall public disturbances of any species or subspecies in the capital. Humans are usually the worst of the bunch, followed by dwarves, the rare vagabond Grey Elf or two, and in a distant last place... vampires. Their only drawback is the low quantities of blood they consume to prevent themselves from going feral. While enlisted, they are required to keep enough blood vials on them for a minimum of one month. One vial can last upwards of a week, making the footprint they leave for maintaining themselves lower than your average soldier. We also pair them with a human just in case they run out, however rare that happens.

In return for overall less food consumption and lower crime rates, vampires rarely need sleep, have flawless night vision, increased strength, and have a guaranteed affinity for the dark element. Between their reduced need for sleep and night vision, the military tries to assign at least one of them to every unit for scouting and night watch responsibilities. We found it cuts down on casualties in the field by an incredible amount. In the past, it was hard to convince the captain of Midgard to release vampires to units… as all vampires hail from that area. Since I came into my position, Leah has loosened how strict she is with such matters. In our case, she personally assigned Alex, and we couldn't be happier. He quickly became our go-to for everything during the nighttime.

"Alex, can you tell if they are hostile?" I asked.

Alex was never much for words; he just executed whatever I told him as if it were his sole mission in life. This can make it hard to tell exactly what is happening when there is no emotional attachment to his actions.

His eyes slowly repositioned from right to left as he scanned the area. "Nothing about them suggests them being ready for battle. However, they don't carry themselves like typical aloof garrison soldiers. They also lack the traditional marching formation of the formal army or knights."

Breaking his usual timidly placid personality, Alex calmly asked, "Did Leah ever tell you why there are so few vampires?"

Alex and I continued to watch the sporadically checkered torches come closer without him taking his red marbles off the approaching group. I wasn't sure what his point was or why he was bringing this up now.

Raising my eyebrow, I said, "No, she doesn't often talk about herself. She's too focused on her job… and harassing me. I'd be remiss if I didn't say she was a breath of fresh air. Can't wait until we get to Midgard."

He explained, "Turning into a vampire requires our court's approval, a magic ritual with several high-class mages, and a willing vampire noble to take responsibility. How often do you think that is approved?"

"Never?" I said, without fully knowing what he was after.

"Not never..." He waited a moment. "It's just incredibly rare. Finding the appropriate noble to vouch for someone is a rare occurrence, and we don't often die, as you can imagine. And it isn't just the noble who is at stake. If the subordinate vampires act out of line, everyone from the noble sponsor on down is severely punished."

This might be one of those bonding moments. "Reliving old memories, are we? Odd time to get sentimental for a stoic hunter of the night."

He replied, "I don't understand sentimentalism anymore. I lost that luxury a while ago. That doesn't mean I can't reminisce a little."

We sat in silence for a moment until he continued. "When I was turned, it was a matter of family. Small villages on Elvania's border are often neglected, and I'm the result of that. As our village was overrun by demons, my friends, acquaintances, and love rivals fought for their lives. Houses burned as they tried to create fire barriers to delay the carnage. Mothers gave their bodies up as food in the hope of buying a few more minutes for their children. How long ago that was."

"A few years ago?" I asked.

"Just over sixty years. I was young back then, maybe five or six, but I can still remember the smell of blood, the taste of ash from the burning of houses and trees, and the feeling of helplessness. Do you know what it's like to see everyone you have ever known being eaten and torn apart? The sound of your mother pleading for you to run as her legs are torn off? These demons that came for us... would you believe me if I told you that they were once also elves and not just wildlife infected with miasma?" I had no idea Alex's past was so troublesome. He's never shared any of this with me before.

My heart started pounding. "That's impossible, isn't it? Nobody has ever said anything about demons being elves or even being able to think for that matter. The implications of what you..."

He interrupted, "Are unheard of, right? Those elves reeked of miasma, and what's worse, those they didn't kill or tear apart, they took with them when they left. I often wonder if my father and sisters are across that wood line into the unknown. No longer in pain... no longer screeching from their misery."

"Do those torches remind you of those fires?" I was probing him a little, hoping he would continue to share his story with me.

Alex's glowing red eyes shifted to meet mine briefly; then they shifted back to the torches. "I won't ask for your reply because I know you have had a rough past as well. For me, it was a calling. A calling to get stronger… and a calling to sacrifice any and everything I had, up to and including my free will. In the end, accepting this fate made me give up my name, past, and even one of the elements I was born with. Funny thing, I used to have affinities with fire and wind, a deadly combination for any elven mage. The pride of my village, even if lacking a third element like many of my peers. But once I turned, the newly awakened vampiric powers converted my wind affinity to the dark element. It took the wind out of my sails and put the darkness into my body."

"What in the… was that the stone-cold Alex making a joke?" I asked. He didn't respond.

I've had Alex under my wing since I was first assigned a bodyguard detail. He's dependable without ever being open to anyone. In just a few minutes, right as daylight was ending, I learned more about him than I had ever known. His age, his family, and how vampires are converted.

Alex's abilities as a Forward Observer are next to none. Scout the enemies, draw strategic maps, set traps, help with additional reconnaissance, and still be ready to assist when we assault. It's a tough job to learn in the academy with a high washout rate. After hearing more about his past, it doesn't surprise me that he has dedicated himself so hard to his craft. Get someone with that much determination and reinforce them with the abilities of a vampire… they are indispensable.

"Do you really miss your wind element that much?" I asked.

He replied, "It's part of the deal. If you aren't born with the dark element, it overwrites one you have an affinity for at random. I knew what was going to happen when I decided to convert. When you lose an element you've had since birth, it's like losing a part of yourself and replacing it with something that will always be foreign."

Recalling one of Marleen's lectures, I added, "I often wondered about that with Marleen if she ever decided to convert. White Elves have three or four affinities, Green Elves have two or three, humans one or none, and Grey Elves and Dwarves both have no affinities. The number is random, but people hypothesize it has to do with your bloodline. That is what originally separated the nobility from the peasants when Alvernia was founded... and what caused the species to refuse to interbreed with each other. That's why it's odd for those with guaranteed affinities to convert. You stick out pretty bad amongst all the human and Grey Elf vampires that converted to get a single affinity."

He mounted up. Before trotting off to meet the oncoming crowd, he clarified. "Changing or losing an affinity isn't the main reason. White Elves and my former kin don't convert because they believe the dark element is a curse. Those who are born with it are culled as soon as they use it once. For this reason, my people despise vampires with self-righteous, loathing hate. Those are the main reasons. Who knows how many elves have been killed to maintain purity? Not that it's my concern anymore."

That last sentence is more like the Alex I know. Although... it seems he's still struggling with emotions that have been suppressed for a long time.

Chapter 8: Marauder's Glory

Alex quickly returned. His horse reared up as he redirected its hooves from landing near me. "Raider, the crowd approaching is the force requested from Lorelei. As expected, they aren't the local garrison. It's more like a ragtag bunch of vigilantes, possibly with a military background. They might also be mercenaries hired by the local population. Our riders are with them."

"Got it. Fall back in with the rest and prepare to move out." The rest of us mounted up after he passed around behind me.

The group wasn't too far behind him. Standing out front of the mob was a remarkably large man with a flowing blonde beard, long braided hair, and muscles for days. He had a huge axe draped over his shoulder, was covered head to toe in grime and dirt, and reeked of alcohol. A walking bulk of everything that is man... I think? My first impression matched up with what Alex thought. He was a former military man who neglected his body and equipment but never got out of the game.

The tall figure stood about three paces in front of me to speak. "Ahoy, General, Sir! I hear great things about you despite your age! I'm Eric Sanders, and these are my men, the Lorelei Marauders."

"Mr. Sanders, glad to meet..." My voice trailed off as he stepped forward.

He raised his hand. "You can call me Eric. I reckon you are the man to talk to about killing some of those bastards stealing our livestock, abducting our women, and disrupting our trade routes. I'd be willing to do all kinds of unspeakable things to get a chance to talk to them in person, man-on-man. Hell, I won't even need a lot of time. Getting to the point all quick like is my specialty."

I grabbed his hand back, barely withstanding his vigorous handshake. "The name is Raider. I can appreciate informalities. It is good to meet you, Eric. Beating around the bush isn't my strongest quality, so I'll be blunt. If you and your men follow my commands, we will wrap this up before dawn."

He agreed to my proposal without me going into any of the details. Their level of anger toward these organized thieves outweighed his desire to broker any deal with me. After our introductions, Eric, his leadership, Alex, and I all went over the finer details of my plan. Judging by Eric's mannerisms, he came off as a man in his mid-forties with an unkempt lust for all things desire-driven. I caught him chuckling multiple times when the underhanded portions of my plan were expressed, all while never missing a prime opportunity to make a dirty joke.

Overall, he was polite and had a carefree and optimistic look at life. At one point, I asked him if he was concerned for the women's well-being beings, and all he said in response was, "Those women? Ha! Those morons couldn't satisfy them if they fucked all night." That pretty much summed up his entire disposition. He even told me he couldn't rightfully send his men into battle until they were at least tipsy. Calling him a marauder might be a bit of an understatement. Eric was wild to the core, and I would love to have a more engaging conversation with him sometime in the future.

For those under his command... they looked surprisingly well-kept in comparison to Eric and his disheveled appearance. If I hadn't known better, they could have easily been mistaken for the real garrison at Lorelei. Beyond their disciplined demeanor, their armor was impressionable. Every piece was well maintained and shined to the max. They even appeared to bathe more than once a month. It's a wonder I have not run into them on my previous stops through here.

The meeting did not take long. I had Eric and his men back brief me on everything we had discussed, and then we set off to the first target. The plan was simple. Hit all three locations back-to-back, so the criminals didn't have time to react. Once we arrive at the first target, we surround the location and kill everyone except potential hostages. When the prisoners are retrieved, we will leave a small group of Eric's men to return any stolen goods and move on to the next target.

Alex and two of Eric's men would act as our scouts. Half of my men would remain dismounted for the frontal assault, while the other half would round up anyone who attempted to exit through escape routes. Since the primary and last target was a large cave, there weren't many places for them to go. We kept our mages free so they could support and rotate as needed. Usually, mages do their own thing on a battlefield, as not many people know what their main role is aside from protecting from magic, lighting up dark areas, or assisting with the occasional spell or two. I'll be the first to admit that I'm not the best at commanding mages. Since Alex is scouting, the only other mage with my group is Lacia. Although green, she has shown herself to have potential... so she can figure her own shit out. When I am with a larger army, I let the black-robed 'Master Mages' lead their groups however they want.

The first location we had to hit was a typical 'hideout.' It was a series of small stand-up houses, each with one or two exit points, minimal ventilation, and extremely poor security. The buildings themselves didn't sound all that impressive. A typical civilian could stand one of them up in the middle of the woods in less than a week. They make for perfect temporary houses for those on the move and trying to remain undetected. If they got tipped off, it would be easy to abandon and move on to the next suitable area with prime pickings.

The marauders urged a cut-and-burn policy to enact their vendettas. Barge in, kill anything moving, and ask questions later. I decided to take an alternate, slightly less brutal approach. Not that their plan was bad; you could tell they had seen enough war and conflict to lose most of their sympathy for the abductees who would get caught in the crossfire.

When we arrived at the first site, it was clear the guy who rolled on his friends was telling the truth... good job, Lacia. It was a series of three buildings, no wall or palisade, very few guards, minimal light, and in the middle of the woods, not too far from the road where we were ambushed. Alex and Eric's scouts could easily sneak up and take out the front three guards from behind. When the rest of us moved into place, just beyond the trees, our scouts quickly took out the remaining guard near the back entrance to the rear building. At least that guy got to smoke his last cigarette.

The rest was as cut and dry as a mission can get. Two groups of seven men stormed from the front of each building while an equal-sized force awaited near the back for anyone who wished to flee. About a dozen criminals were killed upon breach, four were killed trying to flee, no hostages were injured, and we didn't incur a single casualty. One black mark on my record was the one survivor the marauders dragged away. They picked that man apart one body part at a time. They muffled his screams by shoving leaves down his throat as they sliced each piece off. Not something professional soldiery should ever allow to happen on their watch, not that I had a say in the matter. Revenge for what he did to their loved ones, I'm sure.

The second location we hit was even easier and executed more rapidly than the first. A single large building pressed up against the outside of a hill. Whoever built this building did it to expand into an underground cave system eventually. However, when we arrived, there was just one large room on the outside and nothing connected behind it. Storming a single entrance isn't ideal, but with so few guarding it, there wasn't any issue. Here, we discovered two women and one man who had been killed while in captivity. The gruesome sight of their mangled bodies set the marauder's passion ablaze.

The man had been tied to an internal pillar and the woman to the ground. All three had multiple spears or axes stuck in them from multiple angles. The man had spears hurled at him from across the room, while the two women had spears stuck out of their mouths and torsos as though the spears were chucked into the air and fell on them. The blood-soaked floor told us this had gone on for at least a day or two. Once I saw this, I didn't blame them for what they did to the first guy at the previous location.

The final location was the most complicated. This area was their primary headquarters and the best concealed of the three. The whole hideout was located within a large hill… possibly classified as a small mountain. The intel we received said there were only five tunnels, four main areas, and one holding area. These tunnels were dug straight through and included outhouses just outside on the opposite side. That was their weak point. Several outhouses with one or two well-hidden buildings where the forest met the side of the hill. Those buildings being the same size and shape as the ones we just cleared really simplified things.

Our plan of action was modified according to the one weakness they had. Alex and the scouts went to the back entrance with a small contingent consisting of about fifty marauders. The rest of us waited out front until he found the back entrance, correctly emplaced his force, and then shot up a flare to signal that he was ready. The flare would also alert them if any were outside, so it was on us to ensure no guards had arrows or swords in their guts before he was positioned. And it was on him to make sure the guys around back were taken care of before he shot the flare. The timing was everything.

Much to my surprise, a flare never came. Instead, after about an hour of waiting, Alex reappeared by himself through the eerie depths of the woods.

"Alex, what the hell is going on?" I asked.

He peeled himself from the shadows of the trees. "Raider, near the cave exit, we discovered a series of buildings that contained all their captives. We have rescued them with very little resistance. The guards and their captives both claim nobody else that was abducted is left inside the cave system."

Cautiously, I replied, "How did you do that so quietly? We didn't hear shit."

His expressionless face was hard to pair with his words. "Humans are easy to subdue when they are drunk on pleasure…"

I tried to hide my smile from Eric and those around me. My head tilted to the sky to thank my incredible fortune. "Is the back prepared?"

He nodded. "Ready for the smoke-out."

Eric questioned, "Smoke…out?"

I clarified, "Yeah… Alex knows me better than he should… you demon, you. He blockaded the back entryway so they couldn't escape when we started the fire at the front. With the smoke filling the halls, they will have no choice but to flood the entrance. There we will… I don't know. How does a roundhouse boil sound? Lacia, you up for some fun?"

She looked excited. "Yes, General Raider! It's my first time!"

Alex's hand hit his face. "Don't rile her up, please. Let's get to it before they catch on."

Eric interrupted, "Hold up, lad. What do you mean by roundhouse boil? You're using all these terms I don't know. Fill an old man in, will you?"

It's not surprising that he doesn't know textbook military tactics. Although lacking, I even know how to execute rudimentary magical attacks. "It's nothing as far as you're concerned. Just get your men into place and wait for my orders to mop up. Get as many on horseback as you can… this will be over quickly. Alex, take ten of his men and light a bush fire with all those dead leaves and branches."

They both did as I requested. When the fire was lit, it took only a few minutes before the criminals started rushing outside by the dozens. Erics's men had drawn down on them with their bows. Their orders were not to fire until all of them were outside so we could engage them all simultaneously. If they had gotten wind of what we were trying to do, it would have complicated things and led to unnecessary deaths.

Regardless, the first group to come out was hit with loose arrows. Eric quickly scolded them to hold their fire, much to their disappointment. The smoke had blinded and suffocated them. In their delirious state, we wanted them to remain disoriented while trying to form a front line against our group. If they started panicking, then they could charge in any direction. With the frantic, wild swinging, they might score a few hits.

After the initial scolding, their grumbling calmed to a dull roar. These all but ceased when I gave the order to emerge from the woods and form our own line to match theirs. Not a single word of anger or disappointment came after that. On the contrary, they were cheering and goading the enemies as they fumbled over themselves, just opening their eyes. Our side started with loud jeers that slowly became our army's rallying call.

At first, one or two of the marauders banged their shields in unison while screaming, then ten, then all of them. "AHHHHHHHH HUUUUUUUUUUU!"

Eric, spilling his delight all over the place, egged me into it as well. "Nothing like a good blood spilling in the evening. Hard getting old and getting off the front lines, eh? Well, what say you… General Raider? The honors are yours."

I replied, "They only have about fifty. A stand-up fight is probably what you're after, huh? Knock-down, drag-out? As much fun as that sounds… let's do things a bit smarter."

He raised his eyebrow. "Bloodshed is bloodshed. Any way this ends with them dead will satisfy our lusts."

I nodded at Alex. He stood up and threw two simultaneous fireballs into the air above the cave entrance. Everyone watched as they crashed into a large pool of water that was being suspended in the air by Lacia. The clever girl found a way to climb the hill and navigate a ledge about halfway past the entrance. She doesn't seem like the nimble type, but she found a way... clunky robes and all.

Once the fireballs hit, the water boiled in an instant. She released the suspended liquid, pouring scalding-hot water down on the men and women who had no chance of escaping. They were cooked alive. Only the ones along the outside of the tightly huddled group survived for more than a few minutes. Although, surviving is a bit of an overstatement. Their skin was melting, their eyeballs falling out of their sockets, and just general happiness was upon them. The marauder's excitement dwarfed their howling.

I raised my sword. "DEATH BECOMES US!"

To which our entire side echoed, "AND HELL BECOMES THEM."

The front line charged. Axes, swords, spears, and shields were raised at the ready. Unprofessional brawlers looking for a quick kill... and this was exactly what they wanted on the menu. The last seven or so of the bandits still left alive after the live boil died the moment Eric's men rushed the small hill in front of the entrance. Each of them made sure to get one stab, slash, or smash in... even after they had died.

The five men I had on horses waited in the woods. Getting caught in that rumble wouldn't have done us any good, and they may have thought we were trying to take their trophy kills from them. Some of the men took their ears, while others started asking about those who were captured. They all seem to have forgotten that we are on a live battlefield.

I insisted, "Eric, we must push forward and clear the caves. Trophies can wait."

Alex backed me up. "I can assure your men those that were captured have been taken to our temporary camp at Lake Lorelei. There, they can reconcile with those we have found."

He hastily nodded. "Alright, boys! Meat is back on the menu tonight! Let us clear these caves so we can get back home!"

That man commands a great deal of respect from his counterparts. They didn't even think twice before moving. Those who were looting the corpses started stacking them instead, and those who were nervous about the captives received instant clarity. Within a few minutes, we cleared the caves. Like the one we had captured claimed, the caves were mostly empty. Several tunnels had dead ends that went nowhere, while others branched out into rooms.

By the time we had finished clearing the tunnels, it was clear... these weren't very good thieves. Sure, they had taken maybe ten or so caravans worth of shit... small caravans. However, the total cost of everything tallied up to be less than one farmer could make in a year with a good bit of effort. Either their leader didn't know what he was doing, they ditched the goods relatively quickly and spent the coin, or they needed some lessons on how to bandit correctly.

The marauders were excited to find some of them had passed out from the smoke but weren't dead. Just like they did at the previous location, they were dragged outside, strung up, and tortured mercilessly for hours. This gave them the reassurance they needed that there weren't any others that were taken and stashed elsewhere... and that everyone responsible was dead or dying.

The fun didn't end at the cave, either. They insisted on tying the ones still breathing behind our horses until we reached our camp. When we arrived, those who had lost those they cared about picked back up where the others had left off at the cave system. We divided our camp back into two separate groups when we returned to the lake. Eric insisted on them staying until we left the next morning. He made it sound like he wanted to do it to return the favor for us helping him out, but I think it had more to do with what we decided to do with the slaves.

As soon as Eric returned to his side of the camp, Alex and I discussed the matter regarding the slaves. "Make sure there are always guards on them. Did you get the gist of their collars?"

He replied, "All of them are the same. Forgeries."

"So, the rumors are true. How the hell can someone forge a fake slavery pact?" I asked.

Alex looked equally puzzled. "I don't know. If you held a sword to their throat, it would still be impossible to seal a slavery collar around someone's neck. It's almost like they were made to believe that what they were doing was for their own benefit."

I continued, "Just looking at them tells me they wouldn't be the type to do that. Not to mention the Grey Elves, the other humans look to be from Lorelei or someplace close. None of them would give up their freedom like that. What was the color of the forgery collars?"

He gazed over at their group, which was in the middle of our camp. "Red."

"So, the forgeries are prisoner collars, then? Why did it have to be those? Why not yellow, orange, or something else?" I said that, just thinking about what this meant for Alvernia. We might have to investigate every single prisoner to make sure their collars match up with their sentences. There are thousands of prisoners sentenced to hard labor or interned to help our army along the front lines. To verify every one of them would place a complete standstill on our queries, mining, logging, fortifications, and who knows what else. On the other hand, had it been prostitutes with yellow gemmed collars or indentured servants with orange gems in theirs… we could have shut those industries down with minimal impact on our ongoings. The King isn't going to be happy.

Alex seemed confident. "Get some sleep. There's no use in worrying about it now. Control what you can control and let go of everything else. When we get back, report it to the Supreme Commander. Let her figure out what to do from there."

I replied, "Yeah, I suppose so. Whatever… are you going to stay up watching those that Eric's group didn't claim?"

His eyes glossed over. "What else do you think I was going to do? Yes, of course, I'm going to watch them. Now, get some sleep before you put yourself into an early grave. You've been awake far past what a human should. And don't worry about our guys; they will have small rotations tonight."

He was right. As he left to go join the other guards watching over the recovered abductees, I fell asleep to the captured bandit's bone-wrenching wailing from across the small grassy field. Eric's group could be at this all night, from the sounds of it. Something about it seemed so… unnaturally soothing.

Chapter 9: Esoteric Naif

I'm walking in a thick and murky haze, but I'm not quite sure where I'm going. This entire area is like being in a huge, warm cloud… but with a surprisingly enveloping aura to lift and guide me. I can't even remember what I was trying to do before I got here. Is it possible that my troops and I separated in this dense fog? My focus quickly shifts without my consent as I notice something out of the corner of my eye. There's a much taller reflective object standing erect in the distance.

Perhaps if I keep heading towards it, something will begin to make sense. The more I look toward the object, the more my instincts keep telling me this thing contains more than just the answers I am seeking. The problem is, I didn't even know if I had questions that needed answering or answers that needed seeking.

Right now, my state of mind can be compared to this area. It's like I have the capability to find answers if I push through the unknown toward the objective that I didn't know I had. Once I get there, I'll be able to understand both what questions I want to ask and the answers that I need to seek. Am I even making sense anymore?

It's no secret that there is little about magic I find useful or attractive. This whole place could also result from a dark magic user playing tricks on me after I fell asleep. It could be a bandit trying to confuse and alienate me. Or what about Alex trying to place me in a deeper sleep? Maybe a rogue mage or vampire that I pissed off?

"Damn it, shiny object! What is with this sketchy shit? I can't yell or talk to anyone else around here, so it must be your fault!" The object didn't change or move. I'm not sure what I was expecting from that outburst just now. Raider, the 'Slayer of Elven Virtue' and 'Yeller of Mysterious Objects' are far in the distance. What a series of titles. Marleen wants prestigious ones… and I want the hell out of here.

Whatever, I'll continue heading towards the reflective object and fall for whatever scheme I'm getting myself wrapped up inside. As the object came into clear view, it just looked more and more like a normal mirror. As I continued to stare at it, the idea of this whole thing being orchestrated by an outside force faded from my thoughts and was quickly replaced with a form of enlightenment.

If I were to describe the radiating feeling it was giving off, it would be a weird mix of surging power, warmth, and clairvoyance all rolled up and imploding throughout my entire body. Seemingly random, incoherent images swirled around inside the mirror until, finally, they stopped.

I smirked, "Boy, that was anticlimactic. What a letdown. All those rushing pictures as the opening act, and now… my reflection? Let me out, already."

Everything about me looked exactly as it should. I'm roughly six feet tall with short brown hair. My slightly natural spike in the front had my hairline looking unusually kept. Even my slightly muscular build and black leather armor seemed to be accurate. The shoes and red cape were also of the same quality. I was joking at first, but now I'm serious… this is a typical smooth-faced mirror. Or maybe this is just my own mental image of myself? I've been in the field for a few days without shaving, but that isn't reflected here at all.

I asked, "How about showing me as I am now? Don't get me wrong, I love how good I look when I'm in garrison… just testing the waters a bit. You're missing the mud, dirt, and grime on my lovely attire, unkempt stubbles on my face, the blood on my boots and sword… and all that. Hell, you're even missing the shield with two spears tucked away in it that the King gave me. I never go anywhere without that thing."

The mirror didn't budge. It's lacking in its social skills. I stood there staring in silence while rubbing those same stubbles on my chin. It only took another minute or two of me making small talk with it until my reflective self-image withdrew in slow motion… as if I was watching it from a distance. More accurately, this was a top-down view of me running frantically through a hallway. He was breathing hard, panicking, and extremely angry or disappointed about something.

As he rushes through the hallway, he bumps over some servants, cuts corners quickly without looking, ignores someone calling out to him, and bolts toward a room. This desperate… me… is breathing heavier by the second, as if he is going to collapse from anxiety. When he reaches the end of the hallway, he sees a reinforced wooden door common amongst the bedrooms in the castle. The door isn't fully shut, so he peers through without a second of hesitation. The viewpoint shifts from top-down to through his eyes.

Tears well up to cloud the image of the people we are seeing through the slot in the door. A White Elf about five foot four with her hair just past shoulder length is in the room. She is screaming and moaning in ecstasy like she's having the time of her life. For the few seconds he watches, the whole picture in the mirror becomes anything but transparent. As he wipes away the tears, I can once again get a comprehensible picture.

The thunderous performance she is putting on almost seems staged. If I were her partner, I would have to question the sincerity of her exaggerated acting. I can't tell who she is, but strangely, she sounds familiar. Should I watch someone else having fun in their private time like this? As much as I struggle, I can't see the face of either person. The tall, overly muscular blonde guy behind her is giving her the business, or the White Elf in the front, trying to wake the dead.

As I focus harder on her face, it becomes obvious that she doesn't have a single face. It keeps switching between two different people in rapid succession without stopping. But wait a moment… this is… this is, without a doubt, Marleen. One of the faces on that elf is, without question, Marleen's face! The other one isn't important, and I don't know who the blonde guy is. What the hell is going on here? There's no way she would betray me after everything we have been through together. Now, I'm more convinced than ever that some hallucinating spell has been cast on me to cause suffering.

I shook the mirror. "Fucking cut it out! What you're showing me isn't funny in the slightest. If you're trying to infuriate me, it's working! Do you want to die… I mean break… you stupid thing?"

In my efforts to topple the mirror, an electric current shot through my body. The paralysis it caused pushed me to my knees and made me immobile. All I could do was sit and watch this scene play out. The mirror image of me quickly pulled out one of the spears. He looked at it with shaking hands intently, mulling over whether he wanted to throw it at the two in the bedroom or not. His struggle ended when she let out another exasperated laugh as she did nothing but restrain herself.

He pulls a string attached to the bottom of the spear, looks at the tip of it one final time, pulls the door wide open, and throws it.

The spear shot straight through to the headboard of the bed. As soon as he verified it was stuck deep into the wood, he turned around and ran down the hallway where he came from. Moments later, an explosion happens. The door to the bedroom is sent flying in the same direction he was headed... barely missing him. Wait... an explosive spear detonating... without... a fire mage?

  I can't blame the mirror me for his unbridled rage. If that were me, and I saw Marleen doing that completely unexpectedly, I would go on a murderous rampage without any regrets. Watching whatever this isn't good for me because nothing good can possibly come of it. The longer I sit here, the more the mirror me is acting how I would expect myself to act in the same situation. It's unsettlingly... reflective... of my own behavior. However, I don't have a choice but to keep watching. This fucking thing must be taking joy in immobilizing me and sticking me into this dark fantasy.

  What am I supposed to be getting out of watching this? Joy in knowing those two were caught off guard badly enough to receive the justice they deserved? Maybe it wants me to feel some semblance of sorrow for them? Sorry, none of that is to be found here. In this roleplay dream, Marleen got what she deserved, even if it hurt my heart to say that. Nobody survives the shrapnel from a point-blank explosion like that... nobody. Not even Marleen, thinking of deploying pre-sex fire and wind barriers, could have survived that.

  The mirror me cares far more about escaping than he does verifying their deaths. The resemblance is uncanny. He's got to be thinking that it wouldn't do him any good to verify if they were injured or killed. Nothing would alleviate that man's pain. If this was truly a reflection of who I am, I bet he's even wishing he had joined her in death. It would be beyond difficult for me to find a reason to live if she had betrayed me like that. As I watched him running down the hallway while making his harrowing escape, something like a hand reached out from the mirror and violently wrapped around me. As the hand jerked and twisted my body, my legs sprung to the sides of the mirror and latched onto the frame. The pressure ended up being too much. My knees cave in, swiftly buckling under the force.

The next thing I remember is being jolted awake with ice-cold shivers running up and down my body. Lacia was standing over me. "Sir, it's time to get up."

I mumbled, "What time is it?"

She replied, "Just before sun-up. Alex asked me to come and get you in his stead. It seems Eric wants to talk to you, and those we rescued are waiting for your evaluation."

"So much for dreaming about my bride-to-be, huh?" I asked.

She looked puzzled. "I'm sorry, I don't understand."

Slowly getting off the ground, I clarified, "Don't worry about it. Tell Alex I'll be over there in a moment."

The warmth I had been feeling was replaced by icy cold sweat and sporadic convulsing in my right hand. The shaking started small and steady but eventually reverberated up my whole arm. I'm not sure how much I remember from that dream, but I know that whatever was trying to be conveyed to me probably missed its mark. Something about Marleen… and it seemed… important. Doubt, perhaps? I do remember thinking it had something to do with the dark element. A forbidden affinity to the White Elves if there ever was one. Potentially a subconscious play that fed off my reaction to Seventeen's letter. A letter that only I read. There are just too many things to follow up on and not enough mental capacity to handle it all.

Morning always seems to arrive too soon for me. The compounding lack of sleep is just an ordinary, everyday occurrence while in the field. Eric met me when I was in the middle of shaving to insist that we receive half of the horses and other spoils that were retrieved from the bandits. The way he put it, his people thought we should receive even more than that for organizing and successfully quelling their activities. My counterargument was that some of those horses and other items belonged to the people of Lorelei, to begin with… and he just refused to hear me out.

We eventually came to a compromise and decided to only accept six horses for the slaves to ride until we reached Goliad. I still have not had time to sort out all the specifics of the slaves, but at least we can get them some equipment, horses, provisions, and leftover clothes so they can make the trip without too many problems. The rest of the spoils would go back to Lorelei with Eric. After negotiations concluded, we had one final meal together before they returned to doing whatever marauders do.

Before Eric and his crew left, he pulled me off to the side. "You're Laura's disciple, aren't you? I can tell by the way you carry yourself in battle. And the way you establish your command presence? Yeah, that, too. She taught you what you will need to survive and exceed in this harsh world, except... those eyes of hers. The eyes that can look at you fierce enough to make you shit yourself and ask for seconds. However, those aren't something that can be trained; they are earned with a lot of blood."

He chuckled while slapping me on the back. "I bet she was disappointed you decided to go with the tower shield and not take after her unique sword style. But not everyone is cut out for how she brings death with those two blades of hers, so don't take it to heart. Stick with what you're good at, and don't let anyone tell you otherwise."

Eric paused and then put his arm around the back of my neck and pulled me down low. This was a soldier's way to have an isolated private conversation away from prying ears. "If you get a chance, I want you to tell that duel-wielding red-headed war machine that I asked after her. I hope her kid is doing well. Damn shame what happened to her, having to quit her job at the academy and all. But luckily, she was talented enough to be picked up by the King and put to proper use."

My speech was startling. "Kid?"

He raised an eyebrow. "Oh, you didn't know? No matter. We go way back to when we were both in the academy together, and boy, I wish we had become an item. There wasn't a single trainee or instructor there that wouldn't have given up their entire career to wife her. Did she ever tell you she was from around here? Her whole family is held up away from most of the city. The privilege of being a high-born noble."

"She never talked about herself much." My mind was still on Laura having a kid... and this man's foul odor.

He brought me in even closer. "Her extended family doesn't live too far from where mine is along the outskirts of Lorelei. One of those small farming housing collectives they run as a favor for the main branch. Our status isn't low enough not to be considered for a partnership arrangement. The problem is, despite her looks, she has always been completely unapproachable! Practically an ice queen willing to throw daggers into the hearts of all men everywhere. I envy the bastard who knocked her up. I bet that's one fine kid she had."

I asked, "Aren't you a little old for her? What did you do? Did you join the academy in your thirties? I'm not trying to be rude, but she is way too young for you."

It's odd that he was admitted so late in life; he must really have connections. I haven't heard of joining past thirteen or fourteen unless there was a draft. And that happens only when something critical occurs.

He snicked, "Age is just a number! Yeah, I joined late. They pulled my number for the volunteer service when Lorelei got tapped by the capital. Anyway, just her knowing if she ever decides to get into older men and come back home, I still have my second wife's spot reserved just for her. I bet I have the stamina to rival that of her secret lovers!"

"I doubt..." He let go of me so I could stand back up.

He chuckled and rubbed his dirty beard. "Putting Laura aside, if you ever run into a jam and the price is right, we are close enough to the capital to help you out. We won't forget what you did for Lorelei's citizens or my marauders! You can call these goods you gave us a down payment on any future help you request from us. And I mean it! Just name anything at any time, and we will be there to support you!"

Eric laughed, shrugged a little, and waved as he set off with the rest of his guys. He really is a nice guy who likes to play the role of a tough warrior. I'm glad that yesterday he was on my side. But that part about paying him to do anything... let's hope someone else doesn't pay him off to ambush me one of these days. There are too many enemies as it stands.

So, about Laura's child... when did that happen? Why has she never mentioned this? To top off my level of shock, she didn't leave the academy of her own free will but was instead let go. You think you know someone, but you never really do, do you? Even after we reunited several years after we broke up, we have always been exceptionally close. She has always told me everything she has been allowed to tell.

Could Marleen have been told? I'll have to liquor her up until she gives up the goods. I'm not much of a friend if I don't at least give her encouragement and help. Being the top dog in charge of the military is hard enough... let alone doing it while being a single mother. I know... I have just the bottle of mead waiting for me back home to get her to divulge everything.

Shaking my head while vigorously running my hands through my hair, I realized that all this worrying over things I cannot control would detract from my mission and Marleen. Let's focus back on the immediate problem... checking the status of the slaves. We can't move out until we have an initial investigation. If any of the unclaimed slaves really are prisoners, it will change the way we ride into Goliad. We would need more frequent security swaps, so put them in the middle of us just in case. Also, the damned paperwork! Fill this out, sign that, and explain what happened in detail.

It would be nice to avoid dealing with those additional problems when we arrive. Offloading them quickly would allow me to get to what I really want to talk about... corruption and their false reports. 'Dealing' with these estranged four women and two men isn't at the top of my priority list. All those marked as slaves were human except for one male and female Grey Elf. May as well start with them and work my way to the others. Grey Elves aren't all that common this far north, away from their nomadic tribes. Their tribes usually prefer the deserts of the Desolate Plaines.

After getting all the slaves lined up, I sat down on a tree with a natural seat made of its roots and addressed them in a tone that tried to be empathetic to their plight. "Let's start with you two over there. Sorry for running the gambit of questions so early in the morning after what you've all been through. However, I must put everyone through the motions to make sure you were abductees and not escaped prisoners."

They shuffled forward, the female slightly in front of the male. "You two... what are you doing here? What led you to slavery? Do you have any ill intentions? Please be quick with your explanations, as we have a full day's ride ahead of us, and we must make up for lost time.

Regardless of your response, we will verify the inscriptions on your slave collars when we get to our destination. That means lying won't do you a whole lot of good."

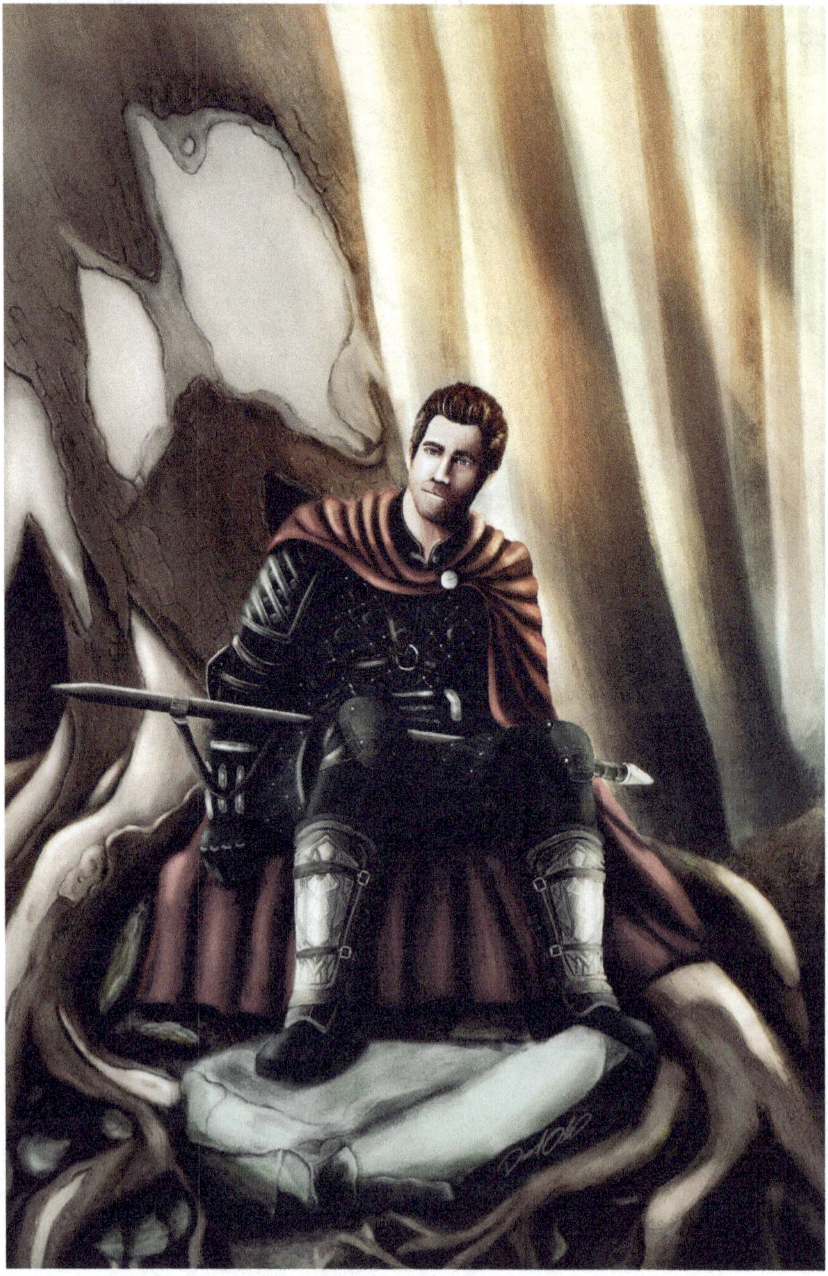

Chapter 10: Forina's Contract

The Grey Elf girl had roughly shoulder-length silver wavy hair, slightly glowing green eyes, and light blueish-grey skin. She was wearing dirty, shabby, torn white clothing that could be found on just about any slave. Both ears were lined with what I assumed were cultural earrings from the bottom to the top. If I wanted to speak honestly with her, my first question would have been why the kidnappers didn't take her earrings. Logically, even if they were worthless, having any personal items was very rare for a slave. The only thing I could think of was that she wouldn't cooperate with them unless they left them alone. Something about her instinctively told me she was a killer, which might line up with why she still had them.

My second question would be about her glowing green eyes. Although I am not familiar with Grey Elves specifically, the few I have met, and even the other one standing behind her, all have what appear to be normal eyes. The only ones I've met with glowing eyes have been vampires with glowing red eyes. Everything about her puts me on edge. The instinct that was telling me she was a killer was also telling me she wasn't from around here, either.

She stepped forward and mawkishly spoke. "Sir, my brother and I are from a nomadic tribe that roams very far south of the most southern city along the desert. Our tribe moves around in the Desolate Plains from one water source to another. We make our living by creating custom crafts from what we find in and around the sands."

I carefully watched for any changes in her facial expression. "I see. Then how did you get this far north? If you are from Arene or even further south, it would take a considerable amount of time to get up here. I doubt slave traders would bother with your kind in Alvernia. No offense, but Grey Elves don't have much to offer slavers or bandits. Sex, maybe, but with no magic and reduced muscular strength... plus the hassle of running you all the way up here... they would be far better off abducting locals."

She shifted her eyes once to each side of the tree behind me. "Yes, sir. That's right. Once a year, we come very far north to Lake Lorelei to stock up on provisions that we may need throughout the hot season. This happens when the temperature begins to change just as it has now. We trade what we can in the local markets."

"Oh?" I asked. "This is the first time word of Grey Elves in Lorelei has reached my ears, not that I've particularly been looking."

She nodded, "We do come up only once a year, which isn't surprising. For how we got captured, these men waited until our hunters had gone out looking for wild game. While they were gone, they snuck in and captured us. I couldn't tell you how because we were both knocked unconscious during the abduction."

Her story is consistent. I might not be giving her the benefit of the doubt as I should. "I see. And was that done recently?"

She shook her head from side to side. "We have been with that group for about a week now. That is why you won't find anyone to claim us. Our tribe has undoubtedly left to go back down south without us."

I replied, "I see. And what about the collars? It's impossible to enslave someone without being at a ManaBank and attuning it while the slave is present. Did they take you to one?"

She shook her head again. "No, we didn't go to a ManaBank. Shortly after being captured, they brought a man in with these collars and forced us to wear them. Will we ever get to see our loved ones again?"

She began to tear up while doing everything she could to hold her emotions back. "Calm down; I'm sure we can figure something out. But to think... someone attuned a slave collar without a ManaBank. This could be disastrous. Alex, we need to send a rider back to the capital quickly. This can't wait for us to finish our rounds."

Alex quickly agreed. He took one of our guys with him, and they disappeared to get him ready to return to the capital. "Oh, and Alex. I'll leave it up to you... but I really do think we should tell the King about elves being infected with miasma. Sentient demon-elves aren't something we have prepared for even in the slightest. I know it happened half a century ago... but if that is what Elvania is facing, it might explain why they are so silent about our struggles. If nothing else, touch base with Seventeen if you run into him."

I have not heard much about the nomadic Grey Elves in Alvernia besides the Desolate Plains being their home. Some rumors say it's because their particular group was persecuted by the White Elves that rule over Elvania, and they wanted to be as far away as possible. Other rumors say they go there because nothing in the desert has mana, putting them on equal footing in a fight. Either way, what she has told me fits the description of several tribes.

This elf's story is flawless. What about her is so offsetting? The way she is standing? Presenting herself? Speaking, perhaps? That's it. Everything about her feels scripted... premeditated, even. Moreover, the male hasn't said one word and is acting as if he doesn't know her or doesn't want to know her. No, more than that... he looks scared of this woman.

I pointed at the male Grey Elf. "You, there, can you shed some light on what she is saying? Anything will be fine. I just need something to back up her statement. The more information we get, the easier it will be to hunt down your tribe."

There's the one kink in her armor if I was looking for one. The other Grey Elf could validate or break apart what she is saying. The more I think about her, the more intoxicating or suffocating her aura becomes. My senses are drawn and enslaved by this woman. It's getting to the point of borderline obsession or a calling. What is it with her that is driving me so mad with anticipation? Our eyes locked only for mere moments, and I'm entranced.

Trying to keep the same pacified air about me, I calmly asked the male again, "Why are you sitting back there and not moving? Please step forward. Again, you are just corroborating her story."

The man didn't move. No, more than that. He was frozen in fear, unable to move even a single step or speak a single word. His posture was slumped over like a marionette. The female waited for me to refocus my attention on her from the man before she continued speaking.

I rested my head on my hand. "It seems he isn't much for words. That's fine; I think I have the gist of it. You all came up here to trade and were abducted from your camp while those that could defend you were out hunting. I guess they just grabbed you because you were easy pickings and then made a dash for it. After all, an elf in hand is worth eighty in the desert. After that, they threw a collar on both of you. Am I missing anything, you two?"

Her head moved left and right again. I continued, "This whole thing reeks of the Empire. Their damned obsession with enslaving any elf they run across. If what you are saying is true, those slavers might have even been smugglers sent over here to traffic you back to the

Empire. The more anger they can sow between our own people and those of Elvania, the better off they are... or so I'm starting to find out."

They were standing there waiting for my verdict. "Well, I hate to say this, but you two are shit out of luck. We don't have time to get the slave collars removed at the local ManaBank, and we cannot deviate from our course to return you to your tribe. We also are not in a position to leave you with the local garrison. I'll spare you the details and tell you it's political, and I don't want to deal with Claire. Never mind all that... for now, I will have to take temporary ownership of you until I can verify with my sources that your story is true. If everything checks out, you will be freed when we get to Goliad. From there, you can figure out your own lives. What are your names and ages?"

Genuinely, I meant what I said. However, the longer this woman stands before me, the more I realize that my life is in danger. That obsessive feeling that I had creeping over my body? I figured out what it was. She moves, evaluates her surroundings, and behaves so much like Seventeen... a trained expert in assassination and intelligence gathering. If I can at least get to that damn collar before she makes a move, then it might be possible to set the owner to me through the blood contract. That would allow me to set the conditions to make it impossible for her to hurt myself or anyone else without it killing her in return.

The conditions of the contract are also for her safety, not that she needs it. A slave with a collar and no master will be actively hunted on suspicion of killing their former master. On the off chance that I am wrong, this would spare her a great deal of grief from anyone else she ran across.

She stood in an offensive stance while moving her hands in an explanatory manner. A normal soldier would have missed it... but not one with Laura's training. "I am Forina D'Sarila, and this is my brother, Julius D'Sarila; we are both sixteen. Our age might be why we were targeted. We can't thank you for saving us."

While tentatively listening to her every word, the male flinched for just a second. "Last question, then I promise we are done here. What all happened to you in captivity? It will help us determine the appropriate level of reparations to give you should your story be upheld. Ultimately, it was our failure because we didn't support

Alvernian citizens' safety. We will be held responsible in its entirety. We can't have this place turning into the Empire where other races aren't welcomed. Had we been more astute and protected you as we should have, then this would never have happened. I will help plead your case to the Regional Lord, but I need details from start to finish."

The thing is, I don't care what happened to them in captivity. When Alex and his crew surrounded the cave with their group, they told me afterward what really happened. All the guards had been killed well in advance. It would have been missed, too, but Alex returned and found the corpses piled deeper into the woods. I didn't think a small thing like this elf could have killed and dragged them that far, but now… I'm not so sure.

Whoever killed them did it with a long, thin blade. An oversized dagger was something that came to mind, even if they aren't widely used. If my suspicions and gut feelings are correct, and this girl is responsible, escaping is impossible as we are all within her killing field. But why? Why go through all this other than possibly setting up a meeting with me? What the hell is her game? Maybe getting her collar removed? No, someone with that skill level wouldn't be subdued so easily.

She replied while slowly positioning herself closer to me, one nuanced half-step at a time. Her hand gestures remained fluidly vigilant during her explanation, indicating she could pull out a blade from her shanty clothing without anyone noticing. "Nothing extreme has happened to us since we were captured. They had us cleaning and tending to the others who were injured during their abductions. This continued for several days… cleaning, sleeping, and tending to the wounded. They fed us regularly and allowed us to talk amongst ourselves but generally left us alone, so their goods weren't damaged. A few of the injured developed a rapidly enveloping sickness, so they also had three of us quarantined with them since we would have already been infected. It is possible they were waiting until the sickness ran its course before taking advantage of us or selling us off."

Her performance is first-rate. Enough to keep increasing my self-doubt the longer her charade continues. I need to confront her and stop this bullshit because it's wasting our time. The way I look at it, if death is coming, then we better not make it wait too long. Many things bother me, but the real issue is that I don't sense any real killing intent leaking from her. Not even skilled assassins can hide their intent this well.

I slid my hand across my blade, resting it in my lap. "Forina, was it? Stop the bullshit games already. What are you after? We don't have time to spend an hour diving into your real motives or to babysit you. It's obvious to any blind man that what you have told us is a lie. Everything about you screams you're an exceptional assassin of sorts. This brings me to my next point. Why are we all still alive, and why do you have that ridiculous slave collar…"

She vanished into thin air, leaving only traces of green mist before I could complete my sentence. There was a puff of green smoke, almost like a ghostly water vapor, leading to her being gone instantly. I couldn't even stand up before I felt it… my own sword's cold blade against my throat.

The words slugged from my mouth. "That… was… impressive. You're going so far as to goad me by taking deep whiffs of my neck like some dog in heat. How far is this mockery going to go?"

Forina whispered into my ear, "I like you, that's why. However, I think you might be a little too clever for your own good. That confident, cocky attitude will get you killed one day… General Raider. However, I admit that I was the first person to underestimate your talents. That gets me excited."

I waved off my men, who had taken up arms and started to surround us. "Lower your weapons and back away. If she wanted us all dead, we would be corpses by now. Let me at least hear her out."

At this point, it was confirmed how out of my league I'm finding myself right now because I have no answers to solve my current predicament. For all I know, she may have even been leading the bandit raids to garner our attention for just this moment. If I were to compare our skill levels, I would be a farmer, and she would be the dragon eating my livestock.

She continued to whisper in my ear, "I know what you're thinking, and no, I have no connection to the humans you killed last night. I really could care less about anyone or anything happening around us right now. For the time being, you need to follow my lead and agree to my terms. Don't ask unnecessary questions and we can go about our merry way."

She doesn't hesitate at all, and she doesn't mince her words. Forina etched the blade of my sword up the side of my neck, slow enough to silently slice right next to my artery. "Showing me just how close you can bring me to death before you negotiate? Smart move, Grey Elf. The problem is… I can't tell if you're trying to seduce or murder me."

Her whisper sunk into my ear, "Why not both?"

"You're not the type… not with that dark, sexy voice of yours. Now that I know you aren't out to kill us…" The smile couldn't escape my face quickly enough.

She interrupted, "You… I don't want to kill you. I already told you once… everyone else here is expendable. It would be wise not to make me repeat myself. I was beginning to have high expectations for you, human."

I cautiously replied, "So, you know my name and position. I would say you picked that up last night, but I know better. This was premeditated days in advance. Inquiring how you got the intel would probably do me no good. So, what do you want? I know at least something you don't want… me dead, but why spare my unit if you're this good?"

"If negotiations break down, they won't be. For now, let's say it's a negotiating courtesy I'm giving you. A show of good standing to establish our rapport." Her response was expectedly sharp and cold-blooded.

I continued to prod her, "Cooperation, then? I'm growing tired of these guessing games with my own sword shaving the tiny whiskers from my neck."

Her smirk could be felt through her words. "The term 'cooperation' is nice, but that isn't what will be the basis of our relationship. Call it… parasitic, but without intent to damage the host. A better word in your language would be commensalism. But that isn't quite right either because parts of you may be damaged in the process, even if unintentional."

"Ok, 'Miss Commensalism'…" The blade instantly cut me deeper to cut off my speech.

She scolded me, "Forina is fine. I'll concede that your cleverness is somewhat charming. But I've seen it all before, so don't go thinking too highly of yourself. Or, rather, I retract my previous statement. Somehow, you deduced my esoteric nature. Things like finding out travel routes, departure dates, and times are trivial when you've been at it a while."

I couldn't see her, but I knew Forina was smiling. The portrait of her that I am painting of her personality indicates that she loves a good challenge. She switched her head over to my other ear and continued her seductive but now somewhat playful tone. "Perhaps you caught onto me this time… the first person in a long while. But really, you still lack evaluative skills, detective. Did you really think I was ever a prisoner?"

I replied, "No?"

She sliced me a little deeper. "Try again, human. I can tell when you're lying. I won't bore you with the details, but I can find out anything about anyone whenever I want… and with very little effort. Sneaking in right before your group showed up, killing a few uselessly clueless humans, and playing dress-up. I could do all this and still find out your darkest sexual fantasies. Intrigued, yet?"

"About my sexual fantasies? I wouldn't be bragging about that, 'Miss Forina'." This time, she flipped her head to my other ear and bit it. The drops of blood rolling down my earlobe startled me.

She whispered, "I said, it's Forina. Next time, it might be that veiny neck of yours. Anyway, that stupid Grey Elf over there was dumb enough to get enslaved. Figured I would use him for leverage. Unfortunately, I went too far, and now the poor thing is scared shitless of me. Too bad, too. He's so… young."

I asked, "Aren't you a Grey Elf? It's weird to refer to someone of your own species by their species…"

Forina interrupted me, "Quiet, now, human. You're only half-right… the rest, you will probably never be alive long enough to find out. Sadly, the way I had envisioned it, we would have had this conversation tonight in your private quarters without our captivated audience gawking at us while we confided in each other. Waiting until we set up camp for this conversation would have given me far more favorable circumstances to persuade you. I may have to resort to my other talents at this rate. Too bad… for you that is…"

Forina paused for a moment, assumingly to regain her composure. I guess even someone as unhinged as her can get worked up. "More on topic, you will trust me for one reason. I'll kill everyone until I get what I want. Friends, family…"

Boldy, I gritted my teeth. "The joke's on you; I don't have any friends or family."

She smelled the side of my face. "Loved ones… yeah, I know you have one. Her scent permeates from your pores. She isn't even human… interesting. Do you think she is unreachable? Think again. I'll find her and everyone else you ever cared about. I'll take pleasure in ripping them up in front of you if you don't comply."

I lost my patience with her. "I've heard this before, psycho. Get to the point. Stop with the threats and just tell me what the fuck you want, already."

"I'm getting there. Being used as a mutually beneficial tool is acceptable until I achieve what I am after. You use me, I use you, we use each other… sounds like quite the bargain, wouldn't you say? The slave collar around my neck was always masterless. I think it makes as good of a contract as anything to complete our agreement, wouldn't you say? If I assessed your character right, it's the only way you will trust me to any degree. The one addendum I have concerns about is how I treat others aside from you. You will allow me to kill, torture, mutilate, kidnap, or even disfigure absolutely anyone I want and for any reason. The moment you interfere with that clause, our agreement is over." Her fingers crept through my hair. Her tone throughout the conversation changed from seductive… to playful-seductive… to straight playful. What a weird elf.

I asked, "If you can kill my people, does that mean it's fair game for me to send people to kill you if you violate your side of the contract? It technically doesn't violate my side, and it stops you from being a permanent headache. I can't have you getting involved in my personal life, after all."

She pretended to take it into consideration. "Saving face, are you? If it helps your people sleep at night, not that it will matter much. We both know you have no room for negotiating. If you push me far enough, I can always finish up here and move on to another target. You aren't the only one who might be willing to negotiate with me."

Regretfully, I nodded. I could feel her delight. "Glad you understand. The contract will be for a minimum of three years. Any violators will be subject to the blade, which means you and I will be held to the same standard. I also encourage you to send anyone you have to me if you have the balls. A rampage killing humans every now and again might just stave off some boredom of mine. But I know that won't happen once you see how useful I am."

She let something slip just now. "I see. The reality is, you need me more than you're letting on."

Her fingers stopped playing with my hair. "Don't get overconfident. We will need each other for what is to come. Ignorance must be the epitome of what it means to be human... blissful, remorseful, ignorance. Don't bother looking too much into that statement. Just know while our goals are somewhat aligned, I might be your closest ally."

While speaking, she was slowly pulling my head back with her other hand, burying her knee in the back of mine. The edge of the blade started near the middle when she first took me hostage, and now it was almost to the hilt with how much she slid the damn thing. She has the nerve to call me arrogant under these circumstances... what a cocky woman. Maybe her, with that dominatrix act, is somehow what I need in my life.

Her failed seduction attempts aside, this contract, in my eyes, will be almost a direct reflection of why I hate magic and magical items. I can't stand gambling, and yet here I am gambling again. She does outclass me in skills, looks, talent, and maybe even her wits. Come on Raider, look at this as objectively as possible. Right now, I can't see any potential benefits to having her along, but that doesn't mean there aren't any. Three years, though? Explaining this psycho elf to Marleen is going to be a real pain in the ass... glowing green eyes and all.

Instead of letting me sort out my thoughts, she preemptively intercepted my internal debate. "I hate to interrupt your internal monologue, but I told you that you have no choice in the matter. And even if you did, didn't you say you had places to be? Or have you lost all that eagerness as well?"

If this psycho could smell Marleen, then I'm sure she's noticed the smell of the sweat dripping down the back of my neck. I'm being facetious, of course... the droplets rolling down my cheeks would have told anyone within eyesight I was in trouble. She knows she has me by the balls, so thinking about this any further really won't help me.

Hesitantly, I admitted defeat. "I'll accept your terms. But I need to know two things if we are to have any positive discourse between us. First, Grey Elves have no magical affinity. How the hell were you able to use dark magic? Second, can you at least give me the common courtesy of refraining from killing my friends, subordinates, or those I love? I'm too young and handsome to fall into despair, lose my job, and live as a vagabond."

Maybe some humor will lighten the mood, or at least make me feel better. If it were anyone else that I could even remotely understand, I would have resisted long enough to take their head. But her? I have no chance of putting up a fight.

She shouted for all to hear, "The contract is signed! Henceforth, we are in agreement! You humans were all witness to it."

I sighed, "Nobody says, 'henceforth'... where the hell are you even from?" Not to my surprise, she ignored me.

I was wrong; humor has no place in her world, only pain. She dug the blade into the side of my neck just a little further until the hilt touched me. The blood she sucked out went immediately into the slave collar. She then cut her hand and did the same thing. The spoken words of the deal were sealed and inscribed into the collar. Yet another absurdity. Inscribing a slave collar without a ManaBank. As if enchanting and attuning them without one wasn't crazy enough, this one was even worse.

She finally let me go. As I turned around, I could see the glowing orange gem surrounded by the gold and silver band around her neck to indicate that both of our fates are now intertwined in an indentured servitude pact. Who could ask for a better start to my two-week vacation? Just thinking about all the fun adventures I'm going to have with this psycho elf chick when she is so hard up on killing people... just has me shaking in anticipation.

Before she vanished again, I felt my sword slide back into its sheath. As I was focusing on her face, her afterimage was a green mist. She was already at one of the makeshift tables over twenty paces away. To add insult to injury, that woman was scarfing down the plate of food I never got a chance to eat. Our relationship keeps getting better and better.

She spoke with her mouth full, but I got the general idea of what she was trying to say. "About my 'Magical Affinity'... it's not magic."

She paused, eating my food for a moment. "We utilize something you humans have never experienced before, so I won't bother explaining it to you now. But seeing as how every one of you humans thinks that Grey Elves have no magical affinity, it gives me the element of surprise. Make your opponent think you're useless, then strike where they don't expect it. You would be... wise... to remember that. If I were you, 'master', I would kill everyone around here right now."

"Don't call me that. We are acquaintances at best." That correction came out of spite... for my food. She could tell I was getting more worked up about her taking my meal than the slice along the side of my neck.

She tried speaking again with her mouth full. "It's so nobody knows what I can do... but suit yourself... master. But that is up to you and how you deal with any potential spies from your adversaries. Think about it... not just your men but also the other slaves are present as well. And we aren't even talking about skilled spies here. None that can shapeshift into shadows or trees or animals or suck blood. Not that they can do much of anything to me. It's a vulnerable human like you that should be worried."

My eyes drooped low in amusement. "Thanks for worrying about me so much. In case you forgot, we aren't friends. Stop trying to be so cordial with me... and put my damn food down."

Forina put my food down. "I suppose you're right. I'll get my fill later anyway. But you see... you should at least think it over. Just give the word, and I'll off the slaves, at the very least. Human prostitutes with nothing to give but what's between their legs."

"Seems rude. How do you know they are prostitutes?" I asked.

"The guys sounded like they were having a lot of fun with them last night. See, look at that; I'm helping you out already." Forina was boasting proudly as if to be applauded or commended.

I'm still a little upset from watching her eat my food, which heavily affects my mood. I replied in an agitated manner, "All right, we aren't killing any of my soldiers, slaves, prostitutes, or otherwise. Also, even if they are prostitutes, that isn't exactly a horrible career for those down on their luck. For now, I'm done talking with you about this shit. We have a tight schedule to keep, and we are already way behind it. I'll have to have someone investigate the remaining slaves along the way. Let's get the hell out of here and get to Goliad. Alex, once your rider has departed for the capital, we will set off."

Truth be told, we aren't that far behind schedule. However, with that weird dream last night that I can somewhat remember, and this elf, I have steadily been feeling more and more uneasy. This is making me want to get this trip over with as soon as I can. Only having made this scenery trip a few times before... and nothing bad happens. This time? I set out, and the world catches on fire in the first few days. Just fantastic. I blame the damn king, and his foreshadows. The King just had to say, 'Hero Summoning,' and suddenly bandits ambush me, huge wolves eat people, and assassin elves are popping out of the woodwork, wanting to form slave contracts with me. We haven't even seen Leah at Midgard yet; boy, I can't wait for that excitement!

We mounted up and took off for Goliad. Forina instantly seemed to be getting even cozier with me as we were riding. It was as if the whole 'holding your sword to your throat' thing never happened.

I broke the ice first. "If we are going to be fighting together for the foreseeable future, you could at least tell me your real name so I can call you by something other than psycho elf internally. Although it has a nice ring to it and suits your personality almost perfectly, it might set the wrong impression when we are in mixed company."

She shrugged and then replied, "So that's what you call me, huh? Personally, I don't care if you name me psycho or crazy or whatever the hell else your human brain comes up with. I gave you the only name I will ever give you, Forina. Use it, or don't. I don't care."

With her refusing to give me her real name, it makes me wonder how much about this woman I can take at face value. I tried again, "Is there some kind of backstory that goes into that name? So much about you and your hostility just boggles my mind. Like, how did you get dressed in those pitch-black leathers from tattered clothes in under two minutes? And... was anything you told me true? For instance, how you're some prodigy teenager who loves to kill people and drink blood. I've never met a non-vampire that drinks blood or a Grey Elf that can vanish."

She boasted, "I don't drink blood, but I did kill some girl with her family a few months ago. The screams the youngling gave off were exhilarating. Also, listening to her brother yelling to let 'Forina' live. 'No, please, don't, stop...' or something like that. Who the hell calls their child 'Forina?' I was so thrown off that I had to ask the brother to enunciate it slowly. Syllable by syllable, he spelled it out... For... een... a. And bam, a dagger through the neck as he hung on to that last letter. Good times, good times. Anyway, I liked her name, so I kept it. To your other questions, just stop. Dwelling on words and ideas like 'trust' will get you killed."

Ok, I stand corrected. She is just some death-hungry psycho-elf with a mindless vendetta against the whole world. And more than that, not a single iota of sympathy for those she murders or kills. Unlike in war, where someone is defending an idea or a cause, she just does whatever the hell she wants and enjoys it. Whatever, I'll call her Forina and just go about business as normal.

"You murdered an innocent girl along with her family and took her name? Our contract doesn't say I can't arrest you for past crimes." I brought my guard back up. This time I put my right hand on my shield just in case I had to grab it. The more I hear, the worse it gets.

A slight smirk crept across her face as she corrected me. "Words, words, words. That's all it is with you humans and your dissections of the irrelevant. The words 'murdered' and 'innocent' are a little too strong when referring to what I did to them. Maybe you could say that I patiently carved up some corrupted nobles, or you could say I was getting better at my favorite hobby. Nobody in this, or any other world, is 'innocent,' you naïve, young human. Never forget that. Everyone has something worth being killed over, it's just a matter of perspective. Besides, they weren't anyone you or anyone in this world would know."

"On... this... world?" She was speaking a foreign language to me. What the hell did she mean by that? The Empire?

"Either way, they are dead, and they deserved it. Is enjoying their deaths a little and taking on one of their names really that bad? Awfully judgmental for a human that would have been dead if not for my 'kindness.'" Yeah, she completely ignored me again as if the statement she just said never came out.

I'm sorry I even asked. That's the last time I pry too deeply into what she does or why she does it. That is unless Marleen goes missing randomly. Forina has officially reduced me into retreating into my own mind as a cave hermit. All that's left is trying to avoid depression for years, followed by a 'mysterious suicide.' The hand-written suicide letter will contain a hurricane of complex emotions, carefully written in someone else's handwriting... elvish... handwriting.

Everyone has a plan until a psycho gets involved. Forina wasn't about to let me isolate myself that easily. She inquired, "By the way, I noticed that rather 'ordinary ring' on your ring finger. Isn't it a bit overzealous to use a magical artifact as your wedding ring? It must be someone pretty important to use an item like that. Did she give it to you because you lack any magical talent of your own? How about me, then? Mind giving me something important since I can't use magic?"

I don't like it when anyone dives into my affairs this abruptly. I'd think if the wrong information got into her hands, it could spell disaster for our sovereignty. Why is the elf so intent on getting close to me so quickly? What makes her think she can ask questions like this just because she forced me into our arrangement?

Snapping at her, I may have let my temper slip a little bit. "That is none of your damn business. Just know that this artifact and the person with whom I share the bond are beyond reprisal in my eyes. Both have saved me more times than I can count. My magical ineptitude has nothing to do with it."

She seemed to expect my response and gave a monotone eye-roll. "Fine, fine. But what about this strange contraption?"

Forina had wrangled one of the spears from my shield without me knowing. "Give that back. It's dangerous. If you handle it inappropriately..."

"It will explode? Yeah, I doubt that. As primitive as it looks, it's missing a detonator. I bet you rely on mages for that, don't you?" She was asking rhetorically.

As she balanced it on her finger, she leaned back from the table. "This spear you all seem to carry on you wherever you go... I like the concept, but it needs a lot of work. Don't you think it's a little half-assed to rely on two people for it to be of any use in battle? Right now, the material that can be ignited inside the shaft is useless without an outside catalyst. I'm not a tactician, but wouldn't it be better to have the one throwing the spear be able to set it off?"

Could it be a coincidence that my dream this morning is reflecting almost exactly what she just said? As if I wasn't already on edge enough, this just makes things even worse. The timing of this woman, the spear in her hand, the similarities... all of it is just too much of a happenstance.

I replied, "Yes, I have been looking into that. Not that it's any of your concern, but we don't know what to use as an igniting agent for our spears. I've tried a few things, such as having mages compress the short spear staff when they are made and then having a cover on the end of the spear. The cover would be made of flint, so when it is ripped off, it will ignite a spark. But the problem..."

She smiled, "Is instant death for anyone holding the spear if it ignites too quickly. Yeah, you all are primitive. Not willing to accept losses to achieve your goals."

I interrupted her. "The alternative... and this is still in the works, is having the pull cord ignite the string on the outside so it is on a timer. The problem with that is its unpredictability. Fox and Anna are looking into... wait, why do you care?"

She elaborated, "Just curious. Always a good time looking at what other cultures try to come up with to survive. I'm sure my people tried it all before we found our own catalyst. Those born with less are always the most creative. That's what my people and yours have in common, isn't it? Increase your lethality or go extinct. The law of the land... the law of nature."

I sighed, "Fair enough. I'll allow you to look at my workshop when we get back to the capital, and you can help me with some of the designs. These spears were a huge step forward from what we had beforehand, and they have only been around for the last few years. My hope is that when I get to Bartad they will have something for me."

She seemed pleased I was giving her some leeway. "I never said I was going to help you discover those means of becoming more lethal. Taking some bold moves, aren't you? But I like it. What's to say there isn't a bit of charm in helping out those in need."

"Where are you going?" I asked as she got up and hopped on one of our horses meant for the other slaves.

She replied chipperly, "I am going to ride ahead of everyone. I'll see you tonight with any suitable gifts I find. Can't you smell it?"

Confused, I questioned, "Smell… what?"

"Filth…" And just like that, both her… and the horse were encompassed in a green mist and vanished. What a creepy nightmare I've found myself inside.

Chapter 11: Golden Goliad Gladiators

If I've said it once, I've said it a thousand times... Goliad is a massive pain in my ass. Because three groups of independent city-states rule our country, all run by independent governing bodies that report to King Forsythe, they tend to be very competitive with each other. Each group believes their people are better than the others, regardless of the fact that they all trained at the same military academy in the capital. This is what causes the root of the problem at Goliad. All three governments want to vie for dominance within the main army. And much like Claire, none of this has anything to do with the actual army or defending the country... it's for the reputation and standing of their houses once they finish military service.

Prestigious positions are difficult to come by in the military. Being an officer or knight commander of the only front-line fort within Alvernia Superior is top among them. You can count on anyone not from an esteemed background, or from Alvernia Superior for that matter, to stand no chance in hell of landing anything other than a standard foot soldier, or maybe a squad leader, position. Even if publicly the positions are available to those from the Tri-Yuli Territories, Alvernia Minor, and commoners, those people stand no chance of being deployed here for any leadership positions... so most don't even try.

Usually, those from the primary territory that the capital rests inside, Alvernia Superior, will use connections, pay people off, or even make back-door deals with other nobles to kickstart their careers by getting stationed here. This directly ties into the kind of people that command here and have for generations. Their corruption is deep, spans centuries, and even starts before they arrive when most are still very young nobles in their late teens or early twenties. For this reason, Goliad has become a hotbed of haughty, stuck-up nobles in charge of other haughty, stuck-up nobles. Every one of them is rotten to the core.

This is where I come into the mix... a commoner by birth, of unknown origins, and a noble by pure, unbridled luck. It doesn't take a genius to realize how welcome they make me feel or how jealous they are that someone of my low standing and youth was given command over them. And, of course, when I do my job by checking in on them, they hate me for it. In the short time I've been over them, I've just about seen it all. Money laundering, illegal prostitution without the appropriate collars or consent of the individual, hazing of new recruits, and much more. What can I do about it? Nothing because they always pin it on the lowest rank possible, which doesn't cut the head off the serpent.

Of the reasons to be disgruntled and angry at me, my birth is probably the most damning in their eyes. This goes back to what happens when studying at the Alvernian Military. Aside from weapon lessons, you study 'Military Arts'. How you place in your class, coupled with your nobility status, determines not only your profession but also your 'station wish list.' The wish list primarily examines nobility status and job category to determine where you go. These jobs, in order from most prestigious to least prestigious, include the Royal Knights, Knight's Order, Engineering Corps, Cavalry Corps, Infantry, and Forward Observers. Or at least, that is how it's supposed to work… before people bend the rules to suit their own desires.

The only people that fall outside the station wish list are the royal family. Royalty can choose anything they want. And again, this is where I came in… I skipped the entire process altogether and was appointed to the Royal Knights. That wouldn't be so bad, but it happened immediately after being knighted while training as a regular infantryman. This action shocked and devastated the nobility, who were the only ones supposed to be appointed to the Royal Knights or the Knight's Order, and only after displaying impeccable performance. The top ten percent of the top ten percent of society are the only ones qualified… and I jumped the line. I'm basically… hated.

People from the commonwealth usually fall into other jobs, like the general soldier slot I was filling, depending on their personal skills and merits. Slaves can also be in the military. However, they are somewhat rare unless they possess extreme talent. If they do, they can be sent to a branch and earn freedom upon graduating. The few times I've run into slaves in the military, they occupied a Forward Observer role. Irreplaceable assets before and during a battle yet shunned by anyone willing to turn their nose up at anyone for any reason. Damn shame too. Without them, we would never know the enemies' movements.

To bring it all back to the main point about Goliad. It is the most desired post because it has the most luxury, is right next to the capital, and has the highest promotion rate. Almost every single soldier stationed here was able to do so based on their connections, their money, or their family… not personal merits. Whenever they see me, it makes them want to vomit just by being within their eyesight. So, they tolerate me only because they know King Forsythe would have their heads if they didn't. Why? He was the one who chose to knight me… but as for why, I still don't know. If asked why Laura and the King tolerate this slime-infested shithole, I would say that I know just as much about that as why I was knighted. Speculating a little, it's probably because it would take way too much work to overhaul the place.

"Thinking about the rider we sent?" Alex asked.

I replied, "No, I know he will make it. I was just pondering over the state Goliad is in."

His red eyes rotated from the road to look at me. "Scum of the earth, not fit to grace these lands?"

"Hmmm… yeah, something like that." His eyes were still on me. Those piercing, bright red glowing marbles. "I was mostly just considering how it all came to be. The difference in how things are run, who's in charge, and so on. Goliad with that son of a bitch, Bartad with one of the most agile leaders ever, and of course, Midgard with Leah."

When her name was mentioned, he moved his eyes back to the road. "Oh? Still a soft spot for her? Is it because you're both vampires?"

He straight-up ignored me. "We are coming up to the last hill now. I would reorganize your thoughts before we come into viewing distance. You know Captain Michael will have something special waiting for you."

"Yeah, yeah. Same old, same old. That man has nothing better to do than to count the coins in his pocket and lie to me. What do you think it will be this time?" I asked.

Alex shrugged, "Guess we will find out. It can't be worse than the 'accidental' ambush from last time. I really do get tired of saving your skin."

The fort sits in a kind of depression in the middle of an open plain. In every direction, flat lands without much of anything else. I am not entirely sure why this location was originally chosen by whatever king or council all those hundreds of years ago, but it holds no obvious strategic value other than its meager ManaBank. It does have three very minor other things it has going for it. Its proximity to Lorelei, the Elvanian border, and a profitable gold mine. Something I had discussed a few times with Laura was dismantling the fort and just rebuilding the whole damn thing on top of the gold mine. More security, easier to defend, closer to Elvania's border, and all you sacrifice is a crappy ManaBank.

Alex sighed, "And we are here. I wish that hill would have taken a little longer. Never a good time in the hotbed of human... filth."

My eyebrows twitched. "I'm getting that a lot lately. Don't look so melancholy, my friend. This is the pinnacle of human achievement! The best of the best... one fort to rule them all! Built with the best resources available to us... a few hundred... years... ago. Reinforced with persistent magic! Yeah, I give up. It's just a large walled settlement with shitty leadership."

I wasn't wrong. They designed the fort well when it was built. Inside each of the four corners of the walled square are four towers about three stories high. Each is always manned by no less than two-to-four mages and a few archers. The mages occupying each tower are usually one of each type if we have the luxury of having them... fire, earth, wind, and water. This allows for increased spell diversity, which increases combinations between the elements that can be used for barriers or attack spells. The forts also have several ManaBank-powered magical items that keep up strong, persistent barriers that cover the sky. These barriers also double as keep warning alarms.

Aside from that, each location comfortably houses roughly ten thousand soldiers. Another key feature they have is a very deep staircase that leads to an extremely secure room under the primary keep. This room is the same in every city or fort because it houses the ManaBank that powers everything. The magical items are easily attuned to them, and they are also accessible to the Master Mage in charge of the fort's defenses for spells. The room is each civilized area's most secure point. Essentially, if the fort or city is going to fall, that is the last bastion of hope. And when that hope fails, the ManaBank can be overloaded with the remaining mana inside of it to cause a very large explosion.

If the small ManaBank ever were detonated, it would completely wreck and irradiate the landscape for at least a day's ride in any direction. The ManaBank would be destroyed in the process and hamper any magic users in the area for over a hundred years. If a much larger one were to detonate, such as the one in the capital, the whole country might be affected one way or another. The radiation would extend to almost Lorelei for sure. Thankfully, there hasn't been a need to detonate a ManaBank for a very long time. Marleen did find some historical records of this occurring once or twice in dire situations, but again, nothing recent.

The overloading technique is a primary factor in nations not going to war. It's clear as day why. All the defending faction must do is eliminate the usefulness of any conquered land. Watch for the enemy's army, wait until they are all inside your city or fort, explode said fort, then counterattack. Then, when your armies approach their cities… they do the same to you. That is why there haven't been any open nationwide invasions in hundreds of years… or at least since before the Unknown Territory appeared.

Alex's voice interrupted my thoughts. "Raider, stop zoning out. We are crossing the draw bridge. Get your human game face on."

Angerly, I spouted, "Two men and a woman have come to greet us… with an entire company in ceremonial armor? What does Captain Michael think this is, a joke?"

"Not a fan of the gold-trimmed blue and silver armor?" He asked.

I replied, "No, it's their stern demeanor practically telling me I'm not welcome. Any one of them is just as likely to put a sword in my back or a shield to my throat as they are to salute me."

He sounded condescending. "I'm not calling you a liar, but their shields are leaning against their legs at their feet, and their swords are sheathed. Being paranoid much?"

"Alex, stop rubbing it in. You know this is all one giant condescending mockery… exactly the kind of thing I wanted to avoid when coming here. Just look at them, the Golden Goliad guys. Each and every one of them is trying to act like they give a shit. None of them want to be here, Alex."

He replied, "None of them? What about that familiar old man in the middle? He looks like he wants to be here. With his strapping grey and black beard and long hair. See? He even looks less grumpy than last time."

I rolled my eyes. "That's enough. Cut it out. You mocking them mocking me isn't going to make this any easier. Let's talk with that 'old man in the middle' and get this over with. If it wasn't for the great Captain Michael coming to greet me himself, I might have bypassed this altogether. But… you know… I must hear him sing his own praises. It's somewhat of a tradition anytime I run into him… or when anyone runs into him…"

Captain Michael stepped forward to address me. "General Raider, it's been far too long. How are you doing? Surely, you must all be tired from your exceedingly long journey. I see it took you two days longer than the correspondence said it would. Did you perhaps walk on foot and find the horses halfway?"

I replied, "Your consideration is too much. Unfortunately, we ran into a little bit of trouble along the way…"

He cut me off, "I see, I see. Terrible business having to stop to utilize the latrine constantly. I dare say, you common… I mean you…"

"You're so right!" I exclaimed. "Taking out the trash that has been accumulating near here is quite exhausting, so I'll take you up on that. You see, my group wore themselves out after dispatching so many more adversaries. What were we outnumbered, Alex? Fifty-to-one?"

He nodded. "Sounds about right, General Raider."

Kicking it up a notch, I really drove my point home. "Captain, please see to it these slaves are very well taken care of while they are in your charge. They are some of the unfortunates that got mixed up in the bandit squabble we took care of in your stead. And one more thing. Their collars may be forgeries. I expect you to launch a full investigation alongside the Royal Ministry. I expect the report to be sent to my desk before I arrive back in the capital."

Captain Michael was stunned. He has probably never been talked to like that in his life. "We can get…"

I stopped him. "It's General, Captain. You will refer to me as my title dictates."

He was biting his lip to keep it from quivering. "Yes, General Raider. We will make the necessary accommodations as you have requested."

"And one more thing." I stopped for a moment to dismount and approach him face-to-face. "We will be discussing these bullshit reports you have been sending. Your lackadaisical attitude, your lackluster responses, and your general disobedience to the greater cause is sickening. We are fucking at war. Treating this fort and this garrison like your own personal toy chest is going to stop."

By now, his whole face was twitching to hold back what he really wanted to say. "Whatever… do you mean… General Raider?"

I whispered into his ear, "You know damn well what I mean. We will start with how you have been wasting the troop surge that you received over half a year ago. Follow that up with unaccounted-for deaths, inaccurate financial reports, and abuse of new recruits. Yeah, I fucking know it all. To squander the King's army is to affront the King himself. I will have an account for those extra five thousand soldiers, or I will have your resignation. I've let you slide until now. But things have changed. You will change."

He took a step back. His eyes shot to the man and woman standing next to them to see if they heard anything I just said. When he was assured they hadn't heard a word, he gathered himself. I suppose he realized I was half bluffing, so he returned to being carelessly smug. That arrogance is going to get a lot of people killed if he doesn't correct his attitude. I bet that man gets it from his wife. The one time I met her, she was the spitting image of him. I bet she gets it from all his soldiers. Another victim of an organized political marriage… and both are equally deserving of each other.

"Ahem…" He cleared his throat. "How would you like to take advantage of our infamous pleasure district? It's the best anywhere outside the capital and would be the best way for you and your soldiers to unwind. Let them take a load off and relax while you stay here. We can clear the air and revisit these topics tomorrow morning."

Ah, yes, the Goliad Pleasure District. I have more respect for the people working there than I do for the villainy in front of me right now. At some point in the past, way before I was born, there was a huge uproar over troops being stationed at these forts and not being able to get any action. The King at the time, probably King Forsythe's grandfather or great-grandfather, decided to legalize prostitution and run a small pleasure district inside each military installation. Those who worked there were usually slaves owned by the state who were trying to pay for their crimes or pay off debts. Others who worked in these districts were commoners just trying to make a living. All of them are more honorable than this man.

    Prostitution isn't my thing, but I tolerate it because It's not a bad deal for a lot of those women and men. I've made it a point to ask several people in several forts if they are treated well, and all of them universally say they have been. Every one of them, even the slaves, gets to choose their clients, have a roof over their heads, can feed themselves, and can relocate if their contracts allow them. Not a bad hand to be dealt when they would otherwise be doing the same thing while living on the streets. I bet the soldiers and the workers roared in approval when that decree was enacted. Imagine being a king and single-handedly solving morale issues for people who are likely to die facing demons at some point in their young lives. My concern comes into play when those who oversee these areas get greedy and try to play around with the rules by exploiting the workers.

    Time to flatter this guy. "I may let my guard take you up on that. Thank you for the abundantly warm hospitality you're showing us. I look forward to meeting with you and the leadership tomorrow morning."

    After I was done speaking to him, the two next to him gave a salute and prepared to escort us. This was very well-rehearsed, much better than the last few times I came here. Their ass-kissing techniques have become top-notch. I'm lying, of course. They sensed the pressure radiating between the two in charge. This was their way of keeping things as formal as possible without worsening the situation.

    He shot me a snarky smile. "We will get you situated in the guest rooms in the primary keep. Please follow my lieutenant. I have instructed her to make sure you and your men are well looked after. I have something I need to attend to, but I look forward to our discussions tomorrow after you have had time to settle down and rest."

After he finished, he quickly turned and left to enter the fort. "Captain, sorry I made you stand on the drawbridge for that long. Next time, we must do introductions over coffee in your private quarters."

My words only made him move quicker in the opposite direction. Damn, he was pissed. His motives were a little too obvious. Assigning his female lieutenant to be my caretaker. What kind of easy bait does he think will lure me in? Granted, he knows about Marleen and my thing for blondes with long hair, but this girl falls short in the elf department... and I love me some elves. Not that I would ever try to be with anyone other than Marleen.

The woman was a little tall for a female. She was about my height, had long blonde hair, and had an amazing figure. She was wearing the same obnoxious plate armor the rest had on, custom fit to accommodate her curves... an unusual breastplate if I've ever seen one.

She sharply turned, approached me, saluted, and introduced herself. "General, I am Lieutenant Helen Winslow. I have been temporarily reassigned from my duties as the primary logistics officer for the fort while you are here. For the duration of your stay, I will be assigned as your secretary to take care of your needs and answer any questions you may have. Please follow me into the fort and over to the room you will stay in."

"Helen, please call me Raider. To my right is my sergeant, Alex. We will be in your care. Since your superior has left in a hurry, would you mind taking those five over there and having your ManaBank Engineers have a look at them? We need their origins investigated. I'm sure you heard we ran across them under some atypical circumstances. Validating if they are really slaves should be your top priority. I didn't have time to check all their stories out, so please be thorough when checking out each of their slave contracts. If they are runaways, then return them. If the contracts were forged, free them and give them enough money to get to their destinations."

She eagerly agreed, escorted us to our rooms, and took the slaves away.

Chapter 12: Frigid Night Blues

It wasn't surprising in the slightest that my guards were given quarters in the barracks across from my room in the main keep. This was to keep me secluded with Helen for as long as we were here, and she already admitted as much. The whole game from Captain Michael was to present her with as many openings as possible to gain my favor. Helen had a room connected to mine but with no door in between, just a see-through curtain. She said it was so she could be within earshot at a moment's notice. Yeah, nice try.

By the time I was settled in, she had already dealt with the slaves and returned to her quarters. In the short time she was gone, I barely had enough time to bid my troops good night and ensure they had a night shift established. Why pull guard when we are in a keep under my command? Foolish questions nobody should ask after seeing that grandiose display earlier. Alex was again taking the burden of most of the shift. I told him to cut it out and share the workload, but he insisted. That man is loyal beyond a fault.

When Helen entered, she did so through my door, not hers. She slowly opened the creaky wooden door with one hand while holding a candle in her other. I was postured on the edge of the cold pallet, attempting to read over the letter Seventeen had given me. But I found it impossible to concentrate because there was a middle-aged man tied up in the middle of the floor. His squirming made it near impossible to concentrate, even in the slightest.

Her shock indicated that she was also not expecting him to be there. This may sound obtuse, but I thought this man was a message to me. Something like, 'Behave or die, asshole.' With her acting so frightened, I didn't know what to think. Did someone just forget their hostage? Maybe this man slept with the wrong woman and got left here? The possibilities were endless.

Seeing him gagged and tied up on the floor ruined any expectation I had for a quiet visit to this place. He was naked with his junk chopped off, lying in a pool of blood while squirming around and making noises. His wrists, waist, and mouth were bound with tightly pulled ropes. I mean, I'm not into bondage, but this was a real masterpiece. Someone took their sweet time chopping this poor sucker up and securing him this way… pure… artwork. Aside from his missing appendage, I might have been almost envious of the artist under normal circumstances.

A dagger flew across the room, blew out the candle, and landed on the wooden door a hair's length away from Helen's head.

Helen immediately drew her sword. "Who's there? Identify yourself. General, quickly get behind me."

Turning the note over to continue reading, I jeered, "Oh, well, aren't you the knight in shining armor? You're too good to me; I don't deserve you. No, really... swinging that long sword in a tight space like this will really do wonders. Keep this up, and I might fall for your gallantry."

"It took you long enough, 'master.' I would recommend you... and your one-night stand... get in here and shut the door." A voice was muttering from the window's ledge.

I tried to act calmly. Truth was, she had me completely taken by surprise. "Forina? Oh, it makes sense now. I assume this is your doing?"

Looking over my shoulder, I could see her slender silhouette. When she leaned forward, I grabbed a clear picture of her in the moonlight. "Why are you wearing our black leather armor? I'm not too sure I want our coat of arms anywhere on your body when you're creating havoc."

She seemed delighted. "I told you I would be here with gifts, didn't I? Why are you acting so surprised? Surely you wouldn't think of me as being a liar, would you? And the clothes... aren't they just adorable? Playing dress-up is such a riveting experience. This style suits me. It has a much deeper hood, allows for more mobility, breathes better, and is stylish... in a human sense."

My unamused side snuck out. "Uh-huh. And you had to play dress-up, looking like one of my shadow agents. How... do you even know what they look like?"

Forina chuckled, "Let's just say... I was able to have one of the most skilled craftsmen in existence replicate your designs but with a few modifications. Neat, huh? The cute thing I had the leatherworker model this outfit after was just about my size, too."

Helen was confused. Her head kept darting between Forina and me. "Helen put that damn thing away and shut the door. Forina, I've known you for what? Maybe a whole day, and you show up with some random guy with his family jewels cut off? What in the hell are you thinking? Putting aside the fact that you almost incriminated someone else for your actions... can't you let me have a somewhat normal life, or is this going to be this chaotic from here on out?"

Forina appeared to be distracted. She was still hunched over on the window's ledge while continuing to toss a large blade up and down. Her posture and overall nonchalantness signaled how little she put stock into our conversation. When she leaned back and placed her back on the wall, all I could make out were her glowing green eyes and shadowy outline breaking the moonlight invading the room.

I couldn't see it, but I knew she was smiling when she replied. "Now, now, don't take that boastful anger out on me. I know deep down you were missing me after the favorable impression I left on you. I can feel our bond growing stronger by the minute. It's as if... we are inseparable from each other."

Her cocky attitude, mixed with the random guy's muffled screams on the ground, was just too much for me. I lost my composure for a moment and snapped. "You on the ground! I know life will suck for however long you are alive... but shut the hell up while I figure out what's going on. I can't think with all that moaning and rolling around you're doing. I have half a mind to kill you... Mr. Nameless person."

The only thing stopping me from doing that is Helen being present. The last thing I need from her is to have this reported back to that asshole and make my life an even bigger trash fire. He wouldn't hesitate to go right to Laura and bitch about my un-officer like conduct. She wouldn't listen, but it would at least give him an edge to gain support from the nobles and, with enough traction, maybe even the King. He would do anything to fuck over the competition.

I thought Forina was too busy cleaning her teeth with her second dagger to give two shits about what was really going on here. I was wrong when she shook her head. "Temper, temper. That attitude isn't very 'General' like. How would you feel if I used that language when addressing you?"

Helen eventually sheathed her sword. This triggered Forina to turn her head and stare off into the vast, empty sky. "Seems I was right... the smell of skank didn't disappear even though you bent the knee."

Helen snapped, "Who the hell…"

Forina interrupted her, "My friend over there oversees the pleasure district. Let's just say that he has been abusing his authority for quite some time, and some of your human women have been suffering because of it."

I was unmoved. "Since when do you care about human women?"

She ignored me as she rattled off, "That meager pain he is experiencing? Well, he hasn't even begun to understand what's about to happen to him. I'm eagerly anticipating every moment of it… the screams, the howling, the laughter… yeah, all of that. What does this have to do with me? Why would I care about the ongoings of this filth? Consider it a down payment on our contract. That's right, it won't be free for you. I'll collect my payment with interest sooner than you think."

I shook my head. "What are you even saying right now? How does you… I don't know… abusing this man… affect me at all? That's like eating someone else's pie while simultaneously saying it benefitted a random person walking on the street."

"An odd comparison, if I might say so." Her head tilted away from the window and toward me. "Seeing as… you know… you're responsible for everything baked in that shop. Don't mistake this for passing some useless righteous judgment of my own accord. It benefits us mutually, just some… more than others."

She began licking that stupid dagger until I could see the drool running down the blade. This again got on my last nerves. "So, you won't tell me the specifics? Fine, I don't need to know the finer details. If you want to deal out punishment to this man, then do it, but don't arbitrarily declare that I owe you something as a result. Even if this guy is as deserving of torture as you're saying, this whole place is full of scum, just like him. Give it a day or a week, and another will take his place. Nothing will change until the source is rooted out. Not that I expect you to know this, but the one who runs this fort won't attempt to fix that issue, so it's self-perpetuating. You're wasting your time."

I briefly looked at Helen, signaling I wanted an explanation for what she was saying, but I kept addressing Forina. "Clean this mess up and get out of here. I can't have some random dickless guy dying in my room on the first night. Can you at least use your head for a moment? Do you even know what some shit like this would do for my reputation?"

Forina replied, "Oh, he isn't dickless. It's just been relocated to a more appropriate location. And I'm not your maid. Ask that slut next to you to do your dirty work, as I'm sure that's right in her area of expertise. I'll take this soon-to-be corpse, but the rest is yours to bask in and relish. Ah, yes, the night is still fresh and unabated. Mouths to feed, moonlight to seek clairvoyance, and humans to tear into... too... perfect. Maybe, just maybe, he might even get lucky."

As she spoke, the man squirmed more. If he wasn't gagged, I'm sure he would be waking the dead right about now. "I love that look upon your face. Please me... and I might get bored and begin chasing down the rest of your friends. Why would I delight in one sacrifice when so many are easy for the picking? The real challenge will come from how I want to entertain him and all his friends. Boiling alive? Slow and steady flaying? Maybe something more... poetic? I'm sure the brothels have plenty of women willing to vent their frustrations. But see, therein lies the problem with you humans. You have no imagination when it comes to inflicting suffering on one another. You're always in such a rush to get to the climax with everything you do. Disappointing, to say the least."

Helen was steadily shuffling her feet towards Forina with her hand on the hilt of her blade. I just told her to cut that shit out, but she was enormously upset at Forina. She spoke in a shaky but steady tone as if to hide the inundated, enshrouding fear caused by the mysterious figure before her.

When she spoke, she did so with an uncertain certainty prominently filled with a fit of disgustful anger. "You think you can come in here and call me a slut, you piece of shit elf? If it were up to me, I would wipe all your kind out for being nothing but garbage. The Empire has it right when they sell your kind into slavery and prostitution while killing all the men so you can't infect the world with your progeny. You vagabonds and your destitute plague Alvernia's deserts! If it weren't for the King being so damn weak, you wouldn't be allowed here!"

She had to be clueless that my fiancée is an elf, or she wouldn't be spewing half of that shit in my presence. For those words alone, I have half of a mind to kill her if Forina doesn't do it first. It's such a pain in my ass to try and be diplomatic in situations like this. Thoughts of decapitating her in several different ways weighed heavily on me. Generally, all of those around me are very accepting of other races, even the brazenly crude dwarves. To express my aura as killing intent would be extremely accurate. If I were a bandit, mercenary, or ruffian, I could get away with an untold number of atrocities on this shithole of a person. Even above my personal feelings, her attitude of slighting the King is not something I have seen in a long time.

    No matter how you look at it, the culture she lives in encourages her to be open with such hatred. She is a direct reflection of her leadership and Fort Goliad's climate. "Helen, your prejudice stops right there. Another word, and I'll rip the life from your cold lips and…"

    Forina jumped off the ledge, loudly interrupting my tirade as her feet hit the ground. Her confidence and tenaciousness are something to be admired, even if she is unhinged. "Well, off I go. Have fun, you two, as it seems I am no longer welcome. I left a bottle for you to celebrate something or another with a few of the other items in the cold box."

    She vanished without even breaking her swaggered stride and reappeared on top of the nameless dickless man. She touched his shoulder, and both disappeared into a green mist, leaving only a pool of blood. What the hell is she? An impromptu vigilante seeking justice? A thrill-seeker? I'll stick with the psycho; it's easier to digest in all the wrong ways. Her violent shifts in civil discord are also impossible to track or understand. Why… wouldn't she have opened Helen's throat after those comments? Not that I wanted death on my first night here… and it was impressive how she didn't let Helen's provocations incite her. Perhaps she is far more levelheaded than I first imagined.

    When my head turned to see her face, I could tell she was angry. She had to be unapologetically furious. Her hand was trembling so badly that she could barely light her candle before screaming, "That elf bitch thinks she can call me a slut and a one-night stand? Does she think she can call me out and get away with that horse shit? She has another thing coming!"

Instinctively, I tried to calm her down before she picked a fight that I knew she couldn't win. I started to talk but was instantly overridden by her broadside rant. "General, I don't know who that woman is, but she just kidnapped and tortured one of the most senior merchants in this town. The sheer impact on our commerce and trade districts…"

"Helen…" I spoke softly until her eyes rotated to meet mine. "Remind me again why there is trade and commerce in a fort on our front line. I'll spoil the ending for you; there shouldn't be any. Your goal, and your mission, is the safety and security of the soldiers in this fort, on patrol, and protecting the citizens of Alvernia. Trade? What a distant thought when confronted with the reality of the deaths that await us should we fail at our jobs here."

She didn't know how to take it. After a few eerie moments of silence, she eventually shot back. "With all due respect, we are getting off track. Her actions are harming the existing commerce, regardless of whether it should or should not exist. Do you want morale to be devastated? Because that is exactly what will happen when the soldiers don't have access to their favorite women in the Wind District. That man controlled everything! We must hunt her down and kill her! And if you don't think crushing our soldier's morale is enough, then send her to the dungeons for defamation of an officer! You can't let her get away with such flagrant disobedience. Whatever magic she used to escape couldn't have gotten her far. Let's notify the guards, corner her, and pull her apart."

She was getting increasingly worked up with every word. Her breaths became deep as she failed to restrain herself. "AND… she's an elf! That disgusting woman with her inferior pedigree was doing all of that while standing in the same room! What else do you need from her? That should be everythin…"

I demanded, "Stop. Just fucking stop while you're already behind. There won't be another mention of her race while I'm in this room. You're entitled to your own beliefs, but not openly in my presence. Do I make myself clear? I swear if you so much as mumble another word damning someone based on their race alone, you won't see the sunrise."

Expectedly, the mood soured. Given what she was saying, she must have been told incorrectly that I shared the same anger toward the elvish race. You wouldn't be able to tell it, but her facial expression was at a crossroads between furiously upset and disappointed. This look was nothing like I originally imagined when we met on the drawbridge earlier. I bet, given the circumstances, she would take the entire garrison after Forina for damaging her pride and questioning her virtue. Her protruding veins along the sides of her forehead were more than enough to support my conclusion.

Time to put the inadequate charms I learned from Ian to the test and mollify her indignation towards Forina. "Look, I... may have overstepped a little. Each person has their own reason for feeling the way they do. Just as I was saved in the past by an elf, you may have had a brush with one that was less than hospitable. Let's move past that and settle down. Perhaps a drink will calm our nerves so we can put this behind us. Starting from square one, if we talk through things, we might be able to find a better compromise than rushing off to kill someone. I'm sure she was not questioning your purity, motives, or your intentions. Instead, think of it as a communication barrier between you two. She was probably trying to get under your skin because I am right here. That seems more like her than intentionally trying to slight your character."

I was, of course, lying my ass off to Helen. Her head returning to its proper place above her shoulders instead of being leaned forward may have lent credit to my attempts, but I knew she was playing along to get back to her original objective. Sacrifice your principles to achieve your mission... admirable. However, my inability to convincingly lie to her lends credit to the fact that I'm not a ladies' man. Between Laura just overpowering me and Marleen's entirely passive nature, I've never had to console a woman before who was this upset at something or someone who wasn't me. It was either to have the punishment dealt to my body or calm my own anger so as not to upset my spouse. Shivers just ran down my spine, remembering Laura's fanatical, hedonistic berserker mode when we were together.

"General Raider... I'll... go... and get someone... to clean... the..." She was still stumbling over her words and hesitating because she was so irate. Before she finished her sentence, she hit her hand on the door near where Forina had thrown her dagger. The oozing hand did little to alter her state of mind. This woman has some real rage issues and may need some professional help.

"I know you're worked up right now, but please call me Raider. Worry about the blood and cleaning up stuff later. Let me look at your hand and see if we can dress it." Maybe if I keep this relaxed pressure on her, it will slowly chip away at that ice barrier she has erected.

I walked over to the cold box, opened it, and pulled out a bottle I knew was worth more than I make in a year. Yup, this was probably in that dickless man's private stash. In this situation, it would be wise to think of the weight of the stolen goods compromising my character and the prestige of my position. With a quick roll of my eyes from the top left to the top right of their sockets, my doubts were shredded as I prioritized dealing with Helen first. If this bottle of whatever doesn't work its magic, I'll have to improvise in another way that doesn't rely on the smooth moves I learned from Ian.

"Hey, Helen?" I asked. "The last time I came here, they hadn't put luxuries like this cold box anywhere inside Goliad. Things like this are reserved for royalty or rich men way above my station. The damn thing even has the water element etched along its sides and handle. What gives?"

It was obvious this thing was built and activated in anticipation of my visit. Well, it could have been for if royalty visited as well, but that was far less likely. The technology for items like this isn't anything new and is no different from other engineered items, but they have generally been considered a poor use of mana. The ManaBank powers these items, but in a practical sense, most people think it is a colossal waste because it keeps a persistent cold barrier cast around either a tightly sealed wooden, clay, or metal box. The advanced ones can even produce ice, but I've only ever seen those in places like the Royal Palace in Prince Wilhelm or Prince Karl's rooms. Very fancy... for a fort.

Helen sat down in the chair next to where I had been seated. "Oh, that? It's something we had custom-made for when esteemed guests decided to pay us a visit. Although it's odd... that box should have been stocked with our local mead, brought in directly from where we produce it. I apologize for that; it was an oversight on my part."

I laughed, "It's fine. I don't usually like drinking heavily on business ventures. The last time I was here, I remember going a little overboard with the stuff. Alex had to carry me to my bed and everything. That wasn't one of the best highlights of my career. Next time I'm around, I'll indulge."

She was completely recomposed. "I'm also... sorry, and I'm doing much better now. Sorry for that outburst just a moment ago. It's true that I get passionate about certain things a little too openly... and I'll work on that. It's obvious you have some form of working relationship with that elf, so it is not my place to say what should and should not happen with her. Maybe... it would be better if I came clean since she did... say more than she should have."

Helen took the bottle before I could pour a glass for myself and started chugging it. I'm not even mad. Her chugging form would impress any adolescent in the academy playing drinking games with each other after they stole a bottle from one of their instructors or seniors.

I began to bandage her hand while serenely speaking to her. "Take your time; there is no need to rush. If something is going on, and you feel I need to know about it, then please tell me. We have a while to kill before I hit the rack."

I reached over to grab the bottle after I finished bandaging her hand. As she released it from her clutches, she took a deep breath. "Everyone knew about what was going on in the pleasure district but did nothing. I have already said that man is a very important nobleman. His appointment was questionable to begin with. First, his origins were from somewhere in Alvernia Minor. Second, he hit it off instantly with the commander and became best friends overnight. They practically do everything together! Splurging on women, importing elven wine that is impossible to get, having secret meetings with nobles from..."

I poured a drink into a glass and took a few sips. Leaning forward, my hand grasped hers to let her know it was fine to continue. "Probably from... the Empire..."

We have a potential hero summoning, major problems with supplies, and raids on villages to worry about. Now, corruption that expands beyond just internal politics? If the Empire was able to secure a partnership with our main line of defense against the demons from the Unknown territory... all the other problems we have going on are but a joke in comparison to what might be coming our way. The Empire wouldn't even have to use their insane numbers to wage war with us... they could open the gates of hell and let us get ravaged to death by our common enemy.

Helen put her bandaged hand on top of mine. She seemed genuinely remorseful. Pausing momentarily, I realized all of this could be some ploy to get me to sympathize with her. If she could get me to slip up bad enough, then no matter what I learn here, it would be relevant. Those bastards back in the capital that were pissed off that I got appointed to this position without being born a noble would be too busy howling about whatever they could to distract from what I would be saying. I can't be careless and let her take advantage of the situation.

Her eyes teared up. "Raider, please put yourself in our shoes! If we had said anything... then... then who knows what would have happened to us?"

Yeah, here comes the act. I was on the fence until just that line. She lacks a certain ardor in her words as she continues to try and bait me into her scheme. "We have nobody willing to listen to our plight! Any of us! Any woman or man who spoke out in the ranks found themselves with a collar slapped around their neck and put into that district, too! Imagine what would happen to an officer like me if I made enemies like that! I'd be served on an open plate, free for all to tarnish! Day in and out, I would be abused until I killed myself."

She was visibly feeling the little bit she had to drink. Her body swayed from left to right as she snatched the bottle from my hand. What a complete lightweight. If you're going to send someone to schmooze and frame an enemy, why would you send someone who couldn't handle a little bit of alcohol? She clearly isn't faking it... not with those wavy arms.

Another two large swigs later, she returned to the topic of Forina. "That Grey Elf...she's..." Her hiccups interrupted her sentence. "She is your fucking pet dog, isn't she? Your dark shadow! I don't like her. Their kind has no sense of loyalty. No... wait, what was I talking about? You know... I hear stories about you all the time. Your features aren't what I was told they would be..."

Her swaying intensified. Wait a moment. I couldn't tell if she was swaying more or if I had gained double vision. There were two, then four of her sitting in front of me. The strength of the concoction was incredible... and the flavor wasn't half bad either. The more I listened to Helen, the tipsier I got, and the more the flavor rolled around, hitting the sides of my mouth in waves. Just what did Forina bring us? Call me heartless; I was more intrigued at how a few sips of this shit got me so inebriated so quickly.

When she realized I wasn't speaking anymore, she began to remove the top parts of her armor. The clanking of the metal pieces mercilessly hit the ground as she undid each of the leather bindings, securing them and throwing them behind her. After the fifth piece slid far enough to hit the door, I was jolted back to focusing on her half-naked body.

"Oh? That got your attention, did it?" She asked with her top fully exposed.

She took my silence as an invitation to move over and sit on my lap. Her swift movements quickly positioned herself above me, fully mounting my hips and jerking me out of my mirage-focused stupor. She was after the kill, but which one of her? The left one looked more dangerous than the right. Wait, which one was the left one again?

I drank the rest of my glass and tried to push her off. Aggressiveness aside, how did she remove that armor so fast? It's almost like she has done this routine a few dozen times and has refined her technique. Perhaps Forina was right, she might only be here to seduce me. That was the trap, and I'm borderline helpless to defend myself.

My arm managed to slam the glass down onto the nightstand next to me. I tried to use that movement to show how disappointed I was that this whole event was so predictable while also encouraging her to knock it off.

However, it was clear she wouldn't give up without a fight. Being naked from the waist up, she was now undoing the straps to my leather armor. I would be lying if I said this wasn't hot and that it was a great attempt, but I need to stop this show. Before I could muster a single word, the multiple Helens slammed together into one and then back out into five. After blinking a few times, the dizziness slapped me harder than the lightheadedness that followed.

I tried to keep my eyes fixated on one of the Helens until I couldn't anymore. Just keeping those marbles open was making me motion sick. Try as I might, they could only remain agape for seconds at a time before I had to shut them for just as long. She was having the same problems, too, but much more severe and to the point that it was throwing her completely off balance. This didn't stop her from continuing her advances and trying to seal the deal. She collapsed into my chest as her lips rolled to a halt on the side of my neck. Landing that kiss cost her dearly as she toppled over, crumbling to the ground. I tried to catch her, but my arms were paralyzed. Before I knew it, I was on the ground next to her, and nothing of mine was responding except my lungs.

    That crazy-ass elf poisoned the bottle. She couldn't even wait a few days before fucking me over, could she? For the thirty or so seconds I'd been laying here waiting to die, I could see that Helen was already out cold. Her breathing wasn't stopping… so at least this wasn't a poison that was meant to kill, just one meant to immobilize. We can only wait and see what she has planned for us next.

    The only reason I think I'm even safe right now is because of our slave contract. Forina can't outright kill me because the collar would do the same in return for her. That's assuming that she cares about her own life, but it would be silly for her to go through all the trouble earlier today to just kill me at a less convenient time later. What… is… her… game…

    A green shimmer materialized into Forina right next to Helen's head. She had a frightening smile draped across her face while giving me a once-over. "Took you long enough… master. Did you really think I was going to let you sleep with this tramp? Tough luck for you."

    She ran her fingernails down the side of my face. "Such a sad state to see you in. Humans and their inability to protect themselves. So… heartbreaking. Look at it this way… at least you won't catch whatever diseases she caught from the other humans around here. Can you smell it? Riddled… riddled with infection and lust. Unlike you, smelling of… another kind of unsavory woman. At least that's the kind of… unsavory… I won't catch from you later. After all, I'm still looking forward to my feast tonight. Now it's nighty-night time."

    I'm getting a handle on her derelict personality when she whispers those sweet nothings to me. She calmly removed her hand from my face and stabbed the back of Helen's back. As her cries of anguish ruptured, both disappeared into another green shimmer.

Chapter 13: Illicit Nightmares

As I am walking through this dense, cold, white haze, every detail from the dream I had before came rushing back to unsuccessfully debilitate me to an enfeebled state. Last time it started with me aimlessly being lost until I found my way to a mirror. Mirror... a reflection of... of something else. Something... troubling, disturbing, unsettling. Do I wish to relive what it showed me last time? I can't take that abuse again; it was too much. But I feel it, the calling, the radiation, the magical permeance. That means it must be around here somewhere. An unavoidable fate calling back to me from an echo I never sent.

There it is... that shiny object in the distance. As I approach the mirror, everything feels far too familiar, too distant... like this isn't just the second time I've done this, but rather like I have been here my whole life. And endless cycle of repeating mirrors elongating my meager existence. I thought my self-pity encroaching on my sanity stopped when I met Marleen, guess I was wrong. When I reached the mirror, the image forming inside this damn thing wasn't like the last projection I witnessed. It's a reckoning of a rugged, war-torn, and discombobulated me. The highlight of this scuffled character is his scraggly-looking beard, and his tattered green, black, and tan armor patched together from who knows what and who knows how. Not too professional of a look for even the lowest soldier on the totem pole. At least the beard is an amazing work of art in all its disorganized curly glory. Plenty of 'I don't give a damn' all over that man's face.

This mirror-me also has prominent dark and light blue tattoos on the exposed parts of his arms and legs. The designs bend and twist up and down every appendage, unapologetically declaring his appreciation of such fine design patterns. There are smooth lines, jagged lines, circles, flames... all of it... and all at once. It is hard to picture the time it took for someone to paint that man and for him to sit still. Days, possibly even weeks, of meticulous scrutiny went into every detail.

Where the woad tattoos ended, his scars began. The tattoos were ripped to pieces along his forearms, elbows, and knees, where there were clear breaks in the armor by large claw-like tears in the skin. With so little visible, the armor is probably concealing far more devastating injuries. His face was even riddled with scars from the top of his eyes to the bottom of his jawline. The man was a monster... probably wrestling demons in his spare time for sport. What a far cry from my current self. I bet he went through the grinder one time or eight to ask for more. Way to get some.

His eyes were also intimidating. A bright glowing yellow deep enough to set the world ablaze with the wink of an eyelid. From my soft blue to a scorching yellow... I like it. As far as I am aware, there aren't any creatures or races that have eyes that unique anywhere in Genesis. All beings that have been turned into demons have black eyes, vampires' eyes glow red, and Forina has glowing green eyes that chill you down to your bones. But none of those are close to yellow... just what did you go through?

He begins to turn away and approach another towering figure slowly. As his back is exposed, his weapon becomes visible... one that didn't make any logical sense. A large, double-bladed broadsword almost as tall as its wielder. Each blade on the sword was facing in the opposite direction, with the one just behind his head facing the ground. The handle was as long as three to four of his hands, and the chips along each of the guards made it clear it had been used through many battles. The stout weapon isn't conventional in the slightest.

On his hip was a modified gladius. A rugged blade with a serrated edge close to the handle... much different from practical use in our military. A short sword that could be used for carving or sawing up prey as easily as it could be used for combat. What I didn't see was Blake Gale, my artifact tower shield. It was an item I swore never to be separated from, no matter the cost. It was given to me by His Highness the moment I was selected to join the Royal Guard. Apparently, those oaths fell by the wayside for this guy.

In time the other figure came into full view. This person was monstrously huge... a damn freak of nature, the likes that shouldn't exist. She is no less than a six-four wall of massive muscle. She had similar blue tattoos spanning the length of her body. Hers, though, were much easier to see due to the scant amount of clothing she had covering her body. Her clothes were a mixture of brown reptilian hide, leather from something similar to cows, and huge teeth on various parts of her single pauldron and belt.

Her hair was wavy, blood orange, came down to in between her shoulders and upper back, and was wildly unkept. This wasn't a woman who spent hours combing her hair every day like Princess Julia or some other prissy noble. Aside from the same yellow-colored eyes, uniquely orange hair, mountains of muscles, and her endless scars, she had a naturally intimidating presence. I wasn't even in the same area she was in, and I knew this woman was dangerous beyond her physical appearance.

She and the man resembling me in the mirror looked as if they were exceedingly close... close enough to be comrades that had bathed in the blood of battle for years. Jealousy doesn't come within earshot of what I am thinking about those two right now. The pain and struggle of being arm and arm with the person next to you. Overcoming insurmountable odds and having the physical indentations to show it. I've got nothing of the sort right now and never have.

Also, watching them set off to their destination feels so... right. Just thinking about how 'complete' those two look together caused an instantaneous shatter in the mirror. A crack began at the top right and rapidly splintered down until it buckled under its own weight, sending pieces flying toward the ground. When the first two were just about to land, I was jolted awake by the sound of a giant crash of glass breaking.

Sweat was rolling down my face on all sides. The sporadic nature of my unilluminated dream was more jarring than it was concerning or painful... like the last one. This event felt like the culmination of the inevitable pulling together of the musclewoman and me into a shared struggle. More than culminating, it felt as though the very nature of companionship bound us. That's saying a lot when looking at one such as her that is so intimidating as to make me piss myself out of fear.

What is the purpose of these fucking dreams invading my... where am I?

"Are you going to sleep all day? I'm starting to get bored, you know. And here I was, up all night taking out the trash for you while you slumbered without any care. Leadership might be a virtue you're missing... master..." Forina smugly spoke as she sat on my back while I was lying face down on the cold hard stone floor.

I tried to respond, but my throat was butchering me. I couldn't get so much as a single word out. First, the poison, then my dreams, and finally, my throat. This is turning out to be a hell of a first stop. The first thing I tried doing was moving my right hand to find it sealed to the ground.

"Why can't my... hand move?" I asked without so much as opening my eyes.

Coming to my senses a little more, being unable to move my hand seems minor. My body seems covered head to toe in an indescribable sticky substance. The hits just keep on coming.

She chuckled, "You can speak, after all. You are an impressive human... a true credit to your species."

A few winks later, I managed to groan out, "Forina, can you explain a few things to me? First, and most importantly, why am I naked with a kind of sticky substance all over me?"

"That's easy..." Forina was positively delighted. "How would I cover you in their delicious honey molasses otherwise? Try some; it's not half-bad in a grimy sort of delicacy way."

"Um... what?" I asked, puzzled beyond her own words.

"This is their famous honey syrup, which they make right here inside the fort. Last night, while I was making my rounds, I found a few hideaway spots that were fermenting this stuff. Don't worry; they were all owned by that merchant. He won't miss it where he's currently enjoying his time. Wouldn't you feel bad if all the hard work the slaves put into making this went to waste? Yeah, me too... so, I decided to help myself to some since none of them will need it anymore."

I grew aggravated. "Uh huh... so why am I covered in it?"

She again chuckled, "I decided you needed some form of punishment for your illicit activities last night. What better way to discipline you than making you into your own honey sandwich? Get it?" Forina started bursting out laughing while slapping her thigh.

My head lifted briefly before falling back into the pile of gooey happiness. "Your puns are as irritating as your personality. Never mind... do you care to explain last night? As I'm sure you can grasp, I'm erupting in enthusiasm over what happened. Fresh start to our cooperative agreement... fresh start to tasting poison for the first time in my life."

She pulled her head down over my shoulders so I could see her upside-down face out of the corner of my eye. "Lying there face down in that shit, and you still have enough energy to try and quip with me? The poison was meant to take the edge off for your first time, unlike the harlot. She had it coming for a whole set of other reasons."

My sticky eyebrow raised. "First... time? Hold on... does this have to do with my throat?"

Forina smiled. "Guess you will never know."

I was trying to speak to her as easily as someone could... with their face being pressed against the floor like mine was. The paralysis poison she gave us was very potent, thus saying all the lingering effects. Forina rocked backward on me and then jumped off into a standing position with her arms stretched outward like she had accomplished some great feat and was expecting praise. She then took her finger and ran it along my back. She outstretched her finger just far enough so the tip of her tongue just barely rolled off the end of it. Then she unleashed that same smile from last night... that evil, unhinged, psychotically subtle smile.

Then, she continued talking while pretending to contain herself. "Everything I did was to guide you onto the right path like any loyal slave would! You must believe me, right master?"

With that, I had had enough. I tried to get off the ground by pushing myself up, only to slip and fall a few times. Every time I got so much as a shoulder off the ground, she would run her finger on a different part of my body and take another sample for her tasting pleasure. And yeah, she ran her finger anywhere that became exposed.

Eventually, one of my knees caught the ground, allowing me to brace on both my elbows and knees. "Stop rubbing salt in my wounds... or honey, whatever. Can we end this charade? If I don't hurry, I may not even have to wash up before I meet Captain Michael. Meanwhile, you are still playing around."

Her head tilted. "You say that as if either one of those is inherently a bad thing. Don't you hate that guy? No, don't respond. Even if you didn't, I've measured his worth."

She was pushing my buttons as hard as she could. The mumbling slipped out of my mouth. "Naked... fucking covered in syrup... going to meet with an asshole... dealing with a psycho elf... and for what? All because I was trying to be slick and find information from the logistics officer. Can't win for not winning. Damn it all."

She ran her finger along the side of my thigh. "No, you can't win because you tried to be charming and failed. Luckily, I'm the only charm you will need while you're here."

I abruptly declared, "You are not, and I mean this, coming with me to meet Captain Michael. Even if he is a pompous asshole, I don't want a dagger in his back. Replacing him would take weeks. Then, there would be rooting out his subordinates and other corrupt officials tied to him. Who knows what else? I don't have that kind of time, and I might end up getting killed as a result."

Forina let out another series of chuckles while following me as I stumbled to my feet. "Well, you're no fun. At least you don't need to worry about the harlot giving you what you want to know at the cost of what little... exposed... dignity you have left. She was prowling in the night... stalking helpless young human males... sinking her teeth into them... and then... she ate them and spit them out. This was a story as old as time itself. A disguised maiden, but secretly, a vampire wannabe who hungers for males. When she strikes, your life is changed forever... dun... dun... duuuuun."

I sighed, "Stop making up bullshit stories and be real for a moment. I'm not even mad at this point; I just want the truth about this fort so I can move on to more important things. So, what intel do you have, and how did you secure it? More death, I assume?"

I could feel all that crap slowly rolling down my body, and it felt gross. She ignored my other questions, so I may as well ask her if she knows anything about the situation here. "You're pathetic, you know that? Took you all that time to stand just to brace yourself on the same chair you were in when you got poisoned. I bet as that sweet honey rolls down your body that you're getting turned on."

"No, I'm not. Although I'm afraid of the answer because of how much damage control I'll have to do, can we stick to what I asked?" If anything, this shit slowly moving down my body would turn me off, regardless of whoever was in front of me.

"Like what specifically?" She was asking rhetorically. My disgusted look let her know to quit messing around. "Maybe about the brothels or the supply lines you care so much about? We could cut straight to the chase and see how they squandered all the goodies you gave them. That's what you really want to know. To you, everything else equates to a meaningless squabble, doesn't it? Your hatred for this place, for the nobles, for this task you've been given when you would rather be with 'her.'"

I was in shock. "How the hell could..."

She interrupted, "I can read your mind. I know all your little secrets. But before we get to that, you must try this wonderful honey. One taste and I'll spill everything... I promise. It would make for an amazing breakfast while also easing and coating your throat."

"What are you now, my doctor or my mother?" I scooped some off my arm and cautiously tried it. "This wouldn't be so bad if I wasn't still standing here naked. Now, stop fucking around."

Forina laughed, "Temper, temper. Something tells me you would really lose it if you knew what I did to you while you were sleeping."

My eyes rolled hard. "I don't ask questions and don't want the answers to them."

Forina wasn't listening. Instead, she was dancing or prancing; I'm not sure which, but it was in circles around me. In between twirls and bows, she would say one sentence or another while swiping more goo from my sides. "Intelligence... intelligence! How much do you worry about an entire society born and bred to hate you right down to your toes? The bigotry and disgust for the lower class... how very human of them. Envy breeds hatred on a whole new level, master."

I snapped, "Look, I have a killer headache, and my throat is so hoarse I can't think. Can you just tell me what you know without all the extra shit? With your incisive gallivanting, I don't even care about how you got it anymore. Damn, this pain!"

She paused mid-dance. "No fun indeed. Fine, aside from their lustful appetites and general hatred of everything you believe in, this fort is wonderful, aside from a little corruption here and there. For all his faults, you are right to put that human in charge of this place. He runs a tight crew. But I would be careful where you travel alone in this city, but I'm sure you already know that. I think they might bribe some mercenaries to fake your capture. That would be swiftly followed by a hefty ransom that goes wrong and gets you killed. Should I take care of the problem and let you be lazy? Hmmmm?"

"Do whatever you want. Just leave me the hell alone for a little while. And please refrain from massacring people all over the fort tonight. You even hinted that what you did last night was already too much." She puckered up into a cheerful elf.

"Oh, and about Helen and…" Forina vanished into a little shimmer again. No answers as to where all the blood or where Helen went out of that woman.

I heard a knock on the door; it was Alex. "Raider, may I enter?"

I replied, "Come in at your own discretion. I'm not responsible for you dying from shock at the sexy man that stands before you." After he opened the door and set eyes on me, he stood there without moving a muscle. This wasn't because he was shocked but because it didn't affect him at all.

"What? I had a rough night last night, and I am still recovering. Alex, were you here at some point last night by chance?" I asked.

In a monotone voice, he replied, "Yes, the slave woman, Forina, asked me to stop by. She mentioned something about a free dinner on the ground and you going at it with that lieutenant until you passed out. Don't worry; I won't let a single word of this reach Marleen. It's to be expected of someone in your position. However… I can't keep this from…"

"Leah… got it. Not that I was expecting you to, given how fond you are of her." Interrupting his line of thought before I heard more didn't help my sadness like I hoped it would.

I sat back down in the chair for a moment. "Well, anyway, Forina told you at least half the truth. Gathering that you cleaned that mess up and took care of the finer details from last night's adventure. Thanks, I appreciate it. Oh, and Helen won't be coming with us today."

He stood there with the same look in the middle of the doorway. Unmoving, unspeaking as if unconvinced that I wasn't a part of Helen's absence. "Right, then. I'm going to wash up, and then I'll meet you all downstairs so we can ride out together. Get the men ready to roll out within the next half hour. I don't want to stay here a second longer than we have to… especially with the psycho causing troubles."

"Very well, I won't dive into your affairs. As for Helen, I think this note that is pinned onto the outside of your door would be adequate proof as to her whereabouts. I'll leave it right here for your viewing pleasure." Alex saluted and then left the room as if to mock me. What he was really saying was, 'Good luck, you'll need it, buddy.' When I read the note, I understood why he did that. But at least I didn't feast on a fast old dead man. Raider and Alex... tied one-to-one.

"Captain Michael,

After spending a wonderful evening with the general, I have decided that my sex life has been too dull! I renounce my position and am moving to an area with manly men who are willing to please me more frequently. It's not you, it's me. My contract with the military was already up anyway, so I was basically deadweight. I am tired of being exploited for your gain. Oh, and the general was able to get all your dark secrets out of me last night while we were locked in heated passion. I wish the best for you and your corrupt plans, but I will no longer be a part of them. Also, all the morally bankrupt nobles you had been taking a cut from are no longer here either. They decided that illegally importing slaves into the pleasure district was no longer what they wanted to do for a living. If you find bloodstains in their residences, just know it was from the good time they had last night paying for their crimes.

Thank you for the lovely memories,

Formerly, Lieutenant Helen"

What... in the... absolute... hell... is that woman thinking? Sure, the note was written and signed in her hand when I compared it to the list she had written and left on top of my dresser drawer... but, really? The authenticity is there, but there isn't a person alive that will think she wasn't coerced. I can't even imagine what that psycho did to her, and probably over a very long and grueling period.

Any moron looking at this would assume I was flexing on Captain Michael as his superior with some point to prove. Weighing the options doesn't give me much, as I know he will ask for her location. Do I have any other choice but to give this ridiculous letter over? Forina got her way while putting me in a spot where I had to become the scapegoat. That son of a bitch really gets off when I squirm, doesn't she? My only hope is to use this to paint me as a law bringer, and if I twist it right, then I can deal with the internal discord later.

Chapter 14: Awkward Riposte

Heading out of my door, which Alex left wide open, and down the stairs, I realized... the damn washroom was next to the barracks outside next to the well. This wasn't very well orchestrated. I just told Alex to muster the men outside, which means I must walk right past all those assholes. Of course, this would turn out to be one of those times that I could take back what I told him. Here's to hoping they are moving sluggish... and no, there they all are.

They did their best to hold back their laughter while I was awkwardly wobbling past them... then scrubbing all this crap off me... then cursing at my life. I suppose if I were them, then I would be cheering on my commander. For all they know, I had a hell of a good time last night with some random hot blonde. Nothing gets the blood going like watching your superior rack in the kills, but on and off the battlefield. The largest obstacle to them treating me like a conquering hero is if word of my exploits gets back to Marleen.

My croaky voice broke and fractured as the words leaped from my mouth. "I hear you back there with all your snickering. Laugh it up! Go on, get it out of your system! You all know this was that psycho elf's doing, so don't even pretend it was anything else. And just for your information, the only reason she was able to get a leg up on me was the poison she drowned down my throat. Don't trust strange women, and don't drink random bottles of high-dollar booze. Learn from my mistakes, or this could happen to you."

That makes it sound like I was with her all-night last night. Depending on how they read into it, they might think I was even double dipping between the two of them. No, I'm thinking too much about it. There's no way they would believe I would go behind Marleen... and with two women. Although Alex was even convinced it was expected of someone in my position, what would the guys really think? The more I got lost in my thoughts, the harder I scrubbed to get this shit off me. Less chatting and more scrubbing! That's going to be my new motto until I get the hell out of this embarrassing situation.

One of my men piped up and yelled, "DEATH BECOMES US," and the rest of the troops burst out laughing while yelling, "AND HELL BECOMES THEM... all night long!". Cocky bastards, but I love every one of them.

Their jeers didn't stop with one chant. I could hear them talking to each other, making honey-related puns. Things such as, 'I bet he enjoyed their comp-honey,' and 'If honey-one can do it, it's you.' Every time one of those puns was just loud enough for me to hear, I tried scrubbing even harder. Just about when I got all the honey off, I thought my skin would peel away.

When I finished washing up, I hurriedly headed back upstairs to get dressed. When I returned to the room, Forina was waiting for me as soon as I opened the door. She was postured on the ledge in front of the window where she had been last night. The only difference was that she looked into the room when I entered, didn't throw a dagger at me, and wasn't licking a blade.

She continued right where she left off, almost like time had stopped for her the moment she dematerialized. "I never answered your last questions, and I promised I would. For all my faults, I do try and be honest… as much as I can be. You wanted to know why your throat is hurting…"

While she was talking, I was getting dressed and sniping at her with harsh language. "No, I said I wouldn't ask the questions to receive the answers I didn't want to know about. I thought those long ears of yours were for hearing better."

Forina taunted, "Oh? An elf joke? I didn't think you had it in you. What would she say about that?"

Continuing my snarky comments, I replied, "Not that it matters, but she would quip about how infatuated I am with their pointiness more than her ability to hear. How do you even know about Marleen?"

Her head turned to face me… her smile had returned. "And we have come full circle! One is directly related to another, you see. But I fear you're too immature to hear the juicy details after your last remark. For now, be thankful you are alive and survived my little test. It's the small things in life that get you the farthest."

I let out a large, encumbered sigh, although she interjected before I could speak. "When the time is right, there is a chance I'll tell you more, but trust is such a hard thing to come by these days. Rest assured, unless you betray me, I'll be next to you for the duration of the contract. And with that look you're giving me, I might stick around for the duration of your short human life. Whatever is in your best interest will probably align with what is in my best interest as well. And when I say that, then I also mean the reverse too. If a prostitute disguised as a logistics officer disappears and is never heard from again, then that means that person is being treated in accordance with what they deserve. You can praise me now, master."

I've noticed she tends to toss that same dagger up and down either while pacing or sitting every time she needs to focus on the conversation. It's like her focusing mechanism, so she doesn't accidentally divulge too much information. It started when she got cold feet about our topic concerning my throat and Marleen. The question is… is she concealing information and taunting me like this for a reason, or did she really think I couldn't handle it?

"Whatever, just more of you leading me around by the nose. Putting what you do or did to me aside, I want to emphasize and reiterate that you need to get my consent before you take hostile actions against those closest to me. You talk about trust, and in the little bit I've known you, you're walking a fine line between garnering mine and losing it. If you want a stable relationship, then don't betray me either. I should tell you that you'll regret it, but that would be a half-hearted threat after seeing what you can do."

I was as firm and polite as possible while still stressing the importance of her compliance. It was enough to make her stop focusing on her dagger-throwing for a second and face me in earnest. I know I can't back up that statement, but if I need to, I could always take my own life. Because I am apparently a 'diamond in the rough,' she sounds like she would do anything to prevent that. Who am I kidding? I have too much going for me to fall that low.

She seemed reluctant when she replied, "Yes… 'Master'. But you must understand that I won't let anyone, and I do mean anyone, threaten my prize. You don't even know how much you are worth to my kind, but don't let it get to your head. If anyone or anything encroaches on your life, I swear they will find my blade. Think about what I just said, and our relationship will only get better."

She just openly admitted to what I thought was the case all along… she found something out last night about me, which made her uneasy. But what was it? Without another second to spare, vanished without giving me a moment to reply. That might be the first time I have had a serious conversation with someone completely naked before. I had even lost track of putting my clothes on, completely facing her in the buff.

I kept thinking about what she said while I got dressed and headed back outside to meet up with my men, who were still waiting for me. I moved to the front of the formation, where my horse was waiting for me and already saddled up. We mounted up, and we began to move to the Captain's Quarters in the middle of the fort. Not that it's far, but I don't want to further embarrass myself by hobbling over there.

When we first walked in, Alex and I were formally greeted. Every lieutenant and senior knight in the fort was present except for those on shift. They formally saluted me as the presiding commanding officer. One person noticeably missing from the formal greeting was the man in charge. He didn't show up until well after we were seated and had started exchanging fake pleasantries. The others present whispered loudly amongst each other about Helen. It seemed it was the best unkept secret that she would be with me all night, and they had already counted on her bedding me. But when we sat down, and Helen did not immediately enter shortly after us, their demeanor changed into a cautious hostility.

Our location was the War Room inside the captain's personalized small keep. I should have expected nothing less from this arrogant man. He purposefully had a four-story tower built separate from the main keep inside the fort for his personal abode. If that wasn't enough, they built it in the last year since I had paid them a visit. It leaves little doubt where all the money, soldiers, food, and abundant other supplies went after they were sent here.

To add further to my headache, while walking through the various rooms to get to the one we are currently in, it was obvious this one was the least spacious by far... the kind reserved for those you want to shit all over. It had only a small space carved out for a mildly accommodating round table in the middle, tight stone walls only four or five paces away from the seats, and it was purposefully designed to squish everyone together and make them as uncomfortable as possible. That is, except for his seat, which was purposefully spaced out from the rest of us and given more than enough legroom for the bastard to stretch out and bask in everyone else's misery as they sweated their balls off. If I were in his shoes, I would have offered that seat to us, you know, his guests that are much higher ranking. Not that anyone was surprised, not even his subordinate officers, that he didn't think twice about it.

Captain Michael started an arrogant, conceited chuckling in anticipation of his small victory. "Where is Helen at? Did you two stay up all night and not get any sleep? It must take some real skills to tucker her out! Color me impressed! I heard from the soldiers in the barracks that you went so hard last night that you came out covered in sticky juices this morning. I don't know what kind of fetishes you have, but isn't it supposed to be the other way around?"

This is where things shift in my favor as I one-eighty this conversation right up his pompous asshole. I slid him the note and then sat back in my seat, eagerly anticipating his reaction. Since this guy is so flamboyant, he could react in any number of ways. My best guess would be him thinking that this was clearly undermining his authority and then acting against me in some form or another.

He didn't take very long, eyeing up and down the small piece of paper. After he had concluded reading the note and made sure there were no mistakes, his eyes met mine and didn't move. Everyone in the room sat in silence for what seemed like forever. Michael occasionally let his eyes wander to the note and then back to me a few times. Nobody else was going to say anything until he spoke first, and his facial expressions were telling me that he couldn't decide if the note was a joke or not.

He must have realized if the note was true, then he lost and lost big. Forina hit him where it would hurt, in his pocketbook. There wasn't going to be a payday today, asshole. Forina also simultaneously took several other pieces of his off the table, including potentially blackmailing me and having him point at my lineage and declare boldly all commoners are scum that fuck their subordinates and cheat on their wives... even though he probably does it as well. Hard to believe just how much turned around in a single night for him.

Finally, he decided to change his attitude and speak in a serious tone. "General, what is the real truth here? There is no possible way Helen would write this abomination. And there is no way that any of the merchants in charge of the commerce would leave overnight… coincidentally right when you show up. Helen might have been a little on the risqué side, but her role was to accommodate you and your personal guards. Her disappearance, along with those merchants, could be considered a big infraction if they are connected to you and the higher-ups found out. Just what should we do about this?"

That was the best he could come up with? A half-assed blackmail attempt? I took out Laura's dagger and slid it across the table to him. This was a direct challenge in front of all the fort's leadership. Culturally, it says, 'Put up and do something about it or shut up.' As part of our customs, he can take the dagger and kill himself as recompense, accept it as part of a duel, or return it and admit he was wrong and give adequate compensation for his false accusations. Overwhelmingly, the person challenged returns the dagger because they realize the seriousness of the situation if they didn't already know. This is only the second time I have used this method and the first time the guy accepted the duel. However, given Captain Michael's disposition and lifestyle, he knows he doesn't stand a chance against me. An old son of a bitch with a big mouth is all he can amount to.

To give him that out, I decided to lay my cards on the table. "Captain, you, and your men, have been wasting time with these childish antics, accusations, and overall bullshit that neither of us have the time or the patience to argue over. This whole endeavor has been a joke since even before I set foot here, and it continues to degrade quickly. Honestly, I am sick and tired of your shit, and I want to move on to more important matters sooner rather than later."

I paused to eye the room a moment before continuing. "If we need to take this to the sparring grounds so I can move on to the next location instead of cleaning up your mess or listening to one more moment of your shit, then we will. You must decide quickly before determining what to do with that dagger. Helen is dead, your corrupt piece of shit nobles are also dead, and it was my men that did it to send you a message. The King means business, and I come representing that business. Our fucking country is at war. War with the demons, potentially war with the Empire, and now, because of you, about to be at war with itself."

He tried to speak, but I cut him off. "If the dagger didn't send you a clear enough message, let me say it bluntly. If you do not comply with absolutely everything I want to be done, without the bullshit games and without you splurging on Alvernia's treasury, then I will have you strung up and quartered as a traitor. The grounds for your execution will be because you are unfit for service as a military officer in the service of Alvernia. Test me. Please, for the love of anything you still care about, I'm begging you to fucking try me."

Captain Michael was taken aback at my abruptness. It's to be expected, as I woke up this morning and chose violence. He had to expect something like my previous visits that were far more of a formality, so it bolstered his ego and gave him the impression he could walk all over me because I'm young, rated lower as a noble, and of common birth.

He clutched the dagger and stood up from the table. His speech was infused with anger as he addressed me. "Who's going to make me? You're in my world, and unlike your last visit, these men are loyal to me. I hear your provocations, and all I see is someone sitting on a throne made of glass with no support. They won't find you or your men because the demons were hungry. I hear the wolf demons especially love the taste of cocky paper generals. You have some balls for being someone who was appointed to a position to be easily manipulated and controlled by the likes of Laura. Don't worry. I'll write a letter to that one specifically and to the King after our patrols find your remains."

As if on cue, Forina appeared behind him with her dagger at his throat. She was still wearing our black leather armor, which undeniably delineated that she belonged with us. The major difference this time was the white skull face mask she had adorned to cover everything except for her glowing green eyes.

She didn't even say a word, which seemed oddly professional and much more like a trained assassin under the tutelage of someone like Seventeen. That one swift movement told me she meant what she said earlier... she had my back. I'm... incredibly grateful... and... beside myself with how badass the psycho elf was acting. This almost, and I mean almost, makes all the crap I went through last night and this morning worthwhile.

Michael's head was being pulled back towards Forina, sharply making him hold himself up by his fingertips on this throne of a chair. An elf that small making a man that tall bend to her will almost gets me off in all the right ways. I'm loving every second of this. The blade was cutting into his flesh to slowly stain his lovely white shirt.

He started choking over his own words as he struggled to get them out. "Ha! It seems you have brought some talent with you. Your subordinates have some impressive abilities, General Raider. Very well, you win this round."

I pushed him further. "Speak in the common tongue, asshole. I said I wasn't playing here!"

He gasped, "What I mean to say is... it's sad to see all those business partners and my logistics officer leave so suddenly. Business... is... business. Nothing else happened here, especially nothing worth losing my head over. I will make sure that in the future, things are run only by your exact orders. I'll also give you appropriate compensation for my outburst."

I nodded, and Forina lifted the dagger and disappeared into a swirl of green mist. I could tell she was disappointed due to the suddenness of her disappearance. That mad woman only thinks about murder. The moment she can't kill, she's like a teenage girl throwing a tantrum. Even now, I bet she is hopeful he would act like a fool so she can pop in and finish the job like she did with Helen. She said it herself; nothing gets her off like cutting people open. You would think that after an entire night of killing people, she would want some rest.

My voice remained stern. "Honesty is still my best policy, even if you don't deserve it. The only reason you are being left alive and retaining your station is because I don't have time to deal with you. I will forget this ever happened, but don't make me regret it."

It was time for the climax. I stood up and hit the table with my fist. "I am dismayed about your lack of maintenance in what is supposed to be our premier frontline fort. From what my men tell me, your barracks are in disarray, your parameter is full of holes, and one of your walls is even in danger of collapsing. All the resources we sent you appear to have been squandered on shit like what we are currently in, and you don't seem to give a shit. Moreover, you need to be more thorough in what happens in your day-to-day activities in your weekly executive officer recaps. Your sad excuse for 'reporting' affairs here is a dishonor to both you and to your men. The next time I see something that pathetic, it's your ass. The more detailed you can get, the more likely we will save lives and ensure you are outfitted appropriately."

Just as I began to speak that last sentence, he even had the guts to give me a 'long blink'. If there is one thing I hate more than anything, it's someone who assumes they are above the chain of command and disrespects those above them. I'm not a stickler for rules, but when someone assumes I'll let it slide by continuing to be a disingenuous asshole, they are asking for my wrath.

I abruptly stood and raised my voice loud enough to alert everyone outside of the keep. "Did I say you could fucking ignore me piece of shit? Stand before me at the position of attention until I am done speaking."

He stood up at a snail's pace and waddled his way directly before me. When he stopped, he handed me back Laura's dagger. I gave him a once-over from top to bottom to make sure he didn't move a muscle and then continued speaking. "Since you want to push the issue. What did you do with the fifty percent increase in soldiers and supplies we sent you? Those resources were meant to combat the 'reported' increasing incursions from the Unknown Territories. I see a hefty amount went into your back pocket, but what about the rest? What about those people? If I've heard about it, then I know you have."

I gave him a line, and he took the bait. "What is that, General Raider? I am not following. What people?"

I shouted, "The villages you're supposed to be protecting! I receive more correspondence from them than I do from you. And it isn't just one or two; it's dozens of local villages and farms in the area. Their letters outline wolf and bear demons attacking and killing citizens. They go so far as to say they don't see patrols sometimes for days to weeks at a time. The whole reason we sent you all those resources was to stop this from happening, so fix it. You may not fucking care, but they sure as hell do. Do you even have a moral compass?"

"No general...I just..." Michael tried to intercept me to defend himself.

I continued, "I didn't ask you to speak! Just a simple yes or no will suffice. Go sit down, shut up, and do as you're told! There is an even more pressing matter that will happen soon, and we haven't even gotten to it yet. We've spent all this time discussing how you 'play house' and haven't even moved on to the main topic yet."

I took a deep breath. "I'll just lay it on you. The King is planning on casting a Hero Summoning Ritual."

The silent room burst into an uproar. Laura's dagger was still in my hand, and my temper was even more inflamed. I had a flashback of how effective it was to break something with it. Following her lead, I unsheathed it and slammed it into the table. "I'm not finished yet, damn it!"

All of them quieted back down and began focusing on me. This might be the first time since I got here that each and every one of them understood the gravity of the situation. They knew nothing like this had happened in modern times, and it meant Alvernia would be ushering in a new, potentially harsh, and chaotic age. A hero summoning could also mean a massive reorganization of the Alvernian Army, which means a high likelihood of it affecting every soldier.

One of the primary reasons that all this corruption in the pleasure district happened so fast was because of the extended tours the soldiers were doing with no real end in sight. If the soldiers are rotated quickly, then that corruption has no time to build. It's a roundabout way of fixing an issue... don't give the corruption enough time to take root. However, when those same soldiers idle on extended deployments, they can act irrationally. The summoning might be their light at the end of the tunnel to bring them back into line, Captain Michael included.

I continued to speak harshly and to the point. "Inadequate reports, mismanagement of troops and supplies, approaching your jobs carelessly, letting civilians die, and overall, just being garbage soldiers ends today. I need you to act according to your station to move forward as an army and nation. If the Hero Summoning Ritual comes to pass, then Alvernia, the King, and I will need your full backing to take the fight to the enemy. Without a doubt, they will want to take the offense instead of being on the defense. We are on the precipice of our salvation... or the collapse of our country. You can join us for the ride or be forcibly replaced. Make your choice because this is your only chance to get it right."

Some of them still had a puzzled look on their faces. There was only one way to make it even more clear so that even a demon wolf could understand. "It's pretty damn simple. Know... Your... Fucking... Place or die. Either way, I don't care."

In a different life, I wouldn't have even left them to the psycho elf. Instead, I would have shredded them into pieces by myself with my killing intent alone. I ripped the dagger from the table and put it back into the sheath in my waistband.

Captain Michael nodded and replied, "I understand. Please forgive me and those under my command for my shortcomings. We will move to immediately rectify our mistakes and act upon your guidance. If there is nothing else to say here, we will convene amongst ourselves and begin preparing. As for the compensation for turning down your duel request... with your permission, we will have to iron that out when you return to the capital, and we have more time."

He sounded sincere, so I nodded and took him at face value. I'll have to have Seventeen send more of his team here to keep track of everything Captain Michael does. As the meeting concluded, Alex and I stood up and exited the room. We headed outside, where the rest of the troops were waiting patiently for us. When I was yelling earlier, it must have reached them because all of them were holding back their smiles. It would be a cold day in the Desolate Plains when I'm pushed to raise my voice to anyone... which meant that may have been the first time any of them had heard me get that serious.

I adjusted my armor, tightened the straps, and cricked my neck. "We will leave as soon as everyone has had something to eat. Fill yourselves up and take two days' worth of rations. We are headed for Fort Midgard. I don't anticipate it taking us any longer than two days, but check your equipment and be prepared for anything just in case we get stopped like we did on the way here. Turbulent times and all that."

The soldiers saluted and began to load their provisions. We were able to leave Goliad before noon and set off to our next destination. Camping out in the cold for one or two nights will also give us an opportunity to see how dangerous it is for others traveling in the area. There was one random thought that had crossed my mind as we were leaving the Goliad. What the hell does Forina do with all the people she takes with her after she vanishes? Better yet, I won't ask her those questions either, or I might end up with another syrup incident.

Chapter 15: Midgard's Inundation

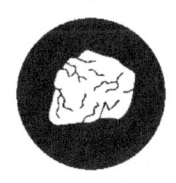

Several days have passed since we left Goliad, and we still haven't reached Fort Midgard. Along the way, we had all kinds of unique and unexpected dilemmas. First, before we crossed into Midgard's territory, we encountered another group of bandits that had the equipment and training of high-class mercenaries. It wouldn't be a stretch to say they were connected to Captain Michael, but I don't have the leeway to investigate or follow up right now. That will end up being a task for Seventeen later. Right about now, I wish he had assigned a messenger to escort me. Hindsight is always perfect, as they say. Besides, it's possible those guys were given the contract before we departed, not that their employer's actions can be forgiven so easily. It's unfortunate that they didn't get the updated memo before they were put into their early graves.

The bandits themselves weren't unusual, but the earth mage with them caught us by surprise. Part of their ambush was to create walls on each side of us to block our escape. When we adapted quicker than they were expecting, the mage shattered one of the walls, crushing one of the men to death and wounding another. The wall missed him, but a high-velocity rock followed up and hit him in the shoulder after he rolled away. He is stable now, but he may lose his arm if we cannot get to the medics quickly enough in Midgard.

Although neither of them specialized in barrier magic in the academy, both Alex and Lacia should have been able to stop a normal projectile. They deployed their elemental barriers to prevent or mitigate damage, but their mage found a way to get through Lacia's the second she was distracted. I've never thought about using mages in a combat role like that before. Their primary responsibility is defense and utility. Using magic to hurl an object fast enough to kill someone... crushing someone with walls... I can almost see why Marleen is so obsessed with researching it.

I spent a considerable amount of time pondering if I should redirect my hobby from inventing non-magical combat weapons, such as the explosive spears we use, or if I should link up with the Mage Tower and work together for a new class of mages to field on a battlefield. There must be a way to take what that mage did and apply it liberally to our formations. Small unit tactics, perhaps? Maybe to cause chaos in larger-scale battles? What could we do with water, wind, or fire mages? We might also be able to combine the two together... like exploding rock fragments instead of metal. Unfortunately, I never landed on a clear course of action. Yet again, something that needs to wait until I return.

The second major issue that kept popping up had started happening just inside the Midgard region several days prior. It seems the several patrols we passed had their attuned magical items stop working. I've never even heard of a ManaBank ceasing to provide mana to the items attuned to it. We depend on this functionality so much in the military that it could even be considered a crutch.

Without their items working, the patrols and even the soldiers at the fort are essentially operating blind. Their rings that show their immediate surroundings are the centerpiece for any forward observer providing cover for their squad. Without them, they could be easily ambushed. Also, their short-range communication earrings would be unable to report back to their command. This means that they could be ambushed, and nobody would know what happened to them until they missed their report time back at the garrison. That could be hours or days later. Effectively, this took us back to being no better than primitive beings that lived thousands of years before recorded history.

Trying to think how it would be possible for a ManaBank to malfunction, I came up with several ideas. The obvious one was that the ManaBank had been abused or the ManaBank Engineers misallocated the amount of mana flowing in and out of it. This could potentially happen if there were a sudden large migration of civilians out of an area. Since ManaBanks operate on siphoning mana from the local population, it is feasible to think that the mana would eventually run dry.

Once this happened, every item would stop functioning almost immediately. This isn't likely, though, because it would take an unbelievable amount of time. Why? Because it's standard practice for each ManaBank to be monitored closely and always kept at least seventy percent full. The only alternative theory I could think of was that the ManaBank was mismanaged for a very long time, and it ended up running dry because of negligence. I find this one even less plausible because I know Leah wouldn't allow that to happen. That leaves the first theory as the front runner, which is cringingly supported by the last problem we have been seeing.

The third and most concerning issue is the large number of refugees fleeing the area. These refugees looked mostly run-down, bewildered, and in dire circumstances. Most were traveling in small family-sized groups that were muddy from head to toe. These small groups were tightly packed along the roads with other similar-sized groups to make for a large crowd. Their numbers were so dense that they covered every section of the brick road for over a quarter-day's ride.

Others among them were bloody and cleaved in what were clear signs of a recent significant struggle, possibly just a day or so before we arrived. We stopped to get statements from several of them along the way, but their backstories were all very similar. They all came from small farming villages along or near the border with the Unknown Territory. When asked if they received help from the fort, most of them began crying while recounting the horrors they saw done to their loved ones. Not a single person we questioned said help arrived in time, which I suspect is directly related to the communication network being offline.

Whenever the garrison did arrive to assist the villages, they were too late and could only help clean up the bodies or kill straggling demons. This amounted to mass casualties, and several of the other villages were abandoned when they heard about the attacks. There was also apparently an uncanny amount of coordination when each location was hit. Horses, dogs, and those putting up the most resistance were killed first. They were then followed by those attempting to coordinate the evacuation efforts. This also explains why almost none of the refugees seem to be carrying a lot and why there weren't any horse-drawn coaches.

The next question asked to them was why they did not return after the fort's garrison was dispatched and their homes were secured. Their answers varied, but generally, they responded that they had lost faith in the garrison's leadership and weren't willing to risk their lives. The patrols had become far less frequent where it mattered, and the local fort's response was now reactive and less proactive. A few of them cited hatred for the vampires that ran the place until I reminded them that we had held a tight-knit alliance for almost a thousand years, making it extremely implausible that they would betray us now out of nowhere.

Aside from the human toll these attacks produce, Alvernia is known for having abundant food because of its large and fertile territory. Annually, we produce enough food to not only provide for our soldiers but also to trade with Tuscany and Elvania for other valuable resources like leather, iron, steel, weapons, horses, spices, and so on.

Neither of their countries can sustain their growing populations by themselves without drastically reforming their agricultural infrastructures. If you listen to the stuck-up Alvernian nobles in charge of internal affairs, we keep the entire continent afloat with our harvests. I think that's mostly gloating, but it's true that these fields have kept us from going broke and all three of our populations fed. However, if these attacks continue, then our fields and what little trade we have left with the elves and those backstabbing Imperials will dry up as well. Luckily, we have already harvested everything for the coming winter months just ahead. This makes it unlikely our own citizens will go hungry this year.

As the sun sets, it looks like tonight will be another night we won't quite make it to Midgard. Our provisions are beginning to run low, and hunting every day hasn't been fruitful because most of the animals are moving out of the area. On a normal trip, two days would be more than enough, making this far more discouraging than it should have been. But, because we are assisting refugees, fighting the endless rain and the creeping cold, progress has been all but halted. I only hope we make it there before the first snow and the deep winter months.

I anticipate that if nothing changes, we will still be at least a half day's ride out. Unlike Captain Michael, Captain Leah Douglas has always been an outstanding officer in my book. When I first got promoted, Leah was the only captain who made a personalized visit to the capital to make a formal appearance. We had met a few times before that and exchanged some... blood... pleasantries. That isn't fair; we also had cordial events where we mingled with one another. However, I wouldn't have called us 'close.' During those brief exchanges, I wasn't a noble, but she sure as hell treated me like one. If I recall correctly, it was after meeting her that the royal family started getting closer to me and others in my class. I owe her a bit more than I let on.

I often found her taking notes of everything I liked and didn't like. She took extra care to jot down how I wished for soldiers to be treated before I got my first command. After I was knighted and received my first unit, she always reminded me of the eternal optimism I expressed to her while in the academy. It seemed like she was being overly familiar, but she just has one of those attentive and charming personalities that weigh on you. For a noble-born vampire, she was someone for me to aspire to be and someone I could count on after she fell under my command.

So, what else makes her a good officer? She addressed all my concerns with the fort's logistics operations and has never once tried to kiss my ass or pander to me. Leah is always in constant communication without even one of her reports being subpar. She even goes through the due diligence of handwriting every report herself instead of delegating it. If I were to list all the traits I desire most in a fellow soldier in arms, then I really cannot think of much she is missing.

That is why this whole situation blows my mind. Refugees, a malfunctioning ManaBank, and demons running rampant through the Midgard province are all things she would never allow. Her last letter arrived two weeks ago and never mentioned anything about any of this. Moreover, I know her well enough to know she wouldn't try to hide something this critical. The only explanation is that all these issues happened back-to-back, and any correspondence sent to the capital arrived after I left or was intercepted. There exists one more possibility. Someone from Midgard has betrayed us and is working as an insider for one of the other countries.

The next morning, we finally arrived just after daybreak. The entire place was overrun with refugees waiting outside of the drawbridge into the fort. The gate guards that were normally just outside the fort patrolling had been pushed back to the inner part of the bridge just inside of the fort. I could tell they were exhausted despite doing their best to tend to the huge crowd that had formed. Every one of those people was pushing to get in to gain some semblance of security. Add in that this morning was so cold that we could see our breaths; the forecast of a bad winter was rolling in fast. The dark clouds were also dense as if they were fulminating the presence of the very little sunlight that made it through.

The refugees had so many tents along the moat's edge and along the road that it resembled some of the worst shanties on the capital's outskirts. This was the beginning of a makeshift city, with several areas being walled off with person-high palisades. Merchants from who knows where were already peddling their overpriced and limited stock of food while soldiers patrolled around and attempted to keep the peace.

I didn't see any obvious signs of starvation or panic going on, which meant that everyone's basic needs here were met. That begged the question that if everyone was being taken care of, then why would so many others be leaving to head north along the mountain ridge where we just came from? And why would any of them have said they lost faith in the garrison? Nobody here looked abused, although there were clearly those who had been injured in the attacks. However, those who looked injured had already been treated or were in line to see the medics. Even if I were trying my best to place blame on the soldiers here, it would be almost impossible.

What else caught my eye was that the soldiers didn't look overly fatigued either, except, of course, those on people-management duty. My first impression was that they were a well-organized unit that cared for the citizens they had promised to protect. The whole thing reeks of Leah's leadership. It just makes me beg the question even more... how did this happen?

It took time, but we were able to part the sea of refugees long enough to get to the fort's main drawbridge, where there was a line of soldiers valiantly holding it together. Both vampire and human soldiers alike took to greeting the citizens who approached and angrily demanded to enter the fort. When one of the vampire soldiers noticed us, he saluted and then sent a small escort with us to guide us to the primary keep, where I had assumed Leah was going to be waiting. I told my men to head to the barracks and get warmed up. Only Alex, Lacia, and one other came with me into the keep. The guards showed us to the War Room and told us the officer in charge would be along shortly.

"Feeling at home yet, Alex?" I asked.

He replied, "Yes, to a degree. It won't be truly home until I see Captain Leah, though."

I smiled, "Do you want to wait for her while I take Lacia with me to peruse the keep? This is her first time into vampire territory, and it might be a good experience for her to get the lay of the land."

His subverted expression never changes. "I will do as you wish, Raider. If waiting for Leah is what you want me to do, then it shall be done."

My eyebrows were dancing back and forth to mock him. "Oh, don't give me that garbage. You want to see her just as bad as anyone, I know it. I'd love to have those people who think vampires can't love to look at you right now. They would be beside themselves with your adolescent way of expressing affection. Very well, come on, Lacia, let's go look around a little bit."

She nodded, and we headed out. I figured it wouldn't be hard to get around without attracting too much attention. The keep was larger than I had remembered, but I knew my way around. I also knew how to get to the primary living areas, the meeting rooms, and, eventually, the barracks. Not bad for a man who has only been here two times before… and was rushed all to high hell both times.

When we arrived on the second floor, where all the officers and influential nobles lived, I saw that all fifteen doors on each side were open all the way down the main coordinator just past the stairwell. As I walked past each one, I saw exhausted human soldiers, vampire maids, stable hands, and others sleeping and recuperating. They were piled all over the place. Some were on the large beds, while others were on the floors. I haven't seen a scene like this since I last went to Fort Bartad and had to crash in the hotel room just above the casino.

The skill needed to coordinate what I was witnessing continued to impress me. As I explained to Lacia how the work-rest cycle works in the military, someone plowed into me at full speed. This person was in such a hurried state that they didn't even bother to stop and address me. Instead, they tried to continue along their way without acknowledging either of us standing before them.

They were wearing the black robes of an Expert Earth Mage. The custom gold embroidery along the edges of the robe was awfully elegant and beautiful for a mage. Perhaps those indicate details were a sign that they were upper-class nobility. Most mages, especially those assigned to the military, are about as well off as a low-ranking knight. This means their robes aren't usually this extravagant.

This mage's robes, their ignorance of who I am, and their hurried state all threw red flags. Could they be a thief taking advantage of those sleeping? I shouted at the mage as they shuffled toward the staircase we had just come from. "Master Earth Mage! Can I please take a moment of your time? I know you are in a hurry, but I would be most appreciative of some assistance."

The mage stopped at the end of the hallway before turning the corner to head down the stairs. Their hood was up, concealing all their features. Having that on indoors is very unusual unless they have something to hide.

The mage finally responded to me after a moment of pause. "General Raider and... Lacia?"

Her feminine voice swiftly paused, giving me a moment to ask, "You know us? I apologize, but I am unfamiliar with those from the Royal Research Academy. Just a handful of mages that unfortunately crossed my path. Have we met before?"

She still hadn't turned around. Her body language suggested she might still be trying to flee. She eventually said, "I am so glad to finally be able to meet you in person! What are you doing up here? Last time you didn't arrive for another day or so. And... how... is Lacia still alive?"

I opened my mouth before I realized what I was even saying. "That might have been the most ominous thing I've ever heard."

I looked at Lacia, who just shrugged back at me as if she didn't care. The mage's response puzzled me, so I kept with the formalities. "Master Earth Mage, have we met before? You seem to know that my name is Raider, and my companion is Lacia, but what do you mean by 'Last time I didn't arrive for another day or so' and 'Lacia is still alive'? Is she supposed to be dead?"

The mage decided to commit to our conversation. She hurriedly turned around and rushed to one knee before me without removing her hood. "General Raider, forgive my impudence. I seem to have forgotten myself. I am Shion D'Garde. Ordinarily, I would have recognized you and given you the proper respect, but I was caught up in the tasks I was given. Please ignore my ramblings about you and your mage counterpart."

I stuttered a bit. "N... No... p... problems at all! I was just startled by your familiarity with Lacia and me. I've never been one for formalities, so it appears at the outset that you knew me quite well. If I know you, then I must apologize for having forgotten who you are or where we met. Sometimes, my memory is a bit fuzzy from all the hits to the head I've taken."

She subconsciously whispered loud enough for me to make out, "Laura..."

Pretending not to hear her, I finished my thought. "I'm sorry, but I still cannot entirely see your face; perhaps I would know you if I could get a good look?" I started rubbing my head out of nervousness.

The mage looked up and turned their head as if bewildered by my response. She kept her hood on and replied, "I'm sorry, we have never met before. I do know who you are through the various rumblings at the Mage Tower. I've also seen you in passing the few times you have come out to Fort Midgard. You see, over the last two years, I have been assigned as a lieutenant in charge of patrolling some of the surrounding villages by Captain Leah. Although there are enough vampires to fill the role, they are almost exclusively embraced by the dark element because they are vampires. They needed a more... agronomic... earthly touch."

She saw I was confused, so she took a breath. "But two days ago, we received a rider that recalled us back to the fort out of concern for the malfunctioning magical items. When we arrived, we also saw the swarms of human refugees flooding in from everywhere."

Patting the mage's shoulder, I chuckled. "You humble me, Master Earth Mage. Please remove your hood and stand up so I can get a good look at you. I want to know more about the problems here, but I have just arrived, so I would greatly appreciate an escort who is more familiar with the area. Let's dispense with the formalities! Feel free to call me Raider. If you need help finishing your tasks, then Lacia can finish what you started while you accompany me. She may not look like it, but she is hearty and a very capable water mage despite only having just graduated."

The mage reluctantly removed their hood and steadily stood up. As her face became visible, my feet instinctively took two steps back. It was the first time I had ever seen a female Green Elf. It was also the first time I had seen one of her kind not already turned into a vampire… Alex was my only other interaction with one before.

Chapter 16: Prosaic Management

She was astonishingly breathtaking, rivaling the looks of any other woman I've ever seen. Her hair was a dark emerald green that slightly lit up and sparkled in the keeps light stones. The wonderful mixture of dark and sparkling green was tucked into her robe, probably going to at least the middle of her back. Her height matched Marleen's, with her head peaking just past my chin. She had green eyes to match her hair, light purple skin, and dark purple ink tattooed below both eyes down past her cheeks like Forina. The difference is that Forina's tattoos looked temporary, while hers looked semi-permanent. Her body was very slender, almost fragile-looking. She also had an hourglass earring in one ear where the sand was on the bottom and one in the other where the sand was on the top. The twisting and turning of time must be rolling in between them.

If I were to say one thing about my first impression of the women of her race, it would be 'jaw-dropping.' I have gotten good at not showing my expressions to others despite what I am thinking... that is until I took two steps back when she uncovered herself. And now I'm standing here like a love-struck moron grasping at the fruits of his youth. If Marleen saw this, I would be in deep shit. There's no way she can't tell what's going on... the words won't come out of my mouth.

It isn't necessarily unheard of that Green Elves would be in our territory or military, but it is not very common because most feel more at home in Elvania. I couldn't help thinking that after meeting her, I had completed my tour of all the elven races. I chuckled a little inside, then nervously outside, then died a little inside when she looked perturbed.

She seemed to understand my internal struggle like she had known me for years. "I'm glad to hear it, Raider. I would be more than happy to accompany you, but with us being extremely short-staffed, I'm afraid your mage companion might be unable to help without supervision. I honestly appreciate the offer of assistance."

"Can you... at least let me know about what's going on before you just dismiss our help?" I asked with my hands still slightly trembling.

She nodded. "Sustainment-wise, our operations in the refugee encampment are at critical levels. The entire garrison, including the mages and soldiers and our ManaBank Engineer, are all beyond exhausted. The barriers around the keep have fluctuated, leaving our mages to fill in the gaps instead of reserving their mana for potential attacks or patrols. If you look around, all the soldiers on this floor just closed their eyes after finishing their shift all night. Helping the refugees and stabilizing the chaos is more than we can handle."

She dodged the topic. "I never heard why Lacia can't assist you while you help me."

"It's all specialized work, and nobody has time to help a new mage fall into the way of things. Are you pressing so hard because is there somewhere in particular you want to go?" She said while reaching into her robe and pulling out a pipe.

Next to the pipe, I saw another unique item... a custom-engraved wand with an unfamiliar emblem. It was almost... like her earrings, but both sides of the hourglass were full of green-speckled sand. While I was dazzled at the engraving, she filled the long pipe with a leafy product before lighting it and taking quick puffs. She savored every moment of the smoke before exhaling.

Thinking for a moment, I replied, "Master Shion..."

She interrupted me, "Shion is fine. I, too, am not one for formalities. Would you like a smoke?"

Who is this, my childhood friend? I continued my question, "... no thank you, I don't smoke. Look, I know my way around a little bit, but it would be an immense help if you could give me a tour of things like the ManaBank. Or, perhaps, is it possible for you to tell me more about what's going on with it? I've heard and seen the items attune to it not working. Any insights would be worth their weight in gold. The way I see it, that takes priority over the refugee issue because if we can solve that, then we can reduce the risk to our soldiers."

Pondering for a minute, she put her hand on her chin and continued to take a few puffs from her pipe. The vibe she gave off indicated that she knew the answer but may not want to relay it to me. "I am afraid I do not have much information regarding the items no longer functioning. I can tell you that the items stopped working almost at the same time as the wolf demons from the Unknown Territory began to invade the surrounding villages. All of this seemed like a coordinated effort because it happened too fast. But that seems highly unlikely because the intelligence level of the minor demons is laughable at best. I don't understand everything, but I would assume Leah would be your best resource to get up to speed quickly."

Her insight is the same as mine. I can already tell we will make a great team. Replying to her, I mistakenly took to her instantly and patted her back like an old drinking buddy. "Thank you, Shion! You and I seem to think a lot alike; I think we will get along just fine. Since you don't know a lot about the items themselves, can you tell me a little bit more about how quickly the items stopped functioning? Did the demons attack and then the items turned off? Or did they malfunction instead of just deactivating? Was it the other way around, and the items deactivated followed by the wolf demon's attack?"

Depending on what came first, it might suggest internal sabotage or straight-out negligence. At first, her eyes shifted from her pipe to me and then back to the pipe. When we locked our eyes, I noticed Green Elves have the same eyes as the other two as far as how they are shaped. You often hear whispers of their 'snake-like' oval pupils that run vertically instead of circular ones like humans have. I knew Marleen had them, and so did Forina, but now… Green Elves as well? No doubt they all come from the same lineage if you go up the ancestry tree far enough.

After a few moments, Shion started pacing back and forth. As she spoke, she addressed 'openly' as if to a crowd instead of just me. She suddenly transformed from a long-lost childhood friend to a stage actor. "I again can't really say. It was almost two days ago, or perhaps a little bit longer, when I was on patrol with my unit to the southwest over a day's ride out. The cold was rolling in, and we were doing our normal rounds from village to village. Then, we saw smoke accompanied by the screams of dying people. When we arrived, we didn't see any demons, but corpses strewn throughout the area with limbs missing and torsos half-eaten. We concluded that if there were any survivors, they had left in fear for their lives." I caught her occasionally glancing at me while giving her grand performance. Don't worry, thespian Shion. I will give you perfect marks for your marketability.

Performer Shion continued her captivating enticement, fully backed up with vivid hand motions and swaying hip movements. She even stopped to relight her pipe mid-presentation. "We set up a parameter and began to investigate what we could when we found several village children in hiding. When we questioned them, we found a similar story to what you might find with any refugees outside. The demons attacked in a huge pack during the nighttime, killed anyone they could sniff out, and disappeared. The children only survived because they were in the stable and covered in filth to mask their scents. Because it was so dark and they were scared, they could barely even describe anything about the demons."

Generally, most 'lesser demons' from the Unknown Territory we have run across look like some form of common animal with a dark aura about them. We don't know as much as we should about these creatures, given how long we have been fighting them. But we know the dark aura surrounding them is the miasma leaking out from the Unknown Territory. This miasma is extremely toxic to humans, elves, dwarves, trees, grass, you name it. In fact, as far as we can tell… it's toxic to everything except the demons that are infected with it.

If the demons are killed and their corpses aren't moved far away to a burn pit, the miasma can get into the ground. Quickly, it will turn the area black where any corpses were left and pollute the surrounding area. Needless to say, they are dangerous, both alive and dead. Any of them that get to our farmlands have the potential of making the land unfarmable for a few years. Marleen and I have had many conversations trying to figure out how these mindless beasts survive. Questions about their reproductivity, or if they can be turned back to normal, often become the brunt of those discussions.

Ultimately, Marleen and I end up on the same topic every time. "…but how do we capture one of those bastards?"

"Excuse me?" Shion asked.

"Oh, sorry…." I collected myself. "Sometimes I think out loud when I am pondering things."

Astonishingly, she giggled. "Yeah, that's just like you. I bet you want to figure out their origin and root them out there. Something like 'breeding them out' or figuring out why they are leaving the Unknown Territory if they slowly die without constant miasma exposure?"

"Just like me?" I shook my head. "Never mind. But yes, I personally think their bodies absorb the miasma as a form of food. Put this together with the chance they can breed, and their population would eventually need to branch out to find another source of miasma once they got to a certain size."

She had a huge smile across her face. "Like they are territorial... just like normal animals?"

Shion was freaking me out with how in tune we are with each other. "You... might have to stop that."

Lacia chimed in. "Are you two like a thing?"

We both replied, "No."

Then Shion and I turned our eyes toward each other. She just continued to smile. "Might have to stop what, exactly?"

I replied while motioning my hand in a circle. "Just continue with your story. You stopped when you said you found some children, and the remaining villages had fled."

Shion looked puzzled, so I clarified, "We were on the topic of items that quit working."

She looked at the ceiling before filling her pipe again and relighting it. "Right... so... it took us half a day to secure any villagers that survived and lock down the area. That's when we realized our items were no longer working. We knew they were operational prior to going to the village, so the assumption was they had been distorted somehow by the residual miasma left behind by the few demon corpses. That wouldn't have been all that unusual..."

I put my hand up for her to stop. "Truth be told, you already told me everything I needed to know. The attuned items went black at almost the same time the demons had attacked. This was a coordinated effort, by the sounds of it. But to militarize demons..."

Lacia gasped, "Unheard of... it's not possible."

Shion raised her right eyebrow. "Not possible, or not heard of? Be careful with your words, young mage. But Raider, why did you jump to that conclusion so quickly?"

I replied, "Just put the pieces together. Items stopped working, demons attacked and killed rapidly before retreating or moving on as a group, and they left you alone when they probably had superior numbers. When have you ever heard of a group of demons ambushing as a group or withdrawing as a group? Something or someone was overseeing these attacks. It could be a smart demon or something similar. It just sucks you didn't at least fight one to see if it had higher-than-normal intelligence from the usual ones."

She nodded. "I see your point. That was swift deductive reasoning. Not bad for a human in the military."

Now that I knew what was going on, I wanted to convince her to come with me even more. "Shion, I understand you are busy and that you are trying to do the right thing here. For that, I commend you. But for the time being, I would like to have you assist me and be part of my escort."

She took one last puff from her pipe before putting it back in her robe. "And if I refuse, then you will forcibly reassign me? It would be just like humans to take what isn't theirs when they think they need it more than anyone else. Fine, my magic and my knowledge are yours… for however long they can assist you."

I insisted, "Seriously, calm down with that. Not even my fiancée knows me that well."

Earth mages are especially beneficial for light cavalry detachments because they can set up makeshift barriers and create Geo Storms that can disorganize and disrupt enemy units. That's to say… even if I don't like magic; they do have a role to play on the battlefield. And deep down, I'm still mulling over the earth mage we fought on the way here. If Shion has a similar talent, I want to see it used on our side. No, I'm greedier than that. I want to use it for myself just in case we get into a fight. I'm also sure Leah won't mind once we meet up with her and give her a proper explanation.

We headed back down the stairs. As we moved, I noticed just how vacant the keep really was on this floor. I didn't see anyone else roaming around, which shows how understaffed or overworked they are here. Moreover, what's impressive is the front that Leah is projecting to the civilians. She has created the illusion that everything is calm and collected. Keeping that façade up will continue the projection that nobody is overburdened and life can return to normal as soon as the problems are solved. However, this will only be temporary if something isn't done to solve the ManaBank and demon issues. With enough time, the refugees will notice the overwhelming stress on the garrison and might even revolt if they feel their security is threatened further.

Eventually, we found ourselves in the barracks where the rest of my unit had already made themselves at home. The barracks here are massive, especially in comparison to Fort Goliad. This isn't because there are more soldiers stationed here but because each soldier gets additional living space allocated to them to make it suck a little less. Whereas Goliad's focus is efficiency, Leah's focus has been on maintaining the soldier's well-being, even if it costs a little bit of space.

Thankfully, the living quarters were placed next to the hallway of the main keep. No more roaming halfway across the fort to be sampled by the local cuisine. Again, quality of life over what might make the most sense from a layout perspective. These two being so close together would make an excellent artillery target, not that we have been at war with a species capable of such a feat anytime in the last thousand years.

When I entered, I was greeted by most of them, almost as if I had been gone for a decade. "Guys, this is Master Shion. She is an earth mage stationed here at Midgard. Please treat her with all the respect due to her position while she is in our company. Shion, these are my soldiers. Until you are reassigned, they will be your comrades in arms. Every one of us will die for each other, and you are now part of that family."

One of my soldiers asked, "How can you be so serious when introducing us to such a beautiful woman? Raider, what is it with you and Elves? Are you starting your personal harem collection or what? Some 'Elf Whisperer' you are. He whispers sweet nothings into their long ears, and all their women become entranced!" All of them started laughing.

Another soldier howled in excitement, "Seriously, though! First, you bagged a White Elf, then that psycho Grey Elf, and now a Green Elf? Awfully ballsy of you, Raider! I also have an elf fetish, can you spread your secrets to me? The rest of us are starting to get envious." All of them continued laughing and carrying on with their fantasies.

Slightly embarrassed by their behavior, my hand couldn't stop itself from hitting the side of my head in disappointment. "Come on, knock it off; you're going to make her feel uncomfortable with those nasty rumors that have no basis in reality. You all are so funny I can hardly contain myself. Try to play nice with Master Shion so we can have a skilled earth mage with us. I am hoping to get and stay on her good side so she might be willing to join us even after we leave here. If you all behave and stop making me look like some deviant with an overdriven elven lust, I might be able to get Leah to reassign her. But if you keep carrying on like that, then who knows what she will tell Leah? Most elves are already cautious of humans… for various reasons… so don't make it worse for one of the few willing to stick around."

I did overhear Shion laughing as we were bantering back and forth. Maybe she appreciates our sense of humor? Being singled out due to her race probably isn't anything new to her since she has been in the Alvernian Military for a while. I wouldn't go so far as to call it discrimination, but there can't be more than a few handfuls of any species of elf in all our armed forces. This probably makes her the topic of conversation wherever she goes.

Clearing my throat, I got us back on topic. "Have you all seen or gotten any information about what is happening here? Maybe some of you also chatted up someone young and innocent?" I was prodding them, knowing full well they probably just put their equipment down and started screwing around.

One of them spoke up. "Nothing yet, Raider. Is it fine if we begin taking shifts with sleeping and recovery until you say otherwise? Nobody knows when we will get another nice barracks like this to kick back for a little while."

I replied, "Go ahead. I still haven't met with Leah, and I have a lot to do. I know you are all comfortable here, but please always keep at least two on watch and be prepared to take off at a moment's notice. I trust this place far more than Goliad, but you never know where enemies might be waiting for us to let our guard down."

"Weary of vampires, are we?" Another one asked while snickering.

Alex replied, "Hardly, or I wouldn't be here."

I smirked, "I trust the vampires here more than most humans in several places. Just get some shuteye, and don't cause too much trouble."

They saluted and then began to unload their equipment. Not that they had any modesty to begin with, but they didn't even wait for Shion and me to leave the barracks before they stripped off their armor and clothes and started washing up. Granted, they are used to a mixed-gender unit where nobody hides anything… which is why Lacia and my one other female soldier were just as quick to strip down. However, it might be offsetting from an outsider's perspective.

All mage units adhere to normal societal standards of gender separation because they are basically 'loaned' out to the military but aren't truly part of it. In the regular military, everything is shared, from the barracks to the washroom, between all species and genders. Put simply, they are afforded the luxury of time while we aren't... lucky bastards. The army has never been afforded such amenities, and it often becomes difficult to remember that once you have been in for a long time. Shion and I exited the barracks and headed back to the War Room.

Shion said, "Raider, you might be a bit disappointed to hear this, but Leah isn't here right now. I'm surprised they didn't tell you when you arrived at the gate."

"What?" I asked. "Why in the hell didn't anyone tell me that before now? What the hell could she be thinking?"

She clarified, "It's not as if she had a choice. She charged one of her lieutenants to take over in her stead. This was done at the last minute, so I am not sure which one of them took over the responsibility. If I were to guess, it would be the one in charge of the infantry, Lieutenant Samuel Articite. Partly because he is human and partly because he is capable."

I nodded in agreement, as this didn't surprise me. Leah is a 'lead from the front' kind of officer. If she needed to get something accomplished and didn't have the resources to delegate, she would take charge herself. Without a doubt, she follows the same style doctrine that I do while also being more practical. Appointing a vampire might not have set well with the humans because it would have shown favoritism. That is why she has always had a human as her second in command.

As we walked, I felt compelled to apologize to her as I remembered the first time Marleen accompanied me on one of our field training exercises. She was mortified at our lack of 'decency,' and it isn't a stretch to think that another mage would feel the same way. Lacia is probably the odd one because she jumps right in with the rest of the crew without a second thought or a care as to what other people think.

This was my attempt to comfort Shion. "Shion, I am sorry for what you saw back there. I hope you can forgive them for their lack of decency in the presence of others. All of them, Lacia included, are used to operating according to the army standard and tend to get a little too relaxed around others."

Lacia chuckled while chiming in, "It was strange when I first arrived, but you get used to it after a while. Besides, nobody has time to admire each other's assets anyway."

I jumped back, clearly startled at Lacia's presence. "How in the hell did you get changed so fast and catch up to us?"

She shrugged. "I skipped the cold-water shower until later. You said you needed me, right? It's not often I get to meet a Master Mage."

"I would say you smell… but I know I reek more. Guess we will hit the water later…" I paused when I remembered Shion was still next to us.

Shion snickered, "It doesn't bother me. I am used to the way the army does things. Our mage unit often gets accompanied by a unit of soldiers or vice versa. While in the field, we shared almost everything, so we adopted your hygiene standards. If anything, I appreciate the efficiency a lot more than the way we were taught back at the academy. As far as modesty, I believe anyone willing to enlist in the army needs to be willing to relinquish such thoughts. I doubt the demons will care about our separation or cleanliness when they gnaw on our bones."

Shion is far more pragmatic than I gave her credit for; I'm beginning to appreciate her company more and more, aside from just her looks and the fact she completes my sentences. Anxiously, I hope she decides to stick around with us after the war council concludes. Come on, my greater luck with elves… come on!

Lacia, Shion, and I exited the barracks area and entered the primary keep together. From there, we went into the War Room instead of taking the tour I had wanted. Learning Leah isn't here put a damper on my explorative inner child. Alex was still waiting for us patiently where I had left him. He was sitting across from someone we did not recognize.

As soon we entered, we were greeted by an unknown individual who spoke formally. "Hello, General. I am Lieutenant

Samuel Articite, and I am here as a representative of Captain Leah Douglas. I was placed in charge of the fort and garrison when she left two days ago. I am here to get you up to speed, so please let me answer any questions you might have."

He seemed to be direct and straight to the point... the way anyone would prefer a competent soldier to act. However, an oddity was Leah leaving in the middle of a crisis and going out on her own. But again, I assumed it was because she was put into a situation where she had no choice. There is no way Leah would abandon her troops; I refuse to believe it. I bet if I even brought it up to her, she would fang me to death out of reprisal.

Probably unprofessional, but I decided to do it anyway to set the mood. I leaned back in my chair and kicked my muddy boots on the table. My hands went on the back of my head, and I started talking straight into the air. "Lieutenant, I don't believe in screwing around when it comes to business, so I'll be blunt and to the point. When I took a tour of the refugee camps outside, it appeared to be set up by someone who was anticipating the attacks to escalate. Even if that wasn't the case, someone was skilled enough to react to the attacks at a moment's notice. The organization, both with the refugees and the shifts of the soldiers, screams Leah's involvement. Am I on the right track?"

I waited for him to nod... a man of few words. "Excellent. Then, if I were to guess further, the surrounding villages and farmland began to see increased demonic activity, and Leah saw that there was some structure to these attacks. As soon as she realized this, she sent out a communication to as many villages to gather here as a safety measure. In the middle of this, it appears some sort of sabotage happened to your ManaBank. Luckily, Leah had already put her plan into action and salvaged most of the situation. Am I getting close to the truth?"

The lieutenant was sweating as he nodded again. "It happened almost exactly as you said. But you left out one minor detail. The attacks against the civilians weren't just coordinated attacks; they had a purpose behind them. I have never seen so many demonic creatures acting in accordance with each other to eradicate a population. Those beings knew exactly where and when to strike for maximum casualties and devastation. After each assault, the survivors reported most of the demons leaving together, like a pack following an alpha. What demons, especially those without any real intelligence, have the capability to do something like that? Leah had an idea, and she acted on it. In the middle of the night, she took her personal guard of two hundred cavalry outriders and went to what she believed to be the source of the attacks. However, since she left, there has been no communication with her. She hasn't been gone long, so maybe worrying just now isn't warranted."

I thought out loud while still looking at the ceiling. "Not even a rider? How... perplexing."

The non-rocking chair I was sitting in made the perfect rocker as I balanced effortlessly on its two hind legs without falling. "So, something or someone has found a way to manipulate the lesser demonic beings and use them to purge our lands of life. A military strategist might go so far as to call this clever. Why would someone attack the military directly when you can hurt their supply chain and economy at the same time?"

I pondered over what I had just said for a moment. "Did Leah mention where she was headed?" A dark figure, which I had not noticed until now, emerged from behind the Lieutenant. It was Forina.

She began to speak. "I can answer that question."

Shion immediately jumped out of her chair and fell back into a defensive stance. She either knew how dangerous Forina was, or she was startled by her sudden appearance.

I put my hand on Shion's back to calm her down. "Relax, she is on our side... kind of."

Forina put her arms around the Lieutenant and rested her head on his right shoulder. She was running her left hand up and down his collarbone. If I hadn't already known better, I would have assumed she was a vampire eyeing her next meal.

She started with her seductive way of speaking. "Your Vampire Princess was not sure what was controlling them. She even suspected that this fort had been infiltrated as well... once the ManaBank went dry and overloaded, her opinion was validated. She knew the outrider company she took with her could not be at fault because they had just returned from a three-week patrol along the border. Not to mention, those outriders are also bloodsuckers since nobody can trust you humans. So... she kept the finer details to herself and only told those she could trust without resorting to emphatic measures. Isn't that right... 'Master Mage'? Or maybe she didn't tell you at all, and you're a fraud looking to coerce my 'Master'?" Forina wanted to provoke Shion as she was shooting her usual unsettling grin.

Forina stood up and walked around the lieutenant until she got to me, never once letting her eyes leave Shion. She gave her a once over as if she were a direct challenger to her territory. "But Miss Mage has a real problem. Can she trust the wayward general to come to her friend's aid? Or does she think there are too many coincidences between his arrival and the current chaos? Or, perhaps the woodling and the Vampire Princess aren't friends at all? That seems more likely... strangers at best."

She disappeared and reappeared on the other side next to Shion. "And what a pretty woodling you are! I hope we can become the best of friends."

Forina knows how to aggravate me, and she knows it. "Stop, Damn it. What is with you and latching on to new people and fucking with them? Get away from her, she isn't used to putting up with your shit yet."

She replied, "Oh? And you're so used to me, are you?"

I sighed and shook my head. "No, I'm not. Anyway, I am guessing you already have a lead as to where Leah went, or you wouldn't be grandstanding in front of our new mage like that."

"Maybe I do... so what's in it for me? You know what will make me happy." Forina took her hand away from Shion's face and turned to look at me. "So, what is your answer?"

"Fine, you can kill anyone you want as long as they are our enemies..." I didn't finish the sentence before she disappeared into a green mist again. I heard that distinct sound of hers when she appeared, but it was outside in the hallway. Both Lieutenant's guards outside of the War Room collapsed. My attention never left the lieutenant because I already knew what that crazy elf was doing. I heard her disappear and reappear again but couldn't tell where she was slithering. Yeah, that was a bit of an elf joke too.

Continuing my conversation about Leah, I started talking with Lieutenant Samuel again. "Fine, back to the main topic. Before we can get a handle on the demon attacks, we must locate Leah and follow up on where she thinks these attacks are coming from. We have a lead as to where Leah went, but she may need to be rescued, especially if she hasn't even sent a rider to inform us that she isn't in trouble. But before focusing on Leah and the attacks, we must first fix the problems with the ManaBank. Aside from attuned items being disabled, the ManaBank itself is a concern. Worst case scenario, it might be permanently damaged or go critical and kill everyone, not to freak you out too much or anything. I need you to call every ManaBank engineer who has been in the fort's vault anytime recently. I'll start interviewing them right away."

    The Lieutenant didn't move a muscle. He was still sitting there with his elbows on the table, his hands clenched in a fist supporting his head. Maybe he is too unnerved to acknowledge me after he saw and heard Forina's abilities? He slowly fell forward and face-planted on the table. There was that signature psycho elf signature stuck into his back. My eyebrows started to twitch in anger when I realized what had happened.

    Raising my voice, I turned toward Forina, who was now in the corner of the room. My finger pointed on its own. "Stop moving around so damn much! Also, don't just sit there and let me talk to a dead man. At least say something like 'He's dead' or 'Are you trying to kill him further with your demands?', or better yet, tell me you're going to kill him before you do. How does that sound? Complicated, right?"

    I forced myself to sit back. Trying to be equanimous with my train of thought, I spoke heartily. "Can you at least tell me why you killed all of them? I don't want to hear because they are human because I know that's the kind of bullshit you would say."

    There is almost nothing she can say that would satisfy me, even though I am restraining myself and trying to keep my cool. The last thing I need is for Shion to think I am unhinged and blow any chance we have of bringing her along. I glanced out of the corner of my eye… and there she sat, completely unphased. Her reaction might even be eerier than Forina's actions.

    Forina just never stops smiling when it comes to killing. She can barely get the words out of her mouth whenever she gets what she wants. "You're just slow like usual. Can't you tell what has been happening here? This guy and several others set the Vampire Princess up to die. She left the fort, knowing full well that you would arrive and clean things up while she did the real work. It must be nice to have that much trust in someone. That captain of yours must place a great deal of trust into the great 'General Raider.' If I were in your boots, I would be angry being the trash man for someone who is supposed to report to you."

She ran her hand through my hair as she stood behind me. "Don't worry, master, I'll be your garbage woman. And yeah… I killed them because they were weak humans."

Forina pulled the dagger out of his back and began to lick the blade. "Tastes like… filthy human corruption. Think I'll wait for something better and give him to the tribe. It does beg the question, though. With all the other bloodsuckers around here, why is she trying so hard to impress you by appointing humans in their territory? It boggles the mind, squalid blood letters."

Moving on, I verbalized my frustration toward Alex. "Alex, don't think you can get away with being silent in the corner about all of this. I want you to go with Shion and figure this shit out right now. Find someone in charge… that Forina won't kill… and bring me the people I need to solve the ManaBank issues. I want any ManaBank or Item Engineer that has gone into the fort's vault in the last three weeks. If we cannot find them, we need anyone familiar with this fort's ManaBank."

He asked with raised eyebrows, "And what, Raider, happens if we can't find the humans responsible, or we find them, and they don't tell us what we need to know?"

I snapped, "I don't care how you do it, but find whoever is responsible, human or not. Interrogate them if you must, but I want to know why it was drained dry with such a large population supporting it. The only way it would run dry is if it was sabotaged or mismanaged… and I know Leah wouldn't let that happen. Get it done quickly… a lot of lives are riding on how swiftly we get that thing operational again."

Shion and Alex were still listening intently. "Look, it's getting late, so we can reconvene here tomorrow at noon. After we finish our discussion, we will try to get the engineers to reset the ManaBank and all items attuned to it so we can power it back up. Shion, I promise we will get to Leah the moment I feel like the situation here is stable. If you have any concerns, feel free to approach me whenever you need."

Alex and Shion nodded and left the room. While they are busy hunting down the engineers, I will work with Forina to map out places that Leah could have gone with her unit. I turned and addressed my two soldiers standing guard inside the room. I honestly hadn't noticed them because they came after Forina killed the Lieutenant's men. Did Forina tell them to come? No, they are vampires, and she doesn't seem all that fond of their kind... even less so than humans for whatever reason.

It was just Lacia and I left. "Lacia, take two of our guys and bring whoever oversees the cavalry, mages, and infantry for this fort tomorrow when we reconvene."

I dismissed her from the room and sat there silently debating with myself over everything going on at Midgard. I don't know where in the room Forina went to, but I am getting good at sensing her presence. "You know... there is a part of me that wonders if deep down you are not a blood-thirsty psycho elf. Could you genuinely be a caring person? Would you at least tell me if you kill for a reason other than just pure enjoyment? I am finding that my world is getting smaller each day. With such unparalleled uncertainty, allies disappearing, and enemies emerging like wildfire... can I trust some random Grey Elf that entered my life wielding unexplainable abilities?"

Forina whispered into my ear, "I guess you will just have to find out." Her presence then vanished from the room.

Chapter 17: Jumbled Confidence

After getting out of the field, I had expected to get some solid rest. The first night, forever dubbed 'Helen's Lustful Fail,' saw that I got some rest but no relaxation. And tonight? Well, I stayed awake for hours on end, thinking about everything we had to do to get this place right. Above all, that was my concern for Leah. Sure, she is what Forina says... a bloodsucker... and sure, she has forcefully taken my blood in the past, something I buried deep in my memory bank, but she is one of the very few people I wish for anything bad to befall. I would put her up there right behind Marleen as far as how much she means to me and our fruitful several-year relationship. Nothing beyond friends and comrades, but still, we bond and support each other extremely well.

When the lingering problems kept me awake past a certain point, I went for a stroll around the compound to check on things. It helps that most soldiers here are vampires, as their eyes light up wherever they are posted. All of them are friendly in the same monotone way that Alex is, although that doesn't detour me in the slightest from getting along with them. In fact, not once have I ever felt insecure or threatened by any of them, unlike many of my counterparts.

My stroll eventually took me into the refugee area outside the keep. In the short time I passed them, the whole place exploded with more people. I would say there are easily ten or fifteen thousand camped outside in their tent city. That makes their numbers rival the garrison... but more realistically, they surpass it.

I ran into a few children running around looking for food. They must be desperate to eat more than the allotted rations if they are scavenging in the middle of the night. I had noticed one of the vampires from the fort was tailing me, so I asked him to come out of hiding. When he reached me, I asked him to fetch my rations for the next day and bring them to me. When he returned, the children scarfed the food down before they got the chance to chew it. Who would have thought a few pieces of bread, a dozen or so slices of meat, and cow's milk would have been so valuable?

Not that I expected them to thank me for the food, but they disappeared the moment their bellies were full. Somewhere in my head, I felt like prolonging even a few children's lives a few days longer might help rectify the mistakes within our ranks that led to their suffering. A fool's errand, I know. Of the six children that ate the food, two would probably die from a disease in the next few days to a week, two from starvation, and one from abuse from other humans. That is, if the demons don't attack, get them first. Life expectancy during these troubling times always tends to bottom out. With a deep breath, I realized that my desensitization to death shouldn't be a natural thing.

The next day, everyone I requested was now sitting at the table from me well in advance of when I requested them to be here. What a stark contrast to what happened at Fort Goliad. Instead of looking at some snobby shitbag sitting on a pedestal, everyone is sitting around a table seemingly as equals. This is such a much better way to tackle problems.

On my side of the table sat Lacia and Alex, and on their side sat several people I didn't recognize. We are getting ready to discuss what actions need to be taken to begin resolving the ManaBank crisis. I assume that everyone present is 'Forina approved' because they were able to show up unharmed. If they wind up missing at some point, then the psycho had her lunch, and I died a little more inside. But I can't always plan around her murderous intentions, so I'll work with what I have. It's probably not good that I've begun to trivialize her actions more and more these last couple of days. I may need to watch that habit of mine.

I remained seated to set the level of comfort amongst everyone here. That's right; I'm not kicking my boots up as I did yesterday. The last thing I need to do is announce a 'my way or the highway' attitude. As far as I could tell, they might be on edge because of the bloodstains in the hallway that couldn't quite be cleaned up from yesterday. That and the fact that most of their leaders were nowhere to be found might suggest I am on a purging mission.

I spoke in earnest, hoping to alleviate some of their fears. "Thank you all for joining me today. I am General Raider, but please call me Raider. I have not had the privilege of speaking with any of you in the past... but due to leadership shortages, you have been placed in charge of your respective sections. I want to clarify that some of your officers stationed here were involved in nefarious activities unbefitting their rank. These individuals have been dealt with accordingly, and I wish to move forward under the pretense of cooperation."

They didn't move a muscle. I'd expect little to no emotion from the vampires, but not the humans. "Keep in mind that we will treat you according to your station so long as you remain trustworthy. From what I can tell, this fort put the supplies sent to you to good use both before and after I got here by aiding the refugees. I had my men determine the fort's stand-to readiness last night and good job... you passed with flying colors. There wasn't a single thing that wasn't in good working order. All your equipment has been maintained, and your soldier's accountability is impeccable. To top that off, your record books are as good as I remember them. You have my utmost respect, which places you in the highest regard amongst those currently serving on the eastern front."

I continued, "Next, I will have Alex take it from here. Alex wears many hats in my unit and always excels at everything I task him with. He is a Green Elf and a vampire who originally reported to me from Fort Midgard. He is also a part of the Forward Observers Core and an excellent fire mage. Above all, he is my second in command, so please treat him as you would anyone else you report to in your chain of command."

Alex stood up next to me and began to speak. "Hello everyone, I am Sergeant Alex Doraleski. I oversee all field scouting operations for General Raider's personal unit. Since you are all now in charge of this fort until Captain Leah returns, you should be made aware of our current situation regarding the unstable ManaBank. Out of the five engineers cleared to enter the vault and perform ManaBank maintenance... two are dead, one is incapacitated and is as good as dead, one is missing, and the last engineer is scared for their life."

A few audible gasps could be heard from the room, but Alex ignored them. "Based on what the last engineer said, we have placed them in the vault, where they will remain in seclusion. The vault's guards have also been doubled as a precautionary measure. That person will remain in the vault and work on the ManaBank alone until we can get them further help. The specifics involving this engineer do not need to be known for their safety. We have begun to place notices out to the refugees and nearby villages for additional engineers familiar with cities or forts ManaBanks to supplement our repair efforts. With any luck, we will find someone to speed up the recovery process."

Alex continued, "On to the next point. From what we understand, the missing engineer is responsible for most, if not all, of the problems that occurred. This individual continually fed false reports up the chain to Captain Leah about how underutilized the mana was. These reports were supported by the second-in-command engineer, who was then later killed. This engineer was more than likely threatened into cooperation, and when their role was over, the mastermind disposed of them."

I interrupted, "Alex, aren't there any more redundancies? I'm a bit ignorant on these matters, but it seems implausible that we have only two people overseeing a ManaBank's entire operation."

He replied, "Yes, there are supposed to be more checks in place two echelons above the engineering level. That would have been the lieutenant, who retired yesterday, and the captain overseeing the fort."

"Did Leah just forget?" I pondered aloud. "Or, perhaps, was something else going on with her? Damage like this had to take what, weeks or months to occur?"

Alex nodded. "You are correct. The amount of requisitioned magical items by these two was unprecedented for a ManaBank this size. Anyone who knows anything about how they operate would have been able to see this coming for at least two months, probably longer. Because the level of depravity was so deep, they were able to pull off their plot and ended up draining the entirety of the mana that was stored."

Questioning lightly, I asked what I shouldn't have. "Why… never mind."

Alex sighed. "It is as you surmised. She put too much faith in…"

"… in humans? I don't blame you for thinking that, given what I've seen over the last few days. It's fine. Continue with your explanation, and we will talk about that another time." Can anyone blame him? Leah can't always micromanage everything. She was likely preoccupied with everything else I'd sent her way. That's right, I've sent her reports about the Empire's activities, shortages of supplies across the board, and just a general overview of our predicament as a country. Her oversight is looking more and more like my fault for overburdening her.

Alex cleared his throat. "The items that drained the ManaBank dry this fast included high mana consumption items with detection, speed enhancements, strength enhancements, magical proficiency enhancements, and even one item for magical nullification."

The room began to chatter amongst themselves. Everyone knew that even a handful of these items would consume more mana than the ManaBank could steadily produce for this area, as items that produce magic nullification, speed enhancements, or proficiency enhancements are usually attuned to a National ManaBank with far more people to draw mana from. This was just in addition to the items already 'standard issue' per unit, such as navigation, armor, and weapon enhancements.

I had to step in, or we might find ourselves in a Goliad situation. "Quiet down; we still have a lot to cover. Once he concludes his brief, you can talk about anything you want. Alex, please continue but summarize as much as you can. We don't have all day."

Alex adjusted himself. "From here on out, to fix the damage that has been done, we are collecting every single one of the items attuned to the fort's ManaBank. From what the last engineer told us, the damage is significant enough that we need to start from scratch. This means it could take several days to restart the core of the ManaBank if we begin immediately. The more items attuned to it, the longer the recovery time… and we don't have an accurate log of everything pulling mana from it. It's much harder to start the ManaBank if its mana supply remains low, and the drain remains even moderate."

Motioning for Alex to sit, I finished the brief. "There you have it. We know roughly why this happened, who was involved, and how to fix it. Begin ordering your subordinates to collect every item systematically. Once they are collected, Shion will be in charge of bringing them to the vault to be disassembled. The good news is that there is currently no risk of the ManaBank overloading to the point of an irradiated mana explosion. But this does not mean we can take our time because lives depend on our celerity."

One of the human lieutenants at the table stood up. "This is outrageous! The front line has never been held without enchanted items! We won't stand a chance of survival without them against intelligent demons, let alone against coordinated ones. You may as well ask us to go without swords, shields, or armor. Hell, let's put blindfolds on and go into battle that way too."

Another human lieutenant stood up and yelled, "He's right! How do you expect us to go to war with our hands tied behind our backs? Next, you will tell us not to use magic or to stay indoors with our thumbs up our asses. It's easy for you to give an order like that when you will eventually disappear back to the capital while we pay for it! How can we do our jobs? We are overworked as it is!"

I stood up and put my hand on my sword's hilt. I was practically daring them to continue running amok. No matter where I go, this same scenario plays out. First, it was Laura running her dagger into the table to shut us up back in the capital. Then it was the dumbasses in Goliad forcing me to resort to challenging their captain to a duel. Now, it's Leah's human leadership doing the same thing while the vampires sit there, not saying a word of defiance. That's when I noticed that my body posture and stance had caused the room to go quiet.

The room was so quiet that I only had to speak softly for everyone to be able to hear me. "Being scared is one thing. However, open dissension amongst the ranks is something else entirely. We don't have time for this. If you interrupt Alex or me again, I will find someone who will listen, one way or another."

Maybe Forina cleaning out some of the riffraff did some good after all. I should put her in charge of a shadow unit that preemptively removes my opposition. No, that is the kind of thing tyrants do, and I'm not one of them. That line of thinking will only lead to fear, oppression, and further rebellions amongst the ranks. I don't have a will or desire to wield a sword that big.

Alex took the hint and moved to wrap the meeting up. "Raider understands how all of you feel, but the items are already inoperable. In other words, they don't currently work, so what we are doing is trying to get them back online so that you aren't fighting blind, or without a sword, or without a shield, or whatever else you were saying. With every mind in or around the fort that knows anything about ManaBanks putting their heads together last night, it was the only way we could figure out how to begin the repair process. Nothing like this has happened in modern times, which makes finding experts nearly impossible."

One of the nameless human lieutenants that spoke out before raised their hand. After my nod, he angrily spoke. "How could the damage be this bad if it hasn't happened before? It's hard to swallow that this is a unique occurrence if it happened so fast."

As I was about to speak, Alex took the question himself. "The engineer that did this knew exactly what they were doing, that's why. Moreover, the corruption went several levels deep, as was mentioned before, and thus escaped Captain Leah's watchful eyes. Had we been here sooner or had one of them made a mistake, then things might have been different. If you want to be thankful for anything, then be thankful for the fact that they did not cause the ManaBank to go critical, or you would all be dead right now, along with anyone within a half-day horse ride."

Alex called on the other human lieutenant when he raised his hand. "Why didn't they, then? If they wanted to kill us, wouldn't that have been much easier?"

He answered, "They must have had another objective in mind. They could have easily overloaded it at any point if they knew the overriding pattern for the runes. If they didn't, that would also explain why they took this route. Moving on, as soon as the core of the ManaBank is filled up to at least twenty percent, we can begin attuning items to it again. We foresee this taking at least two or three days after the attuned items are collected and dismantled. A lot of this work depends on how good the engineer is as well. Dismantling so many attuned items with different runic inscriptions will take a while for someone not extremely skilled."

Alex waited for any more hands, but none came. "If you are looking for good news, there is a little bit. It is possible that it will take less time because so many refugees have arrived. More people will mean less time to fill it out due to the amount absorbed. Again, most of this is hypothetical because we have never seen a ManaBank drained completely dry during our lifetimes. But if we are correct, then military operations may be back to semi-normal sooner rather than later."

One of the lieutenants shot his hand up. "Moving past ManaBanks, as most of us here don't understand them to begin with, do we know a motive?"

My head hit the back of my chair. He should have asked this before we moved on, so I took this question. "You're not wrong that finding out the motive is one of our highest priorities. Whoever is orchestrating these events might have more things planned. But for now, anything we stab at for a reason would be like shooting an arrow in the dark. The ManaBank being run dry was perfectly in sync with coordinated demon attacks, so even a farmer could tell more is probably coming. We understand trying to head that off is important. Alex, you can go now... Shion is just getting back from her assignment."

Shion moved over next to me, where Alex had previously been. "Hello, I am Shion, Master Earth Mage, for those who don't know me. Raider has charged me with two critically important tasks. First, he wants me to get the items that Alex's team collects unattuned to the ManaBank's core with the cooperation of the engineer we have available. Second, he wants me to reorganize our mages to be part of each company and provide support for the main effort."

"Main effort?" One of the silent vampire lieutenants asked.

She nodded, "Yes, and I am sure we will get to that in a moment. Historically, mages fight as part of a separate unit assigned special tasks during a battle. Moving forward, he wants our mages to be separated into small groups and organized as part of each company. This reorganization is a rather revolutionary way of thinking. He is doing this to help cover the loss of our engineered items. Last night, we counted our remaining forces to make sure we could cover our defensive necessities. We currently have about eight thousand infantry, one hundred knights, two thousand cavalry, and two hundred mages."

Shion kept glancing around the room to make sure she had been speaking loud enough. The audience's attentiveness reassured her, so she passed the division of our forces on to me. "Thanks, Shion. Now listen up, the reorganization will go as follows. First, we will divide the garrison into four equal units consisting of knights, cavalry, infantry, and mages. There will be one thousand cavalry and sixteen mages kept out of these units and assigned under me as part of the main effort until we find Leah, or she returns. For those of you assigned to one of the four main units, there will be two shifts each day instead of the existing three shifts per day. Each shift will have one unit in the fort and one out supporting the refugees. We are giving up on the surrounding farmland and villages until we can secure the immediate area first. Please remain after this meeting to verify your assignments."

Chapter 18: Lightfall Part I

With everything said, there was just one thing left to do since Alex wouldn't be coming with me on this trip. That was to assign a knight or an officer who would be my second in command for the outriders. To ensure unit cohesiveness, it really needed to be a knight to incorporate the delicate balance between officers and knights into the chain of command. Since we had four lieutenants now in charge of the fort, vampires to humans proportionately, that just alienated the knights stationed here. Appointment to this role would be tricky because of the class balance structure that is currently in place. The equilibrium between knights and officers can be extremely contentious, but I still err on the side of tradition when all other merits are considered equal.

Usually, knights are nobles in charge of the ground forces engaging in combat. They specialize in heavy armor, heavy weapons, and heavy cavalry tactics. Most think of them as the 'surgeon's scalpel' when utilizing them on the battlefield. Officers are usually talented commoners, but they can also be nobles who are in charge of organizing every other ground unit except knights. It also isn't unheard of for knights to be officers, depending on what the unit's objective is; however, that is exceedingly rare. This structure allows for knights, who are generally proud of their nobility, to operate outside of the general army composed of and led by commoners. Each has their own role to play while garrisoned and while engaging in combat.

This structure has been in place for a long time since commoners have proven themselves capable of being talented strategists, similar to their noble counterparts. In this case, I need an officer who is also on the ground fighting with me, but the knights have been kept completely out of all leadership roles. Add to that… well… that I divided their unit up and made them report to officers, and there might be a bit of animosity. Basically, if I don't appoint a knight and put him in charge as my second in command, I'm liable to piss off a lot of nobility and get stabbed in the back while I'm out looking for Leah.

This all led to the knight standing at attention five paces before me. "Sir Regar Articite. Your peers highly recommend you as a capable leader. Your brother was… Lieutenant Samuel Articite, correct? Will you have a problem standing shoulder to shoulder with me, or do you intend to get revenge for his death? If you want to get vengeance, let me know so we can solve this like men. Truthfully, I am getting tired of all the cloak-and-dagger shit I've had to deal with lately."

Regar is a tall, muscular, brown-haired, and red-bearded man in his late thirties. He distinctively has an eye patch over his right eye and an accent from who knows where. His voice echoed in the courtyard as he responded. "Raider, I am with you until death or until you find someone better. My brother sealed his fate by throwing in with that lot. If I had known what he was up to, I would have stopped him myself before it got to the level it did. I hold no ill will, just a hunger to serve the King and set right the wrongs my family has caused."

This man seems like he knows where it's at. Do honest men really still exist? He's very straightforward, but grudges can go deep... too deep... I know this better than anyone. It would be hard for even me to trust someone responsible for the murder of my brother, regardless of the position they held. Anyway, we are short on competent leaders, and I could use a reputable knight the others will follow to assist me in the mission to come. Worst case scenario, I hope psycho elf still has my back should he turn on me. Wherever she is... that is...

I patted Regar on the shoulder as I passed him and whispered, "You're in charge of outriders, so don't disappoint me. Go get everyone in formation by the front gate within the next half hour. We have demons to slay and vampires to save."

Once the majority had left, I was alone, with only a standing guard outside the room I had commandeered as my office. I called out to Forina. "I know you're here. What do you want?"

Forina appeared in her usual way, but this time sitting on the table in front of me with her legs on either side of my torso. "Tsk Tsk...you know you really should watch your temper. If you can't control yourself, how do you expect me to? At least you are keeping me entertained, and you're getting better at knowing when I'm around. You really do catch on quick."

This time, she was smoking a long pipe, not all that dissimilar from what Shion was smoking. As she spoke, she puffed out in between sentences. Was she high on herbs? Oh, I get it. This might be her way of mellowing out while she isn't busy getting her fix from killing people.

She took an elongated inhale, exhaled, and then began to speak again. "It calms the voices, sometimes."

"Voices..." I jeered.

She inhaled again. "Never mind, you're not ready for that conversation yet. Before you say anything else, no, you can't have any. This is a specially grown herb from my village, and it is extraordinarily toxic to humans. Maybe I can give you some indirectly if you... beg me. But, before you beg, we should talk about how well you can sense me now. If you get any better at it, then I might start to think of you as a real threat. What should I do about that, 'master'? Hmmm...?"

"Get to the point. Where is Leah?" One day, I swear, she will send me over the edge. She isn't making me angry with her flamboyancy; she's just aggravating me.

She shrugged as she replied, "No sense of timing, Raider. Relax for a moment! There will be lots of deaths to come very soon. Endless... death."

She saw how unamused I was and placated me. "She is less than four hours' ride northeast from here as long as your horse isn't overfed. You will know when you have arrived because you will see the great forest's edge with trees as tall as mountains. It's the former ancestral home to the Green Elves... the Forgone Antecedents. I'll tell you the story from thousands of years ago if you want."

She saw the look on my face and was still displeased. She quickly changed the topic back to Leah. "Fine, fine... your Vampire Princess is not in immediate danger. But you better hurry if you want her to be able to bite another day. Those scars on your neck are telling... and I know I didn't leave them. Move swiftly... the ground already begins to tremble... 'master.'"

"The ground begins to tremble? Since when do you speak in riddles? ... annnnd you're gone." She hasn't lied to me yet. Here I am, sitting all alone in the War Room, probably reeking of herbs. I bet the guards in the hallway think I'm getting high and talking to myself. I probably owe them some form of explanation before rumors start spreading about me whispering to dead elves when I get high. Then I'll never live down the 'Elf Whisperer' title.

"You two didn't see anything, right?" They both slightly nodded while whistling and pretending to be oblivious.

"That's right! And that psycho elf doesn't exist either, right?" They again nodded and kept whistling. "Good, you two are dismissed. I better not hear rumors about Elf Whispering." After they left, I realized it would have been better not to say anything at all.

I felt it was best to keep the passionate speech to my newly formed unit to a minimum. Nobody likes long-winded assholes, and I was no exception. Lacia, Regar, and I were standing on top of the wall overlooking the main drawbridge. Regar and all the soldiers were in full battle rattle. Each one was equipped with highly polished plate mail over light chainmail, two explosive spears, and a backup weapon that was usually a sword.

In addition, they each had a round outrider shield on their left arm that could be attached to their horse while they were riding. The mages and I were the only ones not equipped to the teeth. The mages had robes and staves, but everyone's horse had a minimum amount of armor to prevent mortal bites from the wolves. The sun was going down, and the temperature was low enough for the horses to begin getting antsy.

I was drawn to the full moons that were out in full force tonight. One illuminated us in a bright blue gaze, with the other chasing it in a dull red hue. How many people get to say they were alive on a night like tonight? Forina was right; the ground is trembling... not physically, but figuratively. With such a clear layout of the land, I couldn't help but feel some of nature's natural blessings wrapping its arms around us. The men looked fresh, and I couldn't sense any hesitation in any of them. We could be riding directly into oblivion whilst the entire time Leah is already dead, but that wouldn't matter. Tonight is going to be a good night; I can feel it. I kept wavering back and forth on how to explain to them that a crazy vanishing elf told me where we must go... to one of the most dangerous areas known to man, and I would follow that advice unquestionably.

"Riders of Alvernia! I am General Raider. Welcome to my Outriders." As soon as I finished, all the riders smashed the tips of their spears to their shields and shouted, "AHHHHHHHH HUUUUUUUUUUU!". "I won't wrap what we will attempt in useless lies. Tonight, we ride into the endless abyss known as the Unknown Territory. This place is void of anything you have ever known or loved. It is the very essence of what it means to oppose humanity and Alvernia. This is someplace nobody has been to or survived in over a thousand years. This place is so bad that even the demons that live there are constantly trying to leave due to the horrible smell and bad food!" That last one was good for quite a few laughs… and… I got a couple.

After a few seconds, I cleared my throat and resumed my speech. "Something is on the horizon in the dead cold of night, soldiers of Alvernia. I don't know what awaits us, but I can guarantee you we will meet it head-on. I have received intel from my most trusted Forward Observer that we are riding into death itself. We ride into this knowing we have a duty to Alvernia. We ride into this because we have a duty to protect our citizens. And finally, we ride into this hell because we have allies in need. Well, I say, let us wait no longer. What better night is there to die than tonight? What better time to lay one's life down than right now, on the precipice of chaos? So, follow me, soldiers of Alvernia, and we will show Genesis the essence of our mettle and the resolve of our spears."

The soldiers again echoed their war cry. Their cheers included, 'For Alvernia!' and 'For Midgard!' and 'Death to the monsters!'. It worked; they were cheering and hollering loud enough for the demons to hear in the Unknown Territory. My short speech turned into a riled-up mob ready for revenge on those miasma-soaked bastards. Optimistic young soldiers are the only way anything ever gets done for any country. Really, this was just a fancy way of saying Forina told me some stuff, so may as well die proving her right or wrong. The way it came off, even I almost convinced myself.

Regar stepped forward and yelled, "RAIDER'S OUTRIDERS! DEATH BECOMES US!" to which the company echoed, "AND HELL BECOMES THEM! AH HUUUUUUUUUUU!".

And with that, every one of them mounted up. The traveling formation was four blocks of two hundred and fifty cavalry with a row of four mages separating each section. We were fortunate enough to have four fire mages, so we used them to cast two flame balls above themselves to light the way. There was one fire mage in each section to disperse the light evenly. Mana consumption for these spells was low, so we could use them in transit for several hours.

Regar formed at the front of the formation to lead them across the drawbridge. Before I left with them, I noticed Alex was over to the side, waiting to talk to me. I almost didn't recognize him with all the other vampires at Midgard. When I was giving my speech, it was a unique experience to see half of their eyes glowing red. Usually, when I see red eyes in the dead of night, it's Alex.

I tried to reason with him before he could say his peace. Although his expressions are hard to read, his posture wasn't. "Alex, I don't have anyone else I can put in charge of this fort beside you that I can trust. All the leadership Leah had appointed was either conspiring, useless, or killed by miss psycho elf. I need you to build a competent team and continue operations here while I am gone. I don't care what race they are as long as they can get the job done. Who knows what we will find out there, but regardless, we will need to return to a secure fort and able allies."

Alex shook his head from left to right. "It's not that. We believe we know the identity of the saboteur. However, the reports that came in indicated that the culprit was not a human. Not to set you astray, but those who saw him say it was a humanoid that exuded miasma."

I asked, "I see… like the story of your childhood, is it? Demons that look like us, talk like us, and act like us. And why didn't anyone notice this… humanoid demon?"

He continued, "The reason was because of his abilities using dark magic. He was able to cast illusionary magic to appear human, or so I am told. If not for your arrival, this individual wouldn't have been seen escaping by the two remaining engineers."

My hand went to my chin like it does when I think. "They didn't come forward because they didn't think anyone would believe them."

Alex nodded. "Yes, but there is another reason. The one in a coma was injured, while the other one was frightened to the point of debilitation. Both were saved when the guards showed up. If what they are saying is true, there is a strong likelihood he killed the original engineer with the same appearance. This means he had stalked him, learned his habits, and mimicked his appearance so well that nobody knew it wasn't him. When word reaches the crown about this..."

I finished his sentence, "...life as we know it will change. Well, it seems the rider I sent out was for nothing, as that passive man will learn about it anyway. Alex, try to keep this under wraps as much as possible until I return and have time to contemplate my next move. Who knows how many others, across however many countries, are also doppelgangers? Since they haven't made a move until now, we can't make any hasty generalizations. If we play this card wrong, a lot of innocent people could get killed by false accusations."

Alex nodded again and replied, "I understand. But, Raider, be ready for anything out there. We don't know what kind of intelligence the enemy has on us or our movements. As far as taking care of the fort, I've got it covered. Most of the soldiers around here are my kind and won't misalign from the mission. If that isn't convincing enough, we all know of your close relationship with Leah, and we would do anything for her." Alex was always dependable, and I had no idea where I would be without him.

"Now you..." I started to say, then paused. No, I can say it. "Now you have me concerned the vampires might mutiny because I'm too close."

I had a heartfelt chuckle to myself... all to myself.

We had been riding for about two and a half hours when the ground gently palpitated. Could Forina have been speaking... in a nonfigurative way? The vibrations started simultaneously as the clear skies rapidly degenerated into a dark maelstrom of mana and clouds. I have never claimed to have abilities or know magic, but this was shooting off all kinds of what the fuck alarms in my head. I knew it was only a matter of time until some apocalypse befell us, and we were out in the open. Was this on me? Are we caught in the open when someone or something casts tactical-level magic on us?

Regar, like everyone else, was seized in a daze... too focused on the ominous swirling clouds. Snapping him out of it, I finally got his attention after yelling several times. "Order the lead mage to shoot a green flare off! We must pick up the pace and reach the tree line before it's too late. It might be our only chance to avoid whatever is being cast."

He nodded and told the fire mage next to us to signal everyone else in the formation. When the green flare exploded, every other fire mage followed suit. In seconds, all hell broke loose as we pushed our horses to their limits. The massive trees at the start of Tree Mountain grew inexplicably large as our mounts continued to exhaust themselves.

Come on, you bastards. Push harder... faster. You need to make it to at least the tree line! We can walk back if they all die, but they cannot give up now. I thought we would be riding directly into combat, but knowing what I know now, I would have told the knights falling behind to strip all their uselessly heavy armor off themselves and their horses. If I return without any of them alive, there will be a court hearing for sure when I get back to the capital, and my reputation will be further degraded amongst the nobility.

I kept telling myself, 'Leah and her soldiers will be directly in front of us' repeatedly to reassure my hard-hit staggard feelings. We must rally with them; there are no other options. If she hadn't been where Forina said she would be, we would have made this trip into this large miasma-infested death forest for no reason.

The vanguard scouts shot up a yellow flare that exploded and fell to the left and a white flare that exploded and fell to the right. The yellow flare indicated an enemy was near our formation on that side, and the white flare warned us of spotted humanoids that could be potential allies. A green flare was then shot up and to the right, and we shifted the column to head directly to where the possible allies were seen. This shift in direction also meant we had to shift our column formation from two abreast into a single column. Once our formation was organized into a column, we were anchored into our do-or-die charge. When we were close enough, a blue flare was then sent up to signal that they had been verified as allies. The sky couldn't be any more serious.

The clouds had changed from dark to pitch black, with dark blue waves colliding over each other as they struggled for dominance. The temperature plummeted from cold to freezing. And faintly, just faintly, we could see snowflakes falling all around. They were coming down months ahead of schedule, creating an even deeper ominous feeling you couldn't cut with a knife if you tried.

We live in an arid region without much humidity since there aren't many large bodies of water near the capital or Fort Midgard. But along with the unusual snow, the area was blanketed with stiflingly suppressive humidity. Every passing second seemed to push the clouds from slowly crashing into a violent whirlwind of 'stay the hell away.' The only pattern I could pin on them was that they were moving faster and faster to the northwest with what looked like undercurrent clouds racing back in the opposite direction at a quarter of their speed. Within minutes, the light snowflakes were replaced with lightning, rain, and miniature hail. It had happened… this makeshift hurricane formed too fast for us to get outside of its area of devastation before we could make it to safety.

The ground also changed from a mild vibration to something shy of an earthquake. The horses continued to show signs of getting spooked but miraculously didn't throw any of their riders off. The only distraction that made everything better was the glowing red eyes of the people in front of us… vampires. Faint, yet bright enough to make the weakest heart amongst the men jump with joy. Morale rolled from dreadful to upbeat, swifter than the clouds poured into the northwest.

The knights assigned to each section had all fallen out of their ranks. When it became apparent we would make it to the tree line before the spell elapsed, our column started slowing down so they could catch up and so we wouldn't collide with the massive trees. As we got even closer, I could only spot about fifty pairs of red eyes, a far cry from what I was expecting to be here.

Why were they not shooting any flares up to signal us? Where the hell are the rest of them? Were they so underprepared that they left without a plan or the proper supporting elements in their unit? Come on, Leah… what gives?

I yelled to the leadership around me to make sure the appropriate red stop flares were sent to everyone. The order was distributed to all the soldiers to stop inside the tree line and hunker down to wait out this thing. Once we broke the woods, the sergeants in charge of each of their groups yelled fastidious orders with great precision. Their alacrity and unit cohesion are remarkable.

    These soldiers moved fast, removing their equipment and laying the horses on their sides. Once the horses were settled down and their equipment was placed next to them, every soldier's blanket was placed over the top of their horse to prevent weather-related injuries. Leah's cavalry is well coordinated for a group thrown together under my command at the last minute. There was no panic or hesitation remotely visible, and every one of them knew exactly what to do with minimal guidance. This level of discipline far exceeded what was taught at the academy.

    I muttered, "I wish we had this level of discipline across the entire army…"

    "Trouble across the mainland with the new recruits, Raider?" A voice questioned from behind me.

    Leah approached me as I was getting my horse to lie down. She jumped on my back and threw her arms around me. "Long time no see, stud. Did you come to rescue a damsel in distress? You know I'm a big girl and can care for myself, right?"

    Anticipating the bite to my neck, I leaned forward a bit. "I would say you never change, but you've steadily become more attached."

    She licked the back of my neck. "Oh, don't be like that! I would ask if you brought me gifts from the capital, but I can tell you brought me the weather instead. I would be beyond disappointed if you didn't bring me at least some fun after the boring slog we found ourselves in!" Leah was always the wise-ass, but she could get away with it, and she knew it.

    My synergy with her only grows with each passing year. Unparalleled Leadership, sassy charm, good looks, and our well-rounded partnership. She was an odd one with uniquely shoulder-length light purple hair, courted by a red ribbon on one side. She had those vampire red eyes to complement the ribbon, stood about average height for a normal human, five foot seven, and was slenderly built. One more thing about her that stood out… her much larger and very distinct fangs, at least twice the length of any other vampire. I once asked her if it was a birth defect, to which my neck paid the price soon after.

My head tilted to the side to catch a glimpse of her face. "I know it's coming, but can we horse around a little later? The last thing I want is to hear another one of your songs about how you were my first."

"Is it really so bad being with me like this?" She questioned.

I sighed, "No, but every time you hang on me like this, sing those stupid songs, and bite me… it gives people the wrong impression. Besides, we kind of have something going on right now."

Thankfully, she hadn't gone so far as to dance around me with some farfetched made-up dance, too, like she had in the past. Granted, it was all in good fun, but it somehow became an unsettling tradition when we met up. One day she will try to do this shit around Marleen… then I know it's on. Elf versus vampire… one on one… woman on woman. No matter who wins, I lose.

Her fangs aside, I never once knew her to go anywhere without full plate mail on either… much like Laura does when she is in public. Leah resembles a sexy hybrid between Marleen's personality, Laura's sense of style, and my leadership. She would almost be the perfect woman for me if I weren't already spoken for… and she wasn't… a vampire.

She scoffed, "You're no fun. What have you been doing all this time to become such a bore?"

"A bore, huh?" I asked. Quickly, I ferociously pulled her over my shoulder and slammed her to the ground, pinning her with both of my arms on her biceps.

My eyes locked onto her seductive red marbles without flinching for a second. "If I am such a bore, what about your short hairstyle? Since when has the great Leah Douglas defiled her long-flowing locks in such a way? Do you have any clue just how much I appreciated your sassy captain style? How could you possibly pull off the naughty but nice captain without your black long-braided hair? Minus thirty points!"

Leah pretended to blush, easily pushed away my left hand with her monstrous strength, and put her finger to her mouth. "Oh? Don't you know how expensive that hair dye was? I can't keep it black for you all year long when we can only meet once or thrice a year. And don't lie, you like it like this... color and all."

Letting go of her, I realized we couldn't joke around right now. "Don't say the word 'thrice,' it doesn't suit you. Anyway, I suppose we should save the banter for later. I am just glad we made it in time. Do you have any idea what's going on? All we had was a last-minute tip-off to meet you here. The nature of the lead suggested you might be in some danger."

Leah chuckled, "Oh, you really did ride in here like a white knight. Oh, how I miss the gallantry of humans at times! No, nothing has put us in any immediate danger. We are still scouting out the demons, and boy, do we have a story to tell. If anything, you brought the danger with you, weatherman. Maybe Cloudman would be better? No, Lightningman! Swirlman..."

When she gets going like this, there's no stopping her. "Stop it, already! I get it, I get it. But... looking at the sky... if you look close enough, the clouds are all rolling towards the capital. What magic could be responsible for something so powerful? Tactical-level magic, perhaps? I've never heard of anything that grandiose, though... is the capital in immediate danger?" I was clearly letting my minor state of panic leak out a little bit.

Leah got off the ground. Smiling, she forcefully patted me on the back. "A nationwide calamity is happening, and the great prodigy, 'General Acton Escot "Raider" Findlay', doesn't know what's causing it? What a major letdown! Did you think I would have more knowledge than you about these things? By the way, we have an urgent need for..." She was interrupting mid-sentence with the sound of a red flare exploding overhead. Every other mage echoed with their own red flares all along the tree line.

Leah and I turned to scan the area to see if we were being followed. The natural reaction for the soldiers was to begin getting into a quick phalanx formation, but they stopped when they saw me put my hand up to pause. It was a lone rider on a horse bolting towards us. All hell was breaking loose in the skies above them, and they gave no shits about it. If I brought the thunder, then this person brought the whirlwind. As the rider was coming closer into view, I could make out the black robe with gold trim reflecting when lightning struck. It was Shion, but what in the hell was bringing her here?

When she finally got to us, she was out of breath, and her horse fell over from exhaustion. She grabbed me from the ground with my shoulder straps and pulled me down to face level. I pulled back to get her behind our line just inside the trees. I was more worried about her having broken a leg or some ribs from the fall, but she didn't care at all. She was trying to speak to me, and I wasn't listening.

Exasperated, she still managed to get out the words she was looking for once we stopped by my horse. "Get every barrier you can muster up right now! Do it, or we will all die!"

I immediately relayed her orders and heard them echo down the line. Since we did not know what to protect against, each mage put up a barrier for the element they had an affinity for. Fire mages put up firewalls, earth mages erected solid clay and loam walls, water mages made waterwalls, and our wind mages tried their best but couldn't make headway against the strong winds pushing back. Fruitlessly, they tried to create a barrier to make it easier for the other mages to do their work.

Our troops were still divided into four sections, each protected by mages of different affinities. Being prepared has its benefits. The mages continued to cast their magic and focus hard to maintain concentration. Giant domes of red, green, yellow, and blue encompassed all of us once the spells actualized into their protective natures and out of their raw ones.

The clouds were rolling so fast that the blue and black alterations mixed into one fluid color of waving back and forth. It looked exactly like how a huge storm would normally affect ocean waves during a midnight storm. Everything but the clouds had disappeared. There was no sound or rain from the clouds, just howling from the wind and violent shaking from the ground.

The rolling of the clouds, the fast winds, and the shaking ground all worked in tandem in one motion… back and forth. The clouds were still racing towards the same central point northwest near the capital when everything fell dead silent. The shaking, the wind, the lightning, and even the clouds stopped moving simultaneously. The pause after the silence fell on us was crushing. Nobody was even breathing…. it scared the shit out of even me.

The only real answer to a situation like this is to face it head-on. If it was time to die, it may as well be now. That speech I gave earlier wasn't for nothing. The deafening quiet only amplified our anxiety with each passing moment. What better way to go out than to break the tension?

I yelled while pounding my right hand against my chest, "ARE WE GOING TO LET THIS BASTARD INTIMIDATE US?" The troops began to shout in unison over and over, "AHHHHHHHH HUUUUUUUUUUU." That's when it finally happened, as if provoked by a few words of encouragement.

A single light wave scorched the land below with overwhelming, blinding illumination. This light was so bright it temporarily blinded me, and I wasn't even looking directly at it. The light was accompanied by a shock wave so violent that all of us were knocked off our feet and crashed to the ground. We were busy trying to get our bearings and recover when another loud shock wave caught up to us. The shockwaves were enough to cause us to go deaf momentarily. All I could hear was a loud ringing pounding all the way up my spine and into my head. The barriers were still maintained, and the mages were alive, which is probably what saved our lives.

I shouted without even being able to hear myself. "Stand strong, mages, for the lifeblood of our night exists within you! Drink that life, for we will be forever grateful for your struggle!"

Then, another blinding white light overtook the previous one. The new light was big enough that it could have completely encircled the capital with ease. It was hard to look anywhere near it, but I could tell it reached well above the clouds and into the stars. This was one of the most amazing things I have ever seen. The new light originated from the ground. When it shot up, it cleared every cloud in the sky. Nobody could say a word. Probably because we were all deaf and blind, but also because what we did see... was incredible. We just watched this beam reach up into the sky for what seemed like an eternity.

That's when I noticed that the second light wave had broken every barrier and knocked our mages out from mana depletion. Poor bastards gave everything they had and then some. If anything else magical were to hit us now, we may as well find a nice hole and keel over.

Shion got off the ground, looking entirely unaffected. She dusted herself off, patted my horse's neck, and spoke calmly. "They completed the Hero Summoning Ritual in the Mage Tower, and I fear the worst has yet to befall us."

Chapter 19: Lightfall Part II

So many questions come to mind, and it is hard to ask one over the other. If I had to start somewhere, it would probably start with Shion. I'm not quick to anger or to express rage, so when it rears its face, it can creep up unexpectedly and without warning. That beast especially shows its ugly side when it comes to mysterious people showing up, getting involved with me, and then knowing a lot about a kingdom-ending light beam from who knows where. It's like all of this was planned from the beginning. Lure in Raider to a false sense of security, feed him hints about what's going on just long enough to lead him astray, then push him into the Unknown Territory where a spell can easily deal with him.

I shouldn't have done it, but it happened. I struck Shion across the face with my fist and pinned her to the ground. I'm sure my fear of what could have happened to Marleen had much to do with it, but I know my face was unsightly. My entire unit, no, the entire country could have been destroyed... and may still be for all we know. Yet, this mage from nowhere that I trusted so eagerly knew all about it. What a fucking coincidence. It took every ounce of my strength not to beat her unconscious with every bit of my strength.

I stood over her just like I had Leah a few moments before. Her nose had a single drop of blood run out of it and down her cheek. "Shion, start fucking talking."

"What do you..." She tried being coy with me.

I yelled, "No, you don't get to do that! You don't get to play dumb or ask any questions. You start by explaining yourself before I have one of the other mages pull the truth from you one spell at a time. Why the hell do you know what that was? How did you know where to find us? How did you fucking know how to prevent whatever that was from erasing us from this life? Speak, damn it!"

I wasn't sure if I was going to let her talk. I even pulled my arm back, getting ready to hit her again. The blood that had started as a single drop was streaming down her face from her undeniably broken nose. She sat there and didn't say a word or move a muscle. This... this woman knew... she knew I was going to do this, didn't she? She knew how I would react and that no matter what answer I gave her, it wouldn't be good enough.

I yelled again, "Just who the hell are you? How do you know so damn much about everything?"

Leah, clearly the Queen of Placidity, interrupted me. "Who's your pretty elf friend? I love her intensity."

She had stopped me in my tracks. I looked back and saw Leah leaning over the back of my horse with her elbows planted firmly on top of him. Her head was in her hands like some teenager with her obnoxiously huge smile. She is the only one who could have calmed me down in this situation. Her relaxed composure, nonchalant attitude, and her amazing take on how filled with rage I am are something to be admired.

Sometimes, she is so good at what she does that all I can do is step back and hand her the reins. What Leah was signaling to me, in her own way, was that we don't know shit about Shion or why she knows the things she knows. Then it dawned on me... how in the hell does she not know this mage?

Staying on top of Shion, I drew my sword and put it to her throat with the hilt resting just on the other side of her neck. "Just who the fuck are you? Leah clearly doesn't know you, and I sure as hell don't know you either. Everything about you makes me believe you might be from Elvania as a spy."

"Because I'm an elf?" She whispered.

My lips were curling in anger. "No, not because you're a damn elf. It's because it wouldn't make sense if you were from the Empire, and you lied about being from Fort Midgard. Your passive attitude after that light beam hit, your carefree persona about the status of the capital... all of it. I'll only ask once... are you my enemy?"

Without moving a whole lot, she put her hand on my face. Her fingers curled around the side of my jaw and touched the bottom of my ear. Her face was... incredibly lonely. "I never actually said I was stationed here; you just assumed that. I'll tell you everything I can, but after we move somewhere safe."

I whispered, "We aren't going anywhere until you tell me who you are."

Her eyebrows slightly raised only to intensify her isolated expression. "Very well. I am Grand Master Marleen's research assistant. My name is what I've told you, Shion D'Garde."

"You work for my fiancée?" My eyes shifted away from hers to think for a second. "And what just happened?"

She replied, "That phenomenon comes from something called the 'light element.' It happens when…"

She lost me. "There's no such thing, and you know it. You can't just make elements up when you're put on the spot to save your own skin. I don't have time for your bullshit right now, and there's no way Marleen would have either if you really do report to her as you claim."

She kindly asked, "Can you please release me? I'm not fast enough to run away from you without a horse."

My hand released itself, and I steadily sheathed my sword. Deep down, I felt she could have forced me off, potentially lethally, with magic had she really wanted. She slowly got off the ground, popped her nose back into place, brushed the blood off her face, and dusted herself off again. Her response was just as collected as it had ever been. "You know, you get more temperamental every time. How you and the Grand Master ever worked out is a mystery for the stars."

I snapped, "You want to die, you conceited piece of shit? Don't mention Marleen in that condescending tone. I wouldn't take that garbage from the assholes in Goliad, and I sure as hell won't take it from you."

She replied, "A lot is happening here that you are unaware of, but you are the unmistakable key to prosperity. You are not at fault for acting as you are, but we do not have the luxury of time. Time is always against us… always against… me. For now, we need to use Leah's guidance to get to a safe area and quickly."

She looked around and then back at me. "It's my fault I came on so strong without realizing our reset. I apologize, but please place your trust in me."

Reset? I decided to let that go but kept my hand on my sword's hilt. It wanted to cut her down bad enough to give me the shakes. "Even if I trust you, we are in the Unknown Territory. You know, home of the demons and miasma. Anywhere we move will be lethal to us. Vampires might be able to resist a little longer than we can, but we will all die."

She clarified, "Look at the ground and the trees. Until recently, this whole place was encapsulated in a miasma cloud. The miasma has slowly been dissipating. That light wave also neutralized any demon anywhere close to us. This means the lesser demons will either be dead or confused until its effects wear off. So, do you want to sit here and continue to threaten me? Or maybe you want to go to my race's ancestral homeland and get the answers you seek? Personally, I would rather be somewhere secure when the paralysis effects wear off."

I'll admit I was a little dazed and confused by her response, something that has been happening with greater frequency in the last few minutes. Her direct answers are a perfect guideline, shaking my resolve to pin some of the blame on her. This gave me a little time to calm down and reevaluate her threat level. Let's think through this one question at a time.

Why would Marleen send her? Is she also some mage working for Elvania? How can she hold it together like that? How many Hero Summoning Rituals has she been through? "Fine, 'Shion'. I admit I have no solid evidence to automatically label you as an agent of Elvania or, more generally, an enemy of Alvernia. But don't mistake my concession as you getting completely off the hook. You have a lot of shit to explain as soon as we are secure. Leah, is she right, and there is someplace we can hold up around here? We probably won't make it back to the fort in time, especially with all our mages knocked out for a day or two."

A voice responded, "Your precious Vampire Princess has a pretty good spot picked out in the elven tomb up ahead. But if you move now, you might... interrupt her prey."

"Forina? When the hell did you get here?" It seemed like I was the only one a little startled, even if I had gotten used to her antics. Looking at Leah, she knew all along Forina was nearby.

Forina mimicked what Leah was doing but was on the opposite side of my horse. From this distance, they looked like polar opposites in the nighttime. One with her glowing green eyes steadily repelling the other with glowing red eyes. Both were glancing at each other from the sides of their eyes with their heads in their hands. I'm over here worked up and getting ready to kill someone, and they are both fucking around. Leah, I can understand, but Forina too?

Leah then chimed in almost without missing a beat, "Who's your other pretty elf friend?" Her bright smile never dulls with those glistening fangs of hers. "A voidling no less; how unexpected of you, Raider. Quite the attracter of exotic people."

I attempted to ignore Leah's goading, but she had me by the balls. How could I get away without explaining to Forina? "Leah, stuff it and get back to being a good officer. Our priority is moving to this 'safe location.' Forina, while we are on our way there, I need you to level with me on what you know. Somehow, you and Shion have an omnipotent way of gathering information, and we desperately need to tap into it."

Both Leah and Forina, without moving a muscle, moved their eyes back to me and smiled. "Do these two know each other? There's no way Leah is responsible, and Forina is a delinquent. Forina, don't corrupt Leah. She has a lot going for her."

I'm losing the ability to keep my internal monologuing to myself it seems. Actually, maybe it's Leah's playfulness that might corrupt Forina? Forina is crazy, but at least I know what drives her. "On second thought, Leah, don't corrupt Forina. Oh, never mind. Just stay the hell away from each other; I can't handle you two at the same time."

An anonymous voice piped up from the sea of soldiers surrounding us. "Elf Whisperer…"

Of course, Leah couldn't help but instigate further as she howled, "Elf Whisperer…"

Everyone was laughing, completely overshadowing the recent event. By the time it was over, Shion was even chuckling while saying it. I sighed heavily, realizing I was outmatched; there was no winning this one. At least it took my mind off hurting Shion, worrying about Marleen and the capital, and our current predicament.

I chided openly, "Alright, glad you all got that out of your system, and we are all best friends now. Leah, move us out to wherever this safe location is. Catch me up on what's been happening to you along the way."

Turning to face the rest of the troops, I returned to business. "And everyone here, help our mages. They gave everything for you bastards to still be breathing, so the least you can do is treat them with some respect. I need some volunteers to carry them with you and others to tie their horses to yours for the rest of the trip."

Everyone echoed my orders and began getting their horses off the ground and mounting back up. The location we were headed was further into the tall, dense forests of Tree Mountain. I swear each of these trees was taller than the last, with the biggest one so far behind as large as one of the keeps in the capital.

"I wonder… where did they live?" I asked aloud.

Shion mumbled, "You will find out soon enough."

According to Leah, it wasn't very far away. We formed into our single-column formation with Leah, Shion, Forina, Regar, and I riding in front. As we moved out, everyone was still chuckling about my new nickname while stealing glances at the endless, unending, skyward light beam behind us. What a hell of a night this has turned out to be so far.

As we continued to ride, Forina still hadn't 'poofed' somewhere else. This, of course, prompted my curiosity as she never sticks around for longer than thirty minutes to an hour. "Forina, can we ride ahead of the formation a little bit?"

She raised an eager eyebrow without saying a word. We moved in front of the other three just far enough so we wouldn't be overheard. "Is it safe to talk without anyone else overhearing now?"

Forina replied, "I see… this must be important to you. Is this the long-awaited confession? Are you finally giving in to your carnal desires? I haven't heard you complain about your throat in a while. Are you used to it?"

"My throat? It hasn't been hurting in a while, or at least… not since the first two days after I drank your poison. You aren't doing anything to me when I sleep, are you?" She had me panicking a bit as it dawned on me that she had baited me into asking the one thing I had avoided asking since we got together.

Looking up at the moons, she callously answered, "It looks like you have gotten used to it. They do say that a little bit of poison over time builds tolerance. In your case, a lot of poison immediately builds immunity. You get more valuable by the moment, don't you?"

I pretended to completely ignore her with my response and dodged the rest of her answer. "Why are you still with us? Why have you not disappeared? For as short of a time as I have known you, you dislike interacting socially with others. I would go so far as to call you a severe hedonist. So, what gives? I can't seem to get anyone to level with me, and it would do wonders for our partnership if you could cut the shit for a moment and give me a direct answer."

Forina looked a little troubled when she replied to me. "That light disrupted my ability to transfer my physical form to and from the plane my people live in. I still don't know how much I can disclose without talking to the elders first… but I suppose telling you that my people originate from the Void Plane couldn't hurt. That's why we get the name Void-Elves."

I nodded. "Ah, that's why she called you a 'voidling.' It makes sense. But how does she know who or what you are?"

She ignored me. "Right now, I cannot use my tools, so I am stuck here with you. That means we can break down some of those emotional barriers you put up all the time."

Forina leaned over her horse, getting extremely close to my face as she changed to a whisper. She snuck glances behind us towards someone, which made it clear she was more interested in whatever they were doing rather than listening to me prattle on about something she could care less about.

I kept trying to ignore whatever she was engrossed in but caved to look backward, causing her nose to briefly brush my cheek. As soon as I did, that was her cue to grab the back of my head. In one quick jerk, she locked our lips together. There wasn't a choice in the matter. She shoved her tongue down my throat while keeping pressure on the back of my head… almost as if to mash our bodies into one being. The initial stun didn't last long. My mind quickly wandered into less-useful territory.

Were elves' tongues always this long? Not that I had ever asked Marleen how far she could stick her tongue down my throat before, but this was ridiculous. Whatever it was she was doing with her tongue started steadily paralyzing my entire body. Within seconds, the world was splitting in two and blurring together. Like a drunken brawler, I shoved her away with my slovenly self, barely managing to get her back to her horse with my shoulder. Two head nods later, I regained my senses and began wiping off her saliva from my face.

She continued where she left off, a silent whisper in tow. "I think it's adorable how you are beginning to come around. If it's any consolation for you, that's the first time someone didn't instantly succumb to my whiles." I think she has the wrong idea about the direction in which our relationship is heading. I'll be honest and admit I'm too intimidated to speak out against her right now, though.

"What the hell did you do? I felt a pinch at the back of my throat and started to go limp." I was fiercely whispering at her. Call it… an angry whisper.

She winked at me and blew a kiss. "I'm surprised you haven't figured it out by now. My species are parasites that numb their prey before we indulge. Nobody wants their prey to escape, do they?"

Oh, she wants to play that way? I semi-jokingly gestured by running my finger across my throat. "Stop fucking with me. I already get enough of that from everyone else. Just in case you couldn't tell, I'm not in the best of moods right now." All she did was shrug in response.

That's when the jokes behind me clued me into just how much the others had seen. I had to at least make it clear where I stood with Forina, or forever, there be an endless scar on my dwindling reputation. I leaned over and muttered to Forina, "What are the chances you don't leave me high and dry like the asshole I know you are?"

She shrugged again and fell back into formation with the others. I followed suit, quickly avoiding any immediate eye contact with the others. She looked at the other three beside us and slowly licked her lips. This was war, and I was her claimed prize… what a nightmare of epic proportions. Suddenly, I went from the general in charge to the slave of some Grey Elf who was supposed to be my slave. What's more than that, this was almost entirely because she saw how close Leah and I were and just wanted to throw more turmoil into an already hectic situation. That psycho doesn't even give two shits about anyone.

I then glanced over at Leah to see what she was thinking. Leah winked at me and boldly proclaimed, "Don't worry, I won't tell Marleen. If she got wind of what just happened, that storm we just saw wouldn't match her wrath in the slightest! Turmoil and winds combine to form death from the wisest of them all! However…"

She then had her grin run out of control. "However… I bet you'll be the first human to become anything other than raw goods for a voidling; most impressive. Going from a master of a voidling to spouse of one in such a short time. Maybe there is something to that elf whisperer thing…"

I rolled my eyes at her while noticing that Shion was trying to ignore the situation altogether. Her background and her entanglements with Marleen could spell disaster for me. Between her calling Marleen a Grand Master and her familiarity with the Mage Tower, I believe she has a genuine connection to her in some way or another. Between that connection and breaking her nose earlier, I think she may have been Forina's intended target with that stunt of hers. If she holds a grudge in the slightest, it was a well-played sleight of hand... or tongue, rather. But... why? Why drive a wedge between the others, especially Marleen and me?

Since I didn't respond to her, Leah put her face near the harness of her horse to look directly up at me. "It's not like you to stay silent when being poked at. What gives? It's all in good fun."

She snapped me out of my daze. My hand went to my face, and I realized I was frowning far past my usual resting face. "I was just thinking about a long-standing tradition within Alvernia. You know, the one where nobles and those of significant influence try to get with as many women as possible."

Leah snapped her fingers. "Oh yeah, I know the one. Belt-notching or some such childish game. It's the one that the soldiers place bets on... like their commanding officer versus others. The winning team takes the other's money, gets time with their women, or something of the sort? Are you perhaps... thinking of particip..."

There was no completing that sentence for her. "No, and get that out of your head. You know I'll always be loyal to Marleen, come demons or high water. I was thinking that what Forina did could easily be misconstrued by anyone else who got an eyeshot of it. The unsightly feuds that erupt between soldiers from that stupid contest can get out of hand quickly. Not to mention the damage to Marleen's honor."

She burst out laughing. "Leave it to you to worry about someone else's 'honor'. That woman will be fine. Sure, she has chronic anxiety issues when it comes to your safety, but that wouldn't phase her, no matter who reported it."

I raised my eyebrow. "And how would you know? Have you had something similar happen between you and someone else?"

She couldn't help herself. She fell back and slapped her horse. "Me? With someone? Surely you jest! Humans and their wild imaginations. When was the last time you heard about a vampire engaging in romantic endeavors?"

"Never, but then again, you aren't like a normal vampire. You have... clear emotions." I was looking her dead in the eyes. She didn't flinch, and her laughing stopped.

Slowly, the air from her laughing boiled over and caused her to erupt again. "Well, you have me there. No, nobody bets on a vampire in those games. The only woman to ever win one was... well, you know. The undefeated champion herself. Nobody could bed people as fast as she did, and she won her troops a lot of money... or so the rumors go."

She was talking about Laura. Some may behave like that, and it's possible Laura does as well, but I've never personally seen her engage in those competitions. No, Leah was probably right, and I have no leg to stand on if I tried to defend her. I've seen Laura go crazy many times over, and she often brags about how many men she has bagged.

Laura was an absolute savage when it came to our relationship, but to this day, she has never openly told anyone about it herself. With her possessiveness, she once made me feel like a trophy to be hung on a wall. That one piece of the puzzle is what doesn't fit. Why brag so vehemently in the presence of so many people but keep our coupling so close to the chest? Either way, it was entirely because of her that I abhor things like infidelity, multiple wives or husbands, rape, or even trophy hunting of the opposite species.

Leah's more in tune with how this conversation affected me than she lets on. She quickly changed the topic. "Anyway... we aren't far away from our target location. Don't let yourself get too worried about nonsense. It's the small stuff that will eat you up if you let it. How about this to put your mind at ease? There isn't anything scurrying around in the dark anywhere around us right now. Not a critter to be heard or a demon to be smelled."

I scoffed, "Gloating about not smelling demons. How... human... of you."

Unexpectedly, Leah flinched when I said that. It was so subtle that it was hard to notice, but I definitely saw it. The quick action seemed to have been met by a hidden reaction as if he had been provoked and suppressed at the same time.

Leah reached out her right hand and curled her fingers back towards her. "You know how to make a woman in red blush. That is… until you hear about my unit becoming a liability due to running out of provisions."

I half-heartedly smiled. "How long do you have until it turns into a problem?"

She grinned. "Not anytime soon. We can address that issue later; keep it on your priority list… one human… to another. More importantly, we are about to enter the Ancient Elven Ruins in the Ancestral Green Elven lands. Do you or anyone else know anything about this area? Maybe your pretty black-robed woodling friend over there?"

I could tell Forina knew something, but she kept quiet. It seems she will only speak to me and refuses to converse with others unless necessary. Instead, Shion spoke up. "I know my ancestors lived underground. Or, more specifically, our origin race, the Foregone Antecedents. I also know they were killed quickly when the Ancient Miasma Disaster occurred, but I don't know the specifics. While it's true that the progeny of the Foregone Antecedents, my people you call 'Green Elves' or 'woodlings,' originated from this forest, they also had many colonies and cities in the north where Elvania is now."

Leah replied, "How adorable. She breaks it down so you can understand every detail, Raider. She's a keeper for sure."

"Leah…" I sighed in disappointment. "Never mind. Shion, why would your entire 'origin race' only settle in one area? Isn't that asking for extinction if something happens… you know… like it did."

She was quick in her clarification. "That much is well known. Even the vampires know just how strong their affinity was with the earth here. Their ties with earth magic were amplified to an abnormal level, making them practically untouchable by anyone who wished them harm. In this forest, they were the masters, the creators, and…"

Leah interrupted, "They were foolish. But enough about the past. It seems you know more about this area than we learned over the last several days. To fill in the gaps, several very large trees are carved or hollowed out. They go downwards into a set of tunnels made from the tree's roots."

Forina mocked her under her breath. "A bloodsucker doing reconnaissance? What a joke."

Leah ignored her. "Our Forward Observers spent a lot of time cloaking themselves and moving in and out to gain some understanding of the tunnel's layouts. In a nutshell, they blend together to create an enormously elaborate labyrinth. Why? Because every tree has roots, and those roots intersect with each other to create consistent passageways."

Forina mocked her again. "Imagine that… huge trees with huge roots make for passageways big enough to allow people to live there."

This time, Leah didn't ignore her. "More than that… the space was big enough to house entire cities. Although a lot of ones we tried navigating were collapsed or grown over, one of them led to an ancient city larger than half of Fort Midgard."

I also intervened, admonishing Forina in the process. "Forina, please cut the shit. Leah, so there are passageways or hidden chambers that lead to large cities that used to house these elves. What about the miasma that flooded the caves or the demons that have been able to reside here since that disaster?"

Forina replied while tossing her dagger up and down. "You're more concerned with weak demons than the immense ruined metropolis beneath your feet? Why aren't you thinking about treasure like a good human? Become greedier, or it makes me feel guilty."

Leah's eyes rotated from Forina back to me. "We don't know. Demons are present, but no miasma for the first few levels we have gone down. Perhaps… perhaps it's more accurate to say there is very little miasma. It still exists in the roots, but not enough to cause disorientation or death, even when exposed for extended durations."

Forina cut her off again. "Reading between the Blood Princesses' half-truths a little, she is telling you that is what happens when her kind are exposed, not humans."

Finally, Forina hit Leah's nerves. "I was getting to that. It should be safe for humans as well. If it isn't, we can make camp outside in a safe location."

We finally arrived, the first of many trees that Leah had investigated. "Leah, that… that… is… a big fucking tree."

Chapter 20: Lightfall Part III

Leah was humming happily, practically performing the waltz on her horse. "This is one of the trees with the ramp. The tree and the ramp are on the smaller side of the ones we have found around this area, but they are also much safer."

We briefly stopped just outside of the small clearing in front of our target. Leah and I dismounted and unrolled a map she handed me on the ground. This was an area reconnaissance map that had been marked with X's where she had found trees with entrances into the underground labyrinth. The largest tree near us had an 'X' with a circle around it. There were also several arrows pointing to and from it to indicate enemy movement patterns. Elegant proof of intelligence if I've ever seen one.

Leah pointed to several spots. "These are the known entryways into the underground city. We don't know if they are connected, but it's highly probable. We know for sure this one, this one, and this one are all connected. However, two of them have most of their passageways between them collapsed, making both the ideal target to post up shop and wait for our mages to recover. This one to the right is where we are located right now. If we are to make a move, that is the one we should utilize."

"And what about this one?" I pointed to the large X with a circle around it.

She replied, "That is the one we want to avoid the most. That is their nest."

I asked, "A demonic... nest?"

She smiled. "I assume by now you have as many questions as I do about the organized demonic attacks. What if I told you we located the puppet master working these marionettes?"

I replied, "It's hard to understand... although I had my suspicions. Looking at it objectively, there aren't any other possible explanations. I also think you're enjoying this too much. Can you at least try to hide your humming? Are you into this as part of some sick fetish of yours?"

Leah sang, "Beeee-cauusee... myyyyy blooooood... loooongggss foooorrr YoooOUuuuUuUuUUUUUU!"

My eyes drooped. "Are you trying to pull the demons over here, or are you trying to wake the dead?"

She cleared her throat when she realized I wasn't entertained. "Fine, fine. The one controlling the low-grade demons must use an artifact to do it. But this artifact must be putting a tremendous amount of strain on their body. There isn't any race that could withstand the kind of magical energy throughput that bad boy would have to be putting out. Not to mention, if the artifact puts even a quarter of the magical strain as mental strain on its wielder, it could turn them into a vegetable. Isn't it exciting to think about what else they could do?"

"Like..." I paused. "Kill all of us and rip our bodies apart?"

She cheered, "Exactly! With enough focus, they might even be able to kill all of us! Or at least that would have been the case without my big, strong, handsome human knight here to rescue me!" Her mood had turned into an odd mix of pouting and excitement.

I rhetorically asked, "Leah, people are dying. Do you not get that?"

She turned more into her pouting side. "People die all the time; what's the big deal? It's not like I want more people to die; it's just that some sacrifices must be made to understand more about this world. If you keep holding onto that sentimentality of yours, it will burn you alive one day. Not a great trait to own as a 'General of the Eastern Front.'"

I couldn't tell if that response was Marleen's or Forina's. All three of them think alike when it comes to getting what they want. Each is willing to sacrifice something important, such as life or freedom, to reach their goals. Am I the only one still holding on to my useless sense of justice for the common person? Morality can be a tricky thing to navigate, especially across cultures.

I shook my head. "You may have an unusually positive disposition for a vampire, but your views on death and sacrifice differ from mine."

She chided me with that glare of hers. "Just yours. Most humans are... cunningly ruthless."

My nervous chuckle turned the conversation around. "Well, at least all the pieces are beginning to fall into place. Someone got ahold of a lost artifact that almost nobody knows about and is testing its powers. Moreover, this person, or people, has a deep connection rooted in our military… enough so that they can coordinate sabotage efforts with this relic's power. Is there any doubt that this had to be the efforts of another country?"

Forina added, "Efforts of another country, huh? And since when do you know humans or elves that can survive out here? Did they suddenly grow immune to miasma while I wasn't looking?"

"That's true…" I mumbled. "Then what else? Demons that think and understand military tactics infiltrated our defensive line and can operate artifacts we hardly understand ourselves?"

Forina, still mounted on her horse, leaned over and patted my head. "We have a clever one here. It only took giving you everything but the answer."

Leah interrupted. "Right, that's enough speculation. Let's get back to our immediate needs before solving all the deep, dark, mysterious problems of Genesis by ourselves."

I agreed. "We need to secure ourselves first. Let's head to the smaller tree as Leah suggested."

Our column could head up the large, curvy ramp leading into the tree without problems. When we got there, the entirety of the tree was hollowed out except for the walls and the wide-open middle area. In its center, it had a spiral staircase cut out from the bark along its edges. Some parts of the ramp leading down had handrails, but mostly, it was a dead fall into the pitch-black abyss if you happened to make a misstep. Aside from the black center, there was a bluish-green neon hue under the seemingly endless staircase a few flights down. Noting my hesitation to descend, Leah reassured me that this was safe. Each section started to move out, one squad at a time.

Leah, still annoyingly humming, decided to grace us with her knowledge. "It will take us a while to get to where we are going. I forgot to mention that there are enormous larvae here that glow brightly in regular cycles. Whenever the sun is up, the larvae will become dormant, and the glow will eventually fade. And when the sun goes down, the glow will steadily increase until you see that illuminated blue-green hue below. This unique cycle may also be why Green Elves prefer to stay awake at night and sleep during the day, unlike the other elf species. It may also explain why their skin is a light shade of purple."

Shion replied in a melancholy tone, clearly displeased we were talking about Green Elves as if she wasn't here. "I've heard or read a book about these larvae before. Their cycles are directly connected to the tree absorbing the light during the day; then, the larvae absorb the nutrients produced through the roots at night. This cycle happens in tandem with each other every day. Nothing else quite like this exists in Alvernia… it's peculiar that they can even survive the thick miasma that usually fills this place."

"I can see the wheels turning. What is it now, Raider?" Leah asked.

What gave it away? My hand on my chin or my eyes looking at the ground? "Yeah, I was just wondering… now that the miasma is gone from here, this place will be a hotspot for mercenaries from every nation looking to find money and goods. All walks of life will be looking to contest everything from the treasures buried in here to the strongholds to increase their influence and power."

Leah playfully sighed, "Yeah, that's just like you humans. How about we beat them to the punch and make a mercenary group called the 'Woodling Tomb Robbers'?"

Forina rolled her eyes. "Vampires forming mercenary groups with humans? What's next, turning on your colony too?"

I questioned, "Colony?"

Forina pressed, "Yeah, vampires are like ants. They form colonies around centralized…"

Leah nervously laughed, "She is just kidding. You know, a joke…"

Forina replied, "No, I'm not, and you know it."

Forina spiraled me to anger again. "Forina, stop picking fights for once in your life. Both you and Leah don't seem to understand this isn't some joy-riding vacation. There are real concerns here and real questions that need to be answered. Both of you seem to be in the mindset of not giving a crap. And even if you don't, can you at least pretend to while I'm around you? I'm over here concerned we won't make it through the night, and you want to rip her throat out."

"Is that an order, 'master'?" She smirked. "Ripping her throat out wouldn't be a bad idea while she is alone." Both of them were blowing me off in their own way.

Changing the topic back again, I asked, "Leah, how long is this damn thing? We have been riding down for the better part of ten minutes and not a single corridor."

She replied while still eyeing Forina. "Isn't that because we are going in by squad? You're the one who wanted caution when this ramp could easily hold thirty across. Just look how long our column is behind us!"

I clarified, "What I mean is... shouldn't we at least have come by a guard post or a hovel or something? There wasn't anything on the surface either. Wouldn't these elves want a checkpoint in and out of the city like humans do at castle gates?"

Leah nodded. "Being a bit optimistic... given these ruins haven't been inhabited in a long time, aren't you? Anything built on the surface, and probably the initial guard stations, have all but been overgrown by the roots or destroyed. Anyway, there are a few outlets dead ahead. One leads to the city I spoke of that could have housed tens of thousands of citizens, while the one right before it looks like an old military barracks of sorts."

She continued without much of a pause. "My scouts think it might have been the main housing facility for any old guard posts near the city's entrance. So, it's like what you were looking for, only better."

"Is..." I started to ask but stopped when her eyes rolled over to meet mine.

Leah smiled when I cut my own question short. "To preemptively answer your question... no, we couldn't even get close to this city to investigate. We found so many mixed species of lesser demons wandering near the entryway. Attempting to enter with any less than three or four hundred soldiers would have been suicide. The demons still have some uncanny attachment to this area, even after the miasma disappeared. My best guess? The roots have absorbed a decent amount of that poison, and that attracts them."

Forina added, "A much more obvious answer would be that miasma is still down in the deeper levels. The ones on the upper floors might just be trapped."

I could see Leah's eyebrow twitching as Forina slowly chipped away at her emotional armor. "Yes, that is also a possibility, and that's why we were investigating this area further, aside from finding and killing whoever has the artifact."

I pondered further. "Leah, I've been meaning to ask. Did you know the miasma was disappearing from this area before or after everything started happening?"

Her smile reappeared. "Much like you, we only learned about the vanishing miasma once we arrived. Until recently, the miasma extended well beyond the boundaries of Tree Mountain. We were caught completely by surprise when we started investigating the demon attacks and found out they were coming from this area, which was relatively clean. That is why we are here now... dispelling the mysteries behind the dark death cloud. Demon-controlling artifact, vanishing miasma, sabotage... no matter how you look at it, this is the place to be in such troubling times. Don't worry, Leah has it under control!" That last sentence of hers was done in the most teenage girlish voice possible.

"How many times will you get me to roll my eyes at you tonight? Don't refer to yourself in a cutesy voice... or in the third person. So, what do you make of the miasma disappearing from the area?" She can't ever just be normal, can she?

Leah replied, "No clue. Just as the Ancient Miasma Disaster is a complete mystery, so is its undoing. Powerful magic? Maybe the opposite... the magic is subsiding? Wait, no... we don't even know if it was magic. Truthfully, I am at an impasse. It could even be an artifact for all I know."

This time, I couldn't hide my instant facial expression. "You really just glossed over something that important? Rewind your insanity for a moment. If your assumptions are true, finding the miasma-clearing artifact, spell, or whatever it is will be more important than anything else."

Forina yawned, "And why is that? Too weak to deal with a little miasma? Typical humans."

I angrily replied, "We could use that to solidify peace with every other nation! Don't give me that shit. Think about peace between all nations because there is no external threat! We could see an era of prosperity that has never existed before!"

Leah and Forina both replied, "Naiveté."

"Huh?" I asked.

Forina slouched over on her horse and told Leah to explain it. "Raider, darling, there is relative peace because the Unknown Territory and the demons exist. If you recover an artifact that can clear or produce miasma… conflict will only increase. External threats have held the balance of power for the last thousand years."

This was something I vehemently disagreed with. "You can't be serious. There's no evidence to back that up in the slightest. If we weren't having to spend all our budget, time, and effort defending from the demons… then…"

Forina callously interjected, "Then, what? People will just redirect it toward one another. That woman you're so fond of… people like her would research ways to kill each other faster. Every walk of life finds a way to exclude others. Intelligence, location, money, women, breeding, hair color, species, you name it. One day, someone will tell you about the history you are oblivious to. The wars that might follow from the Hero Summoning Ritual might already be coming. That's why you are naive."

Leah quickly nodded before she jerked her head. "Hero Summoning… what now?"

I put my hand up. "Hold it. Let's shelve the hero-summoning question for a moment. That will only put you in a bad mood, and Forina has done that enough by herself."

She put on a pouty face. "Then how about my reward? You know what I want, and you owe me for last time… and the time before that… and…"

I sighed, "Stop, already. I know where you're going. But why bring up saving me from those asshole nobles now of all times? And I already paid you for the dance that one time, and the audience with the Council of Nobles… so it's just the time at the arena. And can't you collect later, we are on a mission and in the middle of nowhere."

Leah insisted, "You are forgetting the last time you came to Midgard and the time you went hunting with Prince Wilhelm and Prince Karl…"

I gave in with a sad nod, which made her very chipper. "Hurray! Besides, I can smell the voidling in you, and I don't mean from earlier. It's only fair… that, or you can try going out with me instead of Marleen to pay for all your debts. Well, I wouldn't even mind if I was the second woman, just because I know how attached you can get. You know we would be a good team."

Chiding her half-seriously, my speech turned playful. "You want to be my second wife as a reward? That smirk on your face isn't taking into account how much I am against multi-partnership marriages, as it stands for everything I hate about the nobility. Oh man... and if Marleen got a hold of what you just said, there would be tactical-class meteor showers across the continent. Can't I just pay in blood like usual? I'd really like to avoid setting up rotating days between you and Marleen."

She continued to fool around. "Oh? Is that because vampires are infertile, and you want little humans running around? Elves aren't much better. Although it's hard for them to get pregnant, it's still possible. You know, if you two have a kid, it will be an elf, right? Not that you're that shallow. If you want kids that badly, we could make something work."

Leah was complimenting her stupid smile with that ridiculously irritatingly positive hum of hers. "Too bad I know you're not serious. And even if you were, I don't share. I'm the queen bee in this hive, and you willingly flew into my territory. That means you adhere to my values, my rules, and my justice... not some random White Elves's whims and desires."

"Hold up... you're the one who..." I stopped. This wasn't a battle worth fighting.

She laughed, "Besides, you seem to forget we already sealed our pact the first time we met; this is just putting it into words."

Forina added, "Queen bee, my ass... more like an ant. Sometimes, I miss the old vampires. Hell-bent on destruction and killing. Those were my kind of adversaries."

I have no idea what either of them were talking about. Leah might be talking about the first time we met. She first ambushed me and damn near sucked me dry. There isn't even such a thing as a 'pact' with vampires unless you go through the official ritual to convert. Her playing goes too far sometimes, but her eyes never left me the entire time she was speaking. Now, there is just a long silence, and she continues to shatter my will with her leering.

Shion cleared her throat. "So, are we almost there? Weren't we discussing demons and the fort we were headed towards?"

I started sweating, thinking Leah might be serious for a moment because of that tone and posture. It made me desperate to capitalize on Shion's redirection... but Forina beat me to it. "Vampire bee... whatever you are... what exactly have you encountered here? Please don't tell me it's just the usual demonic wolves, rabbits, foxes, bears, and other small game because those are just jokes with a bad attitude."

Shion replied, "They become considerably stronger and faster when they convert, though... so that isn't fair."

Leah agreed. "I've personally seen a rabbit rip three humans, so the adorable woodling isn't wrong. But yes, once we got to the tree city, we saw miasma-infected creatures we had never seen before. I'm sure 'punch me two times,' broken nose, and a little adorable woodling over there can attest to some of these creatures being written in books. Minotaurs, treants, chimeras, wyverns, and a type of hostile goblin are all beings we have seen around here. The real winner came when we saw a huge humanoid with horns walking around. It probably had full autonomy, too."

Shion felt slighted. "Hey, now!"

Forina's temperament flared up when she passionately snarled, "To hell with your horned whatever... there were goblins? What did they look like? Did they have eyes like me? Did they communicate with each other? What weapons did they have?"

Leah replied, "Calm down, calm down, don't get your pretty white hair all ruffled. These were low-grade goblins; there was nothing abnormal about them. It is odd how adaptable those things are to their environment, though. Swamps... mountains... miasma... Raider's bedchamber... you name it, they can survive in it, I'm sure."

Forina looked somewhat relaxed as she focused her attention ahead of us. That was the first time I had seen her get that riled up. Here I am, hearing about a potential 'miasma-wyvern' and 'thinking demons' as the worst-case scenario. Meanwhile, Forina freaks out over... goblins? Are goblin's an eternal nemesis to the Void-Elves?

"Leah, can you talk more about the demon displaying signs of intelligence? The one with the horns?" I still couldn't believe what I was hearing.

This is more confirmation that supports what Alex was saying about those who invaded his tribe all those years ago. Something was infected with miasma while retaining its ability to think and reason. Fighting something of that level would rival that of the vampires. No, it would dwarf fighting someone of the vampires' level. Utilizing the power the miasma gives them without becoming completely corrupted and then waging war on others who aren't infected... baffles the mind. It isn't, or shouldn't, be possible.

We finally arrived at the first inlet and headed to the first corridor. Leah signaled for everyone to stop. "Don't worry about sending in your scouts; my observers are still here."

Leah slightly elevated her voice while projecting it into the corridor. "Twenty-Seven, present yourself. Don't keep me waiting all day."

A cloaked individual appeared out of the shadows and kneeled before her. Leah demounted and stepped forward, and they whispered something back and forth. She told the rest of us, "The area ahead is secure, but we will rest here now and send out our scouts in the morning. With all the commotion upstairs, who knows what might happen."

Leah then looked back at the cloaked figure and told them, "Gather all the remaining Reapers in the area and have them set up a parameter. I want to know if so, much as a leaf sprouts from one of these roots."

The cloaked figure replied, "Reaper's Obey." They didn't stay long before stepping back into the shadows from which they came. Leah then signaled us to move forward and begin setting up our forward operating base. When we passed through the corridor, we entered a very wide area. Was it supposed to be a military outpost? It's more like a small city by human standards. Leah's original description didn't do this place justice at all.

The overall space was very cylindrical, with glowing larvae all over the ceiling and walls. There was an area that looked like an old-style stable on the immediate right of the entryway. The primary barracks were against the back wall and occupied most of the space provided. Aside from the stable and the barracks, there wasn't much to see.

Even after all this time being vacant, there was hardly any overgrowth or damage to the structures here. With the sheer size comparison, I could easily have fit the entire Midgard barracks and half of the keep in here with adequate room to spare. The only issue I could see with the design was the ventilation. However, that had to be the last thing on these elves' minds when they lived here because, you know, trees inherently allow you to breathe. But with a single major passageway leading in, it seemed like a major deathtrap. It's always the little things that get you in the end. There's no way they could have seen that leading to mass suffocation from a previously unknown substance flooding their homes like it did.

The pinnacle civilization of the ancient world... eradicated overnight. Tough luck for them, but it's hard to prepare an exit strategy for everything. As for the barracks structure, it was almost identical to the style we use. Thousands of years later, we aren't all that much different. How unlikely of a coincidence is this? It was three stories tall, and the bottom floor bordered what would be an officer's living quarters and recreational room. I didn't even have to explore it to know how most of it was laid out just by the outside architecture. It's almost a letdown, as I thought there would be some unique grand Elvish design like what they apparently have in Elvania. It seems these Green Elves had a much less extravagantly haughty lifestyle.

The rest of us dismounted and left our horses in the stable area. We continued to wander around, looking at both buildings in greater detail. There appears to have been a gate and two small watchtowers near the entrance. It's easy to tell because of how the roots overtook and collapsed what used to be a structure made from this tree's bark. Leah, Forina, Shion, Lacia, and I headed into the officer's area and some form of a council room.

"While Regar is out there supervising our defense, we may as well make this our home for now. It's hard to imagine a more secure room than this one anywhere around this creepy, deserted place. Lacia, I brought you here because I trust you and want you to pick out two or three others you think are trustworthy to help guard us while we sleep." I also wanted us to establish a chain of command as soon as we got the chance... and Leah seems to have picked up on it.

Lacia quickly agreed and left to find others to secure their gear with ours. She was also instructed not to let anyone near the inside of the council room so that we could have a private conversation.

Leah chided, "Trying to hold back that unrelenting yawn? Want to sleep on my lap like last time?"

While we were still unloading our equipment, I remembered Leah had mentioned a critical supply shortage earlier. "I thought we agreed not to mention that again. Anyway, you said there were pressing matters regarding supplies with your troops. It wouldn't take a genius to realize you are all probably short of blood and need to be restocked, am I right?"

Leah responded, "Yeah, you guessed it. Without a resupply shortly, we are no better than humans with an insatiable appetite for blood. We have all the drawbacks of vampirism and none of the benefits. Our blood supply ran out a while ago."

I laughed, "For a two-day trip? That isn't like you."

She looked unamused. "It has more to do with our cravings shooting through the roof since coming to Unknown Territory. It's a side effect of being in an area with a high concentration of miasma for so long. While we have resistance to it to some degree... we also have adverse reactions to it as well. More things are linked in this world than one might realize, right voidling? I get the feeling your people might not be so different... from mine..."

Forina snapped, "Leave me out of your delusions. We are nothing like you bloodsuckers."

Leah had that bright smile on her face when she responded. "Oh, really? Funny how your 'abilities' don't work on us. I wonder why that is. Raider, you see, our species interactions go way, way back." At this point, I asked myself how Leah knew about Forina's abilities or her people and where they come from. They have danced around the conversation a few times but never told me anything.

"I only jest, I have nothing against you and hold no ill will for what happened between our ancestors. You are safe as long as you are with me, but... don't wander too far away, or who knows what trouble you might stir up." She was directly challenging Forina.

Forina laughed, "Miss Blood Princess! You seem to have a grave misunderstanding about our situation. It was our people that let you 'escape' and continue your progeny when we had one of your last queens in our possession. You're always within our grasp, merely playing out your part as we have allowed you to. You may talk a big game, but once one of our elders marks you for retirement, you won't be as fortunate."

I interjected, "I get it. both of you relax. How is this feud relevant to our current predicament? At least tolerate each other until we can solve some of our problems… then I don't care what you do. Forina, I would prefer it if you didn't try to assassinate one of my best captains. Leah, I would prefer it if you didn't piss off the psycho elf following me around and murdering indiscriminately."

Leah sighed, "It's a shame, really. If you want to know, I banked on your swift arrival and your cunning after I had to leave Midgard. And I must say, you didn't disappoint. However, your mediation skills need some work, dear. And since you're so adamant, can we resume talks about how to keep my soldiers from going feral? We must set up daily blood donors to combat the increased desire burdening us. I recommend we move fast, too… before some of us start showing signs of deterioration."

I know she wouldn't let harm come to other vampires unless there was no choice. Every time I saw her in a crowd, she looked like a mother doting on her children. The ever-caring parent attempting to prevent the kids from causing mayhem amongst her friends. She would have made a good mother.

I yelled for Lacia. When she entered, I told her, "Go and find Regar. Tell him to get blood donors lined up. Long story I can't go into, but we need every vampire partnered with a human for a constant blood supply. This whole area increases their hunger, and we can't exactly leave right now. I know it's unusual, but we don't have vials. That means any human volunteers must be directly bitten. If nobody volunteers, I'll feed them all myself until I run dry." She acknowledged me and took off. I do feel bad using her as a messenger, but she's a big girl and must put her time in like everyone else. Despite my slight prejudice towards mages, I wish I had several more like her.

Leaning back on my gear and getting comfortable, I muttered, "Does that address all your concerns? I guarantee the increased hunger won't be an issue with as many soldiers as we currently have. I would love to hear Shion's story now if both of you are satisfied."

"You spoil me. But you know, I need to be fed, too." I didn't see it, but I know Leah was looking at Forina when she said that.

After I let out a sigh, I reluctantly replied, "It wouldn't be the first time. I dare you to keep quarreling with Forina. Your punishment will be having to feed on the nastiest, scummiest, most unclean soldier I can find. At a minimum, they won't have had a bath in a month."

Forina interrupted, "Don't worry, Blood Princess. The difference between you and me is why we need him. You need him as a blood bank for your precious swarm. However, I know his true worth. You can smell it on him, even now… can't you? I know I can. It's gotten more intense since the light beam hit earlier, which caused severe mana fluctuations. But how long will you conceal it from him, I wonder? Will he stay by your side when he finds out?"

I'm done getting in the middle of those two. Leah becoming possessive makes sense because of her cravings and our past relationship, but Forina's insanity knows no bounds. I bet there are times that psycho doesn't even know what comes out of her mouth. With those two at each other's throats, I must try and mend things with Shion, or all of us will be at odds. The only way for us to survive is to get answers out of Shion. However, to thrive, we need to use her knowledge to get those artifacts for Alvernia's future.

Chapter 21: The Dark Marble

Inside, what I am sure are roots as hard as concrete, sit Forina, Shion, Leah, and me on the cold hard ground. Each of us has posted up in the corner of a room no bigger than one that could hold a table to seat ten. There are two entryways into here. One of them leads directly into the main hallway across from the officer's quarters, and one leads out back to a very small courtyard that has nothing in it aside from the root walls.

The four of us stared at each other for the better part of two minutes without saying a word. Eventually, I got tired of counting the cracks in the walls and floor between the tightly woven roots. "A lot has sidetracked us since we got here. Not that it's your fault, Shion, but don't you think it's time for you to spill it? At face value, you set out to save our lives earlier. But I'm no stranger to betrayal, and too much about you is offsetting to just let slide. How could you possibly know the things you know?"

Shion was already smoking her pipe in the corner, fully anticipating this was coming her way. After calling on her, we all continued to sit silently for several more minutes until she started pacing back and forth from her corner to mine. It's a damn good thing she decided to move… Forina was obviously getting antsy. With each passing second, I could feel the anger welling up inside her like a hot iron getting ready to be struck by a blacksmith.

To the rest of us, it was clear that Shion was trying to decide how to methodically explain what she knew without disclosing things she shouldn't. In that regard, she is just like Forina, trying not to disclose anything that might cause problems later. Shion's biggest hurdle would be relaying her intent and the relevant information while keeping us satisfied without digging herself further into a hole.

Truth be told, I also don't know why she even cares about what we are attempting to accomplish out here aside from trying to study things. Couldn't she go back to Elvania if Alvernia falls? The Elvanian Republic would accept any elf, regardless of circumstances, unless she were excommunicated for some reason. But to me, she didn't seem like someone who would have crossed a line like that.

She continued to pick up her pace, and that's when I noticed she had a way of fidgeting with her hair when she got nervous. One hand was on her pipe, and the other was in her green bangs, while the rest of it was kept up in a ponytail. I suppose I haven't paid enough attention to her habits since we met. Right now, all of her 'tells' were expressing a level of uncertainty and uneasiness in her upcoming explanation. The longer this continued, the more impatient Forina got and the more nervous I became.

There was a yawn that had been building up in my system for a while. I let it out by mistake. When she stopped, I rolled my eyes. "Come on already. Humans don't live as long as you do, and we still have shit to do. If all you're going to be doing is pacing around, I'd rather get some sleep."

Shion took a deep breath, slightly hesitating, before she spoke. "Ok... ok... let me first say that the Grand Mage herself theorized everything I am about to discuss. If anything, I am merely a scribe wanting to follow in her footsteps. Let's start with Genesis and the theory of Dark Magic or Dark Magical Affinity."

The thud of Forina's head hitting the wall interrupted her. "Why start there, woodling? This is going to take all night. Just let me kill her instead. She's proving to be useless."

Biting my tongue, I tempered my response. "Forina, let her start where she wants. Continue, Shion."

She went back to pacing and smoking her pipe. "Has anyone ever thought about why Dark Magic exists? What about its opposite, Light Magic? Every element has a counter to it except for Dark Magic. The counter to fire is water, the counter to water is earth, earth is wind, wind is fire. However, almost all elements can also be combined to form powerful spells such as a 'Fire Tornado' or a 'Mudslide'. In this case, the elements can also supplement each other. But... nothing complements or counters Dark Magic."

Leah asked, "What's your point? Are you saying this 'light' magic can combine with or cancel out Dark Magic? That doesn't make any sense. Dark Magic is the strongest element; everyone knows that. It's also why we are the strongest race... because we all have the dark elemental affinity."

Shion nodded and continued, "Right, so... why was Light Magic the only one left out? Also, since you brought it up, why is Dark Magic the only unrivaled affinity? And why is it the only affinity that both demons and vampires have naturally? The Grand Mage thinks that is

Her response this time seemed rushed, as if she was grasping at straws. "Stay with me for a little bit longer, and you will understand why it matters. The Grand Mage thinks that our world is one of the worlds that is severely on the dark side. In the bag of marbles example, we would be on the very bottom of the bag or close to it. This is what caused the miasma to be able to exist in the first place. And, as a byproduct, the Unknown Territory, demons, and vampires also exist... all from the same origin. This means that in a less dark-weighted world, those entities wouldn't be able to exist, or they would die almost immediately."

I got impatient. "I get it... Light Magic doesn't exist because this world is too 'dark'... but what about..."

She interrupted me. "...this also means that you could see light-aligned beings, whatever those are, on other worlds. And, like I said, it's not that the light element doesn't exist here in Genesis. We think it is 'suppressed' or 'overwhelmed' to the point of being unable to manifest. If it was truly absent, I doubt we could see the sun during the day. Now, if our world shifted its location in the bag of marbles, or if, let's say, light energy was to be forcibly pulled into our world..."

Forina murmured something along the lines of, "Fucking angels..."

Leah's restraint became unbearable for her to handle. She tried to get the words out as she held back her laughter. "The woodling is saying that the King and your precious Marleen have invited doom to us all, isn't she? Oh, this is too good to let go. Top that off with her suggesting that demons and vampires are essentially the same; this can't get any better."

"Leah, I'm sure you figured it out by now..." I stopped before I could finish.

She walked over and hugged me by putting her arms around my neck. "I'm sorry, Raider. I had an inkling before you even let it slip back outside. I've known what those two were up to for some time. I'm just... so sorry you have to go through this... and I know you tried your best to reason with them, those damn jackals."

I whispered back, "Yeah... some battles you can't win. But why apologize to me? You and the rest of the vampires are the ones that are going to hurt the most if they have already succeeded with the summoning. This... being... this 'Hero'... will more than likely want to because our world, Genesis, has its own affinity towards the dark element. So much so that the light element is essentially snuffed out. Meaning we can't see, use, or feel its presence like we can the other elements."

Why is it that only Leah and Shion are engaged? Forina has all but tuned out. Shion wrapped up her thoughts. "And stay with me here... if a world can have an affinity, it must also have something to balance it out, just like each element. What's there to stop other worlds from existing that are aligned with the light element?"

I pondered out loud, "Worlds that naturally balance each other out and create a stabilizing harmony with each other? As intriguing as this is, why do we care? This seems like pure speculation."

Shion started embellishing her nervous hand gestures with a side of fidgeting. "We already know other worlds exist because of the past hero summoning, or did you forget that happened? That giant light beam... that was the light element. Light Magic."

She looked at me for physical confirmation of it dawning on me before she elaborated. "So instead of thinking of our world as its own entity, how about we start to think about it in terms of its connection to other parallel worlds? I like to think of it as a bag full of marbles where the marbles on top are light-leaning, and the ones on the bottom are dark-leaning. However, in the end, they all balance each other out inside the bag. That is what maintains balance on the cosmic scale. And this would simultaneously explain why all the other elements are much weaker compared to the dark element."

I questioned, "Is all of this coming to a point? I can follow the general concept of these theories, but again, why do we care? Your general point is that there is this cosmic scale of sorts, and each world has some 'weight' of dark or light magical affinity. This is done so your... bag... doesn't become unbalanced. We are on the dark side of this scale, and this has the consequence of having vampires and demons. Is your point to suggest that not only do light worlds exist, but they are connected or paired with dark worlds? Or is it that light worlds have a light-aligned subspecies to replace vampires and demons? Also, none of this explains the complete absence of light magic. Shouldn't someone be able to use it, if even a little bit?"

eradicate anything aligned with the dark element... if what Shion says is true."

Shion broke the mood. "Ahem... you're jumping to extreme conclusions. Why does one element balancing another element out make them natural enemies? Just like other elements, they can probably complement each other if used correctly. Look at it another way... to keep our world from being overrun by demons, vampires allied themselves with races and beings without a natural dark affinity. Who is to say that the same can't happen between the summoned entity aligned with the light element and a being of the dark element native to Genesis?"

She took a puff from her pipe before adding, "Besides, every being that thinks can think for itself. That means they could be summoned and go against the summoner's wishes. Wasn't this what you feared originally, Raider? Personally, I think this was Leah's way to make a move at you."

Leah's arms relaxed around my neck, and I fell back to her side. "Fair play is good play. Don't be jealous; it doesn't suit your pretty face."

"Stop it, you two... hold on. How did you know that's what I said?" I questioned.

Shion quickly looked away, reluctant to answer me. Forina was again visibly pissed, but I didn't understand why. None of this had anything to do with her... unless... her power, tools, or whatever she uses, being sealed by the light earlier means she is also intimately connected to the dark element. "This theory is why I hate woodlings. They don't know shit and talk a big game. It's not a very populous species, but it's an annoying one, nonetheless. You have circumstantial evidence at best and none at worst. Multiple worlds, fine... I know that's true. But ones designed for specific elements? And we still haven't heard about why we should give a damn about anything you are saying."

Shion's patience with us is something to behold. She cleared her throat to continue her lecture. "I apologize, I still haven't gotten there yet. It's a complex topic. You know how roughly ten to twenty percent of humans and every Grey Elf can't use magic at all?"

I replied, "You're talking about the difference between magical affinity and magical potency? Potency is how strong the magic you can use is, and an affinity is how many elements you can use. Is this by chance in reference to why nobody uses magic because it's so weak, or are you talking about why some people don't have an affinity at all?"

She clarified, "This is regarding magical affinities, or why such a low percentage of the population simply can't use any magic. Maybe they are attuned to light magic, but the world suppression is too much for them to use it. That's the crux of what I am trying to relay. That is the evidence you are all looking for. And the thing is… you all already know it, don't you?"

This perplexed me. "I don't get it. Are you saying a small percentage of the population with no magical affinity is actually attuned to the light element? And even more than that, how would either of you 'know' I had something different about me? I don't mean to scoff in disbelief, but that seems more far-fetched than anything Shion has said so far."

Leah replied, "Isn't it obvious? It's your blood for me… and your mana for the voidling over there. The potency isn't something to be mistaken. And truthfully, the allure has increased tenfold since the light beam came down. It's borderline hard to resist."

"And you would disclose that so easily to your 'prey'?" Forina snarled.

Shion, unabated by Leah and Forina, continued. "It's called Lightfall, and it's what you witnessed earlier. In essence, Lightfall happens when two different parallel worlds are connected, and their elemental balance is rapidly shared between each other to find an equilibrium. If I must spell it out any further… summoning the being from wherever opened the channel and tipped the balance of both worlds by mixing our elements with each other. The stronger the reaction from the Lightfall, the stronger the hero should be because of the distance from their home world. You saw it for yourself… this time, it was severe."

"This time…" I said but was completely ignored. Did she mean that the first time someone was summoned from another world, it wasn't a light-aligned world?

Shion continued her impassioned speech, completely forgetting her audience. "For any mage studying magic at the Royal Research Academy, that event was one in a million and a chance to prove so many theories. There are entire walls covered in various pieces of paper with unsolved riddles and questions. To get the chance to participate in such a spell, then to get the chance to study the person summoned… is a mage's dream. Not to mention, that person is imbued with a foreign element, I envy the Grand Mage to get such an opportunity. Nobody could pass that up."

Shion kept ranting about some magical crap I didn't care about after that. What was stuck in my mind now was how much Marleen knew about my potential light affinity. If Forina and Leah knew about it, even if they didn't know what it was, then Marleen had to know… right? Did she only use me for her research? Is it possible that the happy and fun Marleen, I know, was putting up a front to use me as a lab rat… specifically for this day? The more I think about it, the more I get torn to pieces.

"…anyone who was not in a fort, city, garrison, or was not far enough away is either dead or incapacitated…" I just tuned back into what Shion was saying and found myself in the middle of an important topic.

I interjected, "Stop! I tuned out for a moment. Why are people dead or incapacitated? Don't just gloss over that."

Shion gently sighed at me for not paying attention. She calmly reiterated, "Due to the overwhelming amount of foreign Light Magic that poured into Genesis, anyone who was not in a fort, city, garrison, or was not far enough away is either dead or incapacitated depending on the severity of their body's reaction. Our bodies have gotten so used to how our world works that there isn't any way that much of a foreign element pouring in would have devastating effects. It's like living your entire life in a cave and coming outside to the sun for the first time. If you don't protect yourself, your pale skin will get sunburnt. This is very much the same concept. I also bet every ManaBank is depleted, or close to it, and every mage is out of mana that was too close. Even worse, anyone with an artifact probably cannot use them either." Shion pointed to Forina with her pipe before putting it away.

"That is why your pretty elf friend left Midgard and came after us. The ManaBank was already out of commission, and she knew something big was about to happen. You need to swallow your pride and apologize for going over the top earlier, Raider. She seems a bit odd, but I can't sense any ill intent in her voice or body movements. Maybe if she would share a little of her blood, then I could get an even better read on her; what do you say?" Leah said that, but she was prodding to take advantage of the situation.

Should I bring up Shion's weird habits? Some of her words seem like she knows much more than she will admit to... almost like a premeditated understanding of events. No, we can circle around to that later, as there are much bigger issues to solve. For now, I'll build up a series of events and use them as leverage when she slips up.

My more immediate concern still has to do with Marleen. Was she so predisposed to validate her research that she would do anything? Talking about building up cases, hers is becoming grimmer the longer this trip takes. It started with Seventeen's letter, and now she could be using me for my light affinity while putting the entire kingdom at risk for this 'Lightfall' experiment. There is no way her hubris goes that far; I refuse to believe it.

With that much drive, she could be the single greatest unchecked antagonist in the Alvernia Sovereignty. She has the position, the genius, the ambition, and the resources. It might already be too late if she's the real enemy. Maybe... another actor is pulling her strings? Elvania, perhaps?

I just realized Shion was protecting me the whole time, and Leah was right. The sweating, pacing back and forth, and her hesitation were all because of Marleen's involvement. She knew I would react to this on a personal level, so she wanted to let me down easily. My outburst earlier only further validated her caution.

She might really be a good person. "Shion, I am... very sorry for earlier. I can be a little slow sometimes... so please don't hold it against me. How I treated you was unacceptable; I will have to find a way to make it up to you later." After saying that, I walked over to her and extended my hand. She didn't even pause before she grabbed it as if to say let's put this whole thing behind us and move forward. That's a huge weight off my shoulders... until I find out she secretly holds grudges.

Even given the large possibility that Marleen isn't who I thought she was, I still love her and have to ask Shion about her well-being. "So, what about Marleen? How could she survive all that light energy pouring into her body? She only has the wind and water affinities. She might be torn to shreds along with the entire capital. Do you know if she withstood the magical impact?"

Shion stopped her pacing briefly and looked relieved that I asked about Marleen. "The Grand Mage wouldn't approve of my discussing this, but you know she is a White Elf, right? White Elves have a minimum of three magical affinities. As luck would have it, Marleen is the most powerful dark-element user I have ever seen."

Leah looked astonished. "A White Elf... Dark Magic user? Queen Valporia would never allow such a thing."

Shion quickly continued. "... and she would easily be able to resist that much of the light element. What surprises me is why you never asked about her third and possibly fourth affinities. That goes to show you how much you trust her. Culturally, she has kept her dark affinity a secret because of the discrimination she would have received in Elvania and other White Elves. I only know about it because we have been together for a very long time. However, if her affinity ever got leaked, it could mean the downfall of her family among the other elvish aristocrats."

What she just told me was a prime reason why Marleen could have been blackmailed. The real question is, why did she not tell me this whole time?

Leah grumbled, "More like they would execute her and roll it all under the rug. Moving past that, do you have any ideas about what the light worlds have instead of miasma and demons? And will we get our magic or abilities back anytime soon, Miss Mage? I know several of us are dying to know. Miss former-glowing green eyes in the corner being the main one."

"No clue, I've never made it that far." Shion swiftly replied.

Leah and I said the same thing in response, "Huh?"

She corrected herself, "I mean... our theories can only go so far. Maybe now that Lightfall has happened, we can find out more. If I were to put my best hypothesis forward about your abilities... it would depend on how long the channel between our world and the other world remains open. For all we know, it could still be open, and more light energy is flooding in. If the channel is already closed, you might begin slowly getting your abilities and magical affinities back. Think of it like the lowlands being flooded. The sooner the rain stops, the sooner the lowlands are no longer flooded."

We had been talking for a long time, and we were all tired. It was time to wrap this up. "Fine, that's enough. Everyone needs to take a break. It's been a long day, and we all need time to process everything. Let's get the vampires taken care of and get some sleep." All of them except for Forina left the room to take a walk and check up on things one last time.

Forina was not showing any expressions at all. Her posture and tone had turned monotone, void of emotion. This was in stark contrast to before we started our makeshift meeting. "I'm sure you have noticed our eyes aren't what they used to be. The vampires and I have been cut off from our source of power. I can't feel my home anymore; as in, it doesn't resonate with me at all… almost like it isn't even there. I don't know how to describe it. It's like being cold and stranded without any reason to exist after you have been in a warm house your entire life. And it doesn't make any sense to me; the Void Plane is anchored to this world. How can that pathway be cut off and leave someone abandoned like that? And the whispers… where did they go?"

"The 'Void Plane?' You haven't told me much, but is it like one of those parallel worlds that Shion was talking about?" I feel I'm taking advantage of her situation to prod a bit. But a vulnerable Forina?

She responded, "No, planes aren't the same as parallel worlds. Parallel worlds are independent of each other except for the elemental energy balanced between them. In contrast, planes are dimensional shifts that are attached to worlds. No need to get too deep into it. Just know that planes cannot be disenfranchised from their host worlds. The Void Plane is like this world's shadow; anywhere the world goes… it must take its shadow. If you can survive in one of these planes long enough, your essence becomes attuned, and you are no longer a dweller of the host. That's how I can shift at will using a pathway between the hosting world and my home. The vampires have their own plane of origination; that's why they have a history with my people. One cold, dark, and isolated, while the other is hot and insufferable."

I nodded. "That's a lot to keep track of as well. Tons of planes with tons of different species. My guess is that all of this has to do with why you turned into an assassin and kidnapper. If there's something you want me to know, I'll listen."

She elaborated, "Some things you aren't ready to know yet, others you are. Those of us from a different plane consume a binding type of energy that connects us back to our plane. Vampires have blood, and my people have mana. There are also others out there that can consume a specific type of energy, like miasma or light or dark. If we don't consume enough to hold our connection back to our plane, then we eventually fall into a frenzied state and die. That energy requirement is the same regardless of where we find ourselves."

She started playing with her dagger while continuing. "The problem with the Void Plane is that almost all beings that have even the slightest acumen or mana have been wiped out by the creatures that live there. These creatures that survive are strong. Strong enough for your entire nation to muster its army only to die before landing a single blow. That's why we seek our prey elsewhere... not all that dissimilar to your Blood Princess. The key difference is that we can take our prey back to our origin plane... to my people."

"You're referring to Helen?" I asked.

She let out an elongated sigh. "Yes, prey like Helen. The real problem with you, Genesis dwellers, is your inability to survive in our harsh environment. So, we need a lot of you." As I started to ask why us, she added, "Let's end the conversation there for today." She started slowly walking around me in a circle while gesturing with her hands.

I stayed put, continuing to lean back against my horse saddle. My eyes had been shut for a while now, so it was just her distinct aura and subtle movements that were letting me know where she was. She stopped behind me, pushed me forward, and twisted my wrist behind my back. Now, I was leaning on the ground with a wristlock that I couldn't escape.

"What kind of sick alpha female shit are you trying to pull you psycho?" Not that I cared... she's still unpredictable. This was the first time she had gotten physical with me since we first met.

Forina whispered, "Now, now... that's not very nice. Don't you remember? My kind are parasites. We feed off mana, and you have an enormous amount of it just built up inside of you with nowhere to go. And I have insatiable cravings that can't wait until you fall asleep tonight. Call it a courtesy to spare you from the pain. I only do it because I like you so much. I do wonder... can I feed until I'm reconnected? We shall see..."

Anguishing as she pulled up on my wrist and got closer, I replied, "You weren't lying? What the hell is your problem anyway? I can't use magic and never have been able to. Not to mention, you don't have fangs, so you can't siphon anything. When do you stop screwing around?"

This brings back suppressed memories of Laura and Leah. Every damn alpha female I run across just feels like they can walk all over me. I'm not even that weak; they are just stupid-strong in their own ways and look to use me as an outlet. I've never asked why, but maybe it's because I am in a position of authority? A sick ploy to assert their dominance? Well, that can't be the case with Laura, as she outranks me.

Forina continued, "There's your problem. All you have done is talk, talk, talk all day and all night long. Whenever I feed, I can hear your thoughts."

I muttered, "The whispers..."

She ignored me. "I hear how concerned you are for your bride-to-be. How stressed you are about performing your duties. I can even see the dreams you have of the future. It's not looking too promising for you, now, is it?"

There's another mystery solved. This explains how she always knows who is corrupt and who to kill. When she killed the leadership at Midgard, it always sat in the back of my mind as to how she could target exactly the right people. It might also explain why nothing of mine is off-limits... like she owns me. All those whispers they... must be eating her alive.

There was a break in her tormenting, and then she licked the back of my ear and started to nibble. "You see, if you were ever to go to our plane, your eyes would glow orange just like everyone else from this world. Bright, illustrious orange until their mana is all siphoned off, they fade away one bite at a time. Then, when you run out of mana, you shrivel up and die an agonizingly slow death. Someday, I'll have to let you experience it firsthand, but not before I've had my fill."

Forina released me and swaggered towards the door while doing her usual dagger tossing. She looked back and opened her mouth. There, unlike anything else I've seen, she had her fangs out.

They were as big as Leah's on the top with a complementary set on the bottom. If someone got hooked by both of those, there wouldn't be a way to get out, especially if she injected the same paralysis poison she did to me while we were riding over here. But just looking at her, there was no way she was biting me at night like she was claiming. The scars would still be visible the next morning. That means it was true... she did use her freakishly long tongue on me while I slept to siphon my mana.

"Ok, I believe you. You really do get your fill when I'm asleep. Now I know why you hang around me all the time while knowing so much about everything. Can you humor me? Why would your species have a tongue and fangs that can do the same thing?" I asked while rubbing my wrist. She retracted both the top and bottom fangs so that her teeth looked like a normal elf's mouth. Even vampires can't retract their fangs; she was something else.

"Why do humans and elves have both a nose and a mouth to breathe out of? Both serve the same purpose. Both keep the person alive. Just take comfort that you've been the only one to survive something other than my fangs. The question you should be thinking is... does that alone make you valuable, or is it something else? Others are just fodder to amuse me, while I can get far more from you using my favorite method." She turned back around and strolled out of the room.

Shivers ran up and down my spine just thinking about what was going on in that head of hers, with potentially dozens or hundreds of voices telling her different things. I need to walk to get a breath of stale air. The humidity inside of this damn tree is stifling, and the building is even more stuffy than that. I'm sure getting used to it would take some time, but being cooped up in a structure that's made of roots and inside of a big root won't do much for my mental stability right now.

Here is to hoping someone prepared dinner... I'm straight-up starving to death. I'm not even sure when the last time I ate was. Looking forward to some 'not with psycho elf' potatoes or 'calm and quiet without theoretical nonsense' beans. Hell, at this point, I would even settle for squashed, soggy bread. That is a good point. I think I just decided that thinking about food is how I will make it through this mess. It's much easier to put my mind at ease than thinking about

Marleen or anything else I can't control. We didn't even broach the subject of the Empire and their reaction to that Lightfall.

After thinking a bit, I began to walk out of the door and was immediately pinned against the wall in the hallway by someone from behind. Sporadic assaults seem to be becoming such a common occurrence lately that they aren't even phasing me anymore. I recognized the smell of the person behind me. It was that faint odor that polish gives off when you give your equipment a once over, and there was only one person who does that in this area like it's their birthright.

Crying out with my face against the wall, I must have looked pathetic. "What the fuck, Leah? Did you and Forina coordinate attacks on me tonight, or what? If you two are going to try and compare yourselves to each other, then leave me out of it. I'm getting sick of being treated like a damn belonging."

"I told you; I'm famished. And vials just won't do tonight." Leah bit into my neck and started aggressively sucking.

Being bitten by a vampire isn't a fun experience. Pain shoots through your body instantly and can cause you to convulse if too much is taken out too quickly. The best thing I can relate to is feeling like your entire body's temperature shoots up and sharp needles are injected into your bloodstream. For this reason alone, we distribute vials instead of just lining people up like cattle.

Compound the pain with two, almost finger-length, miniature daggers piercing into your neck, and it's easy to imagine how much life could 'suck' in a hurry. In my case, Leah has a real problem with controlling her desires at times, and her fangs are much bigger than normal. The last two times, I blacked out and woke up several hours later with her caressing my head like I had been a good boy. In her mind, me not speaking out against it is consent… but the pain is so bad it's hard to even say a word, and she knows it.

I kept trying to get the words out but was interrupted by a bone-wrenching screech coming from somewhere deep in this endless tree labyrinth. The wailing bounced off the wooden walls and had to come from something enormous. This sound was unlike any demon I had ever heard before; even Leah was shaken enough to stop her lustful thirsting for a brief moment. Whatever it was, it was very far away and angry. The creature had also encased itself in magic dense enough to cause sound to ricochet off walls that would otherwise absorb it. Aside from the instant fear it invoked in me, I just hoped it wouldn't treat me like a rag doll, too.

"What in the hell was that?" I questioned. But Leah ignored it and stuck her fangs in on the other side of my neck as if two holes weren't enough.

"Le... Le... Leah? Can't we at least see what the hell that thing was?" She didn't hear a word I said. She just kept going at it long enough to make me weak enough for my knees to start to give out. When she noticed I was going limp, she forcefully peeled herself away from me. Before fully breaking off, she licked up all the spare streams coming down from both sides of my neck as if to keep a clean plate.

In an elated tone, she broke away from me and proudly declared, "Just like I remember. It was worth the wait. Next time, don't spoil it with your bickering. It's clear whatever made those sounds would have ruined us if we knew we were here. Those screams you heard were not one of our people, so don't be so worried."

I replied, "Screams? What are you talking about?"

Leah was too busy trying in vain to wipe off her face. Her entire lower half was coated in my blood. "I guess my senses aren't as bad off as I thought they were. Don't worry about it, and get some sleep. You need to recover your strength if you want to keep us in line. Taking better care of yourself is key to a healthy lifestyle... I can really taste your stress. Also, stop being a little girl. I swear you make more noise and struggle worse every time I see you." Says the woman who drains my strength both mentally and physically every time I see her. She released me and finally let me turn around. I could see the light returning to her eyes, albeit very slightly.

"You're bad for my reputation, you know that?" I questioned as I was wobbling back and forth and struggling to keep my footing.

"If anything is going to damage your reputation, it's your squeamishness and your ability to only relate to elvish women. It's no wonder why Laura dumped your ass. She is twice the man you are. But... that might be one of your charming characteristics." Yeah, that's right, I told her about our past relationship one night when I was drunk off my ass. Man, do I regret that decision? She isn't wrong, though; Laura is twice the man of any man.

It dawned on me. "Damn it, I could have overpowered you just now. I forgot you've lost all your luster. You sure know how to put on an aggressive front."

She was still wiping my blood off her face. "I also want to set something straight. Laura didn't 'dump me'; she left for a promotion in the capital. Anybody with any career aspirations would have done the same in her circumstances. And although we had a rocky start, she still means a lot to me. Don't go spreading rumors around; you know barely anyone knows about our past."

"She got reassigned, huh? Amazing how close the academy is to the Royal Guard's headquarters, but she became so distant and never paid you a visit… I wonder why. Anyway, thanks for the meal. I'll see you tomorrow morning." Her playful jesting gets old, but I wouldn't have her any other way.

When she exited, I was left all alone. This was the first time for as long as I can remember that absolutely nobody was around me. There wasn't a bodyguard, a captain, a fiancée… or anything else. Do I want to interrupt my momentary piece of quiet to still go for a walk? Yeah, I better go ahead and check up on everyone and keep up appearances. Maybe my presence will calm a few nerves. And even if it doesn't, it will calm my nerves down.

I reentered the room to grab my canteen, and when I turned around, there was an unfamiliar face standing in front of me. Another Grey Elf? Oh, she is a vampire, so she must be one of Leah's subordinates. But there is no way Leah would trust another vampire with dining on me… that much I know for sure. That's when I noticed the dripping sounds directly below me. I looked away from her alluringly dead eyes to see what was causing that sound. The pool of blood had already started to form from the knife sticking out of my chest. This vampire was an assassin… and she had hit her mark.

Epilogue: Reascend Red

Forward and back... side to side. My already weak knees instantly gave out on me. What had just happened? One foot before the other... the steps hurriedly retreated from the crime scene. The pool welling up under my face was now deep enough to touch the bottom of my eyelid. I couldn't help but laugh as I thought about how tough the floods in this place had to be to retain liquid this well. I bet those elves had a hell of a time with flooding when the rain came down.

"Raider! Raider!" A void roared from beyond my sight.

Ah, which person was it this time? With the world turning dark, I couldn't tell if it was a man or a woman. The pretty black cloth dancing in the pool before me was turning a mild scarlet color. This must already be a dream. A dream I shall not wake up from.

The voice continued to panic. "Get the guards, quickly! We need bandages before he loses too much blood. Don't die on me. Not this time. Not again. The moment you fade from this world, the world will also fade."

What a nice thought. Something you tell someone only to comfort them as they leave the world. The world rotates around you... you are important... you are something that needs to continue to exist. Those words... that sentiment... seems like I've said it a hundred times before, but I don't remember saying it once.

The voice faded to black. "Think about why you're here! Remember the struggles you went through to get to where you are right now! Hold on to it; it will guide you!"

Struggles? Yeah, I had plenty of those growing up as a nobody. That kid I stabbed for bread, the dozens if not hundreds of fights I got into so I could sleep in the sewer with something over my head to protect me from the storm. 'You are trash'... 'you won't amount to anything'... common sentiments.

Then... then there was the academy. It saved my life. Easily rolling over the other commoners in grappling, sword fighting, jousting, horseback riding... all of it. I was... home. A roof over my head, people to follow me, talent from surviving in the streets all those years... all of it. That is until she showed up and put me in my place. Not once, but for years. Dazzling displays I bore physical pain to repeatedly taught me more than any weak opponent.

Another voice rang out, "He's going into shock! We need to stabilize him!"

"Move aside! What are you doing?" Another asked.

One final voice declared, "If he dies, I will kill all of you."

The previous voice asked, "Where are you going? He needs help!"

They replied, "To get my vengeance."

Was that what truly saved me… that red-headed typhoon? Or was it… was it the shy elf? The love I had waited for while suffering all those cold, lonely nights. The one person who was farther from my reach than speaking with nobility or royalty. When I stood there in her defense, and she stood there for mine, that was the day… the day I was saved. My love… Marleen.